PRAISE FOR THE RADIUM AGE SERIES

"New editions of a host of under-discussed classics of the genre."
—*Reactor Magazine*

"Neglected classics of early 20th-century sci-fi in spiffily designed paperback editions."
—*The Financial Times*

"An entertaining, engrossing glimpse into the profound and innovative literature of the early twentieth century."
—*Foreword*

"Shows that 'proto-sf' was being published much more widely, alongside other kinds of fiction, before it emerged as a genre."
—*BSFA Review*

"An excellent start at showcasing the strange wonders offered by the Radium Age."
—*Shelf Awareness*

"Lovingly curated . . . The series' freedom from genre purism lets us see how a specific set of anxieties—channeled through dystopias, Lovecraftian horror, arch social satire, and adventure tales—spurred literary experimentation and the bending of conventions."
—*Los Angeles Review of Books*

"A huge effort to help define a new era of science fiction."
—*Transfer Orbit*

"Admirable . . . and highly recommended."
—*Washington Post*

"Long live the Radium Age."
—*Los Angeles Times*

T0182358

THE HEADS OF CERBERUS AND OTHER STORIES

The Radium Age Book Series
Joshua Glenn

THE HEADS OF CERBERUS AND OTHER STORIES

Francis Stevens

edited and introduced by Lisa Yaszek

THE MIT PRESS
CAMBRIDGE, MASSACHUSETTS
LONDON, ENGLAND

© 2024 Massachusetts Institute of Technology

This edition of *The Heads of Cerberus* follows the text of the 1919 edition published in *The Thrill Book* by Street & Smith Publications, Inc. "The Curious Experience of Thomas Dunbar" was originally published in *The Argosy* in 1904. "Friend Island" and "Behind the Curtain" were originally published in *All-Story Weekly* in 1918. "Unseen—Unfeared" was originally published in *People's Favorite Magazine* in 1919. "The Elf-Trap" was originally published in *The Argosy* in 1919. All works are in the public domain.

All rights reserved. No part of this book may be used to train artificial intelligence systems or reproduced in any form by any electronic or mechanical means (including photocopying, recording, or information storage and retrieval) without permission in writing from the publisher.

This book was set in Arnhem Pro and PF DIN Text Pro by New Best-set Typesetters Ltd. Printed and bound in the United States of America.

Library of Congress Cataloging-in-Publication Data

Names: Stevens, Francis, author. | Yaszek, Lisa, 1969–, editor, writer of introduction.
Title: The heads of Cerberus and other stories / Francis Stevens ; edited and introduced by Lisa Yaszek.
Description: Cambridge, Massachusetts : The MIT Press, 2024. | Series: The radium age book series
Identifiers: LCCN 2023041878 (print) | LCCN 2023041879 (ebook) | ISBN 9780262549066 (paperback) | ISBN 9780262379885 (epub) | ISBN 9780262379892 (pdf)
Subjects: LCSH: Time travel—Fiction. | Authoritarianism—Fiction. | Philadelphia (Pa.)—Fiction. | LCGFT: Dystopian fiction. | Alternative histories (Fiction). | Science fiction. | Novels. | Short stories.
Classification: LCC PS3503.E5472 H43 2024 (print) | LCC PS3503.E5472 (ebook) | DDC 813/.52—dc23/eng/20231030
LC record available at https://lccn.loc.gov/2023041878
LC ebook record available at https://lccn.loc.gov/2023041879

10 9 8 7 6 5 4 3 2 1

CONTENTS

Joshua Glenn

Do we really know science fiction? There were the scientific romance years that stretched from the mid-nineteenth century to circa 1900. And there was the genre's so-called golden age, from circa 1935 through the early 1960s. But between those periods, and overshadowed by them, was an era that has bequeathed us such tropes as the robot (berserk or benevolent), the tyrannical superman, the dystopia, the unfathomable extraterrestrial, the sinister telepath, and the eco-catastrophe. In 2009, writing for the sf blog io9.com at the invitation of Annalee Newitz and Charlie Jane Anders, I became fascinated with the period during which the sf genre as we know it emerged. Inspired by the exactly contemporaneous career of Marie Curie, who shared a Nobel Prize for her discovery of radium in 1903, only to die of radiation-induced leukemia in 1934, I eventually dubbed this three-decade interregnum the "Radium Age."

Curie's development of the theory of radioactivity, which led to the extraordinary, terrifying, awe-inspiring insight that the atom is, at least in part, a state of energy constantly in movement, is an apt metaphor for the twentieth century's first three decades. These years were marked by rising sociocultural strife across various fronts: the founding of the women's suffrage movement, the National Association for the Advancement of Colored People, socialist currents within the labor movement, anticolonial and revolutionary upheaval around the world . . . as well as the associated strengthening of reactionary movements that supported, for example, racial segregation, immigration restriction, eugenics, and sexist policies.

Science—as a system of knowledge, a mode of experimenting, and a method of reasoning—accelerated the pace of change during these years in ways simultaneously liberating and terrifying. As sf author and historian Brian Stableford points out in his 1989 essay "The Plausibility of the Impossible," the universe we discovered by means of the scientific method in the early twentieth century defies common sense: "We are haunted by a sense of the impossibility of ultimately making sense of things." By playing host to certain far-out notions—time travel, faster-than-light travel, and ESP, for example—that we have every reason to judge impossible, science fiction serves as an "instrument of negotiation," Stableford suggests, with which we strive to accomplish "the difficult diplomacy of existence in a scientifically knowable but essentially unimaginable world." This is no less true today than during the Radium Age.

The social, cultural, political, and technological upheavals of the 1900–1935 period are reflected in the proto-sf writings of authors such as Olaf Stapledon, William Hope Hodgson, Muriel Jaeger, Karel Čapek, G. K. Chesterton, Cicely Hamilton, W. E. B. Du Bois, Yevgeny Zamyatin, E. V. Odle, Arthur Conan Doyle, Mikhail Bulgakov,

Pauline Hopkins, Stanisław Ignacy Witkiewicz, Aldous Huxley, Gustave Le Rouge, A. Merritt, Rudyard Kipling, Rose Macaulay, J. D. Beresford, J. J. Connington, S. Fowler Wright, Jack London, Thea von Harbou, and Edgar Rice Burroughs, not to mention the late-period but still incredibly prolific H. G. Wells himself. More cynical than its Victorian precursor yet less hard-boiled than the sf that followed, in the writings of these visionaries we find acerbic social commentary, shock tactics, and also a sense of frustrated idealism—and reactionary cynicism, too—regarding humankind's trajectory.

The MIT Press's Radium Age series represents a much-needed evolution of my own efforts to champion the best proto-sf novels and stories from 1900 to 1935 among scholars already engaged in the fields of utopian and speculative fiction studies, as well as general readers interested in science, technology, history, and thrills and chills. By reissuing literary productions from a time period that hasn't received sufficient attention for its contribution to the emergence of science fiction as a recognizable form—one that exists and has meaning in relation to its own traditions and innovations, as well as within a broader ecosystem of literary genres, each of which, as John Rieder notes in *Science Fiction and the Mass Cultural Genre System* (2017), is itself a product of overlapping "communities of practice"—we hope not only to draw attention to key overlooked works but perhaps also to influence the way scholars and sf fans alike think about this crucial yet neglected and misunderstood moment in the emergence of the sf genre.

John W. Campbell and other Cold War–era sf editors and propagandists dubbed a select group of writers and story types from the pulp era to be the golden age of science fiction. In doing so, they helped fix in the popular imagination a too-narrow understanding of what the sf genre can offer. (In his introduction to the 1974 collection *Before the Golden Age*, for example, Isaac Asimov notes that although it may have possessed a certain exuberance, in general sf from before the mid-1930s moment when Campbell assumed editorship of *Astounding Stories* "seems, to anyone who has experienced the Campbell Revolution, to be clumsy, primitive, naive.") By returning to an international tradition of scientific speculation via fiction from after the Poe–Verne–Wells era and before sf's Golden Age, the Radium Age series will demonstrate— contra Asimov et al.—the breadth, richness, and diversity of the literary works that were responding to a vertiginous historical period, and how they helped innovate a nascent genre (which wouldn't be named until the mid-1920s, by Hugo Gernsback, founder of *Amazing Stories* and namesake of the Hugo Awards) as a mode of speculative imagining.

The MIT Press's Noah J. Springer and I are grateful to the sf writers and scholars who have agreed to serve as this series' advisory board. Aided by their guidance, we'll endeavor to surface a rich variety of texts, along with introductions by a diverse group of sf scholars, sf writers, and others that will situate these remarkable, entertaining, forgotten works within their own social, political, and scientific contexts, while drawing out contemporary parallels.

We hope that reading Radium Age writings, published in times as volatile as our own, will serve to remind us that our own era's seemingly natural, eternal, and inevitable social, economic, and cultural forms and norms are—like Madame Curie's atom—forever in flux.

INTRODUCTION: THE MOTHER OF MODERN GENRE FICTION

Lisa Yaszek

Imagine it. A dystopian government maintains power over the downtrodden population of a postapocalyptic United States through a system of deadly games. Exposure to a strange new element gives an average young man super-strength. Invisible predators from an alternate dimension feed on human evil. A hardy young adventurer forges telepathic connections with a living world to oppose the forces that would brutally exploit them both. And then there are realities that turn out to be nothing more than mere illusions, the projections of angry and excited minds—or *just perhaps*, a nagging voice inside us insists, *they might be real after all.* . . .

These are the dreams that contemporary culture is made of, fueling everything from Hollywood blockbusters to groundbreaking video games and prize-winning literary experiments. And, incredibly, they are all story forms popularized by pioneering genre author Gertrude Mabel Barrows Bennett, who wrote (primarily under the pen name Francis Stevens) in the first decades of the twentieth century. Although she is often celebrated as "the woman who invented dark fantasy," the range of Bennett's groundbreaking stories—produced largely in a six-year period—suggests that she is better understood as the mother of modern genre fiction writ large. Using tales about the clash of alternate worlds and values to reassess scientific ideas and social relations emerging at the turn of the twentieth century (many of which are still very relevant), she innovated in speculative subgenres including but not limited to: the dark fantasy, the parallel worlds story, the superhero origin tale, and the feminist eco-utopia.

Gertrude Barrows was born in 1884, in Minneapolis. She grew up writing poetry and short prose pieces and dreaming of a career as an illustrator. After completing eighth grade, she left school to help support her family but continued to take night classes while working as a department store secretary. In 1904, at the age of 17, she made her literary debut with a short story that appeared in *Argosy*, the premiere all-story magazine of the era. An adventure writer attracted to adventurers, in 1909 Barrows met and married Stewart Bennett, a British journalist and treasurer hunter, and moved with him to Philadelphia. The two separated while Bennett was pregnant, and their marriage was formally terminated by her husband's death in the Florida Keys a year later. Remaining in Philadelphia, Bennett supported her small family as a journalist and secretary at the University of Pennsylvania.

Bennett returned to writing in the late 1910s under a set of conditions that will feel all too familiar to many modern people, especially women: It was one of the few jobs she could do from home while raising her daughter and caring for her ailing mother during a global flu pandemic with minimal social services. She immediately

Lisa Yaszek

sold several stories to *Argosy* and its sister publication, *All-Story Weekly*. Bennett requested that her work be published under the gender-neutral pseudonym "Jean Veil" but editor Robert H. Davis assigned her the masculine "Francis Stevens" instead. She decided to maintain the Stevens pseudonym upon positive reception of her stories by fans, who celebrated her "unsurpassed" ability to create "pure imaginative fantasy" that was "refreshing" in its originality and "exquisite" in its sense of humor. Between 1917 and 1923, Bennett sold five novels and seven short stories to premium venues including *Argosy*, *All-Story*, and *People's Favorite Magazine*; her last publication appeared in one of the first issues of *Weird Tales*, the magazine that would set the standards for modern fantasy and horror fiction. After the pandemic ended, her mother passed away, and her daughter got engaged, Bennett returned to her adventuring ways, exchanging Philadelphia and her writing career for a new life in California; she remained there until her death in 1949.

Like many science fiction authors today, Bennett spent a great deal of time in research—up to seven months for her novel-length works—before drafting her stories. Given her work as a journalist in a major American city and as a secretary at a university known for its cutting-edge zoology, biology, and archeology programs, it is no surprise that Bennett's stories seem ripped from the headlines of her day. This is especially true of *The Heads of Cerberus*, whose dystopian future Philadelphia invokes the Tammany Hall scandals in which Democratic leaders publicly positioned themselves as progressive, working-class reformers while privately encouraging administrative corruption to consolidate their power. At the same time, Bennett's depiction of future Philadelphia as a world analogous to our own but separated in time and space by an interdimensional portal echoes mathematician and science fiction author Charles Howard Hinton's ideas about parallel worlds and the fourth dimension, as explored in *The Fourth Dimension* (1904) and *An Episode of Flatland* (1907).

Indeed, Bennett's entire literary output is characterized by creative engagement with early twentieth-century America's scientific and social obsessions. Her earliest work, 1904's "The Curious Experience of Thomas Dunbar," revolves around the discovery of a powerful element called "stellarite" and was published just one year after Marie Curie won the Nobel Prize for her groundbreaking work in radioactivity, which included the discovery of polonium and radium. Later stories such as "Unseen— Unfeared" (1919) and "Behind the Curtain" (1918) extrapolate from well-publicized scientific accomplishments including the development of infrared photography in 1910 and the Egyptology craze of the early twentieth century (indeed, the University of Pennsylvania launched several major expeditions to Egypt during this period). Meanwhile, 1918's future-oriented feminist sea story, "Friend Island," appeared just one year after Loretta Walsh became the first woman to join the US Navy and the same year that Genevieve and Lucille Baker and Myrtle Hazard became the first enlisted women in the US Coast Guard.

Lisa Yaszek

Bennett was first and foremost a teller of entertaining tales who engaged with the most popular genre traditions of her day. Along with its political and scientific extrapolation, *The Heads of Cerberus* engages in literary extrapolation, paying homage to H.G. Wells' *The Time Machine* (1895) with its concluding image of a shadowy time traveler who may be responsible for dystopian future Philadelphia—all the while exploring how time might run differently in the various worlds created by such travelers. Indeed, Bennett's editors directly compared her to the British literary phenom. The preview for "Friend Island" notes that tales set in the future are common and Wells "has had more than one try at the game," but tantalizingly promises that readers will prefer the story at hand due to the author's "happy combination" of "imagination" and "bubbling . . . humor." Readers also likely noticed that Bennett's subtitle, "A Veracious Tale of an Ancient Mariness," pays homage to Samuel Taylor Coleridge's "Rime of the Ancient Mariner" . . . while the story itself wittily transforms the poet's depiction of nature as feminine, mysterious, and hostile to human reason into a specifically masculine misperception. Elsewhere, Bennett's editors placed her in the emergent pantheon of American speculative superstars, noting that "Behind the Curtain" invokes Edgar Allan Poe's "Cask of Amontillado," but "is a lot better than Poe's story, if we do say it."

When Bennett was not advancing established story forms, she was creating them. Published just one year after Baroness Emma Orczy's wildly popular stage play about a masked avenger called the Scarlet Pimpernel, "The Curious Experience of Thomas Dunbar" was one of the first modern superhero stories and a template for one of America's favorite comic-book tropes: the lab-invented superman. Fifteen years later, Bennett's depiction of elves (in "The Elf-Trap") as human-sized immortals characterized by their "delicate, fascinating beauty" and magical silversmithing abilities would radically transform conventional Victorian depictions of such creatures as miniscule, childish imps. As such, her characters anticipate the rise of the modern fantasy elf popularized by Lord Dunsany's *The King of Elfland's Daughter* (1924) and Tolkien's *The Lord of the Rings* (1954–1955).

Contemporary readers, like their early twentieth-century counterparts, will appreciate Bennett's ability to turn "all the cliches of the hour into a rollicking good laugh"—especially as such cliches are related to gender. For example, "Friend Island" imagines a happy, high-tech matriarchal future where Nature literally rains both silly and serious misfortunes down upon men who refuse to treat her like the dignified lady that the story's swashbuckling, macaroon-consuming woman adventurer knows her to be. *The Heads of Cerberus* provides a more uneven but also more provocative exploration of gender and genre, depicting seventeen-year-old protagonist Viola as both a conventional object of sexual desire and as a sharp-shooting girl genius who regularly outthinks and outacts the older and decidedly less intelligent men around her. Meanwhile, Viola's antagonist, the Philadelphian leader Loveliest, has strange encounters with both the natural

Lisa Yaszek

aging process and unnatural visitors from the past that prompt her to suspect she is being used by men to preserve the dystopian status quo of her world—in other words, that she is what feminist science fiction author Joanna Russ would later call "a female man." Moreover, Viola's concluding realization that Loveliest might be a "distinct reflection" of herself leaves readers wondering what we can do in our own present to prevent ourselves from becoming such creatures and upholding a status quo every bit as problematic as that of Bennett's future Philadelphia.

To a lesser extent, the stories in this anthology also upend racial stereotypes common to early twentieth-century culture. "The Curious Experience of Thomas Dunbar" invokes both Yellow Peril rhetoric and long-standing generic ideals about the mad scientist as ethnic other in its depiction of the half-Japanese Lawrence—a "fantastic vision from the Orient," complete with a "little, weazened body" and "slanted" black eyes that evince "a great deal of scorn for all [Western] doctors." In the end, however, Lawrence emerges as an eccentric but likable scientist "possessed of strange depths" who combats both social and scientific ignorance in his quest for knowledge—much like the decidedly white, Western scientist-heroes populating Wells' own early science fiction. In "Unseen—Unfeared," Bennett's white, liberal protagonist finds himself overwhelmed by a sudden hatred for Philadelphia's African American, Italian, and Jewish communities, which transform from lively if "shabby" neighborhoods to "unhygienic . . . [and] revolting" slums before his very eyes. His subsequent quest to make sense of this experience allows Bennett to thrill her audience with a proto-Lovecraftian vision of a predatory universe while challenging their assumptions about xenophobia as a natural aspect of Darwinian competition between species (and races).

Bennett spent her formative years in Minneapolis and Philadelphia, cities with established Asian, Mediterranean, and Black populations that were home to some of the nation's first attempts at racial integration. Little wonder, then, that she sometimes allows her racial others to speak for themselves, or that she interrogates the roots of white racism. This is not to say, however, that her racial sensitivity did not have its limits. With the notable exception of the very early "Thomas Dunbar," Bennett relegated characters of color to minor positions in her stories, and she remained susceptible to stereotypes about newer immigrant groups such as Eastern Europeans. This is particularly evident in "The Elf-Trap," where the "Negro caretaker" Jake is treated with respect by the narrator and protagonist, but the brilliant, beautiful elves who disguise themselves as Romani are perceived by humans as "dirty and villainous of feature." Even if readers understand that the elves are manipulating human stereotypes to preserve their kingdom from human incursion, the stereotypes themselves are never put into question.

Modern readers might find themselves both tantalized and frustrated by Bennett's tendency to advance scientific and social critique in one paragraph, only to abandon it in the next. This interpretive openness was baked

Lisa Yaszek

into the family-oriented all-story magazines in which Bennett published, and she was an early master of the form. *The Heads of Cerberus* very much revolves around such openness, offering readers four possible interpretations of the novel's events: either our protagonists are the first to travel through time and space; or they are following in the steps of a shadowy time traveler mysteriously changing history as he roams through the astral planes; or they have encountered a "twisted" version of Philadelphia created by one of the "forces that rule" the fourth dimension "for its own sardonic amusement"; or the dust they inhaled caused them to hallucinate the whole adventure. Open endings are central to Bennett's shorter fiction as well: "The Curious Experience of Thomas Dunbar" allows readers to wonder if Lawrence is mad, heroic, or both; if his alienation from the American status quo is an innate characteristic of the scientist or a product of American white supremacy; and if he will abandon or mentor newly minted superhero Thomas Dunbar. At the end of "Unseen—Unfeared," both Bennett's protagonist and readers are left wondering if humankind's racism is innate or implanted by alien forces—and if the narrator in fact encountered aliens, or if it was all a drug-induced hallucination. Likewise, in its exploration of art, science, and perception, "The Elf-Trap" leaves its audience asking if our protagonist's keen observational skills are what allow him to see magic or if his close study of microscopic worlds has driven him insane—just as we wonder, in the concluding pages, whether he is truly dead or has been translated to another world entirely.

Bennett does not give us clear answers to the question of "What world am I in?" and indeed, her stories seem to support all options equally well. Instead, she asks us to answer a much harder question: How do I proceed, regardless of what world I am in? Which is to say: How might my experience of new worlds change my opinions about the "real" world . . . and impel me to work towards winning a better one in my own future?

Works Cited

Ashley, Mike. "Elves." *The Encyclopedia of Fantasy*, edited by John Clute and John Grant. 1997. https://sf-encyclopedia.com/fe/elves. Accessed June 2, 2023.

Barrows, G. M. "The Curious Experience of Thomas Dunbar." *The Argosy* 44.4 (March 4, 1904): 663–669.

Eschbach, Lloyd Arthur. "Introduction." *The Heads of Cerberus*, 13–16. Reading, PA: Polaris Press, 1952 (1919).

"Heart to Heart Talks by the Editor." *All-Story Weekly* 88.1 (August 31, 1918): 189–192.

"Heart to Heart Talks by the Editor." *All-Story Weekly* 88.3 (September 14, 1918): 573–576.

Press, John C. "Letter to the Editor." *The Argosy* 113.1 (October 4, 1919): 176.

Stableford, Brian. "Parallel World." *Science Fact and Science Fiction: An Encyclopedia*. Abingdon, UK: Routledge, 2006. 355–357.

Staples, Mrs. Fred M. "The Best at Any Price." *All-Story Weekly* 98.2 (June 14, 1919): 349.

Stevens, Francis (Gertrude M. Barrows Bennett). "The Elf-Trap." *Famous Fantastic Novels* 3.4 (November 1949 [1919]): 100–112.

———. *The Heads of Cerberus*. Reading, PA: Polaris Press, 1952 (1919).

———. "Unseen–Unfeared." *People's Favorite Magazine* 29.4 (February 10, 1919): 139–148.

Lisa Yaszek thanks Maxanthony Mateer and Diya Patel for their assistance in researching turn-of-the-century immigration patterns and for compiling an extensive list of women who published proto-sf and other genre fiction from 1900–1935. A work in progress, the list can be found here: hilobrow .com/sisters.

THE HEADS OF CERBERUS (1919)

1 "WELCOME, HOWEVER YOU COME!"

Upon a walnut bed in a small, plainly furnished room which dawn had just begun grayly to illuminate, a man lay unconscious.

His thin face, indefinably boyish for all its gauntness, wore that placid, uncaring look which death shares with complete insensibility. Under him his right arm was doubled in an uncomfortable, strained position, while the left hand, slender and well cared for, trailed limp to the floor by the bedside. On his right temple there showed an ugly wound, evidently made by some blunt, heavy instrument, for the skin was burst rather than cut. His fair hair was plastered with blood from the wound, and a good deal of blood had also run down over the side of the face, lending a sinister and tragic aspect to his otherwise not unpleasant countenance. Fully dressed in a rather shabby blue serge, both appearance and attitude suggested that the man had been flung down here and left brutally to die or revive, as he might.

The dawn light grew brighter, and as if in sympathy with its brightening, the face of the man on the bed began to take on a look more akin to that of life. That alien, wax-like placidity of one who is done with pain slowly softened and changed. The features twitched; the lips which had fallen slightly apart, closed firmly. With a sudden contraction of the brows the man opened his eyes.

For several minutes he lay quiet, staring upward. Then he attempted to withdraw his right hand from beneath him, groaned, and by a considerable effort at last raised himself on one elbow. Gazing about the room with bewildered, pain-stricken eyes, he raised his hand to his head and afterward stared stupidly at the blood on his fingers. He seemed like one who, having fallen victim to some powerful drug, awakens in unfamiliar and inexplicable surroundings.

As he again looked about him, however, the expression changed. What he saw, it seemed, had revived some memory that mingled with a new and different bewilderment.

In a corner of the room, near the one window, stood a small, old-fashioned, black steel safe. The door of it was swung wide open, while scattered on the floor before it lay a mass of papers. From between loose pages and folded, elastic-bound documents gleamed a few small articles of jewelry. Two or three empty morocco cases had been carelessly tossed on top of the pile.

With eyes fixed on this heap, the man swung his legs over the side of the bed, and, staggering across to the safe, dropped on his knees beside it. He ran his hand through the papers, uncovered a small brooch which he picked up and examined with a curious frowning intentness; then let it fall and again raised a hand to his head.

In another corner of the room was a doorway through which he glimpsed a porcelain washbowl. Toward this the man dragged himself. Wetting a towel that hung there, he began bathing the wound on his temple. The cold water seemed to relieve the dizziness or nausea from which he suffered. Presently he was able to draw himself erect, and having contemplated his disheveled countenance in the small mirror above the bowl, he proceeded with some care to remove the more obvious traces of disaster. The blood fortunately had clotted and ceased to flow. Having washed, he sought about the room, found his hat, a worn, soft gray felt, on the floor near the bed, and, returning to the mirror, adjusted it with the apparent intent to conceal his wound.

The effort, though attended by a grimace of pain, was successful, and now at length the man returned his attention to that stack of miscellanies which had been the safe's contents.

Ignoring the papers, he began separating from them the few bits of jewelry. Beside the brooch there was a man's heavy gold signet ring, a pair of cuff links set with seed pearls, a bar pin of silver and moonstones, and a few similar trifles. He sorted and searched with an odd scowl, as if the task were unpleasant, though it might equally well have been the pain of his wound which troubled him.

As he found each piece he thrust it in his pocket without examination, until the displacing of a small bundle of insurance policies disclosed the first thing of any real value in the entire collection.

With an astonished ejaculation the man seized upon it, scrutinized it with wide, horrified eyes, and for a moment afterward knelt motionless, while his pallid face slowly flushed until it was nearly crimson in color.

"Good God!"

The man flung the thing from him as if it had burned his fingers. In a sudden frenzy of haste he tore from his pockets the trinkets he had placed there a few moments earlier, threw them all back on the stack of papers, and without another glance for the safe or its contents fairly ran across the room to the door. Flinging it open, he emerged into a short, narrow passageway.

There, however, he paused, listening intently at the head of a narrow stairway that led downward. Two other doors opened off the passage; but both were closed. Behind those doors and throughout the house below all was quiet. Ever and again, from the street, three stories below, there rose the heavy rattle of a passing truck or cart. Within the house there was no sound at all.

Assured of that, the man raised his eyes toward the ceiling. In its center was a closed wooden transom. Frowning, the man tested the transom with his finger tips, found it immovable, and, after some further hesitation, began descending the narrow stairs, a step at a time, very cautiously. They creaked under him, every creak startlingly loud in that otherwise silent place.

Reaching the landing at the floor below, he was about to essay the next flight downward, when abruptly, somewhere in the rear of the ground floor, a door opened and closed. The sound was followed by swift, light footfalls. They crossed the reception hall below, reached the stair, and began to mount.

His face bathed in a sudden sweat of desperation, the man above darted back along the second-floor hallway. One after the other he swiftly turned the handles of three closed doors. One was locked, one opened upon a closet stacked to overflowing with trunks and bags; the third disclosed a large bedroom, apparently empty, though the bed had evidently been slept in.

He sprang inside, shut the door softly, looked for a key, found none, and thereafter stood motionless, his hand gripping the knob, one ear against the panel.

Having ascended the stairs, the footsteps were now advancing along the passage. They reached that very door against which the man stood listening. They halted there. Some one rapped lightly.

With a groan the man inside drew back. Even as he did so he found himself whirled irresistibly about and away from the door.

A great hand had descended upon his shoulder from behind. That large hand, he discovered, belonged to a man immensely tall—a huge, looming giant of a man, who had stolen upon him while he had ears only for those footsteps in the passage.

The fellow's only garment was a Turkish robe, flung loosely about his enormous shoulders. His black hair, damp from the bath, stood out like a fierce, shaggy mane above a dark, savage face in which a pair of singularly bright blue eyes blazed angrily upon the intruder. This forceful and sudden apparition in a room which the latter had believed unoccupied, was sufficiently alarming. In the little sharp cry which escaped the intruder's throat, however, there seemed a note of emotion other than terror—different from and more painful than mere terror.

"You—you!" he muttered, and fell silent.

"For the love of—" began the giant. But he, too, seemed suddenly moved past verbal expression. As a somber landscape lights to the flash of sunshine, his heavy face changed and brightened. The black scowl vanished. Shaggy brows went up in a look of intense surprise, and the fiercely set mouth relaxed to a grin of amazed but supremely good-humored delight.

"Why, it is!" he ejaculated at length. "It surely is—Bob Drayton!"

And then, with a great, pleased laugh, he released the other's shoulder and reached for his hand.

The intruder made no movement of response. Instead, he drew away shrinkingly, and with hands behind him stood leaning against the door. When he spoke it was in the tone of quiet despair with which a man might accept an intolerable situation from which escape has become impossible.

"Yes, Trenmore, it's I," he said. Even as the words left his lips there came another loud rapping from outside. Some one tried the handle, and only Drayton's weight against the door kept it closed.

"Get away from there, Martin!" called the big man peremptorily. "I'll ring again when I want you. Clear out now! It's otherwise engaged I am."

"Very well, sir," came the muffled and somewhat wondering reply.

Staring solemnly at one another, the two in the bedroom stood silent while the invisible Martin's steps receded slowly along the hall and began to descend the stairs.

"And for why will you not take my hand?" demanded the giant with a frown that was bewildered, rather than angry.

The man with the bruised head laughed. "I can't—can't—" Unable to control his voice, he lapsed into miserable silence.

The giant's frown deepened. He drew back a little, hitching the robe up over his bare shoulders.

"What is it ails you, Bobby? Here I'm glad to see you the way I cannot find words to tell it and you will not take my hand! Did you get my letter, and is this a surprise visit? You're welcome, however you've come!"

But the other shrank still closer against the door, while his pallid face grew actually gray. "May I—may I sit down?" he gasped. He was swaying like a drunken man, and his knees seemed to have no strength left in them.

"Sit down! But you may indeed." Trenmore sprang instantly to help him to the nearest chair, one arm about his shoulder in a gentle, kindly pressure. "Tell me now, did you really get my letter?"

"What letter?"

"Then you did not. What ails you, man? You're white as the banshee herself! Is it bad hurt you are, and you not telling me?"

"No—yes. A trifle. It is not that."

"What, then? Have you been ill? Here, take a drop o' the brandy, lad. That's it. A fool could see you're a deathly sick man this minute."

Trenmore's voice was tender as only a woman's or an Irishman's can be; but Drayton shrank away as if its kindness only hurt him the more.

"Don't speak that way!" he cried harshly, and buried his face in his hands.

Very wonderingly, his host laughed and again put his arm about the other's bowed shoulders. "And why not, then?" he asked gently. "I should, perhaps, like to know why you bolt into my room in the early morn, bang to my door behind yourself, and then try to repel my hospitable reception; but you need tell me nothing. For me 'tis enough that you're here at all, whom I've been wanting to see this long while more than any other lad in the world."

"Stop it, I say!" cried Drayton, and raised his head abruptly. His pale face had flushed deeply, and he seemed to flinch at the sound of his own words. "I can't—can't take your welcome. I came here as a thief, Terry Trenmore! And for no other reason."

The Irishman's blue eyes flashed wide.

"A thief?" He laughed shortly. "And pray what of mine did you wish to steal, friend Bobby? Name the thing and it's yours!"

"Terry, I'm not off my head, as you think. Haven't any such excuse. I tell you, I'm a thief. Plain, ugly t-h-i-e-f, thief. I entered this particular house only because I found a way in. I didn't know it was your house."

In the midst of speech Drayton paused and started suddenly to his feet. "Good Lord!" he exclaimed. "I had half forgotten. Terry, I wasn't the only—er—burglar here last night!"

"And what are you meaning now?"

"Your safe was opened!"

Ere he could finish the sentence Trenmore had turned, crossed the room, and was pushing aside a silken curtain, hung from ceiling to floor, near the bed. It disclosed a squared, nickeled-steel door, set flush with the wall. After a moment's scrutiny he turned a freshly bewildered face to his visitor. "Broken open? But it's not! My poor boy, you are out of your mind this morning. It's a doctor you are needing."

"No, no. I don't mean that one. I mean the safe upstairs, in the small room at the front."

"Is there one there?" queried Trenmore. "I didn't know of it."

"What! This isn't your own place, then?"

The giant shook his head, smiling. "For why would you be expecting to find Terence Trenmore tied to a house of his own? It belongs to my cousin, on the mother's side, whom I'll be glad for you to know, though he's not here now. But you say there's been robbery done above-stairs?"

"I'm not exactly sure. There was something so strange about it all. Come up there with me, Terry, and look for yourself."

Either because of the brandy he had swallowed, or because the first shame and shock of confession were over, Drayton seemed to have recovered some measure of strength. He led the way upstairs to the front bedroom, and answered the Irishman's question with a slow gesture toward the violated safe. Trenmore stood thoughtfully over the neglected pile of papers and more or less valuable jewelry, hands thrust deep in the pockets of his bathrobe, brows drawn in a reflective scowl. "And what," he asked, "were they like, these queer thieves that left their plunder behind them?"

"I didn't see them."

"What?"

Drayton's boyish, sensitive mouth quivered. "If you don't believe me, I can't blame you, of course. By Heaven, I think it would be a relief if you would call in the police, Terry, and end the whole rotten affair that way. I wish with all my heart that they'd put me where they put my partner, poor old Warren!"

"And where is that? It's riddles you're talking."

"First in jail and now in his grave," answered Drayton grimly.

The Irishman flung back his great, black-maned head angrily—

"Bobby, my boy, we've had enough of that make of talk! I can see with half an eye that much has happened of which I know nothing, for I've been back in old Ireland this two years past. But for what sort of scoundrel do you take me, to throw over the man I've best liked in my whole life, and just because he chances to be in a bit of trouble? As I said before, 'tis a doctor you are needing, not a policeman. As for this," he pointed to the rifled safe, "it was my thought that you did things here last night of which you have now no memory. Others here? 'Tis not in the bounds of reason that two different thieves—pardon the word; it's your own—should honor this house in one night!"

By way of reply, Drayton removed his hat, and for the first time Trenmore saw the ugly wound its low-drawn brim had concealed. "They gave me that," said Drayton simply. "The room," he continued, "was dark. I came over the roofs and down through the first transom I found unfastened. I had just entered this room and discovered the safe when they, whoever they were, came on me from behind and knocked me out."

Trenmore's lips drew in with a little sympathetic sound. "Ah, and so that's why you're so white and all! But tell me, was the safe open then?"

"No. They must have done the trick afterward. I was left lying on that bed. And I may as well tell you that this morning, when I found myself alone here and that stuff on the floor, I was going to—was going to finish what they had begun."

"And what stopped you?" Trenmore eyed him curiously from beneath lowered brows.

"This." Stooping, Drayton picked up the thing he had flung so desperately away half an hour earlier. It was a thin gold cigarette case, plain save for a monogram done in inlaid platinum.

Trenmore looked, and nodded slowly.

"Your own gift to me, Bobby. I think a power o' that case. But how came it there, I wonder? The other day I mislaid it. Likely Jim found it and put it here while I was in Atlantic City yesterday. When I returned Jim had been called away. I wonder he did not put it in the wall safe, though, that he lent me the use of; but all that's no matter. What did you do after finding the case?"

"I tried to get out, but the transom had been fastened down from above. So I made for the front door. Your servant intercepted me, and I—I hid in your room, hoping he would pass on by."

"And that's the one piece of good luck you had, my boy!" cried Trenmore. Grasping Drayton's shoulder with one great hand, he shook him gently to and fro, as if he had been the child he seemed beside his huge friend.

"Don't look like that now! I'm not so easy shocked, and if you've seen fit to turn burglar, Bob Drayton, I'm only sure 'tis for some very good cause. And let you arrive through the roof or by the front door, it makes no difference at all. You're here now! Martin and I have the place to ourselves for a couple of days. Jimmy Burford's a jolly old bachelor to delight your heart, but he lives at his club mostly and keeps but one man-servant, and him he took to New York with him when he was called away. We'll do fine with Martin, though. The man's a born genius for cooking."

"You mean that you are only visiting here?" asked Drayton hesitantly. Trenmore seemed taking it rather for granted that he was to remain as a guest, who had entered as a very inefficient burglar.

"Just visiting, the while Viola is enjoying herself with some friends in Atlantic City. You know it's no social butterfly I am, and too much of that crowd I will not stand, even for her sake. D'you mind my ever speaking to you of my little sister Viola, that was in the convent school near Los Angeles? But I'm a dog to keep you standing there! Come down to my room while we fix that head of yours and I get myself decently dressed. Then we'll breakfast together, and perhaps you'll tell me a little of what's been troubling your heart? You need not unless—"

"But I will, of course!" broke in Drayton impulsively as he at last grasped the friendly, powerful hand which his innate and self-denied honesty had prevented his taking except on a basis of open understanding.

Gathering up the stuff on the floor in one great armful, Trenmore bore it down to his own bedroom, followed by Drayton.

"I'll advise Jimmy to get him a new safe," chuckled Trenmore as he tossed his burden on the bed. "If there's aught of value here he deserves to be robbed, keeping it in that old tin box of a thing. But perhaps I'm ungrateful. I never thought, so freely he offered it, that he had to clear his own things out of this wall safe to give me the use of it. I'll share it with him from this day, and if there's anything missing from this lot I'll make the value up to him so be he'll let me, which he will not, being proud, stiff-necked, and half a Sassenach, for all he's my mother's third cousin on the O'Shaughnessy side. So I'll do it in a most underhand and secretive manner and get the better of him."

Still running along in a light, commonplace tone which denied any trace of the unusual in the situation, he again rang for Martin, and when that young man appeared bade him prepare breakfast for his guest as well as himself. The servant did his best to conceal a not unnatural amazement; but his imitation of an imperturbable English man-servant was a rather forlorn and weak one.

He went off at last, muttering to himself: "How'd the fellow get in? That's what I want to know! He wasn't here last night, and Mr. Trenmore hasn't been out of his room or I'd have heard him, and I never let his friend in, that's sure!"

Not strangely, perhaps, it did not occur to Martin that Mr. Trenmore's mysterious friend might have come a-visiting through the roof.

2 DUST OF PURGATORY

Less than an hour later, Robert Drayton, amateur burglar and so shortly previous a desperate and hunted man, sat down at table in the respectable Philadelphia residence he had fortunately chosen for his first invasion. His wounded temple was adorned with several neatly adjusted strips of plaster, and if his head ached, at least his heart was lighter than it had been in many a day. This last, as it were, in spite of himself. He felt that he should really be cringing under the table—anywhere out of sight. But with Terence Trenmore sitting opposite, his countenance fairly radiating satisfaction and good cheer, Drayton could not for the life of him either cringe or slink.

The breakfast, moreover, proved Martin to be what his master had boasted—an uncommonly good cook. Before the charms of sweet Virginia ham, fresh eggs, hot muffins, and super-excellent coffee, Drayton's misery and humiliation strangely faded into the background of consciousness.

Trenmore was an older man than he, by ten years of time and thrice their equivalent in rough experience. The two had first met in Chicago during the strenuous period of a strike. Drayton, unwise enough to play peaceful bystander at a full-grown riot, had found himself involved in an embattled medley of muscular slaughter-house men and equally muscular and better-armed police. He had stood an excellent chance of being killed by one party or arrested by the other, and none at all of extricating himself, when Trenmore, overlooking the fight from the steps of a near-by building, and seeing a young, slender, well-dressed man in a struggle in which he obviously had no place, came to his aid and fought a way out for the two of them.

Later they had joined forces on a long vacation in the Canadian woods. Drayton was then a rising young lawyer of considerable independent means, high-strung, nervous, and with a certain disposition toward melancholy. In the Irishman, with his tireless strength and humorous optimism, he found an ideal companion for that outdoor life, while Trenmore, well read, but self-educated, formed a well-nigh extravagant admiration for the young lawyer's intellect and character. And Terence Trenmore, his faith once given, resembled a large, loyal mastiff; he was thenceforth ready to give at need all that was his, goods, gains, or the strength of his great brain and body.

Following those months in Canada, however, Drayton returned to Cincinnati, his home. The two had kept up for some time a desultory correspondence, but Trenmore's fortune, acquired in the Yukon, permitted him to live the roving life which suited his restless temperament. His address changed so frequently that Drayton found it difficult to keep track of him, and as the latter became more and more desperately absorbed in certain ruinous complications of his own affairs, he had allowed his correspondence with Trenmore to lapse to nothing.

Their appetites pleasantly quelled at last, and cigars lighted, the two men adjourned to the library and settled themselves to talk things out.

"You've been in Ireland, you say—" began Drayton, but the other interrupted with raised hand.

"Let that wait. Do you not guess that I'm fair burning up with curiosity? There, there, when you look like that you make me want to cry, you do! Tell me the name of the scoundrel that's been driving you and I'll—I'll obliterate him. But don't act like the world was all black and you at your own wake. Sure, there's no trouble in life that's worth it! Now, what's wrong?"

Drayton smiled in spite of himself. The big man's good humor was too infectious for resistance. His face, however, soon fell again into the tragic lines drawn there by recent events.

"It can be told quickly," he began. "You know we had a very fair legal practice, Simon Warren and I. Up there in the woods I'm afraid I talked a lot about myself, so I don't need to tell you of the early struggles of a couple of cub lawyers. It was Warren, though, who made us what we were. Poor Warren! He had married just before the crash, and his young wife died three days after Simon was sentenced to a ten-year term in the penitentiary."

"So? And what did your partner do to deserve all that?"

"That is the story. We had built up a good clientele among the Cincinnati real-estate men and contractors. Simon specialized on contracts, and I on the real-estate end. We had a pretty fair reputation for success, too.

"Then Warren found out a thing about Interstate General Merchandise which would have put at least five men behind the bars. Unluckily for us they were big men. Too big for us small fry to tackle, though we didn't quite realize that. They tried to settle it amicably by buying us over. We were just the pair they were looking for, they said. And both Warren and I could have cleared over twenty-five thousand a year at the work they offered.

"Well, we'd have liked the money, of course—who wouldn't?—but not enough to take it as blackmail. Simon stuck to his guns and laid the affair before the district attorney. Before we could clinch the matter, Interstate Merchandise came down on us like a triphammer on a soft-boiled egg.

"Oh, yes, they framed us. They got Simon with faked papers on a deal he wouldn't have touched with a ten-foot pair of tongs. Of course we went down together. The disgrace killed his wife. Three weeks ago Simon died in prison of tuberculosis. That or a broken heart—

"And I—well, you see me here. I got off without a jail term. But I'd been disbarred for illegal practice, and what money I had was all gone in the fight. After that—I don't know if it was for revenge or that they were still afraid of me, but Terry, those Interstate devils hounded me out of one job after another—broke me—drove me clean out of life as I knew it.

"Yesterday I landed here in Philadelphia without a cent in my pockets, hungry and with no hope or faith left in anything. Last night I said, 'So be it! They have killed Simon, and they will not let me live as an honest man.

But, by God, I'll live!' And that's the way criminals are created. I've learned it."

Drayton ended with a catch in his voice. His clear, honest eyes were bright with the memory of that desperate resolve, so utterly alien to his nature, and his long, sensitive fingers opened and closed spasmodically.

Then Trenmore did a strangely heartless thing. Having stared at his friend for a moment, he threw back his head and laughed—laughed in a great Olympian peal of merriment that rang through the silent house.

Drayton sprang to his feet. "By heavens, Terry, I wish I could see the joke! But I'm damned if there's anything funny about what I've been through!"

As abruptly as he had begun, his host stopped laughing and forced his face into solemnity. But his blue eyes still twinkled dangerously.

"Sit down—sit down, man, and forgive me for a fool of an Irishman! Should you kill me right here for laughing, I'd not be blaming you and my heart aching this minute the way I can't wait to get at the crooks that have ruined you, and as soon as may be we'll go back to your home, you and I, and see what there is to be done.

"But, sure you're the most original criminal that ever tried to rob a man! You get in, you locate the box—did you call it a box, Bobby?—all in good form. And, by the way, were you thinking of carrying the safe away in your pocket? Or had you a stick of dynamite handy? Well, some obliging professional comes along and works the combination for you and leaves the door open. You awaken from pleasant dreams to find all that was inside, or most of it, lying right at your feet. And what is it you do? You flee as if from the devil himself, and if I hadn't stopped you you'd be straying about the streets this minute as near starvation as you were before!"

Drayton forced a smile for his friend's good-natured raillery. He could not be angry at ridicule so obviously meant to dissipate self-condemnation in laughter. "I could hardly begin on you, Terry," he said. "And speaking of that, I've already enjoyed more hospitality than I have any right to. I'm cured of crime, Terry; but if you have any idea that I am going to load myself down on you—"

Springing up with his usual impetuosity, the big Irishman fairly hurled Drayton back into his chair.

"Sit down! Sit down there where you belong! Is it load yourself you're talking of? It's to be loaded with me you are! Do you know that my very life's been threatened?"

"Please don't joke any more, Terry," protested the other wearily.

"I've not gone into details, but all the fun has been crushed out of me in the last year or so."

"Take shame to yourself, then! But this is no joke. You'll well believe me it's not when you've heard it all. Stay here now a minute, for I've a thing to show you."

In no little wonder, Drayton obeyed while Trenmore left the room and ascended the stairs to his bedchamber. A few minutes later he returned, and, drawing his chair close to Drayton, dropped into it and disclosed the thing he had brought. It seemed to be a glass vial. About six inches in length, it tapered to a point at one end, while the other was capped with silver, daintily carved to the shape of three dogs' heads. These heads, with savage, snarling jaws, all emerged from one collar, set with five small but brilliant rubies. The vial was filled to the top with some substance of the color of gray emery.

"A pretty little thing," commented Drayton.

"Aye, 'tis a pretty little thing," the other assented, staring down at the odd trifle with frowning brows. "Now what would you be thinking it might be?"

"I could hardly say. It looks like a bottle for smelling salts. What is that stuff inside?"

"Ah, now you're asking! And what do you think of the handsome silver cap to it?"

"Really, Terry," replied Drayton with a touch of impatience, "I am no judge of that sort of work. It is intended, I suppose, to represent the three-headed dog, Cerberus—the one that guarded the gates of Pluto's realm in the old mythology. The carving is beautiful."

Trenmore nodded. "It is that. And now I'll tell you how I came by it. You know it's an ignorant, rude man I am; but hid away somewhere inside me there's a great love for little, pretty, delicate things. And though I've no real education like you, Bobby, I've picked up one thing here and another there, and when I happen on some trifle with a bit of a history it just puts the comether on me, and have it I must, whether or no.

"Behind that small steel door you saw in the wall of my room I've some amazing pretty toys that I'd not like to part with. I'll show you them later, if you care, and tell you the tales that go with them. Did you read in the paper last month how Thaddeus B. Crane was after dying and all his great collection to go at auction?"

"I didn't notice."

"You wouldn't. You'd something worse to think of. But I did; so I remembered this which I had heard the fame of, and to that auction I went three days running until they came to the thing I wanted. ',' it's called, just as you named it like the clever lad you are. It's old, and they say ''twas made in Florence centuries ago. But I'll read you the bit of description Crane had for it."

He produced a sheet of time-yellowed paper. "'The Heads of Cerberus,'" he read. "'Said to have been carved by Benvenuto Cellini for his patron, the Duke of Florence. Its contents have never been examined. The legend runs, however, that the gray dust within it was gathered from the rocks at the gates of Purgatory by the poet Dante, and that it was to contain this dust that the duke required the vial. More probably, from a modern viewpoint, the contents are some sort of poison, which a Florentine duke may well have carried in self-protection or for the destruction of his enemies. The vial itself is of rock crystal and the cap—closed with cement—a peculiarly beautiful specimen of sixteenth century work. It is probably a genuine Cellini. It passed into the hands-' But I'll not be reading the rest. It tells the names of those who have owned it, and the astonishing number of them that died violently or disappeared from the face of God's earth, and no more trace left of them than a puff of smoke from your cigar!"

Drayton's lips twisted to an involuntary smile.

"A very extraordinary history," he commented. "Dante, Benvenuto Cellini, and Dust from the Rocks of Purgatory! May I ask what you paid?"

"Only five hundred. There'd word got about that Crane was no good judge and that there were more copies than originals in his collections. The regular collectors bought shy, and I misdoubt Crane's widow realized the half of what he'd spent on the lot. There was little bidding for this. The tale's too extravagant, and most would not believe it a true Cellini. However, no sooner had I got it and walked out of the salesrooms than a gray-haired old party came running after me and caught me by the sleeve.

"'And is it you that bought the Cerberus?' he demands. 'It's myself that did,' I conceded him. 'And will you sell it again to me?' 'I will not,' says I. 'Not for twice what you paid for it?' inquires he with a cunning look in his eye that I did not like. 'No, I'll not,' says I. 'Nor for two or four times what I paid for it. I'm a gentleman collector. I am not a dealer. I bought this for myself and I will keep it. Good day to you, sir,' says I, and with that I walked on.

"But do you believe he would accept my polite rebuff? Not he. He runs along by the side of me, taking three steps to my one. 'If you'll not sell it me you'll be sorry,' he keeps on saying. 'It should be mine. I went to buy it, but my chauffeur ran over a man on Broadway. Confound the fool! The police took my chauffeur and delayed me till I came too late for the bidding. I'd have had it if it cost me five thousand, and that's what I'll give now, if you'll sell.'

"By then I'd taken a real dislike to the man with his persistence and his sharp eyes. In plain words I told him if he'd not desist from following me about I'd be calling an ambulance, for he'd be needing one shortly. 'You can join in the hospital the poor devil your car murdered,' says I. And at that he takes a squint up at me sideways, like I was an elephant he'd just discovered himself to be walking with and him thinking all along I was just a small pigling, and he turns white and stops dead in his tracks. The poor midget! I'd not have laid my little finger on him for fear of crushing him entirely. But for all that he gets courage to shake his fist and call after me, 'You'll be sorry for this. You don't know what you've bought and I do! I'll have it yet!'

"Well, I thought no more of the silly madman that day. But on the next I received a letter that came to me at the hotel where Viola and me were then stopping. It said that if I'd not sell for ten thousand I'd sell for worse than nothing, and to put an ad in the paper if I'd changed my mind.

"Of course, I did nothing. But from that day I've had no peace at all. Twice my baggage has been gone over, and last week two thugs tried to hold me up in Jersey City. The poor devils are in the hospital this minute; but they could not or would not tell the name of the man who employed them.

"There have been two more letters which I'll show you presently, and the last was addressed here, showing how the fellow has watched and spied on my movements. In it he declares that my very life shall not stand in the way, but he must have the Cerberus. I'm a man of peace, and it's fair getting on my nerves.

"Last night they must have tried again, and it's a wonder I was not murdered in my bed! You've come in the nick of time to save me from nervous prostration, Bobby, lad, for it's little they can do against the two of us, your brains and my brawn!"

Now it was Drayton's turn to laugh. The picture of Terence Trenmore suffering from nervous collapse, or caring two straws for all the crooks and madmen in America, was too much for his friend. He laughed and laughed, while the Irishman stared at him in a grieved surprise which only added fuel to his hysterical mirth.

"And why," demanded Trenmore indignantly, "why wouldn't I be thinking of you when I want a lad at my side? Jimmy, my host here, is a fine man, but not the one to consult on such a Mysterious matter, life meaning to him just business, with his club for diversion, heaven help him! And were he not a distant cousin of my own mother on the O'Shaughnessy side, Jimmy and me would have never become acquainted. And wasn't I meaning to go clear to Cincinnati next week, just to be asking your advice? And does that list of folk who have had ill luck from the Cerberus—does that mean nothing at all? I tell you, I need your help and counsel, Bobby, and it's glad I am that you are here to give it."

Drayton suddenly perceived that the Irishman had been entirely serious throughout. The tale was not, as he had believed, a mere excuse seized on with intent to delude him, Drayton, into feeling that he might be of value as an ally. Hidden away in one secret corner of his friend's giant heart there dwelt a small, imaginative and quite credulous child. "Dust from the Rocks of Purgatory!" It was that which had fascinated Trenmore, and it was that more than any dread of midnight assassins which had driven him to appeal to his lawyer friend. What he wished was moral, not physical, backing.

"But, Terry," said Drayton, sobered and really touched by this unexpected demand upon him, "if the thing bothers you so much why not sell and be rid of it?"

Trenmore's mouth set in a straight, obstinate line. "No, I'll not," he declared. "They cannot bully a Trenmore, and Viola says the same. But if I could I'd lay hands on the old villain that's after it the way he'd trouble us no more, so I would!"

"Have you tried the police?"

"To be sure."

"How about the auction rooms where you bought it? If this persecutor of yours is a collector, they might know him there by description."

"That I tried myself before I troubled the police. One young fellow remembered the old villain, and remembered him asking my name. They keep a register at the salesrooms. But as for the villain's own name, no one there seemed to know it."

"Well, then—" Drayton cast about in his mind somewhat vaguely. Then an idea struck him. "By the way, Terry, have you opened the vial and had the contents analyzed?"

Trenmore's blue eyes flashed wide. "I have not!" he exclaimed with considerable energy. "For why would I be intruding on such a matter? Surely, in the place where that Dust came from, they'd not be liking me to meddle with it!"

Drayton firmly suppressed a smile. The price of friendship is tolerance, and he was too grateful and too fond of his Irishman to express ridicule. "I really believe," he said gravely, "that, admitting the Purgatory part of the legend to be true, the Dust is too far separated from its origin, and too many centuries have elapsed since it was placed in this vial for any real danger to attach to it. And who knows? There may be diamonds, or some other jewels, hidden in that close-packed dust. If there is a question of the vial's authenticity as a Cellini it can't be the vial itself that your mysterious collector is ready to pay ten thousand for. Why not open it, anyway, and find out exactly where you are?"

The Irishman scratched his head with a curious expression of indecision. Physical dread was a sensation of which he was happily ignorant; but he possessed a strong disinclination to meddle with any affair that touched on the super-natural. He had bought the vial for the sake of its reputed creator, Cellini. Then his attention had become focused on the "Dust" and the uncanny description accompanying it, and while obstinacy forbade him to let the thing go by force, still it was to him a very uneasy possession. Had no one arisen to dispute its ownership, Trenmore would probably have rid himself of the Cerberus before this.

"Well," he said at length, "if you think opening it is the wise way to be doing, then let us do it and get it over. But myself, I dread it's a foolish trifling with powers we know little of!"

"Nonsense!" laughed Drayton. "That Dante Purgatory stuff has got your goat, Terry. Not," he added hastily, "that I am ridiculing the story, but you will admit that it is slightly—just slightly—improbable. Here!" He snatched a newspaper from a near-by table and spread it on the floor between them. "Give me that vial and I'll see if it is possible to get the cap open without injury. We mustn't risk any vandalism. It is a beautiful piece of work, Cellini or no Cellini."

Feeling in his pocket, he drew out a serviceable pen-knife, opened the large blade, and took the crystal vial from Trenmore's still reluctant hand. As the description had stated, the hinged cover, besides being fastened with a tiny hasp that formed the buckle of the jeweled collar, was cemented down. The cement showed as a thin, reddish line between silver and crystal. The lower sections of hinge and hasp were riveted to the crystal.

Drayton ran the point of his blade cautiously around the red line. "Hard as steel," he commented. "After all, perhaps we can't open it."

A flash of relief lighted Trenmore's heavy, anxious face. He stretched a quick hand to reclaim the vial, but Drayton drew back. Opening a thin small blade, he tried the cement from another angle.

"Aha!" said he triumphantly. "That does it. This stuff is old. I can't cut it, but you see it's easy to separate the cement from the crystal by running the blade underneath. And now—careful does it. There! Let's see how the hasp works."

He fumbled with it for a moment. There came a little snap, and the cover flew up as if propelled by a spring. At the same time a tiny cloud of fine, grayish particles arose from the open vial. They gleamed like diamond dust in the sunlight.

With a quick gasp, Trenmore sat back in his chair. Though the room was cool, his face was shining with perspiration; but Drayton paid him no heed. The ex-lawyer's curiosity was by this time fully aroused, and it was unclouded by any wraith of the superstition which claimed for the gray powder so unnatural an origin.

Without hesitation, he stooped and carefully emptied the vial upon the paper at his feet. The Dust was so finely pulverized that he had to proceed with the utmost care to prevent the stuff from rising into the air. At last the vial was empty. A dark heap, resembling gray flour or powdered emery, had been its sole contents.

"I was wrong," remarked Drayton, sitting up with the Cerberus in his hand. "There was nothing there but the Dust."

Now it was strange that after all his nervous dread and horror of the Dust, Trenmore should have done what he did. Perhaps, having seen Drayton handle it without harm, he had lost this fear; or it might have been the natural heedlessness of his impulsive nature. Whatever the explanation, as Drayton ceased speaking his friend leaned over and deliberately thrust two fingers into the powder, stirring it about and feeling its soft fineness.

And then occurred the first of that series of extraordinary incidents which were to involve both Trenmore and Robert Drayton in adventures so weird, so seemingly inexplicable, that for a time even Drayton came to share his friend's belief in the super-natural quality of that which had been guarded by Cellini's Cerberus.

There sat the two friends in Burford's pleasant sunlit library. Outside the frequent clang or rattle of passing traffic spoke of the "downtown" district which had crept up about Jimmy Burford and some other stubborn old residents of Walnut Street. There they sat, and the city was all about them—commonplace, busy, impatient, and skeptical of the miraculous as Drayton himself. Somewhere at the back of the house Martin was whistling cheerily about his work.

Leaning back in his chair, Drayton's eyes were fixed on his friend, a huge figure in his loose gray morning suit—a very monument of material flesh, bone, and muscle. The sunlight fell full on him as he bent above the Dust, bringing out every kindly line of his heavy, dark face. Drayton saw him stir the Dust with his fingers. And Drayton saw a small cloud of the stuff rise toward Trenmore's face, like a puff of thin, gray smoke.

Then Drayton cried out loudly. He pushed back his chair so sharply as to overset it, and sprang away from the newspaper and its burden.

Above the floor still hovered the thin gray cloud, growing thinner every moment as the particles settled again through the draftless air. But where was Trenmore?

There had been a quivering and a wavering of his great form, as if Drayton saw him through a haze of heat. And with that, as easily and completely as a wraith of smoke from his own cigar, the giant Irishman had vanished!

3 ARRIVALS AND DEPARTURES

In his first moments of stunned surprise it seemed to Drayton that the end of all things had come. The maddest, most impossible surmises flashed across his mind. He scarcely would have felt further amazement had Lucifer himself, in all the traditional panoply of hoofs, tail, and brimstone, risen sudden and flaming through the midst of that dreary-hued heap of mysterious Dust. Had the tables and chairs begun to move about the room on their own legs it would have appeared only the natural sequel to such an event as had just transpired. Indeed, it seemed strangely terrible that nothing more should occur. That Nature, having broken her most sacred law, the indestructibility of matter, should carry her sacrilege no further.

But had that law been broken? Was it possible that by some unheard-of property the gray powder had noiselessly, without shock or visible sign of explosion resolved the great body of his friend into the component gases to which all matter may, in one way or another, be reduced? Or was he, Robert Drayton, stark mad, and had the whole absurd, horrible episode been a part of some delirious dream?

There lay the crystal vial on the floor, where he had dropped it in his first dismay. There was the newspaper, with half of a bargain-sale advertisement extending from beneath the gray heap. And now he became aware that in the library a bell was ringing with regular, monotonous persistence.

Scarcely knowing what he did, Drayton crossed the room and lifted the telephone receiver from its hook.

"Hello, hello! What? Yes, this is James Burford's home. What's that? Mr.-Mr. Trenmore? Yes; he's here. No—I—I mean, he was here a moment ago. No; I don't know where he is or when he will be back. My God, I wish I did! What's that? You are—whom did you say? . . . Oh, my Lord!"

Drayton dropped the receiver and stood staring in blank horror. After a while, leaving the receiver to dangle and click unheeded, he turned and walked slowly back toward the chair on whose broad arm Terence Trenmore's cigar still glowed behind a lengthening ash. With a slight shudder he forced himself to pass his hands carefully over the chair's entire inner surface, seat, arms, and back. The leather covering retained a trace of warmth from its recent occupant; but it was most indubitably empty.

The enormity, the unprecedented horror of the whole situation swept up on Drayton like a rising tide, wiping out for a time all thought of the telephone or the person to whom he had just been speaking. With a dazed, sick look he again circled the newspaper and its burden, righted his own chair, and sat down. He had a queer feeling that some one had just played a particularly cruel practical joke of which he was the victim.

And yet—what if that gray Dust had really possessed just the terrific, unbelievable history with which Trenmore had credited it?

He strove to arrange his facts and premises in a logical and reasonable order, but found himself continually returning to that one scene—he, Drayton, sitting where he now sat; Trenmore opposite, bending over the paper; the cloud that rose, gray and nebulous, and hung in the air *after his friend was gone.*

Presently he was again roused from his stupor, and again by a bell. The sound came faintly from the rear of the house. Drayton waited, thinking to hear Martin pass through the reception hall on his way to the front door. Again the bell rang, and this time in a long, steady, insistent peal. Some one seemed to have placed a finger on the button and determined that it should not be removed until the door opened. Martin must be out, on an errand perhaps.

Half dazedly, as he had answered the phone, Drayton at length responded to this new demand. As he unlocked the front door and opened it a burst of summer sunshine rushed in and with it the small, angry figure of a much perturbed young lady.

"Where is he? What has happened to my brother? Who was that man at the telephone? Answer me instantly, I say! Where is my brother, Terry Trenmore?"

The questions beat upon Drayton's ears like blows, rousing him to some semblance of his normal self-possession.

"You are—you are Miss Trenmore?" he asked in turn, though a sudden conscience-stricken remembrance smote him and assured him that she was. He had terminated that telephone conversation so very abruptly. No doubt the girl had run in from Atlantic City to see her brother, called him up, and—

"I am Viola Trenmore, and I want my brother. Where is he?"

Drayton faced her with a feeling of helpless fright, though in herself, Trenmore's sister was of no terrifying appearance. Nearly as little as her brother was large, she looked even younger than the seventeen years Drayton knew to be hers. She had her brother's eyes, azure as an Italian sky, and her straight, fine brows and curling lashes were black—beautifully so and in vivid contrast to the clear white and rose of her eager face, flushed now like an excited child's. Her small, modish hat, trim pumps, and tailored suit, all matched in color the bright, clear hue of her eyes. Despite his desperate preoccupation, Drayton's first sight of Viola Trenmore brought him the same momentary flash of joy that comes with the sight of a bluebird in springtime. She was like a bluebird, fluttering in from the sunshine. His troubled mind scarcely recognized the thought, but always afterward he remembered that first beauty of her as the flash of a bluebird's wing.

"What have you done with him?" she demanded, while from those blue eyes there blazed the very twin spirit of Terence Trenmore—Terence the impetuous, angered and scorning all caution.

"I hardly know what to tell you, Miss Trenmore," began Drayton hesitatingly. "Your brother is not here. He has gone. Oh, but I don't myself know what has happened, or whether I am sane or crazy! Come in here, Miss Trenmore, and you shall at least hear the story."

Puzzled now, and watching him with a sort of alert wariness, Viola obeyed his gesture and entered the library.

And there, in halting, broken sentences, Drayton told his incredible tale. He showed her the Dust on the paper, the empty crystal vial, the half-smoked cigar, whose fire had expired some minutes since, like a last living trace of the man who had lighted it.

And somehow, as Drayton talked, he knew that it was all true, and that Trenmore was dead. Dead and dissipated to the elements as thoroughly as if, instead of a bare half hour, ten thousand years had slipped by since his going. Grief clutched Drayton's throat and he finished his story in a hoarse, barely audible whisper.

"And so—he was gone! Like that. And nothing left. Nothing but that infernal stuff there that—that murdered him—my friend!"

For one moment the girl stood silent, and Drayton thought that she also was dazed, as he had been. But suddenly she flung back her head with Trenmore's very gesture.

"I don't believe you!" she cried vehemently. "I don't believe you! Did you expect me to believe you? Do you take me for an infant? Who are you that are here in my cousin's house, answer his telephone and his door, and meet me with this mad lie about Terry? I recognize that vial! And I know that some one has been trying to steal it from my brother. Are you that thief, and have you murdered Terry, as you threatened you would?"

She advanced upon him, her eyes two pools of blue, indignant fire; but the man stood his ground. "I am Robert Drayton," he said.

"Robert Drayton! But you can't be. Mr. Drayton is a good friend of Terry's, though I've never met him, and some way you know that and hope to deceive me! Mr. Drayton would not treat me like this. He would not lie to me. He would not—" Sobbing at last, she broke off and clenched her little hands fiercely. "I'll show you!" she cried. "I'll show you what I think of you and your lies, and then I'll make you tell me the true story!"

Before Drayton, springing forward with a cry of wild protest, could prevent, she had dropped on her knees beside the heap of Dust. Another instant and her white-gloved fingers had again raised that ominous gray cloud.

It rose in a spiral swirl—

For a second Drayton still saw her as a vague, translucent blur of blue shading into pink where her face had been. Then the air shimmered and cleared, and once more the unfortunate young man stood alone in Burford's pleasant library. This time not so much as a lighted cigar remained to remind him of recent companionship.

Mr. Robert Drayton began to swear. Serious profanity had never come easily to his lips. Now, however, he heard himself using phrases and words which he had not even been aware that he knew; a steady, low-voiced, earnest stream of expression whose utterance gave him the strangest satisfaction and relief. He swore for two minutes without a pause, then trailed off into silence. The superhuman tension had been broken, however, and he could again think.

This abruptness and totality of disappearance, that left him not so much as a corpse to mourn, awoke in him emotions different from any he had ever experienced. He found that he could not think of Trenmore and his sister as other than alive, nor rid himself of the idea that in some way they were yet present in the library. Not though the very clearest memory informed him that before his eyes those two had been resolved to nothingness.

Pondering on what he should do, however, it came to him that in honor only one course lay open. Had he been content to indulge Trenmore's superstitious regard for that infernal Dust, he would have been left confronting no such ghastly mystery. The fault, by this reckoning, was his. Let him pay, then.

With a firm, resolute tread Drayton approached the sinister gray pile, and of all its victims he alone loosed its deadliness knowingly—or believing that he knew.

Ten seconds later the library was empty of human life.

On the mantelpiece stood a clock which then pointed to the hour of nine-thirty. It ticked on solemnly, dutifully, wholly indifferent to any wonder save the great and perpetual miracle of Time itself. Minute by minute the long and the short hands crept over the dial, and on the vast looms of Eternity thread by thread was added to the universal fabric of the Past.

Ten-twenty-five, and Martin, out marketing among the stalls in the Reading Terminal Market, was very cheerful over some exceptionally large, juicy oranges. Mr. Trenmore liked oranges. He added two dozen of the fruit to his order and started homeward.

Back there in the library the Cerberus still gleamed where Drayton had flung it down. The Dust still lay on its newspaper, whose matter-of-factness seemed to deride all mystery connected with divorce, murder, or the wonderful cheapness of lace blouses and lingerie at Isaac Fineheimer's Stock Clearance Sale.

And as Martin, on his return journey, crossed Juniper Street, five blocks away, a caller arrived at a certain house on Walnut Street.

He was a short, rotund young gentleman. Attired in a suit of dark green, neatly matched by socks, tie, and the ribbon on his wellblocked hat, the one false note in his color scheme was struck by a pair of bright, too-bright tan shoes.

Twice he had passed the house saunteringly; then boldly ascended Mr. Burford's sedate white marble doorsteps. Boldly indeed he walked up and in at the open door; but once inside his demeanor underwent a change. No cat could have slunk more softly through vestibule and hall; no hunting animal could have been more keenly alert for any sound within the quiet, empty house.

He made straight for the stairs; but with one foot on the first step he paused. Through a half-open door he could see part of a large, book-lined room. Was it empty?

After short hesitation the rotund green gentleman stole over and peered cautiously round the edge of that door!

An instant later, and he had darted across the library with a silent, amazing celerity of movement. His attention, it seemed, had been caught by the Cerberus' gleaming in the sunlight. Picking up the vial, he examined it with swift care, thrust it in his pocket, and turned to leave. His cherubic face now wore the look of one who has achieved good fortune with almost suspicious ease; his pleased smile was half doubtful, and as he moved softly toward the door his small, darting eyes glanced from side to side quickly, thoughtful of hidden danger.

Unluckily for him, however, the real danger in that room was not bidden. It lay in full sight on a newspaper, flat on the floor between two chairs that faced one another companionably.

Frequently curiosity has been proved a fatal weakness.

How far the extraordinary affair might have progressed, how many of Philadelphia's citizens, innocent or otherwise, might have entered that library and been tempted to investigate the harmless looking gray peril on its floor, had not Martin been a careful and conscientious individual, is a problem for speculation. Fortunately, however, Martin was what he was. At exactly eleven o'clock he entered the library seeking his employer. Finding the room empty, and having searched the rest of the house in vain, he came to the natural and entirely correct conclusion. Mr. Trenmore was not at home.

The front door had been left open. Martin closed it. Then he returned to straighten the library and empty the ash trays.

Over the fatal Dust he hesitated. Was this gray, floury stuff rubbish left here to be thrown out? Arbitrary and uninstructed action never appealed to Martin. With wise caution—how wise he would have been panic-stricken to learn—he folded the newspaper together, taking pains that its contents be not scattered, made a neat packet of it, and tied it with red tape from the table drawer. This packet he carried upstairs and laid on Trenmore's chiffonier, where there could be no question of its being overlooked.

After that Martin sought the lower regions to prepare luncheon for Trenmore and his guest.

And in the library—that room of abominable and innocent looking emptiness—the clock ticked solemnly on.

4   WHERE THE GRAY DUST LED

What Robert Drayton expected when, without one glance for the world he felt himself to be forever leaving, he so deliberately followed the two Trenmores, he scarcely knew. Death, probably.

As he bent above the Dust, his back to the sunlight and to life, he was conscious of neither regret, fear, nor curiosity. He had reached that blank wall which seems to rise in moments of great crisis—a sense of nowness that cuts off past and future, leaving for standing place only the present, an infinitesimal point.

Carefully copying the actions of those who had preceded him, Drayton touched the Dust, first gently, then, in sudden haste for the end, giving it one vigorous stir with his forefinger.

Had he been a conventional suicide tugging at a trigger the result could have come no more promptly. As he had seen it rise before, so it rose now—that grim cloud which to Drayton presaged dissolution.

It reached his face, was in his eyes, his nostrils. With it came dizziness and a strong physical nausea. His mouth tasted sharply bitter, as if he had swallowed quinine. Drayton shuddered and gasped. He saw everything through a gray mist. The room was filled with it. It was a mist composed of thin, concentric rings, swirling slowly with himself for axis. The rings became thicker, denser—till he could perceive nothing else—till he could not see his hands, when, stretching them out to catch at a chair or table, they came in contact only with the air.

The bitter taste and the sickness increased. His hand was on the floor supporting him, and the floor felt strange; the carpet unlike any weave of human making. Presently even the dizziness and nausea were forgotten. He had attention only for that strange carpet. He could have sworn that what he touched with cautious, investigatory fingers was not carpet at all, but grass! Surely it was grass—long, matted, a tangle of brittle-dry blades.

While he still explored this odd phenomenon, the blinding grayness about him began to thin. All around him appeared the changing outlines of shapes, gray and mutable as the mist itself, but still shapes of a sort. Rapidly now these grew more coherent, solid, and acquired a more than shadowy substance, until, all in a moment, the gray, swirling veil was withdrawn.

Unless every sense of his body lied, Drayton was crouching on the ground in open air. Those gray shapes he had glimpsed were the fallen stones and broken walls of some old, ruined building.

Unspeakably bewildered, Drayton staggered to his feet. There before him stretched the broad level of a wide green plain, across which a low sun stared through a strata of reddened cloud. The ruins near which he stood crowned the summit of a little hill, all overgrown with that dry, tangled grass which had so puzzled him in the mist. Here and there a few small trees had sprung up among the stones. He heard their scant, yellowish foliage rustling stiffly in the slight breeze.

Turning slowly, he perceived that the hill of the gray ruins was the first of a low range of foothills, above whose summits in the east loomed the white peaks of mountains.

Following amazement, Drayton's first impression was one of intolerable loneliness. In the sky of this strange, wide world he had invaded not a bird flew; mountain, hill, and plain lay desolate, empty of any living creature; no sound broke the stillness save the gentle, unhuman whisper of the warm breeze, blowing from the plain upward across the hills.

And yet it was all very real; very convincing and earth-like. The shadows of the ruins stretched long and dark away from the almost level rays of the sinking sun. Stretching forth his hand, Drayton laid it cautiously upon the stone of a broken wall. The rough granite felt dusty and hot beneath his fingers. He broke off a bit of green-gray lichen that grew there, and it was just that—lichen and no more.

If he were dead, if this were the world that awaits the soul when the body perishes, why did he feel so uncommonly like his ordinary, everyday, physical self? How could he feel at all, in any common sense?

He was alive. His feet pressed the earth with the weight of a quite material body. Why, his very clothing denied any spirituality in this experience. There he stood, bare-headed, dressed in the same old blue serge suit he had bought five years ago in Cincinnati, and which now constituted his sole wardrobe. The sun was warm on his face;

the air breathed clear and sweet. Surely he was no spirit, but a living man of flesh and blood.

Nowhere, however, was there hint or sign of other living humanity than himself. He was alone in a land so empty that only the greenness on hills and plain preserved it from utter desolation. The ruins spoke of man, but of man dead and gone so many ages since that their stones remembered his clean chisel strokes but vaguely.

What devilish nature had that Dust possessed, and where had it seen fit to deposit his fellow victims?

Drayton flung out his arms in a gesture of despair. For a long moment he stood so, a desolate figure in a vacant land. Then his hands dropped limp at his sides, and he began an aimless, wandering walk between the ruins.

Here, he thought with a faint flicker of interest, there had once stood a fortress or castle. Centuries ago it had fallen. All that remained were broken columns, heaps of rugged granite and portions of the thick outer walls. Within the latter he could trace the shape of a courtyard, still paved in places with crumbling flagstones.

Presently he came upon the remains of a gateway. The arch had fallen in and upon one of its stones Drayton observed traces of letters. He examined them curiously. Time, however, had done its work too thoroughly, and all he could decipher were the first few letters of two lines:

ULITH—

MC—

There was no clue in that to his whereabouts.

In despair of learning more, he strayed on, vaguely wondering why he should walk at all, until in the matted grass of the courtyard, close to the inner side of the same wall by which he had first found himself kneeling, his foot struck against something.

He stared downward. The sun was very low, the shadow of the wall was dark, and he could see only that there was a long mound there, under the tangled grass. But that soft, heavy resilience of the thing he had stumbled on, coupled with the length and shape of the mound—there was that in the combination which struck him unpleasantly.

He turned to leave it, then came back as if fascinated. Finally he stooped, and with nervous, desperate fingers dragged and tore at the network of dry, tangled fibers that covered the mound. At last he uncovered something that looked and felt like a piece of cloth. But the color of it—the color of it! Out of the dim shadow it gleamed at him, bright, clear, bluest and purest of blues—the hue of a bluebird's wing!

Frantically, with a growing sense of impending horror, Drayton persisted in his task until his worst fears were confirmed.

Beneath that grass lay the body of a woman, face down. Though the face was concealed, he knew her instantly. And she lay there, deathly quiet, face down *and the grass had grown over her*.

How long—good God!—how long a time had passed since he had stood face to face with this girl in James Burford's library? It had been morning there. Here it was sunset. Sunset? How many suns had set since that grass was young and began its task of shroud weaving?

Conquering a sudden and violent impulse to flee, Drayton turned the body over and laughed a little wildly. After all, the grass was a liar. Dead the girl might be—she lay still enough—but if dead she was most recently so. Her face was pale and sweet and perfect as a child's sleeping there in the shadow. The lids were closed softly over her eyes, as if at any moment the curling lashes might quiver and lift.

Scarcely breathing, Drayton knelt and laid his ear above her heart. Surely that was a faint flutter he felt! Raising her head, he sought some other sign of returning consciousness. There was none. He laid a hand on her forehead. It was cool, but not with the chilling coldness he dreaded.

Questioning no longer, but with a great hope in his heart, Drayton sprang to his feet and paused. Where in this empty, houseless land could he obtain any stimulant or even water to revive her? He must have it—he must save her before that faint trace of life should flicker out. Alone he had been nothing. With this small sister of Trenmore's at his side he could face all the mysteries of the universe with a cheerful carelessness. He loved her suddenly and joyously, not because she was the most beautiful creature he had ever seen, but simply because she was *human!*

Yet should he leave her to seek water the girl might die in his absence. Better he had never found her than that! Despairing of other means, Drayton was about to try what resuscitation the chafing of wrists and forehead might effect when, glancing westward to judge how much of day might be left him, he beheld an odd, unlooked-for thing.

On the side of the ruins toward the plain stood the longest and highest fragment of the outer wall. On the left it rose in a jagged slant from the old foundations to a height of six or seven feet, extended level for a distance of four yards or so, then ended in an abrupt vertical line that exactly bisected the red sun, now touching the horizon. And from beyond its black silhouette, against the faint pink of the western sky, a thin puff of smoke was ascending!

It was dissipated by the slight breeze from the plain. Another puff and another followed it. Then the puffs ceased, to be succeeded by a slow, thin column of mysterious vapor.

Who or what was behind that wall?

Standing there alone and weaponless beside the unconscious girl, Drayton was swept by a terror deeper and more vivid than any dread he had ever before experienced. Smoke! The most familiar sight known to man. But in this strange, unhuman place? What vague demon might he not discover if he dared look behind that wall?

Yet his very fear drove him. Night was on its way to lend terror the cloak of invisibility. He must go while the sun befriended him.

Leaving the girl where she was, Drayton stumbled across the grass-hidden stones between him and the fragment of wall. He caught at its top with his hands and cautiously pulled himself up.

Just before his head cleared the ragged stones a voice began speaking. It was a deep, vibrant voice, entirely harmonious with the surroundings.

"Well," it declared, and the tone was somewhat plaintive, "and that is the last of my last cigar. Sure, it's a fine sunset they have here, but 'tis not my idea of Purgatory at all! 'Tis too dull, so it is. I wish—"

"Terry Trenmore!" With joyful, scarce-believing eyes, Drayton was staring over the wall. Then his muscles suddenly gave way and he dropped back on his own side.

For an instant there was dead silence. When the voice was heard again it was with an intonation of profound resignation.

"There now, it's begun at last! Sure, I never should have wished for excitement! But the devils will find Terence Trenmore game. Invisible voices shouting my own name! I wonder now, is that the best they can do? I wonder had I better—"

"Trenmore, it's I—Bob Drayton!"

As Drayton appeared suddenly around the end of the wall, the Irishman faced him calmly without rising. "I'm resigned," he said. "You might take a worse shape than that. What is it you'd be about now?"

Laughing outright, Drayton walked over and shook his giant friend by the shoulder.

"You blessed old idiot! Don't you know me? Have you been sitting here all this time while I mooned about thinking myself—By Heaven, Terry, do you know that Viola is here, too?"

"Viola, is it? Now I tell you straight, my lad, if you're what I suspect you of being you keep your tongue off my little sister or there'll be one devil the less in these parts!"

"Trenmore, have you gone stark mad? I'm no devil! Here, take my hand. Doesn't that feel like flesh and blood? I tell you, Viola is here. She came to the house after—after you went. And before I could prevent her she had stirred up that infernal gray powder."

"She did? Well, tell me then how you reached here yourself, and perhaps I'll begin to believe you."

Drayton shrugged. "I followed, of course. The whole thing was my fault. I thought you were both dead, and I could hardly do less than follow."

Trenmore sprang up and wrung the other's hand with his customary enthusiasm. "And now I do believe you!" he cried. "You're Bobby Drayton and none other, for you've acted like the man I knew you to be. But poor little Viola! And where is she now? Sure, if *she's* in this place, I misdoubt it's the one I took it for, after all!"

"She is over among the ruins, and she seems to have fainted. I found her all buried in grass. She mustn't be left alone another instant. Have you any whisky or brandy about you?"

"I have not—bad luck to me!"

Disappointed, but still hopeful, Drayton led the way, eagerly followed by his friend. The sun had sunk till it glowed like the half of a great, round, red lantern above the horizon's rim. Drayton was wondering what they should do if they failed to revive Viola before night came on; but this anxiety was wasted.

As they crossed the grass-grown court a little figure in blue dashed suddenly from behind a shattered column and flung itself bodily into the arms of Trenmore.

"Terry—oh, Terry, my dear!"

"Little Viola! There, there now. Is it crying you are? And for what?"

"Just for joy, Terry, dear. Don't mind me. There, I'll not cry any more. I waked up—all alone—in the shadow. And Terry, darling, I'd been dreaming that we both were dead!"

5 THE WEAVER OF THE YEARS

When the marvelous oversteps the bounds of known possibility there are three ways of meeting it. Trenmore and his sister, after a grave discussion of certain contingencies connected with the Catholic religion and a dismissal of them on grounds too utterly Celtic and dogmatic for Drayton to follow, took the first way. From that time on they faced every wonder as a fact by itself, to be accepted as such and let go at that.

Drayton, though all his life he had unconsciously so viewed such accustomed marvels as electricity or the phenomenon of his own life, could not here follow his Irish friends. He compromised on the second way, and accepted with a mental reservation, as "I see you now, but I am not at all sure that you are there or that I really believe in you!"

Fortunately there was not one of the three so lacking in mental elasticity as to discover the third way, which is madness.

"And what we should be thinking of," declared Viola presently, "is not how did we come here, but how are we to find our way home?"

This was a truism too obvious for dispute. And yet, to Drayton at least, it seemed that no amount of thinking or action either was likely to be of great service. They were without food or water. Without weapons or compass. Without the faintest glimmering of knowledge as to their actual geographic position upon the earth.

Drayton strained his eyes toward the hills, already purple in the sun's last rays. What hope was there among those desolate heights, more than was offered by the empty flatness of the plain?

How many miles could be traversed by this frail-looking sister of Trenmore's before those dainty, high-heeled pumps of hers were worn to rags? Before she dropped exhausted? How many more miles could he and Trenmore carry her if they found neither food nor water?

"We'll find food as we go," said Terence as if interpreting and answering the thought. "I never did see a green country like this and no sort of food in it. Viola, 'tis a plucky lass you've always been. I've often promised that some day you'd go wandering with me. Let's be starting. And, Bobby, lad, don't look so down-hearted. There's a way out of everything, and aren't we just the three ones to find it, wherever we are?"

Drayton realized that his gloomy countenance must be anything but encouraging to Viola. Determined that henceforth he would be a model adventurer at any cost, he smiled.

"I wasn't really worrying, old man. I was merely thinking—"

But what innocent fabrication he would have devised to account for his despondency they never discovered. His sentence ended abruptly, and the forced smile vanished.

The attention of all three had been caught by a strange, deep, moaning sound. Reaching for his sister, Trenmore drew her close to his side. They all stood very still and listened.

The moaning, which began at first faintly and in a low key, seemed to emanate from a source immediately beneath their feet. Swiftly, however, this source widened and spread outward, extending itself beneath the empty plain and under the hills toward the mountain peaks. As it spread the note rose in key and in volume until it was more than anything else like the sound which might be thrown out by an immense top, whirling with planetary speed.

The intense vibration became agonizing. The listeners clapped their hands over their ears in a vain effort to shut it out. Drayton, for his part, felt that in one more instant either his eardrums or his brain must give way.

Even as he thought it, however, the last segment of the sun's red periphery sank out of sight beneath the horizon. The terrible humming died away, melting into the universal silence in which it had found birth. With scarcely an intervening moment of twilight night swept down.

At first it seemed absolute as blindness, or the end of all created things. Then, as his pupils expanded, Drayton began dimly to perceive his companions, while, on looking upward, he beheld a sky powdered thick with clear, brilliant stars.

He drew a long breath, and heard it echoed by the others.

"They have a strange nightfall in this land," muttered Trenmore, "and they do make a great noise over it!"

"Yes," replied Drayton, the observant, "but those stars look familiar enough."

"Right as usual, Bobby. It's the same old stars they're using. Look, Viola! There's the old bear and her cub!"

"And the Milky Way," said Viola.

Somehow, in spite of all that had occurred, the sight of those familiar stars and constellations brought a feeling of almost-security, of at-homeness and actuality.

"Your talk of Purgatory," laughed Drayton, "and that abominable noise just now sent a few unearthly shivers down my back. Those stars tell a different story. We are surely somewhere on earth. Different longitude, perhaps, but in our own latitude, or nearly, even though night did shut down with such tropical suddenness. If we were in the tropics we should see a sky different from this—"

His astronomical observations were cut short by a low cry from Viola. Dimly he glimpsed her arm, stiffly outstretched and pointing.

"And if this is our own earth," she cried, "is that our own moon? And if it is, what is the moon doing over there? Will you tell me that?"

There was pertinence in her question. From the exact point where the sun had descended five minutes earlier the silver rim of a great white moon was rising. Already the wide plain before it was invaded and dimly illuminated by the flood of its elfin radiance. It was as if, when the sun went down, the moon had been waiting there, and had now slipped past to take his place in the sky.

"Surely a very singular moonrise—in the west!" murmured the ex-lawyer. Inwardly he was more shocked by this apparent misplacement of the lunar orb than by anything which had yet occurred. If the stars had reassured him surely the moon had been prompt to undo their work.

"Is that thing a rock or an animal?"

Again it was Viola who spoke, and again her companions stared where the girl was pointing. Fifteen feet to the right of them was a large, dark object. It lay half in the black shadow of the ruined arch, half in the steadily increasing moonlight.

"That is only a part of the old gateway," began Drayton in a quiet, reassuring tone.

Even as he spoke, however, the dark thing seemed to rear itself slightly from the ground.

Trenmore made a quick movement; but Viola caught his arm.

"Don't go! Don't go near it, Terry! It may be some savage wild beast that's been hiding there!"

"And d'ye think I fear it then?" growled Trenmore.

"Don't be a fool, Trenmore!" Drayton spoke with a brusqueness born of mingled horror and amazement. That uncanny, half-glimpsed thing now appeared to be stretching itself upward, higher and higher in the partial shadow where it stood. "Think of your sister," he cried, "and help me get her away from this unspeakable place before it's too late. Look—look there at that wall!"

The wall he referred to was the same behind which he had first come upon Trenmore. Before their incredulous eyes it seemed to come to life, to rise, and to grow upward.

"They're alive, these stones! They're alive!" cried Viola.

Trenmore held back no longer. Here was something with which even his great strength was not fit to contend. All about them the fallen rocks, the walls, the very flagstones beneath their feet were heaving, moving, and the motion seemed all the more sinister and terrible because of the silence which attended it.

Drayton reached desperately for Viola's arm or hand; but Terry simply plucked her from the ground as one gathers up a child and began running across the court in great leaps and bounds. In one spring he cleared the nearest wall and ran on down the hill. Drayton followed at a speed nearly as great, and only caught up with the Irishman at the foot of the hill, where they both paused as by one impulse to look back.

During his flight Drayton had been filled with a ghastly, unnatural terror. He had feared that the ruins were coming after him, lichenous, soil-incrusted, horribly animate! But now, looking back, that fear at least was banished. The bare hillside, almost white in the moonlight, was crowned still by its broken walls. But were they broken now?

"By heaven, it's like—like—"

"Like a mirage," supplied Viola, who seemed suddenly to have achieved a curious composure. "Put me down, Terry. No, put me down, I say! I wish to see better. Yes, it's growing fast. In a few minutes we shall see the whole castle as it used to be."

Her calm assurance struck Drayton as odd, but only for a moment. After all, why shouldn't a castle grow up like a flower—like a flower with a magic scent? Down here on the plain the grass was filled with flowers and the air with their fragrance. There was something peculiarly soothing and reassuring in the very odor of them.

Drayton no longer felt the least alarm—hardly, even, wonder. Not though a miracle was occurring on the hilltop above.

Rising, ever rising in the white moonlight, the old fortress which they had deemed fallen forever, was rebuilding itself. Up, up shot the walls, battlemented now and perfect. Behind them, tower on tower, pinnacle upon pinnacle, lifted into the clear silver radiance as the white foam of a rising wave might lift—lifted and froze into perfect form—till the vision or mirage or miracle—whatever this marvel might be named—was consummate and growth ceased. Here and there a pennant fluttered in the faint night breeze. From the highest tower of all a great standard drooped, too heavy for so small a wind to raise.

And now it could be seen that close to where they stood a narrow white road led upward from plain to castle, ending at a huge gateway immediately above them. Suddenly the heavy, iron-studded doors of this gateway opened inward and swung slowly back. Beyond them all was darkness. Then came the first sound from the ghost castle—a heavy stamping, a clash and jingle as of metal. Out of the inner darkness a great horse strode into the moonlight. Upon its back sat a gleaming, erect, armed figure. Five more riders followed. Then the gates slowly, silently shut themselves. The company of six came riding down the pale roadway.

Drayton, for his part, felt arising within him a vast curiosity—a curiosity so great that he actually left his companions and walked over to the roadside.

He had advanced with the deliberate intention of questioning those mysterious riders. As they drew near, however, he turned and strode quickly back to Trenmore and his sister.

"What is the matter?" queried Viola. "Why didn't you ask them who they are and the name of the castle?"

Drayton's reply was voiced in a tense, fierce whisper.

"Look at them—only look at them, I tell you!"

His tone seemed to rouse his friends from the strange apathy into which they had all more or less fallen since setting foot on the plain.

They stood no more than eight or nine yards from the road, and could see very well what Drayton had already perceived. The horses were large, heavy brutes, of the type bred centuries ago for battle. They were spirited in a clumsy sort of way, and came curveting and prancing down the road. But the men on their backs—why, those were not men, nor even the ghosts of men! They were mere empty shells of gleaming armor.

The visors of all six were raised, and the watchers could see how the moonlight shimmered inside the helmets.

The armor sat erect, six proud, plumed figures of chivalry, and the joints rattled with a hollow clashing. They were past, and the white moonlight of the plain had swallowed them up. They had melted into it as a ship melts into the sea fog.

Glancing upward, Drayton half expected to see the castle itself dissolve and fade as it had grown; but no such phenomenon occurred. There it stood, massive, solid, dominating the hill.

With a slight shudder, Drayton turned to his companions.

"Somehow," he said, "I don't fancy the idea of asking hospitality at that gate."

"'Twould be madness!" ejaculated Trenmore. "It's fortunate we were to escape from that spook house before the walls grew too high!"

"Yes," conceded his friend simply.

"And what would we be doing now, do you think? Shall we stay here till the sunrise again, or shall we go on?"

It really made very little difference what they did, thought Drayton. Already that pleasant lassitude, from which sight of the riding armor had momentarily shocked him, was returning. By a volition which hardly seemed their own, however, the three of them presently found themselves advancing across the wide green plain.

On the hill the grass had been dry, dead stuff, parched as from long drought. The plain, however, was like a sweet, well-watered meadow. A scent came up from it that told of flowers crushed beneath their feet and growing everywhere in the midst of that lush greenness. They were pale, small flowers, and very fragrant. Viola plucked a few. So delicate were the blossoms that they withered instantly in her hands.

The three walked slowly, for the night had brought warmth rather than coolness. The sweet air breathed soft and languid. Now and then one of them would glance back over his shoulder. The phantom castle remained on the hilltop, as real in appearance as anything looks by moonlight, which casts a veil over all that is not very near.

Now every one knows that moonshine is at best of an uncertain and bewildering quality. Yet it seemed odd—or would have seemed so had they not been past surprise—that in the beginning they had deemed the plain deserted and bare of any moving thing since the empty armor had ridden outward and vanished. For now, as they walked, they perceived that all about them were forms and groups of forms, moving over and through the sweet, flower-sprinkled grass in a weird and noiseless dance, without music or apparent rhythm.

Presently they had blundered fairly into the midst of a group of these shapes, which seemed indeed to form about them from the misty light itself or rise up from the ground.

They were queer, bulky, clumsy-shouldered figures dressed in tight-fitting clothes and hoods and gloves of smooth fur. At least so appeared those directly ahead, black silhouettes against the moon. On looking around, however, the travelers were somewhat startled to find that what they had taken for hooded faces were not faces at all, but just smooth, featureless expanses of fur. The back and the front of the heads were exactly alike, save for one straight, black gash where the mouth might be.

Joining hands, the creatures began to circle with a clumsy, dancing motion. The wanderers, caught in the center of their ring, could proceed no further without using force to break it. Soon the swift, whirling dance began to make Drayton dizzy. Round and round and round. And now over the plain he perceived that there were many other circles like this. They all swung round and round and round. Why had he thought the dance silent? There was music enough, and everywhere the beat, beat of uncounted feet in perfect rhythm with a melody that filled the world. It rose from the scented grass between the beating feet; it flowed from the moon with the sorcery of her light; it circled and circled in rhythmic rings. It caught his feet in a silver snare. He was swept into the net of a great and passionate desire—to dance and dance forever—now!

Before him Drayton saw the circle break apart, and there was just the space for one to join them, to become a link in the mystic ring and satisfy the calling melody. Almost without his will Drayton's feet obeyed the call. His hand caught that of the monster nearest him. He remembered afterward that it felt neither cold nor warm, but rather like a fur glove stuffed with wool. Another hand caught him violently by the shoulder and wrenched him backward.

Drayton cried out and struggled to escape, but Trenmore had him fairly in the grip of his mighty arms. Even as the two strove together all that moonlight madness of sound jarred, broke, and from discord died to silence. The strength went out of Drayton's body. He leaned, weak and panting for breath, against the Irishman's shoulder.

"If you're so fond of dancing," said the latter grimly, "you might at least choose Viola or me for a partner. Are you mad, Bobby, to take hands with those?"

Before Drayton could reply the circle of dancers stopped short in their tracks. Each ungainly figure made a strange, wild gesture as of wrath or despair. Then they separated, scattered, and went dancing wildly away across the grass.

"Hss-ss-ss!"

It was a long-drawn, sibilant sound, and it seemed to come from a little pile of rocks close by. In its black shadow they saw two sparklike eyes gleam redly.

"Hss-ss-ss! Touch not the dancers—go not near them— speak not to them! Strange things be abroad and stranger things be done in the white moonlight of Ulithia! Hss-ss-ss! Go not near!"

"And who and what may you be?" demanded Trenmore, bending down; but the sparklike eyes had vanished. An instant later they reappeared, gleaming dimly through a white cobweb between two tall tufts of grass.

"Hss-ss-ss!" Again that snakelike hissing. "Beware! You have escaped the everlasting dance—beware the Weaver and her song!"

"But who—what are you?" demanded Trenmore again rather wildly.

The red sparks flashed and faded from behind the silver web.

Only a dim voice trailed back to them:

"I am the Voice of Warning in a land of Illusion—beware!"

Drayton, somewhat recovered from his own queer experience, moved as if to follow. Again Trenmore checked him.

"We'd best not traffic with that thing either," he recommended gruffly. "We've no place in this world we've got into—no place at all! And the very best we can do is to keep our own company till we find a way out of it."

"What was it the thing said?" queried Drayton as he fell into step again beside the other two. "Ulithia? That sounds some way familiar—"

Trenmore shook his head. "Not to me. I've traveled many a land, and read not a few books, old and new; but nowhere have I heard that name before."

"Nor I," said Viola.

Drayton was silent a moment, searching his memory. Then his face fell. "I recall the association now," he observed discontentedly. "It's no help. There were some letters—the first letters of that name—carved on the ruins back there. I read them, while the ruins were still ruins."

For a while they walked on in silence. With the breaking of that one ring of dancing forms the plain seemed gradually to have cleared, so that they were again alone with the moonlight and each other. Alone until, long before they saw the White Weaver, they heard her singing.

That was a wondrous, murmurous, liquid song of hers, like shallow summer brooks and rustling fields. They were not surprised to come upon her at last, seated in the moon-frosted grass, tossing a weaver's shuttle between her outstretched hands. They could see neither loom nor thread nor web, however, save a thousand silver cobwebs on the grass. All the plain was agleam with them.

This is the song she was singing, or as much of it as any of them could afterward recall:

"The web lies broad in the weaving room.
    (Fly, little shuttle fly!)

The air is loud with the clashing loom.
    (Fly, little shuttle fly!)"

There was a brief pause in the melody, then:

"Year on year have I woven here.
Green earth, white earth, and autumn sere;
Sitting singing where the earth-props mold;
Weave I, singing, where the world grows old.
Time's a traitor, but the loom is leal—
Time's a liar, but the web is real!
Hear my song and behold my web!
    (Fly, little shuttle—!)"

"But, madam, 'tis no web you have there," broke in Trenmore. "'Tis naught but a little shuttle and no thread to it at all!"

At that the song ceased, and the woman raised her face. It was beautiful as the moon's self, though her hair was silver and her face without a trace of color. Her clear, pale eyes seemed to look through and far beyond them.

"You are strangers," she said in a voice that might have come from very far away, clear and sweet as a silver bell. "Yet your lives, too, are in my web. Aye! They are mine—bound up fast in my web that you see not. From here on go forward—go deeper! Heed not the mockings of the dancing Shadow People. Heed not the voice of mine enemy, who would keep you forever bound in the shallows of Ulithia. Go forward—go deeper—go forward!"

With that she ceased speaking, and, taking up her song where she had left it, she made the empty shuttle fly like a living thing from hand to hand.

Drayton eyed his companions doubtfully. "If the lady would make her advice a little clearer we might try to follow it. We have to go on somewhere, you know, Terry."

But Viola shook her head, staring at the Weaver with a hostile, questioning glance. "Have you so soon forgotten?" she said. "'Beware the Weaver and her song!'"

At that the Weaver again ceased singing. Her thin lips were curled in a smile, but her eyes were like pale blue ice.

"Aye," she murmured, "beware of the Weaver—the White Weaver of the Years—beware! But your feet are set in her web. The door opens before you. There is no way out but on—and what is Ulithia, phantom borderland of life, to such as you? Go forward—go deeper—go forward!"

Trenmore took one step toward her, with what intent he himself scarcely knew. But as he took it Drayton laughed with a touch of weariness.

"You have frightened the lady away, Terry."

It was true. As Trenmore had stepped toward the "White Weaver" that cold-eyed lady had vanished and taken her song and her shuttle with her. As the three again proceeded Viola waved her hand in a wide gesture, indicating the plain they traversed.

"Did either of you notice," she said, "that there were so many of these white spider webs about—before we saw that woman?"

Her brother and Drayton merely stared stupidly, heavy-eyed.

"Before we met the White Weaver," murmured the girl dreamily, "there was only a web here and there, woven between the grass stems. Now it is like—like walking through a silver sea. And the moon. What moon of earth was ever like this of Ulithia?"

"If it is a moon," said Trenmore with no great interest. "She's taking an uncommon long time for her rising."

Blank as a silver shield, the moon, or what they had believed a moon, still rested at the edge of the plain, its lower part bisected by the horizon. More like an enormous archway than a moon it seemed—a sort of celestial door, perhaps, in the edge of the sky.

They neared and neared, walking across a silver sea of web through which the invisible flowers sent up their perpetually increasing incense, almost too sweet now for pleasure. More and more like an arch the moon appeared—an immense, light-filled archway, of the nearly circular Moorish type. About it they began to perceive a certain dim outline of dark substance, behind which the moon itself was just a depth and a blinding expanse of light. Almost unconsciously they hastened their steps. At last, heads swimming with the fragrance of the plain, they had actually reached the splendid thing.

High, high above them curved the perfect arch of stone, black as unpolished ebony and set in what seemed a solid wall of similar rock stretching away to darkness on either hand. Through the opening they could not see, for it was filled with a brilliant mist of pure white light.

"Look!" said Drayton, leaning dizzily against the black stone to which he pointed. "Here on the architrave. There are silver characters—inlaid—aren't they? But they move and writhe like white flame—"

Closing his eyes against the glare, he wished that a great wind might arise—a great, clean wind that would sweep away cobwebs and flowers together.

"Go forward, go deeper, go forward!" murmured a sweet, clear voice. To Drayton it seemed to be Viola's, though with a distant sound, like a far-off silver bell. "Your feet are in the web!" cried the voice. "In the Web of the Weaver of Years. And why linger in the shallows of Ulithia? Go forward—go deeper!"

"Why linger?" echoed Drayton softly.

His feet were in the shallows of a wide, white sea that was carrying him outward—onward.

6 A MATTER OF BUTTONS

When Drayton and his friends walked through the Uli-thian "moon," none of them were either quite uncon-scious nor entirely devoid of sense. Drayton for instance, knew that Viola extended her hand to him; that he took it and that her other hand was held by some one else, an indistinct personality whose identity was of not the slightest interest or importance.

They all knew that with the dizzying fragrance of a mil-lion blossoms in their nostrils; with blinding radiance before them; with behind them only silence and the silver plain, they three joined hands and so passed beneath the black arch which had seemed a moon.

This dim apprehension, however, was wholly dream-like, and unmingled with thought or foreboding. They possessed no faint curiosity, even, as to what might lie beyond that incredible archway.

Active consciousness returned like the shock of a thunderbolt.

They had emerged upon the sidewalk of a wide, paved street. They were but three of a jostling, hurrying throng of very ordinary and solid-looking mortals.

For several moments they experienced a bewilder-ment even greater than had come upon them in passing from a prosaic house on Walnut Street into the uncanny romance land which they knew as "Ulithia." The roar and rattle which now assailed their ears deafened and dazed them. Ulithia had been so silent, so unhuman and divorced from all familiar associations, that in this abrupt escape from it they felt helpless; unpoised as countryfolk who have never seen a city, and to whom its crowds are confusing and vaguely hostile.

In this new place there was none of that bright, dazzling mist which had filled the archway. Instead, it was well and more satisfactorily illuminated by numerous arc lamps. With a thundering clatter an electric train rushed past almost directly overhead.

Before them, the street was a tangle of dodging pedestrians, heavy motor trucks loaded with freight and baggage, arriving and departing autos, and desperately clanging street cars. Above, iron pillars and girders supported an elevated railway system. Close to where they stood a narrow moving stairway carried upward its perpetual stream of passengers, bound for that upper level of traffic where the electric train had passed.

Turning, the dazed wanderers saw behind them, not any vast expanse of silver light, but the wall of a long, low building, pierced with many windows and several doors. From one of those doors, apparently, they had just emerged.

With some difficulty the three extricated themselves from the throng. Finding a comparatively quiet spot by the wall of the building they stood there, very close together.

Suddenly Viola gave a sharp exclamation.

"But this—this is *Philadelphia! This is the entrance to the Market Street Ferry in Philadelphia!*"

Her brother slapped his thigh.

"And to think I did not recognize a place I've been at myself at least three times! But who would have thought we'd get home so easy—or at the other end of the city from where we started?"

Suddenly the melancholy ex-lawyer chuckled aloud.

"I never thought," he said, "that Philadelphia, city of homes or not, would seem homelike to me. By George, I realize now what a charming old place it is! Terry, couldn't you resign wandering and settle down here for the rest of your life—right on this spot, if necessary?"

The Irishman grinned cheerfully.

"I could that, so be there were not a few better spots to be got at. Viola, I'm fair dead of hunger and so must you both be. Is there a cafe in this elegant station building? Or shall we go home and trust Martin? Heaven bless the boy! I never thought to see him again—trust Martin to throw us together some sort of sustaining meal?"

"I'm hungry," confessed Viola frankly, "but it seems to me we should go straight to Cousin Jim's house, rather than to a restaurant. You know that gray powder was left there—"

Trenmore gave a great start and his smile faded.

"That devil dust!" he burst forth. "And all this time it's been laying open and unguarded! Faith, after all we may not find poor Martin to welcome us home!"

"My fault again," said Drayton grimly. "If anything has happened to Martin, I am entirely to blame. In common justice I shall have to follow him—"

Trenmore turned with a growl. "You will not follow him! Is it an endless chain you would establish between this world and that heathenish outland we've escaped from? You after Martin, and myself after you, and Viola after me, I suppose—and there we'll all be again, with nothing to eat and no one but spooks to converse with! No; if Martin is in Ulithia this minute, may his wits and his luck bring him out of it. At least, he's the same chance we had."

"Call a taxi," suggested Viola practically. "It's just possible that Martin hasn't yet fallen into the trap."

"A very sensible suggestion, my dear," commended her brother.

By the curb stood an empty taxicab, its driver loafing near by. The latter was a thin, underfed-looking fellow, clad in a rather startlingly brilliant livery of pale blue and lemon yellow, with a small gilt insignia on the sleeve. A languid cigarette drooped from his lips. Beside his gaudy attire he wore that air of infinite leisure, combined with an eye scornfully alert, with which all true taxi drivers are born.

"Seventeen hundred Walnut Street, my man," directed Trenmore, "and get up what speed you're able."

Drayton had started to open the cab door, since the chauffeur made no move to do so. To his surprise, however, the latter sprang forward and pushed his hand aside.

"You wait a minute, gentlemen!"

"Is this cab engaged? You have the 'Empty' sign out."

"No, we ain't engaged; but wait a minute!"

The fellow was eying them with a curiosity oddly like suspicion. Surely there was little out of the way in their appearance. Viola's attire was the picture of modern propriety. In crossing that ghostly plain nothing had occurred to destroy the respectable appearance with which they had all begun the journey.

"Wait!" ejaculated Trenmore. "And what for? Isn't this a public cab?"

"Yes; it's a public cab, right enough. There ain't nothing the matter with me nor my cab either. The trouble's with you. Why ain't you wearin' your buttons?"

"Wearing our buttons?"

Terence glanced frantically down over himself. Had the rapid transition from one world to another actually removed those necessary adornments from his garments? Everything looked in order. He glanced up angrily.

"Not wearing our buttons, is it? And what in the devil do you mean by that, you fool? Is it fuddled with drink you are?"

The chauffeur's alert eye measured the Irishman. It's owner shrank back against the cab.

"Don't you!" he cried. "Don't you hit me! I don't care who you are, you haven't any right to go about that way. You hit me, and you'll go to the pit for it! I've drove more than one of the Service itself, and they won't stand fer nobody beatin' me up!"

Drayton caught the half-raised arm of his friend.

"Don't, Terry," he cautioned softly. "Why start a row with a lunatic?"

Trenmore shook him off. He was doubly annoyed by Drayton's assumption that he would attack a man of less than half his weight. For an instant he felt inclined to quarrel with his friend on the spot. Then the petty childishness of his irritation struck him, and catching Viola's appealing and astonished glance, he laughed shamefacedly.

"I left my temper behind the moon, Bobby," he grinned, as the three started off down the sidewalk in search of another vehicle. "Somewhere along here there's a bit of an office booth of the taxicab company's. Isn't that it, beyond the escalator?"

"Yes," contributed Viola. "I remember there's a sign over it. 'Quaker City'—Why, but they've changed it to 'Penn Service!' Last week it was the Quaker City Company."

Whether "Penn Service," however, meant taxi service or something different they were not to learn just then. Before they reached the wooden booth beneath that white-lettered signboard, a heavy hand had grasped Drayton's arm from behind, whirling him about. The two others also turned and found themselves confronted by a police officer. At a safe distance in the rear their eccentric acquaintance, the chauffeur, looked on with a satisfied grin.

"And what is this?" demanded Trenmore sternly.

Drayton said nothing at all. With the policeman's hand clutching his arm, fear had him in a yet firmer grip. Was this another phase of the persecution to which he had been recently subjected? Was he about to suffer arrest, here in the presence of Viola Trenmore, upon some such trumped-up charge as had sent his partner to prison and death?

In the bitter grasp of this thought, it was a moment before he comprehended what the officer was replying to Trenmore's question.

"—and if you've lost your buttons, for why have you not reported yourselves at the proper quarters? Sure, 'tis me duty to run ye in without further argument; but 'tis a fair-spoken, soft-hearted man I am. If you've a reason, give it me quick, now!"

Drayton grasped the fact that it was not himself alone who was involved. Equally, it seemed, Trenmore and his sister were objects of the man's absurd though apparently official attention. The lawyer in him leaped to the fore. Here might be some curious local civic ruling of which he, a stranger to the city, had heard nothing.

"What about the buttons, officer?" he queried. "Do you mean that we should be wearing some sort of button as an insignia?"

"Is it crazy ye are all after being? What buttons, d'ye say? Why, what should I be meaning, savin' yer identification buttons? What are yer numbers now? At least ye can tell me that! Or are ye the connections of a family?"

There was a moment's silence. Then Trenmore said heavily, as if in some deep discouragement. "Faith, I myself was born in County Kerry, but till this living minute I never knew the meaning of the words 'a crazy Irishman!' Micky, or Pat, or whatever your name may be, we are connected with families so good that your ignorance never heard tell of them!

"And as for numbers, I do not doubt that you yourself have a number! I do not doubt that the driver of the poor little jitney bus yonder has a number! In jails men have numbers, and perhaps in the lunatic asylum you both came from they have numbers and wear buttons with those same numbers on them; but myself and my friend here and my sister, we have no numbers!

"We have names, my lad, names. And 'tis my own name I'll send in to the poor, unfortunate chief that has charge of you, and you'll find that it is not needful for Terence Trenmore to be given a number in order to have such as you discharged from the force your low intelligence is now disgracing!"

As Trenmore delivered this harangue his voice gradually grew in volume as his sentences grew longer, until it boomed out like the blast of a foghorn. The two or three idlers who had already gathered were reinforced by a rapidly increasing crowd. His last words were delivered to an exceedingly curious and numerous audience.

The policeman, a man of no very powerful physique, quailed before Trenmore's just wrath much as had the taxi driver. He, too, however, had another resource than his unaided strength. His only reply to the threat was a sharp blast on his whistle.

"You've done it now, Terry," groaned Drayton. "Never mind me. Get your sister away from here, if you can—quick!"

The young lady mentioned set her lips.

"Terry shall do not such thing, Mr. Drayton. Officer, surely you won't arrest three harmless people because of some foolish little misunderstanding that could be set right in the twinkle of an eye?"

The policeman eyed her admiringly—too admiringly, in Drayton's estimation.

"Sure, miss," he declared, "'tis myself is most reluctant to place inconvenience on so pretty a lass; but what can I do? Ye know the regulations."

"But indeed we do not," protested the girl truthfully.

Before more could be said on either side, there came an eddy and swirl in the crowd, and two more policemen burst into view. One of them, a sergeant by the stripes on his sleeve, came bustling forward with an air of petty arrogance which Drayton prayed might not collide with his huge friend's rising temper.

"What's this? What's all this, Forty-seven? What have these people been up to? What? No buttons? What do you mean by going about without your buttons? This is a very serious and peculiar offense, Forty-seven! The first I've ever met in this ward, I am glad to say. Under arrest? Certainly you are under arrest! The wagon will be here directly. What did you expect? What are your numbers? What have you done with your buttons, anyway?"

How long the sergeant could have continued this interlocutory monologue, which he delivered at extraordinary speed and without pause for answer or comment, it is impossible to say. He was interrupted by a clanging gong and again the crowd swirled and broke. A motor patrol drew up. Three more officers leaped down and stood at attention.

The accession of numbers drove from Drayton's brain any lingering hope that Trenmore might pick his sister up under his arm and bear her bodily from the shadow of this open disgrace.

That the exasperated Irishman had not acted was due partly to reluctance to leave his friend in the clutches of the law; partly to a rapidly increasing bewilderment. He could now observe that every person in the front ranks of the staring crowd did indeed wear a large yellow button, pinned below the left shoulder, and each bearing a perfectly legible number in black.

He could also see that these numbers ran mostly into five, six and even seven figures; but what those figures represented, or why the wearers should be so adorned, or what bearing the ornamentation might have upon their own liberty, was a puzzle before which the recent mysteries of Ulithia faded.

"Button, button, who's got the button?" he muttered. "Faith, 'tis a wild and barbarous land, this Philadelphia! Sergeant, are you really going to run us in, just for not knowing what you and the rest are talking of?"

The sergeant looked him up and down appreciatively.

"You know very well that I must. But Lord, man, you've nothing to worry over with the contests coming off in a couple of days. Or haven't you any muscle back of that size of yours?"

Distractedly, Trenmore clutched at his black, wild hair.

"Take us to the station, man!" he snarled. "And be quick, as you value your poor, worthless life! Muscle? I've the muscle to pull you to bits, and by all the powers I'll be driven to that act if you do not take me to speak with some sane man this living minute!"

7 A FEW SMALL CHANGES

The ensuing patrol ride, while commonplace and uneventful from the viewpoint of one accustomed to such jaunts, produced in the bosom of at least one of the prisoners emotions of the most painful and poignant nature. It was not for himself that Drayton suffered.

In the recent past he had been too thoroughly seared by the fires of undeserved disgrace to be hurt by so trifling a touch of flame as this. But that Viola Trenmore—Viola of the clear blue eyes and innocent white brow—that she should be forced to enter a common patrol wagon and be carried openly, like any pickpocket, through the city streets, was an intolerable agony in whose endurance he alternately flushed red with shame and paled with ineffective rage.

Trenmore the mighty also sat quiescent; but his was the quiescence of a white-hot anger, held in check for a worthy occasion and object. A pity to waste all that on mere underlings.

Having slowly ascended the short, steep incline where Market Street descended to the ferry, the patrol drove on with increased speed. A mile ahead, at the end of a long, straight, brilliantly lighted perspective, reared the huge bulk of City Hall. The immense building's lower part was sketched in lines of light; its tower gleamed gray and pale against the black sky.

High upon that uttermost pinnacle there brooded a ghostly figure. It was the enormous statue of William Penn, set there to bless the children of his city, with outstretched, benevolent hand.

"Are you taking us to City Hall?" queried Drayton, turning to the officer on his left.

The man nodded. "Your offense is too serious, of course, for a branch temple."

"A—what?"

"A branch," said the man impatiently. "Headquarters will want to handle this; eh, sergeant?"

"They will, but no more conversation, please. Everything you say, my man, will be used against you."

"One would think we were murderers," reflected Drayton bitterly. Of what real offense could they have been guilty? Beneath surface absurdity he had begun to sense something secret and dangerous; something upon which his mind could as yet lay no hold, but which might be revealed to them at City Hall.

The night was fine; the hour eight-thirty by the clock in City Hall tower; the streets well filled. Most of the stores seemed to be open, and innumerable "movie" theaters, saloons and shooting galleries each drew in and expelled its quota of people, like so many lungs breathing prosperity for the owners.

There was a New York Bowery touch to the amusements and the crowds which Drayton did not remember as characteristic of Market Street. The thought, however, was passing and only half-formed.

The patrol clanged its way over the smooth pavement, attracting the usual number of stares and fortunately unheard comments, and presently swung off Market Street into Juniper. They had approached City Hall from the east. Since the patrol entrance was on the western side, it was necessary for them to pass half around the great building to reach it.

As they passed the Broad Street entrance, Drayton chanced to glance upward. Above the arch hung an emblem done in colored lights. It seemed to be a sword crossing a bell. Above the emblem itself glowed a number, consisting of four figures done in glowing red, white and blue—2118.

The bell, thought Drayton, might represent the old Liberty Bell, Philadelphia's most cherished possession; the numerals, however, conveyed to him no more significance than had those on the yellow buttons about which these police were so concerned.

Again turning, the patrol reached Market Street on the western side. Shortly afterward it rolled beneath the portico of City Hall.

The Public Buildings, to use the more ancient name for Philadelphia's proud edifice of administration and justice, are built in the form of an irregular hollow square. The larger inner court may be entered by means of any one of four short tunnels, placed at the four cardinal points of the compass, and passing beneath the walls of the building proper.

As the three prisoners recalled it, that inner court was squarish in shape, paved with gray concrete, and of no very beautiful or imposing appearance. Several old cannon, relics of past wars, adorned the corners and stood at either side of the northward entrance. In the northeast corner there was a sort of pavilion, where various free civic exhibits were perennially on view.

As the center of the place was actually the intersection of those two main arteries of the city, Broad Street and Market, two continuous streams of pedestrians passed through there all day long.

Such was the interior of City Hall as the three prisoners remembered it and into which they now expected to be carried.

While yet in the short, dark entrance tunnel, however, the patrol halted. Rising from their seats, the officers hustled their prisoners from the wagon. A moment later and they all stood together, halted just within the rim of the inner arch.

And there the three received another of those wildly disturbing shocks, of which they had suffered so many in the past few hours.

Instead of a bare gray courtyard, open to the sky, there stood revealed an interior which might have been lifted bodily from an Arabian Nights entertainment.

Above, rounding to a level with the top of the fourth story, curved the golden hollow of a shallow but glorious dome. It seemed to have been carved from the yellow metal itself. The entire under surface was without a seam or trace of ornament, and was polished to almost blinding brilliance.

Striking upward upon it from invisible sources at the sides, light was reflected downward in a diffused glow, yellow as sunshine and giving a curious, almost shadowless appearance to the great chamber below. From the center of the dome, swung at the end of a twenty-foot chain, depended a huge bell. This bell had either been enameled smoothly, or was cast of some strange metal.

The color of it was a brilliant scarlet, so that it hung like an enormous exotic blossom. Some change or repairs to the thing seemed to be in progress for out to it from the southern wall extended narrow suspension bridge of rough planking, that terminated in a partial scaffolding about one side of the bell. No tongue or clapper was within the bell, nor was there any visible means of ringing it.

As for the floor beneath, it was of common gray concrete no longer. An exquisite pavement gleamed there, made of white porcelain or some similar substance, seamless and polished. In it the blood-red bell and certain colored panels of the golden walls were reflected as in a pool of milk. Near the northern wall a design appeared in this floor, set in as a mosaic of varicolored marbles.

Where had been the southern and eastern entrances, short flights of green marble stairs led up to carved golden doors, Gothic in style and all closed. The windowless walls, also of gold, were carved in heavy bas-relief. At regular intervals appeared panels, done in bright enamels, representing various weird figures resembling Chinese gods and heroes. The entire color scheme of red, gold, green and white had a peculiarly barbaric effect, itself entirely out of keeping with the formerly staid and dignified old Public Buildings.

Trenmore, as he gazed, forgot even his anger, and stared open-mouthed. They all had time to stare, for the sergeant, having pressed an electric buzzer near the door, stood at ease, obviously waiting for something or some one to answer the summons.

"And is this the place they have for a courthouse?" Trenmore murmured. "I've seen the Taj Mahal, and I've seen the inside of Westminster Abbey and St. Pauls, but never, never—"

"I can't understand it!" broke in Drayton desperately. Amazement had given place to distress, as the enormity of the change came home to him. "Why, but this is incredible; it's preposterous! I—"

"Here, here!" broke in the sergeant's brusque voice. "None of that. What were you muttering there? Never mind. Be silent. Here comes a gentleman who will dispose of your case in quick order."

At the south, a golden door had opened and a man was seen descending the short flight of green marble steps before it. Even at a distance, he seemed an impressive figure. Over a largely checked vest he wore an exquisitely cut frock coat. His trousers were of a delicate pearl-gray hue, and a pair of white spats surmounted immaculate patent-leather pumps. On his head gleamed a shining silk hat.

Had the gentleman but carried a flag, or Roman candle, he might creditably have adorned a political parade. A large bouquet would have completed his costume for a Bowery wedding. Amid the barbaric splendor which actually surrounded him, he seemed out of place, but happily unconscious of that fact.

Slowly and with dignity he advanced, while in the gleaming porcelain beneath an inverted, silk-hatted replica of him followed every step. At last his majestic progress ceased. He had halted some six paces from the group of prisoners and policemen. Without speaking, he surveyed them with a slow, long, insolent gaze.

He was a small man, handsome in a weak, dissipated way; old with the age of self-indulgence rather than years. His greenish-hazel eyes were close-set and cunning. He possessed a little, pointed mustache, and, in the opinion of the prisoners, an unjustifiably impertinent manner.

Out of the corner of his eye Drayton saw that his Irish friend was bristling anew. Well, if the outbreak had to come, he wished it would burst now and annihilate this silk-hatted monstrosity. No man could eye Viola in just the manner of this stranger and deserve continued life!

The high-hatted one deigned to speak.

"Well, Fifty-three," he drawled languidly, addressing the sergeant, "and why have you brought them here? The chief is in attendance on His Supremity, and there's no one else about who cares to be bothered. I myself came over to warn you that Penn Service is tired of having these trivial cases brought to the Temple. Lately you police chaps seem to consider the Temple a sort of petty court for pickpockets!"

Trenmore passed the sergeant in one stride.

"You miserable, insolent, little whippersnapper!" he thundered in a voice that was amazingly re-echoed from the golden dome above.

Instantly, as if sprung by a single trigger, the six policemen had hurled themselves upon him. High-hat skipped back nimbly out of the way. Drayton, seeing no alternative with honor, flung himself into the combat, and was promptly knocked out by the blow of a policeman's club.

8 LEGAL PROCEDURE EXPEDITED

When his senses returned, Drayton found himself sitting on the polished white floor, his back propped against a golden pillar. He became aware that his head ached horribly; that his wrists were handcuffed behind him; and that his tempestuous Irish ally was no better off than himself. Trenmore, in fact, lay stretched at full length close by. Tears streaming down her face, Viola was wiping ineffectively at his bloody countenance with her pathetic mite of a handkerchief.

Two of the six policemen stood looking on with no evident sympathy. The other four lay or sat about in attitudes of either profound repose or extreme discomfort. Though Terence Trenmore had gone down, he had taken his wounded with him.

"Get an ambulance, one of you chaps!" It was the voice of silk-hatted authority. "You think we want the Temple cluttered up like an accident ward? And bring those crazy prisoners of yours to the Court of Common Pleas. Mr. Virtue is there now, and one court will do as well as another for this sort. Look sharp, now!"

Saluting reverently, the two uninjured officers proceeded to execute high-hat's various behests as best they could. They were forced, however, to leave the wounded while they bore Trenmore across to the southern door.

Viola started to follow, then looked back anxiously toward Drayton. High-hat, following her glance, beckoned imperatively.

With some difficulty, Drayton gained his feet and staggered toward the girl. He felt anything but fit, and he was keenly disappointed. All that shindy had been wasted! The insufferable one yet lived—had not even suffered the knocking off of his intolerable hat!

"Lean on me, Mr. Drayton," he heard Viola's voice, curiously far away and indistinct. The absurdity of such a request moved him to a wry smile; but he certainly did lean on some one, or he could never have crossed that heaving, rocking, slippery floor without falling a dozen times.

Presently blackness descended again, and he knew no more till the strong taste and odor of brandy half-strangled and thoroughly aroused him.

A policeman was holding a tumbler to Drayton's lips, and seemed bent on pouring the entire contents down his throat. Twisting his head away the prisoner sat up. The officer eyed him wonderingly, then drained the glass himself and set it down.

"Feel better?" he queried.

"A little," muttered Drayton. He was seated on a leather-covered couch in a small room, and his only companion was the policeman. "I suppose," he added disconsolately, "that Trenmore was badly hurt. Where are they now?"

The officer laughed. "If Trenmore is your big friend, he came around sooner than you did. Lord, I wish't we had that guy on the force! Can you walk yet?"

Drayton rose unsteadily. "I guess so. Have you put the others in cells?"

"Hardly!" The officers stared at him. "They don't keep a case like this waiting. Your friend won't go in no cell, nor you either. And as for the girl—" He broke off, with a shrug.

"And the girl?" Drayton repeated sharply.

"I dunno. Mr. Mercy was looking her over. I doubt he'll let that beauty go to the Pit. But come along, or we'll keep Mr. Virtue waiting."

"Mr. Virtue!" What a very odd name, thought Drayton, as he walked to the door, leaning heavily on his jailer. And Mr. Mercy, too. Had he fallen into a chapter of Pilgrim's Progress? Had the whole world gone mad while they wandered in Ulithia? And what of this amazing "Temple" that had usurped the interior of City Hall?

On the streets outside, everything had appeared normal—except for those infernal buttons. Surely this was Philadelphia that they had returned to. Who that had ever visited the city could doubt its identity? It was as distinctive as New York, though in a different way. And all the familiar details—the Market Street Ferry, the outer architecture of City Hall, Broad Street—oh, and above all that benevolent, unforgettable statue of William Penn—

The door opened upon a long, low-ceilinged, windowless room, illuminated by hidden lights behind the cornice. The ceiling was a delicate rose-pink, and, like the golden dome, shed its color downward upon a scene of Oriental splendor. Unlike the white-paved court, however, this chamber was far from bare.

The dark, polished floor was strewn with silken rugs of extravagant value and beauty. The many chairs and small tables scattered here and there were of ebony carved in the Chinese fashion, their cushions and covers of rose-pink velvet and silks gleaming richly against the dark austerity of black wood.

Here and there the prevailing rosy tinge was relieved by a touch of dull blue, or by a bit of carved yellow ivory. Several excellent paintings, uniformly framed in dull black, showed well against the unpatterned matte-gold of the walls.

Rather than a courtroom, indeed, this might have been the drawing-room of some wealthy woman with a penchant for the outre in decorative effects. At the chamber's upper end, however, was a sort of dais or platform. There, enthroned on a wonderfully carved ivory chair, a man was seated.

He wore a black gown and a huge white wig, like that of an English justice. He was hawk-nosed, fat-jowled, coarse-featured and repellant. If this was—and Drayton assumed it must be—Mr. Virtue, then his appearance singularly belied his name.

Before the dais were gathered a group consisting of Drayton's fellow-prisoners, a single policeman, and also the little man in the silk hat and frock coat. From above them, Mr. Virtue stared down with an insolent disdain beside which the high-hatted one's languid contempt seemed almost courtesy.

"Come!" whispered Drayton's guardian. "Walk up there and bow to his honor. They've begun the trial."

"The trial!" thought Drayton. There were present neither witnesses, jury, nor counsel.

Having no alternative, however, he obeyed, ranging himself beside Viola and bowing as gracefully as his manacled condition would permit. As a lawyer, though disbarred, he still respected the forms of law, however strangely administered. His own demeanor should be beyond reproach.

Glancing at Trenmore, he saw that the Irishman had suffered no great damage in the recent unpleasantness, and also that he was eying the enthroned judge in anything but a penitent spirit.

As for Viola, she stood with hands folded, eyes meekly downcast, an ideal picture of maidenhood in distress. Drayton, however, caught a sidelong blue flash from beneath her long lashes which hinted that the Trenmores were yet one in spirit.

There was a further moment of awe-inspiring silence. Then the judge, or magistrate, or whatever he might be, cleared his throat portentously.

"Mr. Mercy," he said, "I believe there need be no delay here. From your account and that of Sergeant Fifty-three—by the way, where is Fifty-three?"

"In the hospital, your honor, having his wrist set."

"I see. He should have waited until conclusion of trial. His presence, however, is not essential. As I was saying, from his account and yours there can be no question of either verdict or sentence. In view of the prisoners' conduct within these sacred precincts, there will be no need to appoint counsel or investigate the case further.

"To conform, however, to the letter as well as spirit of the law, and in the interests of purely abstract justice, I now ask you, Mr. Mercy, as sole responsible witness of the worser outrage, if you can bring forward any extenuating circumstances tending to mitigate their obvious culpability and modify the severity of their sentence?"

Drayton wondered if the policeman's billy had addled what sense Ulithia had left him. Had he really understood that speech? He seemed to catch a phrase here and there, stamped with the true legal verbosity. As a whole the speech was incomprehensible. And now Mr. Mercy was replying.

"Your Honor, in the case of the male prisoners, I know of no excuse. Not only have they appeared in public buttonless, but beneath the very Dome of Justice, with their eyes, so to speak, fixed on the scarlet Threat of Penn, they have assaulted and wounded the emissaries of sacred Penn Service. For the third criminal, however—for this mere girl-child—I do desire the mercy for which I am named! Separate her from her evil companions, and who knows? She may become as innocent in fact as in appearance?"

Mr. Mercy uttered this plea solemnly enough; but at the conclusion he deliberately and languidly winked at the judge, and smiled upon the girl prisoner in a way which made Drayton's blood surge to his wounded head.

Were these proceedings in any degree serious? Or was this all part of some elaborate and vicious joke? One hypothesis seemed as impossible as the other. Once more Drayton bowed.

"Your Honor," he said, "surely, even at this preliminary hearing you will permit us—"

But the judge interrupted him. "Preliminary hearing?" he repeated scornfully. "No man within the jurisdiction of Penn Service can be so ignorant of law as your words would indicate. Were there any shadow of doubts as to your guilt, we, in our perfect justice, might grant you a public trial. We might even permit you an appeal to Mr. Justice Supreme himself. But in so obvious and flagrant a case of law-breaking as yours, the Servants of Penn must decline to be further troubled!

"I now, therefore, condemn you, sir, and you, the big fellow there—my soul, Mercy, did you ever see such an enormous brute? I condemn you both to be immediately dropped into the Pit of the Past. And may Penn have mercy on your probably worthless souls!"

Having delivered himself of this remarkable and abrupt sentence his honor arose with a yawn, tossed aside the black robe and removed his wig. Beneath the robe he was dressed in a costume similar to that of their earlier acquaintance, Mr. Mercy. Descending from the dais, Virtue paused to wave an insolent hand toward Viola Trenmore.

"You saw the girl first, Mercy," he addressed his silk-hatted associate. "So I suppose she's yours. You always were a lucky dog!"

9 THE PIT OF THE PAST

Beneath the golden Dome of Justice, directly under the blood-red bell, where looking downward they saw the latter's crimson reflection as in a pool of milk, stood the three prisoners. That Viola was there had been the result of pleadings so passionate that even Mercy the pitiless and Virtue the gross were moved to grant them.

As to why any of them were there, however, or what the queer sentence of that still queerer judge might actually imply, they were yet ignorant.

This was their own world to which the white moon gate of Ulithia had returned them; and yet in some dreadful manner they had been betrayed. Some mighty change had taken place during their brief absence. *How brief had that absence been?*

Beneath the bell, Drayton and his companions had at least a few moments alone together. Their isolation offered no chance of escape. The three doors of the great chamber were shut and locked, while across the old patrol entrance at the west a grate of heavy golden bars had been lowered.

"Viola, my dear," said Trenmore, "my heart aches for you! Whatever this 'Pit' of theirs may be, they've not condemned you to it along with us. I fear 'tis for an ill reason that they have spared you. My own folly and violence have brought me where I can no longer protect you, little sister; but for all you're so young and—and little—you're a Trenmore, Viola. You know what to do when I'm gone? Oh, must I tear out my very heart to be telling you?"

Viola shook her head, smiling bravely.

"I'll never shame you, Terry. When you go, dear, life will be a small thing that I'll not mind to be losing. And, Terry, I've a thought that this world we've come back to is our world no longer. We've no more place here than we had in Ulithia."

Drayton started slightly.

"Then you believe—"

"You must end this now," broke in a languid voice. Mr. Mercy had come up behind them unawares. Back of him appeared the figures of four other men, apparently convicts. They were dressed in loose, ill-fitting costumes, yellow in color and barred with broad black stripes. Their ugly heads were close cropped; their faces stupid and bestially cruel.

"Awfully sorry to interrupt," continued Mercy, fanning himself lazily with a folded newspaper he carried. "But we can't keep the Pit Guard waiting forever, you know. Don't cry, little one! I'll look after you."

Viola turned upon him with flashing, tearless eyes. When roused her temper was as tempestuous as her brother's.

"You insignificant rat of a man!" she stormed fiercely. "Do you believe I would have endured the sight of you even this long, were it not for my brother here, and Mr.

Drayton? Do you believe I'll remain alive one hour after they are gone?"

Mercy looked a trifle surprised.

"Do you know, my dear," he drawled, "I think you're devilish ungrateful! If Virtue and I were not so soft-hearted you wouldn't be here now. Oh, well, I like a girl with a spark of temper about her. You'll get over it. If you really wish to see the last of your heavyweight brother and his pal, come along."

Turning, he strolled off toward that mosaic emblem, set in the northward pavement. The four convicts closed about the prisoners. A moment later, having escorted them a short distance in Mercy's wake, the guard drew aside. The handcuffed prisoners now found themselves standing at the very edge of the mosaic.

The colored marbles, beautifully inlaid, represented a huge chained eagle, pierced with arrows, and reaching vainly with open beak after a flying dove in whose bill appeared the conventional olive branch. On a scroll beneath three words were inscribed in scarlet letters:

"*Sic semper tyrannis.*"

They were the words of Booth, when he bestowed the martyr's crown upon Lincoln. "Thus ever to tyrants!" Incidentally, they were also the motto of a State; but the State was Virginia, not Pennsylvania. What could be their meaning here? And where was this "Pit of the Past" into which the prisoners were to be thrown?

The last question was immediately answered. On the far side of the emblem, Virtue, Mercy and their attendant bluecoats had grouped themselves. Now Virtue stooped, clumsily because of his fat, and pressed a spatulate thumb upon the round eye of the mosaic dove.

Instantly the whole emblem began to sink. It seemed hinged on the base of the scroll. A moment later and there was just a hole in the pavement, shaped like the emblem, and up from which struck a strange, reddish glare.

Edging cautiously closer, Drayton peered downward. Viola and her brother joined him. They stood motionless, the ruddy light striking upward upon their shocked, fascinated faces.

What they saw was a straight-sided pit, some thirty-five feet in depth. From top to bottom the walls were lined with tiny, ruby-colored electric bulbs. At the very bottom sat a squat gigantic thing.

With shoulders and head thrown back, the face of it glared up at them. The mouth distended to an opening of some six feet across, was lined with sharp steel spikes, slanting upward. The tongue was a keen, curved edge of steel. In its taloned hands the monster held two spears upright. A tail, also spiked, reared itself at one side, and the narrow forehead bore two needle-pointed horns of steel.

So the space at the bottom of the Pit was filled. Anything falling there must of necessity be impaled—if not fatally, so much the worse for the thing.

Trenmore growled in his throat.

"For sure," said he at last, "you murderers have gone to needless trouble! Why do you not cut our throats with your own hands? The deed would fit your natures!"

Virtue and Mercy only smiled complacently.

"Sorry you aren't amused," drawled the latter gentleman. "This little joke was not invented for your special benefit. Do you know who that is down there?"

"The statue of the devil you worship!" hazarded Trenmore viciously.

"Oh, no indeed! Quite the contrary. The statue of the devil you worship, my bellicose friend. That is the God of War, and as he can no longer stride loose about the world, we have made it convenient for his devotees to drop in on him. In other words, break the Peace of Penn, and you'll get more of war than you like. '*Sic semper tyrannis!*' Any man who assaults another is a tyrant by intent, at least, so down you go."

"It was your police who attacked me!" accused Trenmore hotly.

Mercy's brows lifted.

"Was it? I had rather forgotten. That does spoil my parable, eh? But we shan't let it interfere with your invaluable opportunity to worship the God of War."

"Do you actually throw people—living people—into that vile trap?" Drayton's voice was incredulous. So theatrical, so tawdry seemed this Pit of theirs: like a stage dragon at which one may shudder, but not sincerely.

"We most assuredly do," smiled Virtue. He continued speaking, but his words were drowned and rendered indistinguishable by a great rattling roar, which seemed to rise from the open Pit itself. The prisoners instinctively sprang back from the edge.

There was nothing vocal in the noise, but if a bronze demon like that below should start into hungry life, just such a mechanical, reverberating roar might issue from its resounding throat.

The sound died away. "What was that?" demanded Trenmore sharply.

Mercy laughed.

"The subway, of course. The trains pass under the Temple foundations. You are the most curiously ignorant crooks that were ever brought in here. Where have you been living?"

Virtue glanced at his watch. "Mercy, if you are interested in their histories, would you mind obtaining them from the young lady later on? I'm due at a banquet in half an hour and I'm not dressed."

"Go ahead," shrugged Mercy. "We can finish without you."

Frowning, the judge shook his head. "His Supremity demands regularity in these affairs, and you know very well that the presence of the condemning judge is required here." Then he added in a lower tone, which nevertheless carried across the Pit, "I tell you frankly, Mercy, that he didn't like that business last week. You are growing too careless of his opinion, my dear fellow."

"Oh, he's an old—Hello; there comes Lovely. Now we shall have to hold the execution till she has looked the prisoners over. If we don't, she'll be deeply offended."

"A lot I care," muttered Virtue. Nevertheless, he lowered his hand, raised as if in direction to the guard.

A woman was approaching from the doorway beyond the open Pit. Tall, slender, a striking blonde in hair and complexion, she was dressed in an evening gown of soft, droopy lines, sea-green and deeply slitted to show slender limbs clad in pale gold.

At first glance and at a distance, Drayton fancied that "Lovely" well deserved her name. But as she drew near two facts became painfully apparent. The color in her cheeks was not the kind limited by nature, and her golden hair, waved back under a jade-green net, was of that suspicious straw gold, easily bought but very seldom grown. Her features, however, were regular and clean-cut, and her eyes really beautiful. They were large, well-shaped, and almost the very green of her gown.

Smiling sweetly upon Mr. Virtue, the lady extended her hand to Mr. Mercy, and afterward swept the prisoners across the Pit with a cold, indifferent gaze. When it rested upon Trenmore, however, her expression changed. A sudden light leaped into the sea-green eyes. The pupils expanded darkly.

"What a perfectly gorgeous giant, Virty!" she exclaimed, turning to the judge. "Where on earth did you get him? Surely, you were not about to waste that on the Pit?"

"Why not?" His Honor bestowed another covert, annoyed glance upon his watch.

"He has already beaten up four of our blue boys," laughed Mercy.

"Indeed? How so?"

Mercy related the incident briefly, giving Trenmore full credit and even exaggerating his feats for narrative effect. The lady laughed, a silvery peal of light-hearted merriment.

"And you meant to throw all that away in the Pit! How extravagant you boys are. It's fortunate I came out here.

Now, what I should like to know is this. Why hasn't at least that one," she pointed at Trenmore, "taken condemned right and entered for the contests day after tomorrow? Why didn't you, Number—Number, whatever your number may be?"

Trenmore eyed her, frowning.

"Madam, I can't so much as guess at your meaning. If there's some way out of this murderous business for my sister, my friend and myself, we'd take it more than kindly if you'll explain."

"Lovely," Virtue protested, snapping shut his watch, "I really must leave here immediately."

"Just a minute," she flung him, and called across to Trenmore. "You must know the laws!"

Believing that their fate hung in a delicate balance, Drayton intervened.

"We are strangers here. They haven't allowed us to speak or defend ourselves, but we certainly do not understand the laws, and we have not offended intentionally."

"Strangers! Strangers in Philadelphia?"

"Certainly. This gentleman only recently arrived from Ireland; his sister has spent the last few years in the West, and I myself am from Cincinnati."

The woman shook her head, looking more puzzled than before.

"Those names mean nothing. If you are really from outside the boundaries, how did you get in?"

Drayton hesitated. A diplomatic answer to that was, under the circumstances, difficult. Before he could frame a sentence sufficiently noncommittal, a new figure had thrust its way through the police guard and walked to the woman's side.

He was a man of about thirty-five, sharp-featured, cunning-eyed, and with a thin-lipped mouth which closed tight as a trap. Unlike Virtue and Mercy, the newcomer was attired in full evening dress. A light cloak, black and lined with flame-colored silk, was flung across one arm.

Without troubling to salute her companions, and without the slightest evidence of interest in the meaning of the scene in general, he addressed the green-clad woman.

"Lovely," he demanded in barely repressed impatience, "are you intending to go out this evening or not? If you don't wish to dance, for heaven's sake, say so! I can take some one else."

She turned upon him a glance of indolent scorn.

"Do that, if you think best. All my life I've been looking for a full-grown man to share my responsibility under Penn Service. Now that I have found one, do you think I will let him be lost in the Pit?"

At this speech Mr. Virtue gave a sharp exclamation, and Mercy laughed outright.

"So that's what you're up to, Lovely! Cleverest, I'm sorry for you! Goodnight!"

The thin lips of "Cleverest" parted in an unpleasant smile.

"I always knew you'd throw me over if you found a chance, Lovely. You mean to enter your protege for Strongest, I suppose?"

"Certainly."

"And you believe he will be able to supplant the present incumbent?"

"I know he will!"

"Ah, well, I shan't despair. You may close the Pit now, but it can also be opened again after the contests. And what of these other prisoners?"

The woman laughed defiantly.

"They shall have their chance, too! Virty, I don't often question your decisions, do I? But this time I wish you to close your ugly old Pit and," with a glance of disdain, "not oblige Clever by reopening it."

Mr. Virtue glanced very dubiously toward the thin-lipped man. He appeared not at all enthusiastic. Mercy scowled.

"Don't forget me, please, Virty! I've a very personal interest in this execution, and even Lovely shan't do me out of it!"

"Oh, shut up, Mercy," broke in the woman impatiently. "I can imagine what your interest is. You're afraid this girl's brother won't let you have her. But the law is the law and they have their contest right. You never think of any one but yourself Virty, turn these people loose and I'll be responsible for their appearance Wednesday."

"Cleverest, are you going to stand for this?" demanded Mercy angrily.

But Cleverest, who had himself been eying Viola, now smiled a strange, fox-like, tight-lipped smile.

"Why not?" he asked simply. "If Lovely prefers the fellow's strength to my brains, what can I do but gracefully withdraw?"

The woman looked at him with a trace of suspicion.

"Such amiability is really touching, Clever. But I'll take you up on it. That thin chap can go in for Swiftest, I think, and as for the girl—" She frowned at Viola with a look of mingled dislike and reluctant admiration. "Oh, well," she finished, "the girl can enter the contest for Domestic Excellence."

Slapping his fat thigh, Virtue burst into a sudden roar of laughter.

"Splendid, Lovely! You have it all arranged, eh? Mercy, you and Cleverest are down and out! Take 'em—take your charming proteges, Lovely, my child; and shut up the Pit. Old War must go hungry to-night. And now you'll excuse me, Lovely. You've already made me miss at least one full course!"

"It would do you no harm to miss more than that," she retorted with a disparaging glance at his waist-line; but Virtue only chuckled without taking offense and hurried away.

10 THE FOURTH VICTIM

The three quondam prisoners, seated about a table where they had done full justice to an excellent repast, were alone. The scene about them was no longer of barbaric magnificence, but presented the more comfortable and familiar luxury of a good hotel. Lovely, or rather Loveliest, for such they had discovered the lady's full title to be, had done her work with surprising thoroughness and munificence. Having made herself responsible for their custody, she had ordered the two men freed, carried them all in her own motor car to a large hotel on South Broad Street, and there engaged for them a suite consisting of bedrooms, private baths and a large parlor.

Her exact standing in this new Philadelphia, so like the old and so unlike, was as yet unknown to them. So far as their needs were concerned, she seemed to possess a power of command practically unlimited.

The hotel in itself presented no apparent difference to any other large, metropolitan hostelry. Drayton, in fact, who had once before stopped at this identical hotel, could have sworn that even the furnishings were the same as upon his former visit. The clerk at the desk was perhaps a trifle too obsequious for a normal hotel clerk. Otherwise, their introduction had been attended by no bizarre circumstance. Having seen them comfortably established, having begged them to send out for anything they might require and have the price charged to "Penn Service"—that mysterious, ubiquitous Service again!—their odd protectress had assured Trenmore that she would look in on them early next day and departed.

The lady had whirled them so rapidly through this period of change in their fortunes that they had been able to ask no questions, and though she had talked almost incessantly, the monologue had conveyed little meaning. They found themselves continually bewildered by references, simple in themselves, and yet cryptic for lack of a key to them.

The conclusion of their late dinner, served in their own rooms, at least found them more comfortable than at any time since that fatal hour when the Cerberus was uncapped. If they were still under police surveillance, there was no evidence to show it. By common consent, however, they had abjured for the present any idea of escape. Precarious though their position might be, such an attempt in their state of ignorance was predoomed to failure.

The meal finished, and the servant having departed for the last time, Drayton asked a question which had been in the back of his head for two hours past.

"Miss Viola, what were you saying about Ulithia when Mercy interrupted? Before the pit was opened, I mean, while we stood beneath the Red Bell?"

"I remember. It was merely a notion of mine, Mr. Drayton."

"But tell it," urged her brother.

"When we meddled with that strange dust," the girl said softly, "I think we intruded upon that which was never meant for mortals. The White Weaver said it—she said we had no place in Ulithia. And she told us to go forward, go deeper, and that the door was open before us."

"Yes, she did," sighed Drayton.

"And so," continued the girl, "we escaped from Ulithia, but went *forward*. Just how far is what we have yet to discover."

"You mean," said the ex-lawyer slowly, "that some six hours ago by my watch—which has not been wound by the way, yet is still running—we practically stepped out of space and time as we know them into a realm where those words have no meaning? And that when we passed through the moon gate, we returned into space at almost the place from which we started, but into time at a point perhaps many years later?"

"Yes. You say it better than I, but that is what I believe."

Drayton shook his head, smiling. "Something like that occurred to me, Miss Viola, but the more I think of it the more impossible it seems."

"And why, Bobby?" queried Trenmore impatiently. "Sure, 'tis the only moderately reasonable explanation of all the unreasonability we have met!"

"Because if enough years had passed to so completely change the laws, the customs, even the value of human life, why is it that Time has left costumes, language, even buildings, except for City Hall, exactly as we have always known them? Why, this very hotel has not so much as changed the livery of its bell boys since I was here three years ago!"

"That is a difficulty," admitted Viola. Then she added quickly, "How very stupid I am! Terry, won't you ring for one of those same bell boys and ask him to bring us an evening paper?"

So obvious a source of information and so easily obtainable! Drayton and Trenmore sprang as one man for the push button. Just as they reached it, however, there came a loud crash, as of something heavy and breakable falling upon a bare floor. The sound issued from the bedroom assigned to Trenmore. A moment later that gentleman had flung open the door. The chamber within was dark, save for what light entered it from the parlor. Peering uncertainly, Trenmore stood poised for a moment. Then he had hurled himself through the doorway. There was another crash, this time of an overturned chair.

Drayton, following, ran his hand along the wall inside the door. An instant later he had thrown on the light. The illumination disclosed the Irishman clasping a kicking man to his bosom with both mighty arms. Though the fellow fought desperately, he might as well have contended with an Alaskan bear. Trenmore simply squeezed the tighter. The breath left the captive's lungs in a despairing groan, and he was tossed, limp as a wrung rag, upon the bed.

By now Viola was in the room. "I hope you haven't hurt him, Terry," she cried. "The man might be a policeman in plain clothes!"

"If he is, he might better have watched us openly," growled Trenmore. "Here, you! Why were you after hiding in my bedroom? Was it eavesdropping you were?"

The figure on the bed sat up weakly.

"You can bet your sweet life I'd of been somewhere else, if I'd knowed you was around, chum! Why not tackle a guy your own size?"

Drayton burst out laughing, and after a moment Terence joined him.

The man on the bed could hardly have been over five feet in height, but what he lacked in length was made up in rotundity. His round face was smooth-shaven and wore an expression of abused innocence which would have done credit to an injured cherub. Though disheveled, the captive's dark-green suit was of good material and irreproachable cut. Socks and tie matched it in color. His one false color note was the glaring yellow of a large identification button, pinned duly beneath the left shoulder, and the too-brilliant tan of his broad-soled Oxfords.

"I say," repeated Trenmore, "what are you doing in my room? Or did you but come here to break the cut-glass carafe, and the noise of it betrayed you?"

"I came here—" The man on the bed hesitated, but only for a moment. "I came here," he announced with great dignity, "because I believed this to be my own room, sir. The numbers in this corridor are confusing! I shall speak to the management in the morning. If I have disturbed you, I'm sorry."

The little fellow had assumed a quaint dignity of manner and phraseology which for a moment took them all aback. Then Trenmore walked over to the outer door and tried it. The door was locked.

"And how's this?" demanded Terence, his blue eyes twinkling.

"I—er—locked it, sir, when I entered."

"Yes? And have you the key, then?"

The man made a pretense of searching his pockets; then smiled wryly and threw up his hands.

"Oh, what's the use? You got me! I came in through the window."

"Just so. Well, Bobby, 'tis the same old world, after all. Take a glance through the lad's pockets, will you? Something of interest might be there."

Catching the man's wrists he twisted them back and held the two easily in one hand. This time Trenmore's victim knew better than to struggle. He stood quiet while Drayton conducted the suggested search.

Viola wondered why the lawyer's face was suddenly so red. She had been told nothing of the episode at the house on Walnut Street; but Drayton had remembered, and the memory sickened him. The parallel to be drawn between this sneak thief and himself was not pleasant to contemplate.

His search was at first rewarded by nothing more interesting than a silk handkerchief, a plain gold watch, some loose change and a bunch of rather peculiar-looking keys. Then, while exploring the captive's right-hand coat pocket, Drayton came on a thing which could have shocked him no more had it been a coiled live rattlesnake.

"Why—why—" he stammered, extending it in a suddenly tremulous hand. "Look at this, Terry. *Look at what I found in his pocket!*"

"'Tis the Cerberus! The Cerberus vial itself!" The Irishman's voice was no more than awed whisper.

"Where did you get this?" Drayton uttered the demand so fiercely that the captive shrank back. "Where?" cried Drayton again, brandishing the vial as though intending to brain the man with it.

"Where did you get it?"

"Don't hit me! I ain't done nothing! I picked it up in street."

Trenmore twisted him around and glared in a manner so fiendishly terrifying that the little man's ruddy face paled to a sickly greenish white.

"The truth, little rat! Where did you get it?"

"I—I—Leggo my arm; you're twisting it off! I'll tell you."

Terence, who had not really meant to torture the little round man, released him but continued to glare.

"I got it over in a house on Walnut Street."

"You did? When?"

The man glanced from one to the other. His cherubic face assumed a look of sudden, piteous doubt, like a child about to cry.

"Well, as near as I can make things out, it was about two hundred years ago I done that! But I'd of took oath it was no later than this morning! Now send me to the bug-house if you want. I'm down and out!"

"Two-hundred-years!" This from Drayton. "Terry, I begin to see daylight in one direction, at least. My man, where did you acquire that yellow button you are wearing?"

The captive glanced down at his lapel. "I lifted it off a guy that had been hittin' up the booze. Everybody else in town was wearing one, and I got pinched for not; but I shook the cop and then I got in style." He grinned deprecatingly.

"I thought the button was obtained in some such manner. Terry, this fellow is the crook, or one of the crooks, who were hired by your unknown collector friend to steal the Cerberus! He is here by the same route as ourselves." He whirled upon the thief. "Did you or did you not pass through a kind of dream, or place, or condition called Ulithia?"

"Say," demanded the prisoner in turn, "is either of you fellows the guy that owns that bottle? Are you the guys that left that gray, dusty stuff laying on a newspaper on the floor?"

"We are those very identical guys," retorted Drayton solemnly.

"Suppose we all compare notes, Mr. Burglar," suggested Viola. "Perhaps we can help each other."

It was after three a.m. before the suggested conference ended. Any animosity which might have existed between robber and robbed was by then buried in the grave of that distant, unregainable past from which all four of them had been so ruthlessly uprooted. From the moment when the three first-comers became assured that Arnold Bertram—self-introduced, and a very fine name to be sure, as Trenmore commented—was actually a man of their own old, lost world, they welcomed him almost as a brother. There was surprising satisfaction and relief in relating their recent adventures to him. So far as they knew, Bertram was the only man living in whom they could confide, unbranded as outrageous liars. Bertram understood and believed them, and Bertram had good reason to do so. At the conclusion of their story, he frankly explained about the vial.

"I was near down and out," said he. "Nothing doing for weeks, and whatever I put my hand to fizzling like wet firecrackers. Then an old guy comes along and says to me and Tim—Tim's my sidekick—'Boys, there's a little glass bottle with three dogs' heads on the top. A guy named Trenmore stole it off me. Get it back and there's two thousand bucks layin' in the bank for each of you!' Well, he didn't put that 'stole it' stuff over on me and Tim. We're wise, all right, but most anybody'd crack a box for two grand, and he let on the job was an easy one. So we tried it that night and the old boy with us. He would come along, but we wished later we'd made him stay behind. We was going to jimmy the trap off the roof, but when we got to your house, Mr. Trenmore, darned if the trap wasn't open. Down we go, the old guy making a noise like a ton of brick; but nobody wakes up. Then we seen the light of a bull's-eye in the front bedroom on the top floor. We sneaks in quiet. There's a guy and his torch just showin' up the neatest kind of an easy, old-fashioned safe. So we knocks this convenient competition on the noggin, and opens the box. There's some ice there, but no bottle. Me an' Tim, we was satisfied to take the ice; but what does this old guy that brung us there do? Why, he flashes a rod, and makes us beat it and leave the stuff layin' there!"

Here Trenmore glanced quizzically at his friend, and again Drayton blushed. Viola, however, was far too intent on the burglar's tale to give heed.

"That must have happened before my brother and Mr. Drayton opened the vial," she observed. "How did you come—"

"I'll get to that in a minute, lady. We'd missed the bottle some way, and the old guy was scared to look any further that night. Next day, though, I goes back on my own, just for a glance around, and there was the front door of your house, Mr. Trenmore, standing wide open. 'Dear me, but these people are friendly,' thinks I. 'Come at it from the roof or the street, it's Welcome Home!' So up I goes, and once inside I seen this here bottle, right out in the middle of the floor. Things seem most too easy, but I picks it up, and then, like the nut I am, I have to go meddling with the gray stuff on the floor, wondering what it is and does the boss want that, too. He'd let on the bottle was full of gray powder.

"Next thing I knowed the room went all foggy. Then I found I was somewhere else than I ought to be, and hell— beg pardon, lady—but honest, if what I went through didn't send me off my nut nothin' ever will!"

It seemed he had almost exactly trod in their footsteps so far as the Market Street Ferry. Beyond that, however, Bertram's adaptable ingenuity had spared him a duplication of their more painful adventures. Though arrested soon after his arrival, he had escaped with proud ease, legalized his status with the "borrowed" identification button, and shortly thereafter a newspaper filched from a convenient pocket had furnished him with a date. "It put me down for the count," said Bertram, "but it give me the dope I needed." That date had been September 21st, 2118.

"Two centuries!" interpolated Drayton in a sort of groaning undertone.

"Yep. Twenty-one eighteen! Old Rip had nothin' on us eh?"

Recovering from the shock, Bertram had determined to recoup his fortunes. Hence, very naturally, the incident of the fire escape, the open window, and Terence Trenmore's hotel bedroom.

"And now," he concluded, "I've come clean; but hell!— beg pardon, lady—what I want to know is this: What was that gray stuff you guys left layin' on the floor?"

"I'll tell you," responded Drayton gravely. "It was dust from the rocks of Purgatory, gathered by the great poet Dante, and placed in this crystal vial by a certain Florentine nobleman. Any other little thing you'd like to learn?"

"I guess not!" The burglar's eyes were fairly popping from his head. "Gee, if I'd heard about that Purgatory stuff, I wouldn't have touched the thing with a ten foot pole!"

"Don't let Mr. Drayton frighten you," laughed Viola. "He has no more idea than yourself what that dust is—or was. That's a foolish old legend, and even Terry doesn't really believe in it."

The Irishman shook his head dubiously. "And if it was not that, then what was it, Viola, my dear?"

Drayton sprang to his feet.

"If we continue talking and thinking about the dust, we shall all end in the madhouse! We are in a tight spot and must make the best of it. Before I for my part can believe that this is the year A.D. 2118, some one will need to explain how the Hotel Belleclaire has remained the Hotel Belleclaire two centuries, without the change of a button on a bell-hop's coat. But that can wait. I move that we spend what's left of the night in sleep. Perhaps"—he smiled grimly—"whichever one of us is dreaming this nightmare will wake up sane to-morrow, and we'll get out of it that way!"

11 MINE AND COUNTERMINE

Dreaming or not, they all slept late the following morning, and would probably have slept much later had not Trenmore been roused shortly after nine by the house phone. After answering it, he awakened first Viola, then Drayton and Bertram.

"The foxy-faced gentleman—the one they name the Cleverest—he'll be calling on us it seems. Will you dress yourselves? This is a business that no doubt concerns us all."

Five minutes later, Terence emerged to find their tight-mouthed, cunning-eyed acquaintance awaiting him in their private parlor.

"'Tis a fine morning," greeted the Irishman cheerfully. After the few hours' rest, he had risen his usual optimistic, easy-going self, sure that A.D. 2118 was as good as any other year to live in. "Will you be seated, sir," he suggested, "and maybe have a bit of breakfast with the four of us?"

"Thank you, no. I have already eaten and shall only detain you a few minutes. Did I understand you to say there are four of you? I was informed of only three."

Trenmore's bushy brows rose in childlike surprise.

"Four," he corrected simply. "Myself and my sister, my friend Bobby Drayton and Mr. Arnold Bertram. Here they are all joining us now. Viola, my dear, this gentleman is Mr. Cleverest, and—"

The man checked him with upraised, deprecating hand.

"Not Mr. Cleverest I am only a Superlative as yet. But I am charmed to meet you—er—Viola. What a delightful title! May I ask what it signifies in your own city?"

Trenmore frowned and scratched his head.

"We shall never get anywhere at this rate!" he complained.

Drayton came to the rescue. "It might be better, sir, if we begin by making allowances for entirely different customs, here and where we came from. 'Viola' is a given name; it is proper to address the lady as Miss Trenmore. My own name is Robert Drayton; that gentleman is Mr. Terence Trenmore, and this is Mr. Arnold Bertram."

Cleverest bowed, though still with a puzzled expression.

"I admit that to me your titles appear to have no meaning, and seem rather long for convenience. As you say, however, it may be best to leave explanations till later. Time presses. Forgive me for dragging you out of bed so early, but there is something you should know before Her Loveliness plunges you into difficulties. She is likely to be here at any moment. May I ask your attention?"

The man was making a patent effort to appear friendly, though after a somewhat condescending manner.

"You are very kind," said Viola, speaking for the first time, "to put yourself out for us, Mr.—How would you wish us to call you, sir?"

"Just Cleverest—or Clever, to my friends," he added with a smirk of his traplike mouth. "I believe my presence and errand are sufficient proof that I wish you for friends. It is well enough for you, Mr.—er—Trenmore, to enter the contest for Strongest. Lovely knows her own hand in that respect. There will be no question of failure. But for you, Miss Trenmore, it is a different pair of shoes. Have you any idea of the duties connected with the position of Superlatively Domestic?"

"We know nothing," interpolated Trenmore, "about your system of government or your customs at all. 'Tis ignorant children we are, sir, in respect of all those matters."

The man regarded him with narrow, doubting eyes.

"It seems incredible," he murmured. "But your being here at all is incredible. However, I shall take you at your word. You must at least have observed that all our citizens wear a numbered mark of identification?"

"We have that," conceded Trenmore grimly. "I also observe that you yourself wear a red one, that is blank of any number."

"Oh, I am a Superlative." The man smiled tolerantly. "We officials, like the Servants themselves, have our own distinctive insignia. But the commonalty, who have no titles and are known only as numbers, must conform to the law. Otherwise we should have anarchy, instead of ordered government. From what Mr. Mercy has told me, I gather that you considered the penalty for dereliction in this respect too severe. But our people need to be kept under with a strong hand, or they would turn on us like wolves. They have their opportunity to be of those who make the laws. Most of them, however, are far too lazy or vicious to compete.

"Now these competitions—the Civic Service Examinations, as they are properly named—are conducted on a perfectly fair basis. It is a system as democratic as it is natural and logical. The Superlatives are chosen from the people according to fitness and supreme merit. Thus, our legal fraternity is ruled by the Cleverest—my unworthy self. The Quickest has command of the police force. The Sweetest Singer conducts the civic music. So on through all the offices. Above all, under Penn Service, the Loveliest Woman rules, with a consort who may be at her option either the Cleverest or Strongest of men. The system is really ideal, and whoever originated it deserves the congratulations of all good Philadelphians. You, sir," turning to Drayton, "if you pass as Swiftest, will have control of the City Messenger Service."

"And the Most Domestic?" queried Viola, smiling in spite of herself at this odd distribution of offices.

"Ah, there we come to the rub. The Superlatively Domestic is nominally Superintendent of Scrubwomen and City Scavengers. In practice, she is expected to take a very active and personal part in the Temple housekeeping, while the administrative work really falls to the department of police. When I tell you that the office is at present unfilled, and that the latest incumbent died some time ago from overwork, you will agree with me that you, Miss Trenmore, are unfitted for such a post. Your social position would be intolerable. The other Superlatives would ignore you, while as for the common Numbers, I, for one, would never dream of permitting you to associate with that ill-bred herd!"

"And yet," thought Drayton, "by his own account he must once have been only a Number himself!"

"Now, I," continued the Superlative, "have a very different and more attractive proposal to submit."

"And that is?"

Leaning forward, Cleverest's eyes became more cunningly eager.

"I propose that you, Miss Trenmore, supplant the Loveliest herself! It is perfectly feasible. She only holds the position—I mean, there is no chance of your being defeated. Let the woman go to the pit! Her beauty is a thing outworn years ago. But you—Listen: she threw me over for you, Mr. Trenmore, because she is so sure of herself that she believes she cannot be supplanted. But she is like every other woman; her skill at politics is limited by her own self-esteem and vanity. She has dallied along for years, putting off her choice of a male consort for one excuse or another, but really because she likes her selfish independence and prefers to keep her very considerable power to herself.

"At one time she was a great favorite with His Supremity, and in consequence more or less deferred to by even the Service. At present, however, Mr. Virtue is the only real friend she has among the Servants, and he is growing rather tired of it. Without realizing it, she has for three years been walking on the very thin ice of His Supremity's tolerance. It is true that six months ago she pledged herself to me, which shows that even she is not quite blind. But that was a contract which I, for my part, have never intended to fulfill. I had almost despaired, however, of discovering any really desirable candidate to take her place. Last night when I looked across the Pit I could hardly trust my eyes, Miss Trenmore. You seemed too good to be true. No, really you did! If she had thought about it at all, Lovely would have guessed then that her day was over. Your friends, Miss Trenmore, are my friends, and if you will follow my advice, you and I will end by having this city under our thumbs—like that!"

He made a crushing gesture, which somehow suggested an ultimate cruelty and tyranny beyond anything which Drayton, even, had encountered in his own proper century.

"The Penn Service will give you a free hand," continued the man. "I can promise that as no other living man save one could do. I am—But never mind that now. Will you take me on as a friend?"

Viola was eying him curiously.

"And this Loveliest—you say she must take her choice in marriage of just those two, Strongest or Cleverest? But Terry will be one of those, and he is my brother!"

"I am not your brother," said Cleverest insinuatingly.

Drayton sprang to his feet, and Trenmore, already standing, made a sudden forward motion. But to their surprise Viola herself waved them to be quiet and smiled very sweetly upon this foxy-faced and cold-blooded suitor.

"I think I may thank you, sir, and accept your alternative. If you are sure that I shall win in this strange competition. And now I am thinking, what do you do with the people who lose their high office? I suppose they go back among the Numbers again?"

The man laughed. "That would never do. Penn Service could never allow that. Any one who fails at a competition, whether he is a candidate or an actual incumbent of office, goes into the pit!"

"Gee!" muttered Bertram succinctly. Then aloud, "Say, Mister, I shouldn't think these here Super-what-you-may-call-'em jobs would ever get to be real popular!"

"We are not exactly crowded with applicants," acknowledged the Superlative. "But do not allow yourselves to be troubled on that score. I have excellent reasons for prophesying your success. And now I had best leave you, before her worn-out Loveliness catches me here. She might just possibly upset the apple cart yet! May I rely on you?"

He looked from one to the other with a shifty, yet piercing gaze.

"I think you may." Again Viola smiled upon him in a way that made Drayton writhe inwardly. What hidden side of this beautiful, innocent, girl-child's nature was now being brought to the surface? Did she realize the implications of this thing to which she was so sweetly agreeing? Her brother stood glum and silent, eyes fixed on the floor. Cleverest, however, his ax having been produced and successfully ground, extended a thin, cold hand to Viola.

"It is refreshing," he declared, "to find brains and the faculty of decision in conjunction with such beauty!"

Viola accepted the hand and the crude compliment with equal cordiality. "May we hope to see you soon again?"

"As early as circumstances allow. Don't let Lovely suspect what's in the wind. Just let her imagine that everything is drifting her way. I'll look after you. Be sure of that!"

And the Superlative departed, leaving behind him a brewing storm which broke almost as quickly as the door closed on his retreating back.

"Viola," growled her brother, and it said much for his anger that there was no endearment in his tone, "is it crazy you have gone? Or is it your intention to offer me that for a brother-in-law? Can you not see—"

"Now, just a minute, Terry. What is the title and position of the pleasant-faced gentleman who was here?"

"Cleverest, of course, the cunning-eyed rat! And he said he was at the head of the lawyers, bad luck to the lot of them—begging your sole pardon, Bobby, my boy!"

"Exactly. And is there no one of us who is better fitted for that same office than he that was just now here? Who is it that you've told me was the cleverest lad you ever met, Terry, and the prince of all lawyers?" She smiled mischievously at Drayton. "And why," she continued, "should Loveliest be the only one to receive a surprise on Wednesday? Let Mr. Drayton try for the office he's best trained for. I have faith that this Cleverest of theirs is not the man to win against him."

"I might try—" began Drayton. Then as the full inference struck him he started, staring with incredulous eyes at Trenmore's sister.

Though a slow flush mounted in her delicate cheeks, she returned his gaze unwaveringly.

"And why not, Mr. Drayton? Would you have me give myself to the present incumbent of that office? And I am asking of you only the protection betrothal would offer me until we may escape from these unkindly folk. Are

The Heads of Cerberus (1919)

you not my brother's trusted friend, and may I not trust you also?"

"Before Heaven, you may, Miss Viola," said Drayton simply, but with all the intensity of one taking a holy vow. "Terry, are you willing that I should attempt this thing?"

Trenmore nodded. "As a possible brother-in-law, Bobby, I do certainly prefer you to the other candidate. And by the powers, 'twill be worth all the troubles we've had to see that sly rat's face when you oust him from his precious job!"

"If I oust him," corrected Drayton.

"You'll do it. You've the brains of three of him packed in that handsome skull of yours. But Bertram, man, wherever did you get that watch? 'Tis a beautiful timepiece and all, but never the one you had last night!"

"It is, though." The most recent addition to their party turned away, at the same time sliding the watch in his pocket.

"It is not! Let me see it." The Irishman held out his hand with a peremptory gesture.

Somewhat sullenly the little round man obeyed the command. It was, as Trenmore had said, a beautiful watch; a thin hunting-case model and engraved "J. S. to C. June 16, 2114." The watch was attached to a plain fob of black silk, terminating in a ruby of remarkable size and brilliance, set in platinum. Trenmore looked up from his examination sternly.

"Who is 'C'? Never mind. I can guess! I remember how you brushed against the man as you went to open the door for him to go out."

"Well, and what if I did?" grumbled Bertram. "That Cleverest guy ain't no real friend of yours, is he?"

To Drayton's surprise, Viola laughed outright. "Mr. Burglar, you should change your habits once in two thousand years at least! Had you looked into that pit of theirs, as we did, you'd not be lifting things from a man who can send you there. Terry, how would it do to let Mr. Bertram try for the office of Quickest? He is that, by this piece of work, and on the police force he'd be—"

Her brother drowned the sentence in a great shout of mirth.

"You've the right of it, little sister! 'Tis the very post for him. Bertram, my round little lad, would that keep you out of mischief, do you think?"

Bertram grinned sheepishly. "It ain't such a bad idea," he conceded. "They tell me there's lots of graft to be picked up on the force. And say, it would be some fun to be ordering a bunch of cops around! I'm on, Mr. Trenmore!"

12   THE NEW CITY

By the evening of that day the four castaways of Time had acquired a better knowledge of the city, its odd customs and odder laws, than had been theirs during Cleverest's morning call. The Loveliest had kept her word and more than kept it. She had called for them in her car, amiably accepted their rather lame excuses for Bertram's presence, and insisted on an immediate shopping expedition to supply their more pressing needs in the way of clothing and toilette necessities.

On leaving the hotel she bestowed upon each of her proteges a plain green button. These, she explained, denoted that the wearer was of the immediate family of a Superlative. She had arranged with "Virty" to stretch a point for convenience sake, and so protect her wards *pro tempore*. Connections of Penn Servants, it seemed, wore similar buttons, but purple in color. No wearer of a button of either hue, she assured them, would ever be troubled by the police unless at the direct command of a Servant. This seemed a sweeping assertion, but they assumed that it did not cover such a person in the commission of actual crime. Later they were not so sure.

The most curious impression which Drayton received upon this brief expedition was that of the intense, commonplace familiarity of everything he saw, complicated by a secret undercurrent of differences too deep to be more than guessed at. The stores—most of them—were the same. The streets were the same. The people were not quite the same. Not only did both men and women appear to have undergone positive physical deterioration, but the look in their eyes was different.

These nameless, yellow-tagged Numbers who thronged the streets had a hangdog, spiritless appearance, as if caring little what their labor or their goings to and fro might bring them.

Everywhere the most profound, even slavish, respect was accorded to the Loveliest and her party. Evidently she was well known throughout the city.

Before entering the stores, she took them to luncheon and played the part of munificent hostess so well that all of them, save perhaps, Mr. Bertram, were more than half ashamed of their secret alliance with her jilted betrothed, the Cleverest.

One thing she did later, however, which cleared Viola's conscience. At one of the larger department stores, she insisted on purchasing for the girl a great supply of gingham aprons and plain, practical house dresses.

"You will need them, my dear," she assured affectionately. "Now, don't object! If you are to keep up your position as Superlatively Domestic you will require at least four dozen of each!"

Viola, more amused than annoyed, let the woman have her way. "Just picture me," she murmured aside to Drayton. "Picture poor little me cleaning the whole inside of City Hall! Isn't she the dear, though?"

Everything was to be charged, they discovered, to that benevolent institution "Penn Service." Trenmore, who made it a practice to carry a considerable amount of money about him, wished to pay. The woman scoffed at the notion.

"You'll soon get over the idea of paying for anything," she declared. "But tell me; how do you come to have money? I thought you said you had just reached the city. Is it money you brought with you? May I see it?"

Trenmore handed her some silver and a ten-dollar bill.

"Why, what curious little medals—and how pretty they are! Would you mind giving me these as a keepsake?"

"Not at all, madam," Trenmore responded gravely. Despite her obvious efforts to please, the woman's company and her open devotion to himself were becoming increasingly distasteful. As he complained to Drayton, he did not like the green eyes of her! "I suppose your own coins are different?" he queried.

"We don't use coins—is that what you call them?—for exchange. The common Numbers have their certificates of labor, somewhat like this piece of paper of yours. They are not green and yellow, though, but red, stamped with the number of hours in black. They are free to spend these as they please. But the Servants of Penn and we Superlatives charge everything to the Service."

"You mean the city pays?"

"Oh, no. These stores must do their part toward the government upkeep. That is only just. We levy on all the people equally—on the merchant and property-holder for goods; on the laborer for a portion of his time, if we require it. Penn Service makes no exceptions."

She said this with an air of great virtue, but Drayton commented, "That must be rather hard on any merchant or worker you particularly favor—especially a man of small capital or large family."

"It keeps them in line," she retorted, with a somewhat cruel set to her thin red lips.

"But," objected Drayton, harking back to the matter of money, "if your currency is not based on gold or silver, how does it possess any stability?"

"I don't know what you mean. The Service sets a valuation on the different sorts of labor. For instance, if an expert accountant and a street cleaner each work one hour, the accountant will receive credit for ten hours and the scavenger credit for half an hour. I suppose you might say the system is based on working time."

"And the value is not set by either employer or employed?"

Her eyes widened. "Let the Numbers say how much a man's labor is worth? Whoever heard of such a thing! Why, they would grind each other into the ground."

"They are at least free to work for each other or not as they please, I suppose?"

"Certainly. Why, they are perfectly free in every way. They even own all the property except the Temple itself and the officials' private residences."

Drayton was hopelessly at sea. Was this system a tyranny, as he had indefinitely suspected, or was it the freest and most orderly of governments?

"Forgive my stupidity," he apologized. "I don't even yet understand. Instead of the dollar you make an hour's labor the unit and then set a fixed schedule of labor value. But the work of two men at the same job is hardly ever of equal worth. How do you—"

"Wait," she broke in impatiently. "When you are yourself one of us, sir, you may understand these arrangements better. Penn Service owns practically nothing; but it rules everything. It is perfectly impartial. One man's labor is as good as another's. Any one who refused to give or take a certificate would have the Service to deal with."

"And yet the Service itself never pays for anything and takes what it likes of goods or labor. But according to that your whole population are mere slaves, and their ownership of property a mockery! Who are these Servants of Penn that hold such power?"

She stared at him, a hard look in her green eyes.

"The Masters of the City," she retorted briefly. "It is not suitable that we discuss them here and now. Wait until to-morrow. Then you yourself will become, I hope, a Superlative, and as such will receive all the necessary information."

The ex-lawyer accepted the snub meekly, but dared one further question.

"Are Mercy and Judge Virtue Servants of Penn?"

"Mr. Mercy and Mr. Virtue are both of the Inner Order. You will do very well not to cross their path—er—Drayton."

He made no further comment, but determined to use every opportunity to get at the true inwardness of this singular system and the toleration of it by the so-called "Numbers." Were all other cities like this? They must be, he thought, or no one would choose this one to live in.

The Loveliest herself seemed strangely devoid of curiosity regarding her proteges' past lives and histories. Indeed, twice she checked Trenmore when he would have volunteered information along this line. "You must not tell me these things," she declared. "Even we Superlatives are not permitted to learn of other places and customs— are not supposed to know that such exist!"

At this preposterous statement Bertram, who had been going about with an air of pained boredom, became interested.

"Say, lady, don't you folks ever go traveling anywheres?"

Had he suggested something indelicate, she could have looked no more horrified.

"Traveling outside of Philadelphia? I should hope not! Besides, such an outrage would never be permitted, I assure you."

"But you must have some communication with the outer world?" puzzled Viola. "We saw the trains and the passengers at the ferry. And where do all these things come from that we see in the stores?"

"My dear, we have many local trains, of course, but the interstate commerce is entirely in the hands of Penn Service. Our laborers here manufacture certain articles; our farmers raise certain produce. These things are turned over to the Service who reserve a share to themselves for expense. Then they exchange it outside the boundaries; but it is all done by the secret agents and I have never bothered my head about it. The matter is outside the province of my administration."

"How long has this sort of thing gone on?" persisted Drayton.

"My dear sir, and all of you, why will you ask such absurd and impossible questions? Can't you understand that we Philadelphians have no concern either with the past or with anything outside our own boundaries? The law says, let every good citizen live his own life. It is forbidden that he should do more than that."

"Do you mean to tell us," gasped the lawyer, "that you know nothing of this city's history?"

"Certainly I mean that. Most of these people that you see would not understand your meaning should you ask them such a question. I was educated privately by one of the Servants of Penn." She said it as one might boast of having been brought up by the King of England in person. "I am able to converse intelligently, I hope, on any reasonable subject. But even I never received such absurdly needless instruction as that."

"But what are the children taught in your schools?"

"The natural, useful things. Cooking, carpentry, weaving—all the necessary trades. What use would any more be to them? It would only make them dissatisfied, and goodness knows they are already dissatisfied and ungrateful enough!"

"Well," sighed Trenmore, "whoever has done these things to your people has certainly hit a new low in autocratic government."

Half playfully, she shook her head at him.

"Big man," she rebuked, "I don't altogether understand you, but take care of your words. I like you too well to wish to see you die! Penn Service is sacred. Never speak against it, even when you believe yourself alone or in the safest company. It has a million eyes and a million ears, and they are everywhere. And now, let me take you back to the Belleclaire. After to-morrow I will see you more suitably lodged. To-night, however, you must put up as best you may with its inconvenience and bareness."

Its "inconvenience and bareness," however, amounted to luxury in the eyes of these benighted wanderers from another age. They were very well content to have one more evening alone together. The Loveliest, it seemed, was attending an important social function to which, until they had actually claimed their laurels in the approaching competition, she could not take them.

"Nobody is anybody here," she said, "except the Servants themselves, the Superlatives and the family connections of each. There are only three or four hundred of us, all told, but we manage to keep the social ball rolling. I can promise you a gay winter. Now, don't attempt to go out on the streets."

Trenmore frowned. He had a secret desire to visit a certain house on Walnut Street and of course he wouldn't find the place unchanged, and the dust still lying there on the library floor. But he wished to look, at least. "Why not?" he inquired.

"Because I am responsible for your appearance at the contests to-morrow. Don't be offended. Should anything happen to you it would not only make me very unhappy, but might cause me serious trouble. The competitions are held in the Temple to-morrow at high noon. I'll call for you early and see to it that everything goes through just right. You've no idea what a pleasant future lies in store for you, big man!"

"Oh, haven't I, though?" muttered Trenmore as he stood with the others in the lobby and watched her retreating back. "Madam Green-eyes, it's yourself has a pleasant surprise on its way to you, and I'm the sorry man to see trouble come to any woman, but it's yourself deserves it, I'm thinking—and anyway, I couldn't let my little sister Viola be made the slave you'd gladly see her, or I've misread the green eyes of you!"

"What's that you're saying, Terry?" queried Drayton.

"Just a benediction on the kind-hearted lady, Bobby. Bertram, where are you off to? Didn't you hear herself saying we are all to stop inside?"

"Aw, say, boss, I'm fair smothered. That doll would talk the hind wheel off a street car. It wasn't me she went bail for and I won't get into trouble."

"See that you don't, then," counseled Trenmore, and let him go.

13 PENN SERVICE

Their day had been so fully occupied that none of the three had found time to seek that purveyor of plentiful information, the newspaper. Indeed, now that he thought of it, Drayton could not recall having seen any newsboy or news stands, and on consulting his friends they, too, denied any such memory. Yet that papers were still published in the city was certain. Mercy had carried one in the golden Court of Justice. Bertram had accounted for his knowledge of the date by reference to a "borrowed" newspaper.

Drayton went to the house phone and made his request. Something seemed wrong with the wire. While he could perfectly hear the girl at the other end, that young lady appeared unable to catch his meaning. Suddenly she cut him off, and though he snapped the receiver hook impatiently, it produced no further response.

"Ring for a boy, Bobby," suggested Trenmore. As he said it, however, there came a rapping at the door. Trenmore opened it and there stood a dignified gentleman who bowed courteously and stepped inside.

"I am the assistant manager," he explained. "There was some trouble over the phone just now. The management desires, of course, that guests of Penn Service shall receive every attention. What were you trying to make that stupid operator understand?"

"Nothing very difficult," smiled Drayton. "I asked for an evening paper."

"I beg your pardon. A—what?"

"A paper—a newspaper," retorted the lawyer impatiently.

"But, my dear sir! Surely you can't mean to make such an extraordinary request! Or—perhaps you have a special permit?"

A dazed silence ensued. "Are you telling me," burst forth Terence, "that in this God-forsaken place you need a permit to read the news of the day?"

"Every one knows," protested the manager placatingly, "that only Servants or their families are permitted to read the newspaper issued for their benefit."

Trenmore made a violent forward movement, and Drayton, after one glance at the giant's darkening countenance, hastily pushed the manager into the hall, assured him that their request was withdrawn and closed the door.

Not five minutes later, Cleverest was again announced. He followed the phone call so closely that Drayton had hardly hung up the receiver before he was at the door. He entered with a frown and a very pale face.

"See here," he began without greeting or preamble, "are you people trying to commit suicide? How can you expect protection if you persist in running foul of every law in the city?"

"Why the excitement?" queried Drayton coolly.

"The excitement, as you call it, is of your making. How dare you attempt to pry among the secret affairs of Penn Service?"

Drayton shook his head. "Can't imagine what you mean. We've not been out of this suite since the Loveliest brought us back to the hotel."

"That may be. But you were trying to bribe the manager to supply you with a copy of the *Penn Bulletin*!"

Enlightenment dawned in the minds of his three hearers.

"And is that all?" asked Trenmore scornfully. "As for bribe, we never offered the lad a cent. Did he claim we tried to bribe him?"

"He hinted at it. He met me at the door, and by Jove, it was a good thing he did! He was on his way to report you at the Temple!"

"Is it a capital crime, then, to wish to read a paper?"

Still frowning, Cleverest sank into a chair.

"What you need is a little common or kindergarten instruction. A bit more and you'll have us all in the pit for conspiracy. To begin, then, are you aware that no one in this city, barring those born in Penn Service or the officials under their control, is allowed to read any literature more informing than a sign post, an instruction pamphlet or a telephone directory? The only books, the only papers, the only manuscripts in existence are circulated and confined strictly to the Temple and the Temple people. The Supreme Servant himself is the only man having access to the more important documents and books, although there is a lesser library open to officials who care for study.

"Furthermore, the City of Philadelphia having reached a state of perfection under the beneficent power of Penn, his Servants have made it their business to keep it so. Advance or retrogression would be alike objectionable. That is obvious and logical. Everything is most exquisitely standardized. To change so much as a syllable of the language, a style in garments, the architecture or interior arrangement of a building, is rightly regarded as a capital offense. No man, saving the Servants or their emissaries, is allowed to pass outside city limits. No stranger in my time or knowledge has ever crossed them from without. You yourselves are the sole exceptions."

"But," puzzled Drayton, "how does Penn Service keep the city in subjection? We come from a place of far different customs and spirit, where innumerable armed troops would be required for such a business. You have only the usual police."

The man laughed. "There is a fear more restraining than the fear of bullets. Penn, the mighty All-Father, stands behind his Servants and justifies their acts." The Superlative spoke reverently, but it was a threadbare reverence through which gleamed more than a hint of mockery. "Do you recall," he continued, "that great Red Bell which hangs beneath the golden Dome of Justice? There is a saying in this city, 'When the Bell strikes, we die.' It is named the Threat of Penn. The people believe implicitly that should the Servants become incensed and strike that Bell, the city, the people, the very earth itself would dissolve into air like thin smoke! I myself can't tell you how this supersti—I should say, this faith originated. But it is a very deep-rooted and convenient one. Have you any other questions?"

"One more, and it is this. During the day I have heard Penn Service referred to as sacred. Last night the judge spoke of the 'sacred precincts.' What we called City Hall you call the Temple. Just now you referred to 'Penn, the mighty All-Father.' Is Penn Service a religious organization?"

The other stared. "Religious? That is a word I have never before heard. Penn is the All-Father. The Numbers worship and pray to him. Immobile and benevolent he stands, high above our petty affairs, speaking to none save his Servants. Through his wisdom they, the twelve great Servants of Penn, are the Supreme and only power—the Masters of his City!"

Drayton sighed deeply. "We are indebted to you, sir, for your frankness. In future we will certainly try to keep out of trouble."

"I trust you will." Cleverest rose to take his departure. "I've set my heart on upsetting Lovely's little game. By the way, where is that other chap—Bertram, you call him?"

"He went out. He'll be back soon. We had thought of entering Bertram for Quickest—that is, if you have no objection?"

The Superlative looked startled, then smiled oddly.

"Oh, no possible objection, of course. Good day to you all. And to you, dearest lady! I shall be first at your side when you reach the Temple to-morrow."

Speaking of Bertram, however, had recalled something to Viola. "Just a moment, Mr. Cleverest. I beg your pardon. Cleverest, then. Terry, have you that watch?"

"Did I lose it here?" Cleverest's eyes lighted as Trenmore extended the expensive timepiece.

"It fell from your pocket perhaps?" suggested Viola demurely.

"I am a thousand times obliged to you, Miss Trenmore. That watch was given me by my uncle, Mr. Justice Supreme. The old gentleman would never have forgiven me if I had lost it."

"So, he's the nephew of Mr. Justice Supreme, is he?" murmured Viola, when the Superlative had at last departed. "Now I wonder if that relationship is the card he has up his sleeve?"

"Viola, if you've an inkling of further mystery, save it till I'm rested from what we've had," protested her brother. "Let's ring for the servant the way we'll be having our suppers. I think we do need them!"

14 THE THREAT OF PENN

That night Mr. Arnold Bertram did not return to the Hotel Belleclaire. Moreover, Trenmore discovered with some annoyance that the Cerberus was again missing. He had thrust the thing in his pocket and forgotten it. Now the vial was gone, either lost in the streets, or, more probably, again confiscated by their rotund and assimilative friend the burglar.

Morning came, but no Bertram. Drayton was first dressed, and he was waiting in the parlor when the others appeared. A moment of silence was followed by a sudden deep chuckle from Trenmore and a little shriek from Viola.

"Why, you two absurd men!" she cried. "You're wearing exactly the same things as yesterday! You haven't even had them pressed! Terry, your trousers look as if you'd slept in them—not a sign of a crease. What will your true love be thinking?"

Trenmore flung back his head with a comical look of defiance. "Let her think what she likes. I've no liking for goods no better than stole, Penn Service or no Penn Service! I pay for my clothes, or I'll wear none. But you've no cause to be talking, Viola. Where's the pretty new gown you were to be wearing? And Bobby, what about those fine ash-grays you were choosing so carefully yesterday?"

"I meant to wear them. If we intended to keep faith with the lady who provided them, I should certainly have worn them. As it is—" Drayton shrugged.

"And I," confessed Viola, "couldn't bring myself to touch anything that woman gave me. She must take us as we are or not at all. It's ten o'clock—and there's the telephone. I expect that is my Lady Green-eyes."

It was. She looked disappointed and more than a trifle hurt when she saw their costumes and learned their intention not to change. She herself was resplendent in a gown of pale-yellow satin, under a magnificent fitted coat of Irish lace. Trenmore placated her for their shabby appearance as best he could, and dropping that subject, though with obvious annoyance, the Loveliest inquired for the missing Bertram.

"We've no idea at all where he is, madam. He went out last night, though I argued it with him, and we've seen neither hide nor hair of the lad since that time."

She seemed little concerned. "He will probably show up at the Temple. If he has lost his green button and got himself arrested, he is sure to be there. Shall we go now?"

Descending to the lady's car, they found Broad Street crowded with an immense and mostly stationary throng. Narrow lanes had been cleared by the police for such pedestrians and motor cars as might prefer moving along. A few cars belonging, they were informed, to various officials, were parked in the middle of the street.

"What are they all waiting for?" queried Viola.

"For the competitions. They don't often take so much interest. This time the Numbers have a candidate for musical director, and they are waiting for blocks around until the result is announced."

Drayton wondered why such a large percentage of the population were concerned over an apparently unimportant office; but he made no comment.

The run from the hotel to the former City Hall was a short one. As the car swung into the open traffic lane, Drayton looked ahead. There, closing the brief vista, loomed that huge gray bulk of masonry which is the heart—the center—the very soul, as one might say, of the ancient Quaker City.

From the street no sign of the golden dome was visible, nor any exterior hint of the vast innovations within. There rose the tower upon whose pinnacle, visible for many a mile around, stood the giant figure of that good old Quaker, his vast hand forever outstretched in gentle blessing. There he stood, as he had stood for troublous centuries. Below him was the familiar clock and a wraith of white mist obscured its face. Drayton remembered how, on previous visits to Philadelphia, that wraith of mist had prevented him from seeing the time. The wind was perpetually blowing it across. And Broad Street—he had once been here through a city election. All Broad Street had been crowded, just as it was crowded now, with people in fixed masses before the bulletin boards. The bulletins were missing now, but what other difference was there in appearance?

A yellow multiplicity of numbered buttons and yes, the emblem displayed above the Public Building's southern entrance. Then it had a huge replica of the Knight Templar insignia, with "Welcome K. T." in varicolored bulbs. Now the emblem was a sword-crossed bell. Above it gleamed four ominous figures—2118. *That* was the difference.

Drayton emerged from his homesick comparisons to find that the car was drawing up at the curb. Where had once been an open archway were doors of studded iron. A traffic policeman hurried forward and hustled the crowd aside. He used his stick freely, but the crowd did not even growl. It sickened Drayton—not so much the blows, as the spirit in which they were taken. Had the backbone of this people been entirely softened in the vinegar of even two centuries of oppression? And these were his own people, or their descendants—his fellow Americans! That hurt.

Doubtless, however, as he became adjusted to new usages, the injustice and oppressions of the year A.D. 2118 would seem no more intolerable than the tyrannies and injustices of the twentieth century.

The iron doors swung wide and closed silently behind the little party. They found themselves in a long corridor, walled and floored with polished red marble, artificially lighted and lined with doors, paneled with frosted glass. "Part of the administrative section," explained the Loveliest, as she hurried them along the passage. "These are all offices of the different departments. Would you care to see the crowd under the Dome from the balcony?"

Without waiting for assent, she led the way up a short flight of red marble stairs. Suddenly they emerged from beneath a low arch and looked out into the space beneath the Dome of Justice. They stood upon a little balcony. Out from it extended a narrow bridge of planking to the rough scaffold that hung about the Red Bell.

Beneath the Dome the milk-white floor was no longer visible. They looked down upon a sea of heads. The people were packed so closely that had there come one of those swaying motions common to crowds many must inevitably have been trampled. Only at the northern side was a space cleared and roped off. In the center of this space was the eagle and dove symbol that hid the pit. At the far side a throne of carved and jeweled gold had been set on a high dais, draped with pale blue and yellow banners. Throne and dais were empty, but close about the roped-off space was drawn a cordon of uniformed police. Save for these who wore their regulation caps, not a head in the great hall was covered. Silent, patient, bareheaded, they stood—the despised "Numbers," packed too tightly for even the slight relief of motion, waiting.

Drayton wondered what it was about them that seemed so strange—so unearthly. Then it came to him. They were silent. Except for a faint rustling sound, like dry leaves in a breeze, the space beneath the golden dome was entirely silent. One could have closed one's eyes and fancied oneself alone.

Said Trenmore, "Are they dumb, these people of yours?"

Low though he had spoken, his voice reverberated from the shallow Dome as from a sounding board. The dark sea of heads became flecked with white, as faces were turned toward the balcony. Leaning her gloved elbows on the golden rail, the Loveliest looked indifferently down.

"They are not permitted to speak within the sacred precincts. Most of them have stood these three hours past, and they have another two hours to wait. They are all so lazy that I don't imagine they mind. Anything, rather than to be at work!"

"Some of those women have babies in their arms," observed Viola pityingly.

The Loveliest shrugged. "Don't ask me why they are here. It's a foolish old custom, and I am glad to say this is the last of it. Mr. Justice Supreme has ordered that hereafter the competitions shall be held in private. We had best go around to the north side now. I'll find out if Mr. J. S. is ready to receive you. I persuaded Virty to arrange for a presentation. Mr. J. S. is just a trifle difficult in his old age, but he won't interfere."

Interfere with what? Drayton wondered. Then the question slipped from his mind as his eye lighted on a curious thing at the back of the balcony.

It was a sword; a huge, unwieldy weapon, fully seven feet in length. The broad blade was of polished blue steel, inlaid to the hilt with gold. The grip, such of it as could be seen, was of gold studded with rough turquoise. Too large and heavy, surely, for human wielding, the sword was held upright in the grip of a great bronze hand, the wrist of which terminated in the wall at about the height of a man's chest from the floor.

"And what weapon is that?" inquired Trenmore.

"That? Oh, that is part of the Threat. You see the hand that holds it? That is the so-called 'Hand of Penn.' From the tower above, his hand is extended in blessing.

Down here it grasps the sword. It is attached to a sort of mechanical arm, long enough to pass halfway across the Hall of Justice. The arm runs back through the wall there, between the ceiling of the corridor and the floor above. It is controlled by a mechanism to which only the Servants hold a key."

"And what happens when the queer machine is used?" asked Trenmore. It seemed a useless invention, on the face of it.

"It isn't used," she replied with an amused smile. "If it ever were, the hand would drop so that the sword was level; then shoot out and the sword's point would strike the edge of that Red Bell and recoil. Of course, it couldn't strike now, because of the scaffolding. Mr. J. S. has an idea that the bell will look well with a ring of red electric lamps around it. They are wiring it for that."

"The sword is a kind of elaborate gong-striking device then," commented Drayton. He recalled Cleverest's description of the singular dread in which the Red Bell was held by the Numbers. "What would happen if it were used?" he queried in turn.

"Oh, the city would go up in smoke, I suppose." The woman laughed as she said it. Clearly she herself had no great faith in the probability of such a catastrophe.

"But how do your people imagine that a miracle of that sort could be brought about?" persisted Drayton.

"You do ask such questions! By a special dispensation of our Lord Penn, I suppose. Will you come with me, please? Under no circumstances must His Supremacy be kept waiting."

They followed her, back into the red corridor, and thence through a long series of luxurious living apartments, smoking, lounging, and drawing-rooms, each furnished in a style compatible only with great wealth or the system of "credit" peculiar to Penn Service. Crossing the old patrol entrance, they at last reached that part of the Temple which was held consecrate to the use of the highest Servant, Mr. Justice Supreme. While possessing several residences in various pleasant locations, he preferred, the lady informed them, to live almost entirely in the Temple. To the visitors, this "Temple," with its more or less resident "Servants," bore a close resemblance to a clubhouse for luxury-loving millionaires.

They waited in an anteroom with their guide, who had given her card and a penciled message to one of the half-dozen uniformed page boys who lounged there. The lad returned with a verbal message to the effect that Mr. Justice Supreme begged to be excused.

At almost the same moment Cleverest emerged from the door leading to the inner sanctum. He came straight to them with a smile of welcome which made him look almost good humored. Close behind appeared the plethoric Mr. Virtue.

"I declare, Virty, it's too bad!" began Loveliest indignantly. "You promised that you would arrange a presentation."

Mr. Virtue, looking worried and more than a little annoyed, shook his head. "I can't help it. I couldn't see him myself, Lovely. Clever's been with him all morning. Ask him what the trouble is!"

She turned a glance of sharp suspicion upon her fellow Superlative. "Did you have anything to do with this, Clever? If you did—"

"To do with what?" inquired Cleverest blandly. "His Supremity is somewhat indisposed, and is conserving his strength for the ceremonies. You have no cause for anxiety. I explained things to him myself. There will be no trouble. You really owe me a debt of gratitude, Lovely. The dear old gentleman has always been rather fond of the present Strongest. I had quite a little job persuading him that your candidate was in every way more deserving."

She watched him with a puzzled frown. Then her brow cleared, her eyes opened wide with that dark distension of the pupils which was a trick of theirs.

"Why, Clever," she beamed, "I'm tremendously obliged to you. I never thought you really cared enough to do anything like that for me. Particularly now!"

He smiled, with a barefaced assumption of hurt tenderness which would have deceived none but the most vain and assured of women.

"You've never done me justice Lovely. Don't thank me until the competitions are over. When the job's done I shall feel more worthy! Come along to the Green Room. Nearly every one else is there."

The "Green Room" proved to be a long, wide chamber with windows on one side only, opening out upon the Hall of Justice. In the center of that side, level with the pavement, opened the northern door, which varied from the other two in being of the same scarlet hue as the Red Bell.

The room itself was done entirely in green, a thick velvet carpet of that color covering the floor like moss, and the walls being decorated in a simulation of foliage. The place was well filled. By the law, it seemed, every Superlative physically able to be present must appear at the Civic Service Examinations, held once in four years. Most of them had brought members of their families.

All wore the green or red buttons of Superlativism, and all were dressed with a gayety which verged—in many cases more than verged—on distinct vulgarity. For some reason of etiquette none of the Servants' womenfolk were present. The three visitors were therefore unable to pass judgment on those greatest of great ladies. The gathering present, however, represented if not the cream, at least the top milk of twenty-second century society. Though it was morning, the only women present whose gowns were not almost painfully decollate were Viola Trenmore, Loveliest, and two or three very young girls. Colors shrieked at one another, or were gagged to silence by an overpowering display of jewelry. Some of the older and plainer ladies were quite masked in the enamel of their complexions.

The Loveliest took her proteges about the room, presenting them to the various officials and their wives. She seemed on the most familiar terms with the men, but the women, while they addressed her with formal respect, cast glances at her back tinged with anything but affection.

The only Superlative not present was the Swiftest, Chief of the Messenger Service. "Laid up with another bad attack of rheumatism," Mr. Virtue explained sympathetically.

"He'll be laid up with worse than that after the contests," grinned Cleverest, with a meaning wink at Drayton.

The latter smiled back, but the effort was mechanical. They boasted of the fair and open nature of these contests, and at the same time talked of the results as a foregone conclusion. One ex-lawyer wondered what ghost of a chance he had to supplant this man, nephew of Justice Supreme, and so sure of his ability to undermine Loveliest, herself a person of influence and evident power. He had the ghastly feeling of a man walking on a thin crust above unknown fires. There was too little that they understood; too much that hinted of subterranean movements and powers which at any moment might writhe and cast them all into that theatrical, deadly pit, beneath the Dove of Peace.

Then he heard the green-eyed lady's voice again, speaking in the silkiest of tones. "And this, my friends, is our Chief of Contractors, the Strongest. Stringy, let me make you acquainted with Mr. Trenmore. And Miss Trenmore. This little lady is to try her hand at domesticity, Stringy. I don't imagine there will be any competition—not for *that* office."

The official whom she disrespectfully misaddressed as "Stringy" fitted his nickname better than his real title of Strongest. He was a tall, long-limbed, lean man, with a very red face and sunburned neck. He glanced pityingly at Viola. From her his gaze turned anxiously to the huge giant of a man with whom he was shortly to contend not only for continuance in office, but life itself. He started to say something, choked, and, turning abruptly, hurried off to lose himself in the crowd of his more fortunate fellows.

"Somebody has tipped Stringy off," laughed Mr. Virtue. "Hi, there, Merry! Whither away?"

But the ineffable Mr. Mercy jerked roughly from his friend's detaining hand and without a glance for the rest of the party passed on through the door leading to the inner sanctuary.

"He's sore, too," growled Virtue. "Lovely, you're getting me in bad all around."

"Merry will get over it," she replied indifferently. "He never thinks of any one but himself. Outside of that he's a good sort. I'll square things for you, Virty, once this examination is over. What was it you said, Mr. Drayton?"

"Is there any objection," repeated Drayton, "to my wandering about a bit? The decorative schemes of these rooms are wonderful. I used to be interested in such things, as a boy. You don't mind?"

"Not at all. Go over toward the eastern side, though, away from Mr. J. S.'s sanctum. And be back here within the half hour."

"I will. Terry, you don't mind if I leave you?"

"Go ahead," assented the Irishman, and Viola nodded abstractedly. She was staring out at that pathetically silent multitude in the Hall of Justice.

As a matter of fact, the lawyer craved solitude for thought. The more time he spent in this Temple of Justice, the more he became convinced of the puerility of their own light-hearted schemes.

Viola's reflections, had he known it, were no shade less gloomy than his own. Quick-brained, intuitive to a degree, the psychic atmosphere of the place, combined with hints picked up here and there, had shaken her assurance to its foundations. She could think of nothing but Drayton's well-nigh certain failure and its inevitable toll of disaster. She herself would then be the promised bride of a man she instinctively loathed, while Drayton— but there she halted, unable to contemplate the hideous fate which once more threatened.

Her reverie was interrupted by her brother. The Loveliest had deserted him temporarily and was engaged with some of her friends across the room. The two Trenmores conversed for some time undisturbed; then Terry drew out his watch.

"Viola, it's 11:45 and Bobby is not yet back. Where can the lad be lingering, do you think?"

Before the girl could reply, Loveliest hurried over to them.

"You must go out into the hall now, big man. You, too, my dear."

"Not without Mr. Drayton," stipulated Viola firmly. "He has not returned!"

Loveliest frowned. "We certainly cannot wait for him! I warned him to be back here by half past eleven."

"I'll go look for him," volunteered Trenmore; but Lady Green-eyes checked him.

"I can send an officer if you really can't get along without him. He is probably lost somewhere in the corridors. Here comes Mr. Justice Supreme. I told you it was late!"

A green baize door at the end of the room had swung open. Through it filed several men, all attired in the same frock coats, light trousers, patent-leather pumps and spats which distinguished Mercy and Virtue from the common herd. They also possessed similar silk hats, and wore them, though they and the police were the only male persons within the Temple with covered heads. The hats, evidently, were further marks of distinction, like a bishop's miter or the splendid crown of royalty.

Having passed through the door, they divided into two ranks, the last man at the end on each side holding wide the two halves of the door. There followed a pause, during which a solemn hush settled throughout the Green Room.

Through the open doorway emerged the figure of a very old man. He was bent, shaking, decrepit with a loathsome senility. His face was shaven and his clothes the apotheosis of dandyism. His coat curved in at the waist, his shoes were two mirrors, his hat another. He wore a yellow chrysanthemum as a boutonniere, and from his eyeglasses depended a broad black ribbon. His vest was of white flowered satin. His hands were ungloved yellow claws, and in one of them he carried an ivory-headed ebony cane. With the latter he felt his way like a blind man, and supported himself in his slow and tremulous progress.

His face! It was lined and scarred by every vice of which Clever's younger countenance had hinted. His pale-blue eyes, rheumy and red-rimmed, blinked evilly above purple pouches. Over ragged yellow teeth his mouth worked and snarled, as though mumbling a continuous, silent curse against life and all mankind.

Looking neither to right nor left, he hobbled between the ranks of the lesser Servants. Promptly, as he passed, they closed in behind and followed him on and across the Green Room toward the door which led to his great golden throne, set in the Hall of Justice.

And the people in the room bowed very reverently as he passed by—bowed and looked relieved that he had gone without a word to them.

Staring fascinated, Viola and her brother were startled by a whisper at their shoulders.

"Old J. S. has had a bad night. He looks grouchier than usual!"

It was the irrepressible Loveliest. "Come over to the window," she continued as the door closed behind the last of the Servants. "I'll tell you exactly who's who. You see that man helping His Supremity up the steps of the dais? That is Mr. Courage, his right-hand man. And just behind is Mr. Kindness. That short, thin one is Mr. Power; the old fellow that drags one leg is Mr. Purity. Then come Mr. Pity, Mr. Contentment, and Mr. Love. And there goes good old Virty, looking as if his last friend had died; just because Mercy cut him, I suppose, and he blames me for it. But they're all alike—they never think of any one but themselves. I suppose Merry is sulking somewhere, too.

"Those are all the Servants who are here to-day. There are twelve altogether. And now you really must go to your places. I've sent a man to look for your friend and I'll have him brought out to you as soon as he is found. I have to stay here with the other Superlatives until my place is called; but of course that is merely a formality. The only candidates up are yourselves, and that boy the Numbers are trying to wedge in as Musical Director. Here,

Fifty-three," she addressed their old acquaintance, the police sergeant, "look after my friends, will you? Well the nerve of him! Will you look at Clever? He's gone right up on the dais with the Servants! I don't care if Mr. J. S. is his uncle, Clever has no right to push himself forward like that—not while he's holding a Superlative office!"

She was still talking as they left her, but so obviously to herself that they felt guilty of no discourtesy. Following Sergeant Fifty-three, they were led to a place at one side of the roped-off enclosure. No one else was there, save a slim, graceful boy of about nineteen or twenty. This was the Numbers' candidate for Musical Director. He was plainly, though not shabbily dressed, and his face was of such unusual beauty that Viola was really startled. As she said afterward, that face was the first thing she had seen in the city which reminded her that somewhere still there really was a Heaven.

15 THE JUSTICE OF PENN SERVICE

The Supreme Servant had already seated himself on his throne of gold. His virtuous subordinates occupied lesser seats to his right and left, while the chairs on the pavement, at either side of the dais, were by now pretty well filled, mostly by the womenfolk of the Superlatives. The Numbers still waited in their silent, terrible patience. When Mr. Justice Supreme took his seat they had knelt and again risen, a feat only possible because it was done as one surging motion. Here and there a cry or groan, quickly stifled, gave testimony that, even so, the weaker folk must have suffered.

Between the candidates and the front ranks of the crowd ran the enclosing plush rope. Against it, on the outside, the police guard had now faced about toward the dais. None of the Numbers, save those immediately behind the police, could hope to see what went on before the dais. They could hear, however, and for that privilege they had stood five hours, silent.

Trenmore glanced at his watch. It pointed to eleven fifty-nine.

And now Courage, whom the Loveliest had designated as Mr. Justice Supreme's right-hand man, arose and walked to the front of the platform. In his hands he held a document from which depended the red ribbons of an official seal. Without a preliminary word the Servant began reading:

"To all whom it may concern: Be it known by these presents that I, Justice Supreme and Spiritual Director of the City of Philadelphia under our dread lord, Penn, do hereby decree that upon the twenty-third day of September, in the year twenty-one hundred and eighteen, there shall be held in the sacred temple of Penn, beneath the Golden Dome of Justice, a series of examinations by which—"

The document proceeded to enumerate the various offices for which candidates might contest, related in detail the ghastly penalty of failure, and concluded abruptly with the signature and seal of Mr. Justice Supreme.

Mr. Courage—and Trenmore thought it must have required considerable courage to read a document of that nature, with its numerous references to "this democratic and blessed institution, the bulwark of your liberties!"—finished and resumed his seat. There was a moment's pause. Then Pity took the place of Courage on the platform.

"The first examination will be held in the superlative quality of Kindness."

A short, stocky, heavily built man emerged from behind the dais and took his place, standing fairly upon the eagle and dove symbol that covered the pit. Either his features or his title, in Trenmore's opinion, must be misleading. Those thin, cruel lips, narrow-set eyes, and low, slightly protruding forehead indicated several possible qualities; but benevolence was hardly of the number. As agreeably as his facial limitations would permit, the gentleman smiled up toward Mr. Pity.

"Is there any other candidate for this office?" droned the latter in his high, singsong voice. "It entails the management and control, under Penn Service, of the Bureau of Penn Charities for Philadelphia and environing suburbs. Any candidate? There is no other candidate for Kindest! Present incumbent of the office may retire."

Having reached this foregone conclusion, Pity returned Kindness' smile, and the latter did retire, as far as the chairs at one side, where he sat down beside a very fleshy, be-diamonded and prosperous looking lady whom Viola remembered to be his wife.

Three other offices followed: the Wisest, appropriately superintendent of the Board of Education; the Bravest, chief of the Electrical Bureau; and Most Ingenious, this latter holding the curious office of providing entertainment for the Servants of Penn themselves. The holders of these positions came out one by one, stood upon the fatal symbol, and retired, their right to superlativism unquestioned.

"The fifth quality upon my list is Sweetness of Voice. This office carries with it the honor, duties, and emoluments of Director of Civic Music."

Out to the eagle with assured tread waddled a mountain of flesh, crowned by a head of flowing black hair which Svengali might have envied, with a beard of astounding proportions, and somewhere between hair and beard a pair of small, piglike eyes.

"Is there any candidate for this office?" droned the bored voice of Mr. Pity. "Is there any other candidate for this—"

"Go on out there, boy," muttered Trenmore, giving the Numbers' candidate a friendly push. As they waited, he, like Viola, had conceived a strong sympathy for this solitary, youthful champion of the despised Numbers.

"Go on out, boy! Go out and give 'em hell!" was the Irishman's ambiguous encouragement.

The candidate, however, cast him a grateful glance, sensing the spirit behind the words. As Mr. Pity uttered the third and last call for candidates, the young man advanced boldly into the arena. He was greeted by a low, thunderous mutter of applause, starting at the front ranks of the crowd and spreading backward in a resonant wave. Mr. Justice Supreme grasped the arms of his throne-like chair and half arose.

"Silence!" he snarled. "Silence, my children! You are committing sacrilege! Do you know the penalty?"

His answer was the silence he had commanded, and the faces in the front rows went very white. Their vantage point was uncomfortably close to the pit.

"Mr. Pity," muttered the old man, sinking back, "will you kindly proceed?"

Bowing, the master of ceremonies turned once more to the contestants.

"Candidate, what is your number, place of residence, employment, and age? Answer in order, please, and speak clearly." He held a fountain pen poised over the list in his hand.

"My number is 57403. My—my—I live at 709 Race Street." The boy's clear tenor, faltering at first, grew firmer. "I am a carpenter's apprentice. I was nineteen years old in June."

"Nineteen years and four months, odd." Mr. Pity wrote it down forthwith. He capped his pen, replaced it in his vest pocket, and smiled down upon the young carpenter with such a friendly look that Viola's heart gave a leap. Perhaps, after all, the boy was to have a fair chance.

"Very well, young man." In Mr. Pity's tone was a distinct note of encouragement and approval. "If you have the best voice in Philadelphia, now is the time to prove it. Sing your best. Don't be afraid of hurting any one's feelings."

He smiled wickedly upon the fat man, who suddenly lost his composure and glanced downward rather anxiously at the deadly trap under his feet.

"As you know," continued Pity, "you must sing without notes or accompaniment, as must your opponent. His Supremity is waiting. Penn, the august, will decide through him this free and democratic contest! Sing!"

There was a second's pause. Then the boy, standing above Death and before the Throne of Justice, raised his clear young voice and sang. His was a ballad of the people, unwritten, passed from mouth to mouth. It redounded in rhymes of "love" and "dove," "thee," and "me." It was sentiment—crass, vulgar, common sentiment—but the air had a certain redeeming birdlike lilt.

The tenor rose to its final high note, held it, and died away. No. 57403 bowed, stepped back one pace, and folded his arms. His face was flushed, alight, and his clear eyes looked fearlessly upward to his judge. No cheering followed, but a great sigh rose from the Numbers—a long, simultaneous exhalation, as if each man and woman had been holding breath throughout that last high, sweet note.

"Very good!" exclaimed Mr. Pity, again smiling. "There might be some criticism of your selection, but to give it is not in my province. And now, having heard this high-voiced young candidate, let us listen to his rival, our present esteemed musical director." He bowed to the hairy mountain. "His Supremity is waiting. Penn, the benevolent All-Father, will through him decide this contest. Sing!"

Straightway an aperture appeared in the black beard. White teeth flashed. A burst of sound ascended to the golden dome and rebounded therefrom, assaulting the ears of the multitude beneath. It was a cannonade in bass; the roar of awakened hungry lions; the commingled tumult of a hundred phonographs all playing bass records with rasping needles—a song intensified past endurance by a gigantic sounding board, and also— alas!—hopelessly off key. With an inaudible cry Viola clapped her small hands over her music-loving ears. She saw Sergeant 53 grinning at her, saw his lips move, but he might as well have talked in a Kansas cyclone.

The roar crescendoed to a terrible disharmonic laugh. At last Viola recognized the music he was murdering. Of all selections he had chosen the "Serenade of Mephistopheles," from Counoud's "Faust," a number demanding the most refined, sardonic, and genuinely superlative of voices for an endurable rendering.

Before he ended, Viola was sure she must fall upon the porcelain floor and writhe in anguish. Fortunately her powers of endurance were greater than she believed possible. The final burst of demoniac mirth died an awful death, and Viola's endurance received its reward. Henceforth she could appreciate the bliss of silence.

Looking around, the girl half expected to see the audience flat, like a field of wheat after a wind storm; but though even the policemen wore a somewhat chastened appearance, they still stood. She glanced toward the dais. Mr. Pity, with a pained, faraway expression, was scribbling at his list. Mr. Justice Supreme opened his eyes with a start, like a man unexpectedly relieved from torment. He snarled incoherently and flapped a yellow hand at Mr. Pity. The bull of Basban stood his ground, his eyes blinking, his beard once more a dark, unbroken jungle. As the two Trenmores learned later, his complacence was not without foundation. His wife was a third cousin of Mr. Justice Supreme, and he himself was distantly connected with the family of Mr. Purity, of the dragging leg.

The master of ceremonies lifted up his own thin, piercing voice, like the piping of a reed after the bellow of thunders.

"Sir, His Supremity thanks you for your wonderful rendering of—er—sound." He turned to the throne. "Mr. Justice Supreme, the contestants in all humility submit their respective merits to the high decision of our lord and father, Penn!"

The old dandy dragged himself to his feet. The audience was more than hushed; it wasn't even breathing now. No. 57403 cast a pitying glance at the bearded mountain and fearlessly eyed his judge.

"Children of Penn," began that snarling, senile voice, "in due legal and sacred form two contestants have striven before the father and protector of us all. One is young. He should have further perfected his attainments before presuming to air them in this sacred Hall. Yet his very youth excuses him, and Penn the All-Father is merciful. He can forgive even presumption. For the magnificent bass voice which we have just been privileged to—hm!—enjoy, in a rendering of the work of a great composer, so exalted above the paltry, sentimental balderdash of the other contestant—I—I—words fail me!"

Mr. Justice Supreme glared down at the contestant he was praising with eyes so malevolent that the mountain actually cringed—if a mountain can be said to cringe.

"The decision of Penn," snarled Mr. Justice Supreme, "is that No. 57403 be dropped into the Pit of the Past. Mercy may extend to his immortal soul, but not to his presumptuous body! And the present musical director will continue in office."

Dropping back on his throne with a gasp of exhaustion, he recovered sufficiently to rasp out: "Go! And Penn bless you!" to the victorious contestant.

Then, with the air of one who has got through a tedious but necessary duty, he let his ancient, villainous body relax and his bleared eyes close.

The mountain removed itself with suspicious alacrity. If the look in its porcine eyes went for anything, that musical director valued the "blessing of Penn" less than the permission to vacate an unexpectedly dangerous neighborhood.

But for poor No. 57403 no such retreat was possible. For an instant he seemed unable to believe his ears. He reddened and glanced uneasily about, as if to question others of this injustice, this incredible decision. Then the color faded, he drew himself to his slender height and bowed to the condemning judge with a dignity worthy of some classic young Greek.

Viola clutched at Terry's arm in frantic appeal, but one mightier even than Terence Trenmore was present there—a giant crushed, betrayed, bound down in fetters of ignorance; but a giant none the less. A low growl was the first intimation that he had awakened. It was the voice of the Numbers; a warning protest against this blackest wrong. They surged forward. It was a little motion—half a step—but before it the police were crushed irresistibly back against the plush rope. Alarmed, they faced about with threatening clubs. The eyes of the enthroned figure on the dais snapped open.

"Silence!" he snarled. "Guard, open the pit!"

A crouching, striped form stole forth, leaned over the Dove, and the symbol dropped. But the young man did not drop with it as ordained. He had, quite instinctively and naturally, stepped backward from the danger.

"In with him!"

"No—no—no!" This time it was a roaring negative from hundreds of throats. Heedless now of sacrilege, the Numbers again surged. The plush rope stretched and broke. In an instant clubs were rising and falling desperately. The police might as well have attempted to dam Niagara with a toothpick. A few Numbers in the front ranks went down, it is true, but over their bodies came their fellows, pushed irresistibly by the mass behind.

The former enclosure disappeared. A series of piercing shrieks cut the uproar like knife stabs. They came from below, and Viola, shuddering in her brother's arm, knew that some unfortunate had been pushed into the Pit of the Past.

Mr. Pity, finding himself confronted by a myriad of upturned, glaring eyes, retreated precipitately. But the dais was not stormed—not yet. Too many years of ground-in teaching, too thorough a dread of the awful power of Penn Service held them back.

"Go to it—go to it, boys!" yelled Trenmore, holding Viola in one arm and shaking his other fist excitedly. "Down with the murdering hounds! Scrape the platform like a dirty dish!"

His great voice merged indistinguishably with the swelling roar beneath the echoing dome. The police were down, or helplessly packed in. One more surge and the wave would have broken over the platform, performing the very feat suggested by Trenmore. But in that fatal instant of superstitious hesitance the blare of a bugle rang high above the din. It was followed by a rattling, crashing sound, mingled with shrieks, screams, and horrible, echoing sounds of pain and fear unutterable.

Turning its eyes from the dais, the mob knew that its moment of power was past. Each one of those colored panels in the walls, enameled with the figures of strange gods or demons, had slid to one side. Each had hidden the muzzle of a machine gun. Three of them were already in action, spitting curses that killed. There were women and even babies there, but what cared Penn Service for that? They were merely Numbers. And Numbers in revolt must be crushed—massacred if need be.

The growl of the giant was transmuted into frantic prayer. Those close to the dais flung themselves on their knees and stretched supplicating hands toward the throne they had all but overturned.

A moment Mr. Justice Supreme waited, while the guns still spat and swore. Then both his hands went up, palms outward. The crashing rattle ceased. Only the prayers and shrieks continued, increased, and echoed from the Dome of Justice to the wail of a great city, sacked and full of bloody wrongs.

Again the old man raised his yellow, skinny hands, this time with a silencing, pacifying gesture, and silence followed, spreading from before the dais as the first growl had spread. Even the wounded, so great is the power of life-long submission, ceased presently to shriek. Only the occasional wail of some infant, too young to recognize the supremacy of ruthless force, broke the ghastly quiet.

"My children," began the High Priest of Evil, "you have sinned grievously." The excitement had invigorated and ennobled his voice, so that it was no longer a snarl, but a dreadful threat. "You have been punished a little," he cried. "Beware lest the great and tender patience of Penn be strained to breaking and you be punished past any power to remedy!"

He pointed solemnly upward at the Red Bell. A shivering groan swept the hall.

"You have broken the sacred silence. Beware that it be not broken by a voice more awful! Beware that it be not broken by a tongue at whose speaking you and your sons and your daughters, your women and your men, shall fall into the ignoble dust from which you sprang! Ungrateful Children of Penn, gather up your wounded and your dead. Depart from this temple which you have desecrated. Go home, and on your knees thank the old and faithful servant who intercedes for you—even you, the graceless children of a kind and merciful father! But first yield up the body of that young man whose vanity and presumption have caused your sorrow and his. Yield him, I say! Where is he?"

Mr. Justice Supreme actually tottered forward to the platform edge. Like a bloodthirsty old ferret, questing some particular tender rabbit, he scanned the faces nearest him. The crowd gave back. Here and there the head and blue shoulders of a policeman bobbed into view. But No. 57403 was not produced.

"Give him up!" yelled the old man. Dignity forgotten, he brandished his ebony cane like a sword. "Yield him up, you—whoever is concealing him! Or the guns shall talk to you!"

He was answered by a low mutter, then silence. The Numbers stood with set, dogged faces, staring back at their oppressor.

Trenmore gave Viola a sudden squeeze. "Powers o' darkness!" he whispered exultantly. "The pups have the makings of men in them, after all! They'll not give him up, their sweet-voiced lad. They'll die by the guns, men, women, and babes, but—"

"Surrender him!" The high priest's voice crackled ominously. "I'll give you while I count three. One—two—three! Oh, very well there!"

His right hand started slowly up, palm out. A second more and the guns would resume their devilish chatter. There came a swirl in the crowd, a struggle, and out into the little open area by the pit sprang the singer, disheveled but triumphant.

"Don't shoot!" he cried. "Don't shoot! Friends, I thank you for everything—what you wished for me, what you have given, and what you would give if I would let you! But you," he turned upon Justice Supreme with the look and face of a deathless young god, unfearing and scornful, "you I do not even hate! You poor wreck of what was one time a man, you are already dead and damned in the rottenness of your vile body and viler spirit! If you are the servant of Penn, then I am his enemy. I go to tell him so!"

And before any man could stir a hand the boy had dived, head foremost, into the pit.

A moaning sigh rose, echoed, and fell. Those nearest the pit turned aside and covered their ears with their hands; but the shriek they dreaded never came. Presently one of the pit guard, lurking out of sight behind the dais, sneaked cautiously around, crept to the pit, and looked down. Then he raised his eyes to the purple, raging face of Mr. Justice Supreme. The high priest made a gesture with his cane. A moment later and the eagle and dove symbol swung into place again.

16 DISASTER

In barely thirty minutes the hall was emptied, cleansed of blood and debris, and the ceremony of the "examinations" resumed.

Mr. Justice Supreme had waited, dozing, on his throne. The lesser servants perforce waited also, albeit impatiently and with much glancing at watches and sotto voce complaint about the delay.

Sad, silent, and defeated, the Numbers had retired, bearing with them their injured and their dead. When the hall was at last cleared the lovely, milk-white pavement resembled more nearly the pit of a slaughter house than the floor of a temple. It was smeared and slimy with trampled blood, fragments of clothing, and other fragments less pleasant to contemplate. The temple force of "white wings," however, made short work of it. They dragged out a few lengths of hose, turned on a powerful water pressure and in less than five minutes the blood and debris were washed down three drains to which the pavement imperceptibly sloped. The wet floor gleamed whiter than ever, and the Red Bell and wonderful walls were reflected with redoubled glory. A corps of scrubwomen went to work on hands and knees to dry and polish the cleansed floor, while Mr. Pity, with a final glance at his watch, again rose and advanced to the platform edge.

"The next superlative quality on my list," droned the master of ceremonies, disregarding the fact that he addressed only the bent backs of five inattentive scrubwomen, "is that of Quickest. This office entails management and control, under Penn Service, of the Department of Police, involving responsibility for the keeping of peace in Philadelphia and outlying suburbs."

A slim, alert-looking man of about forty-five advanced to the pit.

"Is there any other candidate for this office? Any other candidate?"

Came the click of hurrying heels, and round the dais appeared a small, rotund figure, surmounted by a cherubic but troubled countenance. Trenmore growled disappointedly. He had hoped for Drayton, not Bertram. What misadventure was keeping his friend away?

Bertram came up just as the master of ceremonies commenced his stereotyped conclusion: "No other candidate for this office. Present holder may—"

"Wait a minute there!" cried Trenmore, and thrust Bertram forward. "Go on—go on in, you fat rascal!" he added in a forceful whisper. "Here's the contest for Quickest now. You've not quite missed it. Go on!"

Though Bertram struggled vainly to face about, the Irishman still pushed him forward. He was not wasting such an opportunity to delay the proceedings in his absent friend's interest.

"I—I've changed my mind!" the burglar protested.

"Are we to understand," cut in Mr. Pity, "that this person does or does not wish to compete? Just a minute, chief. I don't know whether or not you have a rival."

"Certainly not!" spluttered Bertram.

"Certainly he does!" Trenmore's affirmative drowned out the burglar's plaintive negative. "If you don't," he added in his victim's ear, "I'll wring the round head off you!"

Mr. Arnold Bertram succumbed. Between two dangers, he chose the pit.

"Very well, y'r honor," he stammered. "I—I guess I'll have a go at it."

"Come forward then," snapped the master of ceremonies impatiently. "What is your number, place of residence, occupation, and age? Answer in order and speak clearly, please."

"My—Say, I ain't got no number."

"What?" Pity glanced frowningly at Bertram's lapel, and saw the green button with which Loveliest had supplied him. "With whose family are you connected?"

Just then Cleverest, who had been sitting quietly among the servants, rose and strolled to the front. He looked Bertram over; then turned to the throne.

"Your Supremity, this is one of those four strangers of whom you are already informed. Is it permitted that the usual questions be omitted?"

Both Mr. Pity and the Superlative seemed to interpret the inarticulate snarl which replied as assent. The latter gentleman, after giving Viola an encouraging smirk, sauntered back to his seat.

"Very well," said Pity. "But I must call you something you know. Haven't you any title?"

"Me name's Bertram," conceded the burglar.

"Well—er—Bertram, you now have an opportunity to prove yourself the quickest man in the city. Bring around that machine there."

At the word a thing like a penny-in-the-slot scales was trundled over the porcelain by two pit guards. They brought it to a halt just before Mr. Pity. Following it came Mr. Virtue, who drew the chief of police aside, whispered earnestly to him, and stepped back. Suspiciously Bertram eyed the contrivance, with its platform and large dial.

"Now, Bertram, place yourself on that platform and grasp the lever at the right. That's it. Now. Raise your left hand and snap finger and thumb nine times!"

With a dazed look the burglar obeyed. The needle on the dial jerked, swept around once, quivered, and stopped. By the servant's instructions, Bertram performed a number of similar feats, all equally trivial. Each time the needle made its mysterious record. At last Mr. Pity seemed satisfied.

"Very good. Mr. Virtue, would you mind making a note of that percentage? You may step off, Bertram."

Still dazed, Bertram again obeyed.

"You next, chief. Thank you."

The mysterious rites of the grasped lever and foolish-looking calisthenics were repeated.

"What is the comparison, Mr. Virtue?"

The servant figured for a moment on the back of an envelope.

"Ninety-eight for friend Bertram; ninety-five for the chief. Congratulations to you, my man! Sorry, chief. I fear you're getting old!"

The alert man who had been so unceremoniously superseded stepped off the little platform. He did not look particularly concerned, thought Trenmore—not at all like a man condemned to lose both means of living and life.

"It's all in the game, Mr. Virtue," he observed cheerfully. "Tell the boys to send lilies of the valley. When's the funeral?"

"Some other time, chief," retorted Virtue with equal jocosity. "The pit is not working right to-day."

"The cheerful liar!" muttered Trenmore. "Now tell me, Viola, what's the meaning of yonder small comedy?"

The girl, white-lipped and sick at heart, laughed mirthlessly. "What does it matter? At least, neither Bertram nor the other is to be murdered. Terry, if Mr. Drayton does not return soon, what shall we do when our time comes?"

"He will return—he must—but now what's wrong with the little round man?"

It was evident that Bertram was in a difficulty of some sort. The displaced chief of police had him firmly by the collar. Mr. Virtue was glaring at him with an expression of incredulous wrath, while Cleverest strode toward them, anxiety in every line of his sharp features.

Terence and Viola were at that time unable to understand the disgrace of Bertram and his immediately subsequent condemnation. It appeared only that during their three minutes' conversation with one another the burglar had committed some act so unpardonable that even the intercession of Cleverest did not avail him. Apparently the act had been witnessed by every one present save the two remaining candidates. The accusation was not even formulated in words.

"In three hours' time let him be cast into the pit," came the inexorable judgment from the throne. "Let him have that three hours to consider and repent of his sacrilege. Penn is just and all-merciful. Take the prisoner away! Let the former chief resume his official duties."

The chief celebrated his rehabilitation by dragging his presumptuous successor off the scene, the latter still sputtering and expostulating, his captor wearing an expression of serene amusement.

"What next?" questioned Viola hopelessly.

The next arrived with great promptness. Mr. Pity had no more than glanced at his list, after the prisoner's removal, when there came the tramp of feet and the sound of an excited voice.

"Bring him along, men," it commanded. "Drag the sacrilegious beast before the throne! Let his Supremity judge the dog!"

Then appeared the triumphant Mr. Mercy, waving on a cohort of four policemen. In their midst was another and much disheveled prisoner.

"'Tis Bobby!" groaned the Irishman.

Loveliest appeared, crossed behind the guarded prisoner, and defiantly took her stand beside Trenmore. Evidently the downfall of two of her four proteges had alarmed the woman. As much occasion for formality had vanished with the Numbers' exit, she had chanced the anger of the throne and come to her "big man's" assistance. Once more Mr. Justice Supreme was roused from somnolence.

"Well, well," he demanded crossly of Mercy. "What's all this about? Are we never to have a moment's peace to finish these examinations? Who is that fellow you have there?"

Mr. Mercy bowed gracefully, silk hat for once removed and pressed to his triumphant bosom. He cast one glance of joyous malice at Loveliest, and addressed the throne:

"Your Supremity, I have a well-nigh unbelievable charge to lay against this prisoner. Because of the magnitude, the incredible audacity of his crime, and because one—I might say two—of our own number have actually stood his sponsor—because of these things, I say, I have presumed to interrupt the proceedings of this Board of Examiners in the full faith that—"

"Get to the point—get to the point, man," cut in the high priest petulantly. "What has he done?"

Again Mercy bowed. "Your Supremity, to waste no words, this mad and audacious stranger, this insolent abuser of Your Supremity's hospitality, who now faces the very throne with such brazen effrontery—"

"Well—well? Mr. Mercy, if you can't tell it, step aside, please, and allow me to question the prisoner himself!"

"He has invaded the holy Library of Penn," retorted Mercy, "and perused the sacred books!"

There was a general movement of interest among the bored servants. Several of the women auditors rose from their chairs and walked forward to obtain a better view of the prisoner. Even His Supremity was aroused. His face purpled with a rage greater than that awakened by the presumptuous Numbers, his mouth worked horribly, and it was some moments before he could sufficiently control his voice to speak. "How do you know this?" he at last enunciated hoarsely.

"Because I caught him at it," replied Mercy unguardedly.

"You? You found him? What were you doing in the library?"

Mr. Mercy started and gasped at the trap in which he had caught himself. "Why—I—I was passing by and the door was open. I looked in and—and—"

"Your Supremity, have I permission to speak?"

The interrupter was one of the police officers holding Drayton. Mercy turned upon him with furious face, but Justice Supreme waved him to silence. "You may speak, Forty-five. Mr. Mercy, I am conducting this inquiry. Kindly refrain from intimidating the witness."

"Your Supremity, two hours ago or thereabouts, Mr. Mercy come to me and says 'Forty-five, is the door of the library locked to-day?' I says, no, I thought not, as Your Supremity had been in there reading. On days when you cared to read, you very seldom kept it locked. No one would ever dare go in there, anyway. Then he says—"

"Wait a minute!" came a voice of repressed fury from the throne. "Mr. Pity, will you take this down, please?"

Pity drew forth his fountain pen and a small blank book. He began to scribble furiously.

"'Your Supremity,' he says then, 'is the door actually open?' I didn't believe so, but I walked over into Corridor 27 just to have a look. Of course the door was shut. Mr. Mercy, he followed right along behind. 'If I were you,' he says, 'I'd open that door and turn on the fan at the end of the corridor. His Supremity was complaining to me it was that stifling in the library it pretty near made him sick.' Well, I thought it was a queer thing Your Supremity hadn't spoke to me if you wished the room ventilated. But

Mr. Mercy, being one of the Inner Order, and of such high authority—"

"I understand," snapped the high priest. "Get on. You opened it?"

"I did, Your Supremity, with Mr. Mercy looking on. Then I went to turn on the fan, and Mr. Mercy strolled off. Without meaning to spy on him, I followed. My rubber soles don't make much noise, of course, and I guess he didn't hear me. He went around a corner. Just before I reached it myself I heard him speaking. Thinking he would blame me if he thought I was spying on him, I stopped where I was. He was talking to this prisoner here, as I found out later. First he says, 'Were you looking for some one, Mr. Drayton?' The prisoner, he says no; he was merely strolling around and got lost and can't find his way back to the Green Room. 'I'll take you there myself,' says Mr. Mercy. 'But have you seen the library?'"

At this a sort of gasp came from Mercy. He staggered slightly where he stood. He dared not interrupt, however, and the policeman continued.

"This Mr. Drayton says, no, he ain't saw it, but he'd be real glad to—in fact, there wasn't anything much he'd rather see. So Mr. Mercy says, 'You go on around that corner straight along the corridor and you'll come to it. The door is open and you can go right in.' This Mr. Drayton says he's understood strangers was not allowed in there. Mr. Mercy says, 'Oh, you're as good as a Superlative already. This library is open to officials.'

"The gentleman thanked him and come on around the corner and past me, but Mr. Mercy he goes the other way."

Mr. Justice Supreme interrupted, "Why did you not stop this man? Do you mean you allowed him to enter without any protest?"

"I did, Your Supremity. Mr. Mercy is my superior, sir, and while I intended reporting to Your Supremity—as I am doing now—it wasn't for me to interfere with his commands or permissions. The stranger, he went in the library. I stuck around, thinking I'd keep my eye on him, at least, to see that he didn't remove none of the books. That would be going it a little too strong. But he stayed and stayed. Once or twice I strolled by, and there he was, reading for all he was worth.

"Then, a while ago, Mr. Mercy comes hurrying along again. He stops short, like he was surprised. 'Haven't you got that door shut yet?' he snaps at me. Before I could answer he runs to the door, looks in, and shouts, 'What's that fellow doing in there? Forty-five, go in there and get that man! Did you know he was there?' Before I had a chance to say anything he blows his whistle. Twenty-seven and Seventy-nine comes on the run. Sixty-three got there later. We go in and grab this Mr. Drayton. He seems surprised like, and starts to say something about Mr. Mercy telling him to go right in and read. Mr. Mercy tells him to shut up, if he don't want rough handling, and he shuts up. Then Mr. Mercy orders us to bring the man here. That's all I have to say, Your Supremity. If I have taken a liberty in reporting just at this time—"

"Don't be a fool," snarled His Supremity. "You are about the only honest man on the force and the one man I have never caught in a lie. Mr. Mercy, have you any defense?"

"Simply that this is a fabrication on the part of No. 45," drawled Mercy. Having passed through the various stages of rage, surprise, and fear, he had emerged in a mood of dangerous calm. "I had occasion to discipline the fellow recently. This, I presume, is his revenge."

Mr. Justice Supreme glared at him. His next words showed that while the servants as a body might be "Masters of the City," Mr. Justice Supreme was in turn their very arbitrary tyrant. Whether he held this power because of his own malignant personality, or because of hereditary authority, it was power absolute. No. 45 had made no mistake when he braved the certain wrath of Mr. Mercy and thereby gained the favor of His Supremity.

"Mr. Mercy," said the latter with snarling bluntness, "you are a liar and No. 45 is not! Again and again you have recently overstepped the mark, thinking, perhaps, that I have no eyes and no ears but my own, and that they are growing defective with old age. We will go into your case fully at a more appropriate time and try to correct that impression. You will find that the exposing of state secrets to help along some petty intrigue of your own is not the light offense you appear to believe it.

"Let this prisoner be held as a witness—no, I do not care to have him held. One who has desecrated the realm of sacred knowledge cannot die too quickly. Cast him into the pit!"

A trifle pale, but entirely self-possessed, Drayton had stood silent. Even now, hearing that by-this-time monotonous decree, he made no attempt to defend himself. Indeed he found composure for a certain whimsical reflection.

Twice before he had been condemned to the pit—once, two days ago, by Judge Virtue, in this very temple; once, in a distant place and age, before a tribunal whose proceedings, though less promptly fatal, were strangely similar in spirit. And of the two, Penn Service was the kindlier. Its condemned neither endured imprisonment nor had time to suffer the bitterness of unjust disgrace.

Breaking from her brother's sustaining arm, Viola Trenmore pushed her way between the police and caught Drayton's cold hand in hers.

"Mr. Justice Supreme," she called, "may I make an appeal?"

Drayton turned with a gesture of protest. "Viola," he said earnestly, "go back to your brother. You can do nothing for me."

"And do you think we would let you die alone?" she whispered fiercely.

Mr. Justice Supreme gazed down upon her, and as he looked his loose old mouth spread in a ghastly smile. A gleam brightened his lecherous old eyes.

"Are you the young lady who is destined to assume the title of Loveliest? My nephew has spoken to me of you. He spoke very highly—very highly indeed. My own eyes confirm his claims for your fitness. Your examination is next on the list, I believe, and I assure you that you need fear nothing from your rival. You will make many friends, my child, and you must count me as one of the first."

At the words, Lady Green-eyes, standing by Trenmore, gasped and turned very white beneath her rouge. Even before the high priest had finished, however, her green eyes were flashing. A surge of real color backed the artificial on her thin cheeks. With catlike quickness she had comprehended the situation. As though he had grown suddenly loathsome, she drew away from Trenmore.

"So!" she spat out. "You were planning to betray me, were you? After all I have done for you, you meant to put that sly puss of a sister of yours in my place! You were planning to have me thrown in that very pit I saved you from such a little while ago! And I thought you were honest. Because you were so big and strong I took you for a real man! Bah! You are no better than the rest of these swine—you are no better than Mercy or Clever or any of the others!"

Her voice had steadily risen until every eye in the hall was focused upon them.

Trenmore could say nothing. His face was suffused by a deep, burning flood of painful color. At this moment what had looked right and just enough when Cleverest proposed it appeared in a different light. No matter if the woman had planned a disagreeable future for Viola, she had also unquestionably saved the girl from a choice between death and dishonor; saved himself and Drayton from immediate destruction.

What miasma of treachery existed in this ancient city that he, who prided himself on his loyalty, had become so horribly infected?

Up went his head in that old gesture of defiant decision. He strode to his sister's side, sweeping two policemen out of his way, and flung an arm about Viola and his friend together.

"Your honor," he thundered, "that lady yonder is right! We have been in danger of making ourselves no better than the Servants of Penn, Heaven judge them for their sins and their murderings! No better than your honor's self, and I take shame to admit it! But that is over. We three want no favors. We want nothing at all from any of you, save to go our way clean and straight. If you choose to murder us, then we will go by way of that pit you're so infatuated with. Terence Trenmore has been mad these two days past, but he's sane again now, thank Heaven, and can speak for himself and his own!"

Viola drew a long breath, and stood up proudly between the two men. She had meant making a desperate plea for Drayton's life, and if that failed she had meant to die with him. But this was far better—that they three go together, not forced, but proudly and avoiding shame. From her eyes also the scales had been swept away. She knew now that this ending had been inevitable—that she could never have stood by and seen another woman, however hateful, murdered that she might go safe.

The semi-amiable expression on the High Priest's face twisted back to its habitual snarl. Cleverest stood glowering like a thundercloud.

"Nephew," said Mr. Justice Supreme, "your clemency and kindness have been thrown away. Do you still wish to raise this girl to your side?"

"Yes!" came the prompt reply. The trap mouth clicked shut on the bare affirmative.

"You do?"

"I do, Your Supremity. As a personal favor, I ask that Miss Trenmore be urged to speak for herself and that her brother be not yet condemned. That woman whom we have tolerated too long as one of us has insulted him so grossly that I cannot wonder at his taking umbrage. I ask that she"—he leveled a thin forefinger at the indignant Loveliest—"be removed beyond further power to poison with her venom, and that this girl and her brother be given time to consider before they hurl themselves to destruction. I even ask that you grant this other stranger—this Drayton—reprieve that he may bid his friends farewell. It cannot be that he would wish so young and lovely a girl to share his fate. If he is a man he will urge his friends to accept the life, wealth, and high honors which Penn Service can bestow. Your Supremity, may I hope that my prayer is granted?"

The high priest bowed his head. It was clear that Cleverest had a tremendous influence with his uncle and a hold on Penn Service far stronger than was indicated by his official position.

"You ask a great deal, my boy, but you always did that. After all, there can be no harm in granting your wish. The girl is too pretty to be the bride of the old war god. If, however"—and his voice rose to the shrill impatience of the aged—"if after due respite they still refuse your kindness, then I decline to be troubled any further. If they refuse they shall all die, and that green-eyed she-cat with them. I'm tired of seeing the painted fool about."

"Take these three people away. Lock them all up together and let them make up their minds once for all.

At ten to-morrow morning they may either die or accept. No great matter which. Hold that other man—Bertram—for the same hour. Take them away! And now, Mr. Pity, there are no further candidates. You may omit the rest of the proceedings. I want my luncheon. I'm an old man, Clever, and all this excitement is bad for my heart. If you ever had any consideration for anyone but yourself—"

His snarling whine was shut from their ears as the three prisoners passed into the Green Room, and the red door closed behind the last of their guards.

17 THEIR LAST CHANCE

When Justice Supreme commanded that the former candidates for Superlativism be "all locked up together," the police evidently construed the command as including Bertram. It was into the bare, steel-walled room where that rotund gentleman awaited his fate that Trenmore, his sister, and Robert Drayton were presently escorted. They were little surprised at this. What did amaze them was to find their fellow victim not alone. Seated on the floor with his back to the wall, he was engaged in earnest conversation with a small female person, enthroned upon the only chair in the room. Moreover, the latter was wagging an admonitory finger at Bertram as if delivering a "curtain lecture" of the most approved domestic type.

The chair comprised the entire furnishing of the cell. There was not even the moldy straw, without which no medieval dungeon was complete. It might be merely a detention cell; or perhaps prisoners of the Temple passed to their doom too swiftly to require sleeping accommodations.

In costume Bertram's companion emulated the rainbow for color. Her large hat was bright green, lined with pink. She wore an old rose silk sweater over a soiled lace blouse, and crumpled blue linen skirt; her hosiery was golden yellow, and her down-at-heel pumps had once been very elegant green buckskins. As the door clanged shut behind the newcomers, she turned upon them large inquiring eyes, whose size was accentuated by the thinness of her face. Her complexion, however, was as fine as Viola's own. The yellow button displayed upon her old-rose lapel bore the number 23000.

Bertram's first expression of surprise changed to one of genuine concern.

"Say, boss," he questioned Trenmore. "What's up? Did they frame you, too? Or have you come to kiss your old college chump good-by?"

"We'll be saying good-by this day the way we'll be troubled with no more farewells at all," retorted Trenmore grimly.

"Are you really in bad, all of you?"

"We are that. And who's the lady, Bertram?"

"A pal of mine," replied the burglar. Taking the small person's hand, he forthwith presented her. "Skidoo, these here are the three friends of mine I was telling you about. Miss Trenmore and Mr. Trenmore and Mr. Drayton. Gents and lady, let me make you acquainted with the brightest, best-hearted, prettiest kid in this bughouse burg. Her Number is 23000, but that ain't no handle for a lady. I call her Miss Skidoo."

His round face shone with such whole-hearted pride in the human rainbow; he was so clearly assured of her cordial reception by any one possessing brains and eyes that Viola, who had at first hung back a trifle, extended her hand.

"We are very glad to meet you, Miss Skidoo," she said gravely, "but sorry it has to be in such a place."

Terry's eyes were twinkling. He followed his sister's lead, however, as did Drayton. "Any friend of Mr. Bertram's," Terry contributed, "is bound to be most interesting. 'Tis charmed we all are, Miss Skidoo!"

"Same here," responded No. 23000, eying them with a sort of childlike solemnity. "Bert's been talking about you folks ever since I met him. But, gee! The lookout's bad for this bunch, ain't it?"

"I fear it is about as bad as possible," sighed Viola. "At least for four of us here."

"Count me in," announced the girl. "They drug me in, just for comin' to the Temple with Bert. I ain't done nothin'."

"I couldn't help it," Bertram defended himself. "I wasn't going to fall for the game, but Mr. Trenmore here, he says I must. Say, won't you tell the kid that I didn't want to go in the game? She won't believe anything I say."

The Irishman, somewhat conscience-stricken, hastened to assure No. 23000 that the blame for Bertram's downfall lay entirely on his shoulders. "He appeared to have no desire at all for it, but I did not and do not yet understand what happened."

"Aw, I didn't do anything to get sent up for," said the burglar disgustedly. "I did cop a medal thing one of them guys was wearing on his watch chain, but I was going to give it right back to him. That weighing machine of theirs was a crazy way to test speed. I wanted to show 'em what quick really meant. So I copped this medal thing off the one they call Mr. Virtue. Then I flashed it, and was going to explain. They didn't give me no chance. They just jumped on me and said I'd been and done sacri—sacri-something or other, and that was all."

"They was just waitin' for a chance to land you," commented Miss Skidoo wisely. "They didn't mean you should have that job really. Sooner or later they'd have framed you. Say, folks, let's set on the floor and fight this thing out right."

Acquiescing willingly enough, Terence and Viola between them related the various events occurring between Drayton's departure from the Green Room and his return in the custody of Mercy. The story of cold-blooded cruelty, the hints of internecine warfare among the Servants and Superlatives—united only against their common enemy, the Numbers—was interesting and startling enough to call forth many exclamations from Drayton and Bertram. Miss Skidoo, however, listened with the bored look of one who hears an oft-told and wearisome tale.

"Say," she commented at the end, "a ordinary person like you or us"—indicating herself and Bertram—"got no business mixing in with that gang of highbinders. They're always layin' for each other an' scrapping among themselves; but say, a snowball's got a better chance in a bucket of hot water than a straight guy or a plain Number around this joint. As I've been telling Bert here—"

"Pardon me," interrupted Drayton curiously, "but where did you happen to meet Mr. Bertram?"

She flushed so red that Drayton wished he had not asked the question. Catching the look in the lawyer's eye, Bertram bristled instantly.

"Say," he blurted, "I want you to know that Miss Skidoo here is a straight, nice kid. I was in a movie last night, and she was there with her dad. I got talking to the old man. He says, come along and get some home cooking; them hotels ain't no good. I stayed so late—talkin' and playin' seven-up—that they let me bunk out in the spare room. That's all. Straight, decent folks, just like there used to be, even if they are tagged with numbers instead of proper monikers. Get me?"

They got him. Drayton apologized silently with his eyes for the equally unvoiced suspicion.

It seemed that Bertram had bragged to these chance acquaintances of his pull with the Superlative, Cleverest. Miss Skidoo had warned him earnestly against any attempt to supersede the chief of police, no matter what his pull might be. The present Quickest, it seemed, like the musical director and most of the other Superlatives, was a distant connection of "Penn Service." She revealed to him many facts regarding that "democratic institution," Superlativism—how every man of the Superlatives, save Cleverest, held his job by pure favor, aided by the pull he could exercise through family connections.

"Cleverest, he's a Servant by birth," the girl explained. "He only took on that Superlative job because the next Justice Supreme can't be chose from the Servants in office. He's the old man's nephew. When the old man dies Cleverest will chuck the law and run this city. He was aimin' to marry Loveliest because he wants to be high man anywhere he is, and the Loveliest's husband, when she has one, is supposed to run this town, outside of the Service.

But I guess he meant to chuck her as soon as the old man passes over.

"Them Servants, they keep the Service itself right in their own families, father to son like. Only Mr. J. S. as is, he ain't got no son. Say, me sister's a scrublady an' she's got a swell job scrubbin' floors right here in the temple. Course, she don't get paid nothing, but she's fed good, and as for clothes, the ladies round here gives her a lot. That's how I get these glad rags I'm wearin'—from sis. But I tell you a job like hers is great for gettin' wiser. Folks don't take much more notice of a scrublady than if she was a chair or sump'n. She's told me a lot o' things.

"Servants of Penn! Say, I reckon if that big image o' Penn could get a peep at what goes on under his feet he'd jump right down on top of the dome and smash the bell and everything else!"

The flow of her eloquence was interrupted by Drayton, who had been listening with even greater interest than the others. "Tell me, Miss Skidoo, have you or any of your friends an idea of who William Penn really is, or rather was?"

"I don't know nothin' about that Will-thing. Penn is the All-Father. He runs heaven and hell just like the Servants run us. I don't believe in him no more. I think there ain't nothing but Philadelphia, and when you die you stay dead?"

"Well, religion aside," said Drayton, "I myself have learned a great deal since this morning. The Penn Service library was really most informing. If its doors could be thrown open to the Numbers, I believe they are men enough yet to overthrow this government of false priests and their sycophants and come into their own. It would be worth living, just to see it done." He sighed. "However, that is not to be. We can help the sorrow of this age no more than we could cure the grief of our own."

"Get on with it, Bobby," said Trenmore. "Sure, I've a load of curiosity I'd hate to die burdened with!"

"I'll tell it as briefly as I can. There are big gaps in the story as I collated it, but the general run is clear enough. I became so absorbed that I forgot the time and the competitions and everything else. Remember, this is their history.

"It seems that after the close of the World Wars there followed a few years of respite. Then Communism had its way of Europe. Class war, which spells social chaos, ensued.

"The U.S.A. very sensibly and hastily declined to be further involved, but unfortunately did not stop there. The country had been largely militarized; but this new European outbreak swung the pacifists back into the saddle. You know the delirious possibilities which may spring from the brain of a full-fledged pacifist. The president then in office was a weakling, a dreamer, and completely under the influence of a man named Andrew Power. I'll tell you more of that later. Congress—I don't know what they were thinking of, but they backed this sawdust president, or rather the man behind his chair. According to the records, it appeared to all these wise rulers that the only safety lay in complete severance of relations with mad-dog Europe. So they severed them. They deliberately stopped all traffic and communication between the United States and Europe. Later, in logical sequence, they dropped communication with our nearest neighbors, Canada, Mexico, Central and South America."

"Why, Mr. Drayton!" exclaimed Viola incredulously. "How could they?"

"They did. I am telling you what I read in books and old newspapers of those times. Now this man I spoke of, this Andrew Power, who stood behind the presidential chair, seems to have been a sort of sublimified madman. His personality was of the Napoleonic order raised to the nth power. He was a madman, but he was a reasoning madman. Taking the theories and work of the pacifists, he carried them to a logical conclusion.

"The trouble with the world, he said, was that its communities, its nations, had grown too bulky and unwieldy. He pointed to the case of Switzerland, a small, therefore manageable, republic, with its efficient, well-equipped army, its contented people and high rate of wealth per capita. The United States was a republic, but it could never be like that. It was too big. All the really big countries, he said, were ill-balanced, ill-governed, and with a high percentage of poor and unemployed. The ideal nation would consist of not over three or four million souls, with a democratic government. It should be completely isolated from the world in a space compelling it to keep the population within that limit of three or four million. Each State in the Union, he argued, was a potential ideal republic, given the isolation which was apparently—but only apparently—impossible."

"But," cried Viola, her eyes wide and incredulous, "that was a hundred times worse than the secession of the South from the North!"

"I have told you," replied Drayton wearily, "that this man was mad. The whole world, I think, was mad. In this country, too, Communism had been lifting its disorganizing clamor. The madman carried the mad people with him. State by State, it seemed, they might handle what was daily becoming more ungovernable. If some States were rotten, let them rot alone; not infect the others. It was necessary to redistribute the population, but that does not appear to have troubled their maniacal energy. There were riots and battles. What sane people remained objected strenuously to the whole scheme. But Power—this Andrew Power, who stood behind the president—had the majority with him. I think that many clever, wealthy men foresaw opportunities for absolute despotism under open colors. At any rate, the scheme was carried out, each State accepting a population within its powers to feed."

"But that meant the end of civilization, the end of exchange!"

"Oh, they arranged for exchange of products in a limited degree, but all other intercommunication, all exchange of ideas or moving about of people from one State to another, was cut off under heavy penalty."

"Their coast line, man—their coast line?" broke in Trenmore. "What was Europe doing then?"

"I don't know. The history of the world ends in that library with the isolation of Pennsylvania. For all I know, the nations of Europe may have emulated the Kilkenny cats and devoured one another, or perhaps they are still fighting. Anyway, what these people call 'Philadelphia and its environing suburbs' really includes the whole of Pennsylvania.

"They began here under a sort of commission government, but the 'contractor gang'—Philadelphia was always you know, peculiarly—"

He never told them, however, what it was that Philadelphia was peculiar in. There came a sound at the door. The heavy bolts slid back, and a man entered, partly closing the door behind him. The man was Cleverest. For an instant he stood, arms folded, glaring majestically upon them.

The captives rose and faced him with more or less composure. Had the high priest's nephew come to announce an advance of execution or to offer them further terms?

"You've stared long enough," said Trenmore brusquely. "What is it you want with us?"

"A little fair and decent treatment perhaps," snapped Cleverest. "Do you realize what a very unpleasant position you have placed me in? Every man in the Temple is laughing at me behind his hand for standing by a gang of beggars and getting insulted for my pains!"

Viola interposed quietly. "You are mistaken, sir. None of us has ever said a word to or about you that could be construed as an insult."

"Your brother meant to include me in his tirade addressed to my uncle," the man retorted gloomily.

Terry eyed him in obstinate dislike. "You led me to forget my honor, sir, and conspire against a woman. I'm not blaming you so much as myself; but 'twas a dirty deal, and well you know it!"

"You were ready enough at the time," sneered Cleverest with more truth than was pleasant. "However, matters are not yet too late to mend. Your death won't help Loveliest now. My uncle has settled that once for all. You've blundered and blundered until the best I can do is to save you and your sister. Miss Trenmore"—he eyed the girl with a coldly calculating eye—"I love you. I am offering you more than any other man in this city could offer. I desire a beautiful and accomplished wife, and you are better qualified than any one I have met. If you marry me you will be not merely Loveliest, which is in one sense an empty title, but the future Mrs. Justice Supreme!"

"Unless," replied Viola very coolly and not at all impressed, "you should see fit to depose me before your uncle's death. You could do that, couldn't you?"

His face expressed surprise, mingled with a kind of vulpine admiration. "You knew all the time," he exclaimed with a laugh, "and hid it from me! No danger, my dear. You play fair with me and I'll stick to you. I've never seen a woman yet that could touch you for looks, brains, or manner. As an added inducement, remember that I offer your brother's life!"

Viola looked from Drayton to Terry and back again at Drayton.

"Terry!" she whispered at last. "I—I can't. Oh, forgive me, Terry! Yes, I'll do it for you. But he must save Mr. Drayton, too!"

"You'll do no such thing!" stormed the Irishman. "I'd rather see you dead, Viola, than wedded to that fox!"

"Don't consider me, Miss Viola," put in Drayton. "Save yourself if you wish and can. But not—for Heaven's sake, not in that way—not for *my* sake!"

The girl and the lawyer were looking into each other's eyes. The faint rose of Viola's cheeks brightened to a livelier hue. Cleverest saw, and jumped at the conclusion most natural to a born Servant of Penn.

"Oh, is that it?" he demanded angrily. "Is this man your reason for declining my offers? Perhaps I have been a bit hasty, after all. The wife of Justice Supreme can have had no former lovers, dead or living!"

Viola uttered a little, horrified cry. The pink flush became a burning flood of color. Drayton sprang, but Terry was before him. One second later the Superlative's body crashed against the steel wall of the cell and dropped in a limp heap to the floor.

At the sound of his fall, the door was again flung open. The occupants of the cell found themselves covered by four leveled rifle barrels. Cleverest had not come here alone, and it looked as if the guards were in a mood to fire upon them and clear the cell of life forthwith. But finding, upon examination, that their superior was merely stunned and had suffered no broken bones, they decided to leave punishment to their masters. With many threats they retired, bearing the insensible Cleverest with them.

"That settles it!" said Drayton. "Nobody can ever mistake your feelings toward them, Terry!"

"I only wish that I'd killed him," growled the Irishman.

It was seven p.m., and they were beginning to wonder if Penn Service wasted not even bread and water on condemned prisoners, when the door bolts again clicked smoothly.

"Our supper at last!" commented Terry with satisfaction.

He was mistaken. No food-bearing jailer appeared, but the chief of police himself, alert and smiling. Behind him the light glinted on a dozen rifle barrels. They were taking no further chances, it appeared, with the Trenmore temper.

"I have come to make a rather unpleasant announcement," began Quickest. He spoke with quiet courtesy, but firmly and as one prepared for an outbreak. "You were to have been passed to the All-Father in the morning, I believe. His Supremity has instructed that the time be advanced. Will you accompany me without resistance? If so, you may go unfettered."

18   THE SWORD AND THE BELL

It was with a dull feeling of despair that Drayton, recovering from the first momentary shock, heard Trenmore accept the chief's condition for the freedom of their limbs.

"We'll go with you quietly, chief, to the very door of your bloody slaughter-house. You've the word of Terence Trenmore for every one of us."

And then Trenmore had looked from one to the other of his friends with a fiery glance that commanded their obedience. He was first to leave the cell, not even taking Viola's hand, which she stretched out like a small child, brave but knowing its own helplessness.

Drayton went to her, and then, in the face of such near death he did what he would not have permitted himself to do had fate been more kind. He remembered that look in her eyes, before Terry had flung Cleverest across the cell, and putting his arm about the little sister of Trenmore, he drew her to him.

"Viola," he said, very softly and with a great, quiet tenderness, "I love you, dear, so much that death with you is mere happiness!"

And she answered, "You are my world, Bobby Drayton! If death was needed to show us this love, then death can never rob us of it!"

"Skidoo," said Bertram the burglar to the young lady he designated by that name. "I guess our numbers are up. I meant right by you, kid, and I'm darned sorry!"

"It ain't your fault," retorted Miss Skidoo, of the solemn, childlike eyes. "I guess I got a right to die with a good, straight guy like you!"

With ironical politeness, the chief of police broke in. "His Supremity might be willing to wait if he knew how much sad romance is going on here, but my own time is valuable. Two abreast, please—that's right. You can continue your farewells as you walk. I guess I can stand it! Twenty-nine, turn out that light before you close the door."

In front, between two of the rifle-bearing guards, marched Terence Trenmore. His dark, heavy face was sullen. His lids drooped over narrowed, fire-blue eyes. When his guards brushed against him, in a narrow passage, he shuddered away from them as one in mortal fear. They laughed, and one of them murmured, "The bigger they are the harder they fall, eh, Forty-nine?"

Having passed through two steel-lined corridors, the party of guards and prisoners came presently to a stair, ascended one flight and so reached the red marble passage of the administrative offices on the southern side. Tramping along this, they passed the open door of Mr. Virtue's darkened "courtroom," and came to the southern entrance of the Hall of Justice.

Quickest, who was now in the lead, laid his hand on the door to push it open. As he did so Trenmore, standing between his guards, spoke for the first time since leaving the cell. "Chief, before we go in I've a word for your ear alone."

The chief shook his head, smiling. "Sorry, but I have no time to listen, my man." And he pushed at the door so that it opened a trifle.

"I'll say it aloud, then!" snapped Trenmore. "You can listen or not as you please. I gave my promise just now that I'd come unresisting to the very door of your slaughter pen. There is the door and here am I to take my word back again!"

For all his bulk, Trenmore had the speed of a springing tiger. He was on the chief before any one realized that he had begun to move. He had swung that startled official before him with one arm about his chest. His right hand dragged from the holster at his captive's side a revolver of pleasantly efficient caliber. He clapped the muzzle to the chief's head, behind the ear.

"Shoot now and be damned to you, you scum of the earth!" Trenmore roared. "But the first finger that crooks at a trigger, I'll scatter this scut's brains the way he'll be dead before any of us!"

Twelve astonished and dismayed guards stood agape, with rifles half raised. After a moment two of them turned their weapons on Drayton and Bertram. The other prisoners, however, as much taken by surprise as the guards, were quiet enough.

The chief was quiet, too. He was helpless as in the grip of a gorilla, and he could feel the cold nose of his own weapon nuzzling behind his ear. He was not smiling now.

"You've a grain of sense after all," observed Trenmore approvingly. "And now the chief and myself will be taking a bit of a walk. Just don't interfere. And don't you harm the hair of a head of one of my friends there—mind that now!"

He began sidling along the wall, still holding his human shield before him. In a moment more he had regained the red corridor and begun backing down it. After him came the guards. One of them, on a sudden thought, dashed back to the golden door and through it.

"Your friend's gone for help," said Trenmore to the chief conversationally. "He's a bright lad and I'd counsel you to advance him. You need help the way you'd sell your mouse of a soul to get it; don't you, my fine policeman? Don't you? Answer me, you scum!"

"Y-yes!" gasped the chief.

The breath was half squeezed out of him, and his feet stumbled and dragged as he backed with his relentless captor along the corridor. And still the guards followed, step for step, rifles half raised, and in their midst the prisoners.

A minute and Trenmore had reached a break in the red wall. Beyond it was a short flight of stairs. Terry backed around the corner. With a little rush, the pursuing guard came after. They found him halfway up the flight, still dragging their reluctant chief. He had reached the landing at the top. Behind it was an arched doorway, of which the heavy bronze doors stood open, fastened back flat to the wall.

Feeling with his foot for the floor catch, Trenmore found it and trod down. The door, released, swung out a trifle. Standing to one side and again feeling backward with his foot, Terry caught the edge with his toe and gave the door a pull. It moved easily on well-oiled hinges. Next instant, without once having turned his back on the guard, he was able to get his shoulder behind the door and push it to. The other door he treated in the same way, leaving an aperture between.

Then, without warning and with lightning speed, he lowered the gun, stooped, picked the chief up by the ankles and collar, gave him one mighty swing and pitched him headlong down upon his allies.

The hurtling body struck two of the foremost, knocking them backward. There were shouts, and somebody's rifle exploded accidentally. Another guard fired intentionally toward the stair head. But the space there was empty. The bullet splashed on the innocent bronze nose of a cupid in bas-relief, flying across a door shut tight and already bolted from the inside.

Trenmore, panting on the little balcony of the Threat of Penn, congratulated himself that earlier in the day he had observed those doors and those strangely placed inner bolts. Already men were banging and shouting outside; but Trenmore only chuckled.

"They'll need dynamite for that little job," he murmured happily. "I'm thinking the Servants put those doors there for just the purpose they're now serving. Sword, you were made for the hand of a man, not the grip of this cold metal thing!"

He was examining the bronze fist that held the great sword upright. Though the heavy door shook and clanged to the besiegers' futile blows, he was cool as if alone in the Temple. He had not yet even glanced down into the Hall of Justice.

Across the knuckles of the Hand of Penn ran a tiny line, green-edged with verdigris. It was a flaw, a crack in the age-old bronze.

His inspection completed, Trenmore sprang into action with the sudden wholeheartedness which was a disconcerting factor in his make-up. Throwing off his coat he removed a large handkerchief from the pocket, wadded it in his right hand and grasped the blade high up. Seizing the pommel in his left hand, slowly but with gathering force, he twisted at the sword. It did not move. His white shirt stood out in bulging lumps over his laboring shoulders. His face went dark red. The purple veins rose and throbbed on a forehead beaded with great drops of perspiration. He did not jerk or heave at the thing. He merely twisted and the leverage was terrific.

There came a loud crack, like the report of a pistol. Within the wall something dropped clanging, and the sword gave way so suddenly that Trenmore was hurled to the floor. Picking himself up, he calmly resumed his coat and stooped for the famous weapon. Not only had the bronze hand fallen in two pieces, freeing the grip, but the whole wrist had broken loose from the wall, leaving only a blank black hole.

Trenmore was not concerned for the mechanism so ruthlessly shattered. He cared only for the shining prisoner he had released. He raised it with both hands to the roughened grip. As he did so the yellow light from the dome slid flamelike down the long blade. It was a weight for any two ordinary men to carry; but the Irishman swung it up and over his shoulder with hardly an effort.

"You're a heavy one, my beauty, and no mistake," he muttered. "Even Terence Trenmore would not care to swing you many times together. But that which you struck would never strike back, I'm thinking."

And then at last, with the sword on his shoulder, he turned and looked down from the railing. The blows on the door had ceased. He now perceived the reason. Midway across the hall, with upturned faces and raised rifles, waited every man of the prison guard he had so successfully eluded. Trenmore's appearance was greeted with shouts and a scattering volley. Unhurt but considerably startled, he skipped back.

"Powers o' darkness!" he gasped. "I'm a fool or I'd have expected it. And now what am I to do, will you tell me that, Sword of Battle?"

But the sword was silent.

He was safe where he now stood, for the balcony was high enough and deep enough to be out of range from any place on the floor. And it was made of metal too heavy for bullets to penetrate.

"They'll not use those machine guns," reflected Trenmore, "for they couldn't and not hit the bell. But if they've the brains of a rat—and they have just about that—they'll send riflemen up where the guns are placed and pick me off like a cat on a wall. Before they do that, we'll rush it, Sword o' Beauty. And if they fire on us after—well, they'll hit their own bell, and that's a thing I don't think they'll want. Now, then!"

Balancing the sword on his shoulder, he dashed at the rail and vaulted to the narrow plank bridge left by the electricians. Though it bent and swayed sickeningly under the double weight of Trenmore and the huge sword, he ran its length as if it were a brick causeway. A moment later he brought up clinging to the scaffold about the bell. His speed had not averted another volley, but all the harm done was to the golden carvings on the wall around the balcony.

"You're but poor marksmen," growled Trenmore between his teeth. "You've a beautiful target now, though. The question is, will you dare shoot at it?"

The guard scattered and spread out. Several men aimed at Trenmore on the bell, but a sharp command caused them to lower their weapons. The word came from none other than the chief himself, who now walked to a place whence he could look up at Trenmore and Trenmore down at him. If the chief's fall had injured him he showed no signs of it.

"Praise Heaven, your neck wasn't broke at all, chief," called the Irishman cheerfully. "I was afeared for you so I could scarce do my work; but I got me a pretty plaything for all that!"

That the chief might see, he raised the sword and balanced it in his hands.

"Where—How did you get that?"

"From the Hand of Penn," came the Irishman's gay reply. "Sure, for all he was a Quaker, Penn's the kind-hearted old gentleman that would never withhold a weapon from a lad in a tight place!"

And he swung the sword about his head till it glittered like a wheel of fire. "'Twill make a world o' noise when it strikes the bell. Eh, my little policeman?"

"You must not—you dare not!" shrieked Quickest. The last shred of his composure had dropped off like a torn cloak. He at least seemed to share the superstition of the Numbers with regard to the old Threat of Penn.

Trenmore, however, felt that he had given the police sufficient attention. He was casting for bigger fish than they. Why had his bait not yet been taken? The bell, scaffolding and all, swung alarmingly against the electricians' tethering ropes; but Trenmore cautiously made his way a step or so along the planking.

There was the dais, and before it yawned the pit, open again and glaring upward like a red eye set in the milk-white floor. Close by, under guard, stood his four companions watching the bell with anxious eyes.

Drayton and Viola greeted Terry's appearance with a cheer and waved their hands encouragingly. In response Terry raised the sword, called a hearty greeting, and looked at the dais.

On the throne sat that decrepit, hateful figure, Mr. Justice Supreme. There sat also every one of the Servants who had witnessed the examinations, earlier in the day, including Mr. Mercy, looking depressed but interested. Cleverest was there, too, standing beside his uncle.

Then Trenmore spoke, with the great voice of an Angel of Doom.

"You devils below there!" he shouted. "Take heed to my words! I've a warning to give you."

There came a deafening roar behind him. Glancing over his shoulder he saw a billowing, greenish cloud issuing from the balcony. It cleared slowly, revealing a pair of explosion-shattered doors, sagging from their hinges. A crowd of his enemies poured through the aperture and on to the balcony. At the rail, however, they paused, glaring across at Trenmore.

"Sword o' Battle," he murmured softly, "do you not wish they may try to cross on our bridge? Do you not hope it, little sword?"

Between his men the Quickest pushed his way to the railing. He had secured another revolver and he leveled it at Trenmore. "Surrender, my man, or you'll be shot where you stand!" came his terse command.

"Surrender is it? And why don't you shoot me, then? Sure, am I not a condemned man, chief, darling?"

"His Supremity has instructed me to grant you a reprieve if you will surrender. There has already been damage enough done."

Said Trenmore, "I'll wager my life against your marksmanship, chief. Shoot now! And see if you can kill Terence Trenmore before he can strike the bell!" Once more he heaved up the sword.

The chief turned pale and lowered his own weapon. "You are a madman!" he shouted. "Strike that bell and your friends and you will perish with the rest of us!"

"A quick death and a happy one! In dying we'll rid the earth of its worst scum, if all they say is true. No, no, little man. I'll not come over to you. And if you shoot, you'll strike the bell yourself in a small way—or cause me to do it in earnest. I've no time to be exchanging pleasantries. I'll just guard my back and go on with my business."

He brought the sword crashing down on the frail bridge. With a splintering sound it broke loose. Trenmore's end fell to the floor, carrying with it some of the scaffolding. Trenmore barely saved himself from going down. Regaining his footing neatly, he waved a hand at the furious chief and climbed around the bell to a place where it partly shielded him from the balcony. Thence he could face his more important enemies on the dais.

"You'll pardon me," he shouted. "There was a small interruption. Now, tell me, you old scoundrel on the throne there, have I the upper hand, or have I not?"

19 TRENMORE STRIKES

It was Cleverest who replied, scornfully and with no sign of fear.

"You fool," he cried, "strike the bell if you like. Do you think we care for that? We are waiting for you to be brought down here to die with these other vermin!"

"And is that the way you regard it?" inquired Trenmore with a laugh, but his heart sank. He was bluffing on a large and glorious scale, and if the bluff was to be called, he might as well leap from his place and be done with it. However, the Irishman was a firm believer in the motto: Fight to a finish whatever the odds! "Then I'll strike and settle the matter," he added defiantly.

Just beyond where he stood, the Red Bell was naked of scaffolding. He swung up the sword for a great blow. But there was at least one man in the hall whose faith was equal to that of the Numbers themselves. That man was Mr. Justice Supreme, High Servant of Penn.

As the sword flashed up, the old man leaped from his chair. With galvanic energy and upraised, clawlike hands, he stumbled to the edge of the dais. "No, no, no!" he shrieked. "Don't strike! For mercy's sake don't strike the bell; don't strike—"

The words died on his lips. The yellow claws clutched at his heart and he flung back his head, mouth open. As his knees sagged under him, Cleverest barely saved his uncle from falling to the pavement below. Holding the limp form in his arms, he felt for the old man's heart. Then he laid him down on the dais and turned to the Servants.

"Gentlemen," he said very solemnly. "Mr. Justice Supreme has passed to the arms of Penn!"

Every man on the platform rose and gravely removed his high hat; then, with the utmost tranquility, reseated himself. Full tribute to the dead having been rendered, business might proceed as before.

Cleverest turned again and shook his fist at Trenmore. "It is you who have done this!" he cried. "It is you who shall pay for it! Gentlemen"—he whirled to his seated fellows—"have you any objection—any fear of this world or the next—which causes you to dread the striking of that bell?"

They all smiled. One or two laughed outright. Mr. Pity arose in his place. "Mr. Justice Supreme," he said, "Pardon me if I forestall your ordination under that title, but this is an uncommon emergency. Your Supremity, I am sure I speak for all of us when I say that the gentleman on the bell is welcome to hammer at it all night, if that will relieve his feelings. He gives us credit for an uncommonly large slice of his own superstition!"

"You hear?" yelled Cleverest at the Irishman. "Strike if you please! For every stroke you will see one of your friends here dropped screaming down the pit!"

This was checkmate with a vengeance. Trenmore hesitated, feeling suddenly rather foolish. If he struck, they would throw Viola in first. Already she had been dragged to the very edge by a burly tiger of a pit guard. A dozen men had their hands on the other prisoners. If he did not strike, they would still be thrown in. This was the end.

A sickening weariness replaced the exaltation which had upheld Trenmore till this moment. He let the sword sink slowly, until its point rested on the edge of the Red Bell.

Cleverest smiled sneeringly and half turned. He meant to seat himself on the throne and thenceforward give his orders from the place he had long coveted. Then an earnest, ringing voice arose from the group below him.

"Terry—Terry! For the love of Heaven, don't give up! That man is wrong! They are all wrong! Only that old man knew the truth. Strike that bell and no man in all the city will be alive one moment after! Strike, I say! Kill us and avenge us with one blow!"

"Stop that man's mouth!" cut in Cleverest savagely. "Proceed with the executions!"

But now his fellow Servants intervened. Perhaps they remembered that for all their pride they were only mortal men; or perhaps they were merely curious. At least, several of them rose in open protest.

"No! Wait a minute, Clever—beg pardon, Your Supremity, I should say. Let's hear what the fellow has to say."

"Wait!" This from Mr. Courage, the former High Priest's lieutenant. He was a dignified man with cold gray eyes and features which indicated a character of considerable determination. "Remember, sir, that until the ordination, the Council of Twelve holds power. Let the man speak!"

"Let him speak!"

The chorus was too unanimous for even Cleverest to overlook. With a scowl he stalked to the throne. "Very well, gentleman," he snapped. "Have your way, but no good will come of it. Bring that man up here!"

Leaning on the sword Trenmore looked on with renewed hope in his optimistic soul. "I wonder," thought he, "does the boy know some real secret about this red thing here? Or is he bluffing? If he is, good luck and a power of invention to the tongue of him!"

Drayton was escorted around to the dais steps by two blue-clad policemen. When he stood before the throne, Cleverest gestured impatiently.

"I have no wish to question this man. Gentlemen, since you have taken the matter on yourselves, will you kindly conclude it?"

"We will." The imperturbable Mr. Courage turned to Drayton. "Young man, what is it that you know about the Threat of Penn which we, the Servants of Penn, do not already know?"

"It's history," retorted Drayton boldly. He spoke up loudly, so that Trenmore also might hear. "To be convincing I must go back a long way in the history of Philadelphia—back to the very beginning of her isolation from the rest of the United States. You know nothing of that?"

Leaning from his throne, Cleverest whispered in the ear of Mr. Courage. The latter nodded.

"Stick to the bell itself, please," he said sternly. "We are not interested in the history of Philadelphia."

"I'll try to but you won't understand. Well, then, in that distant age there was a certain group of men practically, though not openly, in control of this city. They were called 'grafters,' 'the contractor gang,' and 'the gang.' Those were titles of high honors then—like Servants and Superlatives, you know."

Here, Trenmore, on the bell, almost dropped the sword for sheer delight.

"These grafters," continued Drayton, "got hold of a man who had made a certain discovery. He was professor of physics in a university here. You know—or rather probably you don't know—that all matter in its atomic structure vibrates, and that different sorts of energy waves can affect that vibration. I am no physicist myself, and I can't tell you this in scientific terms. As I understood it, however, he discovered a combination of metals which, when treated in a certain way, would give off sound waves of the exact length of the vibration not of atoms, but of the electrons. That is to say—"

"This is madness," broke in Cleverest impatiently. "It is a jargon of senseless words!"

"Tell us about the bell," seconded Mr. Courage, and "Yes, the bell—the bell!" came from half a dozen other Servants.

"I *am* telling you of the bell," protested Drayton. "But you are too ignorant to grasp even a simple idea of it. Perhaps you can understand if I put it another way. This man—this professor had discovered a secret power by which metal, reverberating to a blow, might destroy not only other metal but human flesh, clothes, wood, marble, the very air you breathe! And these grafters, of whom you yourselves are the lineal descendants, forced the man to use his discovery for their benefit.

"With refined irony they took the old Liberty Bell. They had it recast. They made this professor recast the Liberty Bell itself, with other metal and in his new secret way— recast it as a much larger bell. It came out red as blood. Then they built this dome. They said Philadelphia should have the most glorious city hall in the world. They hung the bell there and they put the sword there. And then they set guards at the doors, and guns behind those panels. They invited the leading citizens to a demonstration. They forced the professor to play showman to his discovery, but they betrayed him so that his precautions for his own safety were annulled at the critical moment. Before the citizens' horrified eyes the professor, and the little gong he used for the experiment, and all the solid matter around it dissolved, disintegrated, vanished. He stood right there, where your pit yawns now. When he was gone there was a hole in the pavement as if made by a great explosion.

"And they—the grafters—set themselves up as masters of the city under threat of its complete destruction. They called themselves the Servants of Penn. They curtailed the education of the people as needless and too expensive. When the people complained, they placated them by abolishing all grades above the primary and turning the schools into dance halls and free moving-picture theaters. City hall they remodeled into a luxurious clubhouse where they themselves lived and reveled.

"Two generations later—generations of unschooled, iron-ruled citizens—and Penn had become a god. The poor, good old Quaker! His Servants made him the god of Lust, of Vice, of Drunkenness, of every sort of foul debauchery. The Servants were his priests and this his temple. In mockery they named themselves for the cardinal virtues—Mercy, Pity, Justice, Love. But they were tyrants without mercy, revelers in vice—"

"Stop!"

The command came from a livid, furious Cleverest, and the hand of a policeman cut off Drayton's flow of eloquence effectively. Cleverest was not the only angry man present. Drayton faced eight Servants who would have cheerfully torn him to pieces.

"Mr. Courage," Cleverest turned whitely to his uncle's lieutenant, "are you satisfied now, or do you desire further insult from this—this lying dog who would blacken the name of Penn and of Penn Service?"

"You were right, sir," conceded Courage. "I had not supposed that the brain of a human being could compass such a tissue of lies and blasphemy! We cannot be too quickly rid of the whole sacrilegious horde!"

Now was Cleverest's hour of triumph. With sickening certainty, Drayton realized that he had carried his tirade too far. He had not convinced; only enraged. Nothing but death remained. He wrenched his face away from the officer's hand.

"Strike, Terry!" he shouted. "I have spoken only the truth! Strike!"

Then did Terence Trenmore raise the Sword of Penn in good earnest. The fury that had been in him this hour past rose in his heart like boiling lava. Though he believed, no more than the Servants, he must strike at something. He could reach nothing human. There was the Red Bell!

As the sword swung up, even the disbelieving Servants stared fascinated. The police and pit guards dropped their prisoners and raised one beastlike wail of fear.

Up whirled the sword and descended, a yellow flash of flame. It rose again.

A strange reverberation shook the air. It was not like the note of a bell, nor of a gong, nor of any man-made thing. It was more than sound—worse than sound. It was a feeling; an emotion; the sickening pang of a spirit wrenching itself from a body racked with pain.

Every living being in that great place save one dropped where he was, and lay writhing feebly beneath the awful, echoing dome.

But Trenmore, standing against the bell itself, did not fall. Perhaps he was too close to be affected. Perhaps the scaffolding which pressed on the bell, preventing its full reverberation, broke the sound waves for him. At least he still stood; and now he seemed to be peering through a crimson haze of fury. Though after that first blow he might have brought even Penn Service to terms, he cared not to temporize. He cared only to destroy. Again he brought down the sword with all his terrible strength.

His foothold sagged beneath him. Looking upward he beheld an awe-inspiring thing. The golden Dome of Justice was sinking; crumpling inward. It was growing transparent, like a sheet of gold leaf beaten too thin. A moment later and he could see through it on upward.

He saw the high, gray-white tower, with its illuminated clock face, and still above that the circle of white lights about the feet of Penn. He saw the huge statue sway and stagger like a drunken man. Beneath it the tower began to bend like a tallow candle set in an oven thrice heated.

A warning quiver shot through the scaffold. With one yell of sheer, savage delight, Trenmore heaved up the sword. For the third and last time it smote the blood-red Threat of Penn!

Then the air was sucked out of his lungs; sight was wiped from his eyes. His muscles relaxed and he lost all power to feel; but he knew in the deathless soul of him that his body was falling and that the created world had dissolved, disintegrated into formless chaos!

Trenmore fell but not into the empty void created when the Red Bell dissolved itself, its temple and its world.

He struck feet first on some kind of hard surface, jarred in every bone and nerve by the impact. As light flashed up all around him, he staggered against a man.

The next incident can only be explained by the fact that Trenmore was still "seeing red." The fight had been by no means knocked out of him by the recent catastrophe. He grasped one fact and one only. The man against whom he had stumbled wore a black coat and a silk hat, accursed insignia of Penn Service. Promptly grappling with this individual, they went to the pavement together. While Terry reached for his adversary's throat, the latter let out yell after yell of terror and dismay.

It was fortunate that the Irishman had been so thoroughly shaken by his fall that his customary efficiency was somewhat impaired. Two scandalized policemen dashing upon the struggling pair were able to pull him off before he could inflict more than a bad fright upon his victim.

Dragged to his knees, Trenmore shook his head like an angry bull of the wild Irish breed. He got his feet under him and rose so suddenly that the policemen lost their grip, thrown off like a couple of terriers.

Then would bloody battle have raged indeed in the very precincts of law and order, had not a new figure rushed up and fairly flung itself into Trenmore's arms. It was a small figure to quell so huge an adversary. Even the maddest of Irishmen, however, could hardly go on fighting while a pair of slim arms reached for his neck, a soft cheek pressed against his coat, and a loved voice cried softly:

"Look about you! Terry, oh, Terry! Look about you!"

Folding an arm about Viola, Trenmore dashed a hand across his eyes and at last did look. On four sides rose the gray, irregular, many-windowed walls of a huge building. Beneath his feet lay a pavement of uneven gray concrete. The place was bright with the white glare of electric lights. Where had been the four doors of the temple, he saw through open archways to the streets beyond.

Above was no golden dome, but the open starlit sky. Up toward it pointed a high, gray tower, almost white in the rays of a searchlight somewhere on the lower walls. The tower was surmounted by the foreshortened but identifiable statue of William Penn, not falling but very solid and majestically beneficent as usual. Then Trenmore became aware of a nasal, high-pitched voice.

"I tell you I've got to catch my train!" it wailed. "Arrest that lunatic or let him go, just as you please. But if you make me miss that train, you'll regret it! Your own men there will testify that I did nothing. I was simply hurrying through the public buildings on my way to Broad Street Station. Then that wild man jumped on me from behind. Chief Hannigan is my brother-in-law. If you make me miss that last train I'll get your stripes for it, or I'm a Dutchman!"

Viewing the speaker with new eyes, Trenmore perceived him to be a tall, thin man; who had already rescued his hat from where it had rolled, and retrieved a small black suit case. He was handing his card to the sergeant. That officer promptly capitulated.

"Beg your pardon, Mr. Flynn. Meant no offense, I'm sure. Trying to catch the ten-five? You can get it yet!"

Making no reply, the man fled so precipitately toward Broad Street Station that his coat tails stood out behind.

"That's Mr. Charles Flynn, the undertaker," observed the sergeant to a group of four or five policemen who had now gathered and were regarding Trenmore with mingled wonder and menace. "He lives out at Media. Now, my man, you come along quietly. What were you trying to do—provide Mr. Flynn as a corpse for one of his own funerals?"

The jest brought a laugh from his subordinates. Trenmore was silent. He had lost all desire to fight, and the smallest policeman there could have led him away by one hand. But Viola's quick wits again saved the situation. Releasing herself gently from her brother's arm, she addressed the sergeant with quiet dignity.

"Officer, this gentleman is my brother. He is subject to epileptic seizures. Just now he became separated from me and from his—his attendant. The fit came on him and he fell against the other gentleman. He is ill, and all he needs is to be taken home and put to bed. Mr. Drayton, here, is his nurse. Please, sergeant! You wouldn't arrest my poor brother?"

Trenmore perceived that Drayton had indeed taken his place at his other side. Over the heads of the police he saw Arnold Bertram and Miss Skidoo!

Feeling remarkably foolish, he began to wonder if what Viola was saying might not be actual fact. Could it be that he had been ill—mad—and had dreamed that whole wild vision of the year 2118?

Fortunately Viola's pleadings, in which Drayton presently joined, proved effective. With a number of good-natured warnings that she "keep her crazy brother at home, or at least under better restraint," the sergeant wrote down the name and address and called off his myrmidons.

Robert Drayton and the two Trenmores were free at last to walk quietly out of the southern entrance into Broad Street. They hastened to do so. They had, in fact, seen quite enough of Philadelphia city hall, in any century. Behind followed Bertram and his companion.

It was then a little after ten, and the street was by no means crowded. Nevertheless, as Drayton and Trenmore were more than a little disheveled, the party were glad to turn off from brightly lighted Broad into the comparative emptiness and gloom of Sansom Street. Just before they did so, Drayton paused for one glance backward at the enormous pile of gray masonry terminating the short vista of Broad Street. Had they really, as he hopefully surmised, returned into the safe protection of their own day and age?

High above, like a white ghost in the searchlight, brooded the giant figure of that old Quaker, his stony hand outstretched in petrified blessing. And below him, across the face of the yellow-lighted clock, a wraith of vapor drifted, obscuring the figures. What difference was there between it all as he saw it now and as he had seen it that very morning, as it seemed to him? The difference stared him in the face.

There was still an emblem above the southern arch. That morning it had been the ominous, sword-crossed Red Bell. Now it was a shield with the city colors, pale yellow and blue; above it glowed a huge "Welcome" and the letters "A. A. M. W."; beneath it the one word "TRUTH."

"Associated Advertising Men of the World," he muttered half aloud, "and their convention was here—I mean is here. Yes, we're back in our own century again."

Half a block farther they all walked, in the silence of prisoners too suddenly released to believe their own good fortune. Then Trenmore abruptly halted. Bertram and Miss Skidoo coming up, they all stood grouped in the friendly shadow of an awning.

"Viola," exclaimed Trenmore, "tell me the facts and don't spare me! Was that thing you said to the policemen back there—was it really so?"

Her eyes opened wide. "What do you mean?"

"I mean that if I've been crazy, dreaming—"

"Then we've all been dreaming together," broke in Drayton soberly. "I was never more astounded in my life than when that gorgeous temple suddenly dissolved, melted, and reformed as the old familiar public buildings. It's lucky for us that there were only a few people passing through at the time. We must have dropped into the scene like figures in one of these faked movie reels. It's a wonder no one noticed!"

"An' me," put in Bertram. "I've been talkin' my head off tryin' to explain to the kid here how she's got back about two hundred years before she was born. I know it by that 'Welcoming Advertising Men' thing over the city hall entrance. 'Truth.' it says under it. Gee, it's mighty hard to make some folks believe the truth!"

"Miss Skidoo!" ejaculated Terence. Again he brushed his eyes with his hand, staring blankly at that bewildered but defiant young lady.

"Yes," she retorted sharply, "and you can't kid me, neither! Sump'n certainly happened, but it couldn't be what Bert said. Why, I know this place where we're standing like it was my own kitchen!"

There she stood, certainly, green hat, silk sweater, and all. The yellow button, insignia of the enslaved Numbers of a future age, glared like a nightmare eye from her lapel. Yet how, granting that all the rest was so—that they had actually lived through some forty-eight hours in a century yet unborn—how had she survived the oblivion which had swallowed her fellow citizens? Servants, Superlatives, police, Numbers, and all had dissolved and vanished. But No. 23000 had made the two-century jump unscathed. Could it be that future, past, and present were all one, as he had once read in some book, tossed aside after ten minutes of incredulous attention?

"Let's get home," exclaimed Trenmore abruptly. "I feel my reason is slipping. And let's walk, for it's not far and 'tis agreeable to be loose in a sane world again. At least," Terry corrected himself after a moment's sober reflection, "a comparatively sane world. Yes, let's be moving, friends, for I'm thinking we need a good meal and a night's sleep to save our own sanity!"

21 THE LAST OF THE GRAY DUST

At ten-thirty, five tired and hungry people ascended the steps of No. 17 Walnut Street and rang the bell. It was not immediately answered. Then Drayton noticed that the door was not latched. They all entered and became aware that in the library on the right something unusual was going on. A gurgling, choking noise was punctuated by several thumps, followed by the crash of furniture violently overthrown.

Trenmore was first at the door. He flung it open and rushed inside. The room seemed empty. As the noises continued, however, Trenmore passed around the big reading table and stooping over plucked his man, Martin, from the prostrate body of an unknown antagonist. He did it with the air of one who separates his bull pup from the mangled corpse of the neighbor's Pomeranian. With a sad, disgusted face Terry glanced from the pugnacious one to the figure on the floor.

"Ah now, boy," he demanded, "are you not ashamed to be choking a man old enough to be your own grand-dad?" Then he dropped Martin, with an exclamation. "Sure, 'tis my old friend the little collector man!"

"Mr. Trenmore," began Martin in excited self-defense, "he come in here and he—"

"Never mind what he did till I count what's left of the pieces, my boy. I take back what I said, though. Be he alive or dead, the old rascal's got no more than was coming to him."

Kneeling down, while the rest gathered in an interested group, he put his hand to the man's heart. He was an elderly, smooth-shaven, gray-haired person, with sharp, clean-cut features. The forehead was high and sloping, the mouth thin and tight-pressed even in unconsciousness. He was well dressed, and a gold pince-nez lay on the floor near by, miraculously unbroken.

"He's all right," announced Trenmore. "Martin, a drop of liquor now and we'll have the old scoundrel up and able for an explanation."

His prophecy proved correct. Five minutes later the gray-haired collector sat in an armchair, shaken but able to talk and be talked to.

"And now," said Trenmore, "I'll ask you, Martin, to tell your share in this, and then you'll go out and you'll get everything in the house that is eatable and you'll set it out in the dining room, for it's starved to death we are, every one of us."

"Yes, Mr. Trenmore, I'll tend to it. This old man broke in on me about half an hour ago. He asked for you, Sir. I told him you'd been out since this morning—"

"This morning!" The exclamation broke from three pairs of lips simultaneously. Martin stared.

"Never mind," said Terry hastily. "And then?"

"He wanted to know where you were. I said I didn't know, as you didn't say anything to me. And then we got talking and—I'm sorry, sir—but I let out that it seemed mighty queer, your going that way. And then he asked me questions about where I'd last seen you and all that. I told him about finding this gray stuff—it's wrapped up in that newspaper on the table, sir—and not knowing what it was or whether you wanted it kept or thrown out.

"And then—honest, I don't know how he did it, but he got me to show it to him. I brought it in here. And then he said I'd never see you again, and would I sell him the stuff. I said no, of course. Then he pulled a gun on me—here it is—and I jumped on him—and then you came in. I didn't want to hurt the old guy, but he got me wild and—"

"That's all right, Martin. You did very well, but don't ever be doing any of it again. Now hurry up that supper. What's coming next would likely strain your poor brain. Get along with you."

Reluctantly, Martin vanished kitchenward. The rest of the company pulled up chairs and made themselves comfortable. For a time they found the captive of Martin's prowess inclined to an attitude of silent defiance. Upon Terry's threat, however, to turn him over to the police on charges of housebreaking, he expressed a willingness to listen to reason. Bertram's presence had a very chastening effect. He knew the burglar for one of the men he had hired to steal the Cerberus, and realized that should his former accomplice go on the stand, his testimony, together with the attack on Martin, would mean penitentiary stripes for himself.

"By the way," Drayton broke in, picking up the newspaper package which contained the Dust of Purgatory and weighing it in his hand, "did you ever ask Bertram, Terry, if he knew what had become of the vial this was in?"

The burglar started and flushed. "Say, I done a mean trick then. I didn't mean to keep the thing, but you left it laying on your bureau that day at the Belleclaire, Mr. Trenmore, and I—well, I took it along. I give it to Skidoo here for a keepsake. I didn't have anything else pretty to give her. But she's a straight girl and I shouldn't't've done it. Skidoo, have you got that bottle I give you for bath salts?"

"Sure." No. 23000 promptly produced it from her sweater pocket. "Why, Bert, wasn't it yours?"

Bertram admitted that it was not. With a reproachful glance for Bertram, she extended the Cerberus vial to Trenmore. Trenmore reached for it and took it in his hand. In the flash of an eye the space before him was empty. Miss Skidoo had vanished more abruptly than he had himself disappeared, upon his first experience with the dust!

With a startled yell, Terence leaped to his feet and flung the Cerberus across the room. His feelings were shared by all present, save the old collector, who put up a thin, protesting hand.

"Now, don't—I beg of you, don't become excited! Mr. Trenmore, my nerves are not in shape to stand this sort of thing. There is no harm done—unless the beautiful little curio is broken, which would be a pity. Tell me, did that violently costumed young lady come here from—well, from the place you have been in since this morning?"

"She did that!"

"Then she has simply returned there," announced the collector and he settled placidly back in his chair.

But Bertram, who had been stricken temporarily dumb and paralyzed by the abrupt vanishment of his beloved "kid," gave vent to one anguished cry of grief and rage. Springing upon Drayton, he wrenched from him the newspaper packet.

"What the deuce are you doing?" exclaimed the lawyer.

"You lemme alone!" panted the burglar, backing away. "I want a dose of this dust, that's what. I'm goin' after Skidoo, I am!"

"You are not!"

Trenmore pounced on him and recovered the dangerous package. "You poor little maniac," he said. "Do you think that I rang the Red Bell in that temple for nothing? Don't you realize that the place where we were *isn't anywhere now*, wherever it was before?"

A moment the burglar stood cogitating this puzzling statement, his face the picture of woe. Then he sank slowly into a chair and dropped his head in his hands.

"The brightest kid!" he muttered despairingly. "The best kid and now she's nothing! Hell—beg pardon, lady, but this's fierce! I don't care what happens now!"

They all sincerely pitied him. As, however, there is no known remedy for the loss of a sweetheart who has melted into the circumambient atmosphere, and as he repulsed their sympathy with almost savage impatience, they once more turned their attention to the gray-haired collector.

Trenmore began by asking his name.

The old fellow fumbled in his pockets a moment. "I find I have left my card case," he said, "but I am Phineas

Dodd Scarboro. By profession I am an oculist. I am willing to tell you the history and nature of that dust. In order that I may do so intelligently, however, I must ask that you first relate your own experience with it."

There seemed nothing unreasonable in this request. Beginning with the first uncapping of the vial, they unfolded their remarkable narrative. Long before that tale was done, Martin had announced supper. The collector adjourned with them to the dining room. Bertram, however, declined, saying that he had no appetite and preferred to stay where he was. So he was left alone, hunched over in his chair, a figure of sorrow inconsolable. Trenmore took the precaution of bringing the packet of dust into the dining room.

"And so," concluded Trenmore over the coffee cups, "we got back to our own day again, and a very good job it was. I'd sooner put up with any hardships of our own time, than live out my life in the year 2118!"

Phineas Scarboro sniffed scornfully at Terry's last remark.

"The year fiddlesticks!" he exclaimed impatiently. "You might, if you had used that powder intelligently, have reached a plane where the vibration was so rapid that a year there was the equivalent of one day here. That, however, is the only form of trick you could play with time. To talk of time as a dimension through which one might travel is the merest nonsense. Time is not a dimension. It is a sequence, or rather a comparative sequence, of vibrations."

Trenmore threw up his hand. "Man, man, don't confuse us that way; we'll be worse off than we are now!"

"The sun rose and set at least twice while we were there," said Drayton.

"And if it was not the year 2118, then what was it and where were we?" This from Viola.

Scarboro placed his fingers together, tip to tip. He contemplated them for a moment without replying.

"Perhaps," he said at last, "I had best begin where your adventures began—with the Dust of Purgatory. In my freshman year at Harvard I made the acquaintance of a young man destined to influence my life in a very remarkable manner. His name was Andrew Power. You appear startled. That was the name, was it not, which you, Mr. Drayton, encountered in the temple library as the man who had carried out the scheme for state isolation? The appearance of that name is one of those inexplicable circumstances which in my own investigations have often obtruded themselves.

"Andrew Power, then, was a young man of very unusual abilities. He was, in fact, a theorist along lines so novel that he became persona non grata to more than one member of the faculty. In those days they were convinced that science had achieved her ultimate victories. Any one who pointed out new worlds to conquer was a heretic or worse. Finding no sympathy in his instructors, Power brought his theories to me and to Thaddeus B. Crane, who was then my roommate. The three of us struck up one of those intense friendships of boyhood. On many a night we argued and wrangled into the small hours over subjects of whose very existence Thaddeus and I would scarcely have been aware, save for Andrew Power.

"His chief interest lay in the fields of the occult, which he approached from the angle of sheer materialism. To expound his theories even in brief would require more time than you, I am sure, would care to expend in listening. Enough that he was deeply interested in the Eastern religions—he was born in India, by the way, and had studied under some of their greatest pundits—and contended that their mysticism was based on scientifically demonstrable facts."

In spite of himself, Trenmore yawned. Was the man never going to reach the dust?

"In his own words," continued Scarboro, "Power believed it possible to 'reduce psychic experiences to a material basis! You smile"—They hadn't—"but Andrew Power, whom we secretly considered a mad theorist, proved himself far more practical than Crane and I, who merely talked. The faculty objected to experiments along any line not in the regular curriculum. Power, however, had set up for himself a small private laboratory.

"One night he came to us ablaze with excitement. In his hand was a glass specimen jar, half filled with this gray, powdery stuff. 'Fellows,' he said, 'I've done the thing at last. I've precipitated RI.' Though we hadn't the vaguest idea what he was talking about, we managed not to give ourselves away. We led him on to explanation. This powder, he said, was of a substance more magical than the fabled philosopher's stone, which could at most but transmute one element into another. Taken into the system of a living creature this substance so altered the vibrations of the electrons—he called them atomic corpuscles, but electrons is the modern term—of not only the body but of any other matter within the immediate radius of its magnetism that these vibrations were modified to function on an entirely different plane from this with which we are familiar from birth. This other world, or rather these worlds, lie within or in the same place as our own. The old axiom, that two bodies cannot exist simultaneously in the same place, was, according to Power, an axiom no more. Two bodies, a hundred bodies, could by inter-vibration exist in precisely the same place. And therein lay the explanation of every materialization, every 'miracle,' every 'super-natural' wonder since the world began. Mediums, clairvoyants, prophets, and yogis, all had their occasional spiritual glimpses of these hidden planes or worlds. What Power desired—what he had accomplished—was the actual physical entry.

"Needless to say, we scoffed. We angered Power to the point where he was ready to actually demonstrate. Later we learned from his notes that he had only translated an unlucky cat or so to these secret realms, and was personally inexperienced. Driven, however, by our laughter, Power took about ten grains of the powder and placed it on his tongue. He disappeared. From that day to this no one, not even I, who have many times gone the same road and returned, has ever seen Andrew Power.

"We two escaped arrest only because our unfortunate friend had not been seen coming to our rooms that night. There was a great fuss made over his supposed murder, and the country for miles around was searched for days. Thaddeus and I, two frightened boys, kept still. The first day or so we had access to his laboratory, where we read his notes in the hope of being able to reverse his disastrous experiment on himself. Then everything was locked up and later his effects were shipped to his only living relative, an uncle in Delhi. But the formula for the dust was not among them. That, before my eyes and in the face of my frantic protest, Thaddeus Crane had destroyed.

"He would have destroyed the powder also, had I not persuaded him that it was our moral duty to hold it in case of Andrew Power's return. He was always a bit afraid of Andrew. In the face of that contingency he suddenly saw his arbitrary act with the formula in its true light. So Crane and I divided the powder between us, promising each other to hold it in case Power should ever return.

"But Crane had had enough and more than enough. He would never afterward discuss even with me the theories which had cost humanity that great and daring mind. I think Crane privately considered that the devil had taken his own. He became very religious, a rigid church member, and died in a firm conviction of grace.

"But I was of different stuff. Power's notes had given me a few ideas of my own. For fifteen years, though I followed the profession for which I had trained myself, I worked, studied, and experimented. At last I felt that I, too, had solved a problem, not of this dust, the secret of which passed with its creator, but of a means to recover the original vibratory rhythm after it had been altered by the dust, that is, a means to return to our own world.

"I am proud to say that I had the courage to make the trial. I, too, have wandered across the wide Ulithian plain. I, too, have passed the Gateway of the Moon into places and amid peoples more strange than even you can dream. The thought of those wanderings became to me an obsession. I was like a drug fiend, who can neither rest nor sleep unless he knows that the means are at hand to rebuild his dream castles—reanimate his wondrous and seductive houris.

"But the time came when my share of the dust was at last exhausted. Naturally I went to Crane. I think I hinted to you that he was a superstitious fool. He had bought that vial, the Cerberus, and he dumped out the absurdly impossible relic of Dante, replacing it with Power's stuff. 'Dust from the Rocks of Purgatory' appealed to him, I suppose, as better applicable to this powder than to the very earthy dust the vial had before contained.

"Well, I found Crane utterly unapproachable on the subject. I begged, pleaded, threatened, offered him all in my power to give; but he would not let me have it. At his death I was wild with rage when I learned of its sale to a mere collector of curios. You know the rest of that episode. Can you blame me now?

"To-day science herself is steadily approaching the magic boundaries of those realms which were once my familiar playground. Soon she can no longer ignore the actual, material existence of the 'astral plane' as it has been misnamed by investigators who only recognize it as a Psychical possibility.

"But I—in the flesh, I have known such adventures as only you in all the world would credit! There, ever changing, continually forming, are born the nuclei of events, conditions, inventions, ideas, which later 'break through' as it were and recreate this more stable world to which we are born. The inspiration of the poet, the philosopher, or the inventor, is no more than a flicker from that swifter, different vibration within our own.

"And those lands have their monsters—devils, even. The spirit can at times attune itself and in our world a prophet arises. But let him beware! They are wild realms which he glimpses, neither good nor bad, but alive with their own never-ceasing, half-aimless, half-purposeful activities. I know them as no other man save Andrew Power alone. Many times have I sought him there. Many times has his name come up in some such fantastic connection at it came to you. I have seen, as it were, the shadow of his thought sketched in the tangible phantasmagoria which surrounded me. But either he eludes me purposely, or he is dead, and only his mind endures as an invisible force. But if he still lives and we meet, he can make this stuff that I can't make; I can show him the way back to our own world; and after that the door will be open for all to pass!

"Think of the discoveries that will be hastened—the miracles that may be wrought by knowledge acquired at first hand across that threshold! I could almost kill myself for sheer rage when I think how I wasted glorious opportunities in the pursuit of mere unprofitable adventure! Why, you yourselves brought back at least one idea—the idea of matter-destroying sound waves. Had it been Andrew Power or I, we would have searched those archives until we found the formula by which the Red Bell was made. We would have brought that back, instead of the bare and useless idea!"

"And a fine lot of good that would have been to the world!" exploded Trenmore. "I'd as soon give matches to a child and bid it go play in the nice powder mill, as turn loose the men of this world in that one we've come from, if all you say is true. This dust here I'll toss in the river, so no man shall go that road again. 'Tis not right nor decent, Mr. Scarboro, that one should so thrust oneself into the very workshop of the Almighty!"

By the gleam in Scarboro's eye hostilities threatened.

Drayton intervened. "Before we discuss the ultimate fate of the dust, Mr. Scarboro, won't you run over our own experience and explain a few little things? Now, in the first place you say that Andrew Power placed the powder on his tongue and disappeared! I am sure none of us even tried to taste the stuff."

"I said," corrected Scarboro, "that it must enter the system of a living creature! It is equally effective when breathed into the lungs. That is the way every one of you went. As to what you found, Ulithia is a place, or rather a condition, which is the one invariable prelude to every adventure I have had. Its phantasmagoria are well-nigh as fixed in their nature as what we please to call 'reality.' But of the character of its inhabitants or of the laws which govern its various phenomena, I can tell you but little.

"After living in this commonplace world of ours so many thousand centuries, mankind stands blank-faced before its greater mysteries. How can I, then, who have but one lifetime, and of that have spent but a small proportion in this other world, be expected to explain Ulithia? It is there. Every one present has seen it. We have seen its starry sky that is like our own sky; its sun that is not our sun; its moon that is a mystic gateway. While in our world the sun set once, you passed three days and two whole nights in Ulithia and the next inner world. Our astronomy is not theirs, however much it may resemble it in appearance. And we have all talked with Ulithia's ghostly, phantasmal inhabitants. Spirits? Demons? Elves? I do not know. That they are more familiar with our nature than we with theirs is certain. In Ulithia they recognize our alien passing. As the whim pleases them, they speed or hinder us. But, just as happened to all of you, one always does finally pass through there.

"What lies beyond varies. Those worlds are real. Their matter is solid while it lasts. But the form passes. 'The hills are shadows and they flow from form to form and nothing stands. They melt like mists, the solid lands; like clouds they shape themselves and go!' That was written of earth as we know it. How much better it applies to those inner, wilder realms!

"To one who knows the conditions, who has power to go and come at will, their perils are negligible; their wonder and delight inexhaustible. But 'woe to the stranger in the Hollow Lands!' You people were singularly fortunate. By a millionth chance, when the great Red Bell dissolved the astral vibrations, you were restored to your own. The distance which you had moved through space, even the direction was the same. In traversing Ulithia you actually traversed Philadelphia. When you went through the moon gate, you turned inward upon another plane and came back through the false city as if it were the real one. Thus, because your temple occupied the same space as the real city hall, it was there you finally found yourselves.

"That girl who returned with you came because she was temporarily in contact with a thing of this world—the Cerberus. When contact with that particular object ceased she went. I say 'she,' but she was nothing—a phantasm—the materialized figment of a dream. All those phantasmagoria which you met, touched, which might and would have slain you had not the Red Bell been one of them—they were the changing forms of a world which may be created and recreated in a single day.

"A prophecy of the actual future of this city and nation? Perhaps. More likely some one of the forces that rule there, for its own sardonic amusement, twisted the fluent astral matter into a distorted and mocking reflection of the real city. Oh, yes, there are forces there, as here, at whose nature we can only guess. Matter does not form or vivify itself, either in those worlds or in this.

"As to the general moral tone of your Philadelphia in the year A.D. 2118—pardon me—but that moral tone seems to have been a distinct reflection of your own. At least, you met guile with treachery, and the inference is not hard to draw!"

At this gratuitous and unexpected insult, Drayton flushed uncomfortably, Viola drew herself up with great dignity, and Trenmore rose from the table so violently that his chair crashed over.

"You old scalawag—"

Just here the door was flung open. There stood Martin, panting and stammering incoherently.

"What is it now?" demanded his employer.

"Is it Mr. Bertram, Martin?" queried Viola, turning quite pale. A vision had flashed up of the disconsolate burglar, lying in a pool of blood, slain by his own hand in excessive grief for the loss of his phantasmal sweetheart.

"Y-yes, ma'am! At least, I guess so. Was Mr. Bertram that other party that didn't want supper?"

By now Viola's fears had communicated themselves to her brother and Drayton. Without pausing, all three pushed past Martin and reached the library. Bertram's chair was empty. His body was nowhere in sight.

Trenmore turned on Martin. "Where is he, then?"

"I don't know, sir. I'm not saying anything against a guest of yours, Mr. Trenmore, but all I know is he went upstairs a while back and I just now went to your room, sir, to lay out your pajamas, and—and the safe's open, sir—and—"

But Trenmore waited for no more. He bounded up the stairs three steps at a time. Martin's tale proved only too true. The silk curtain was pushed back, the steel door in the wall swung wide, and the floor was as littered as that of the third-floor bedroom upon Drayton's first awakening in this much-burglarized house.

"The money," moaned Martin, wringing his hands. "All the money I saw you put in there yesterday—it's gone!"

Trenmore was rapidly running over the leather boxes, trays, and the like which were scattered about. He rose with a sigh of relief. "At least, he's taken nothing else. The money was only a couple of hundred that I can spare; but these trinkets of mine I could not easily replace."

"I don't believe it was Bertram," broke in Viola, with the eager loyalty of youth for one who has been, if not a friend, at least a companion. "He couldn't rob you, Terry, after all we've been through together!"

"What's this?" Drayton had picked up a folded scrap of paper from the dresser. "Why it's addressed to you, Terry!"

The Irishman took the paper, hastily opened it, and read:

"Dear Mr. Trenmore, I heard what Mr. Scarboro said. Skidoo wasn't anything. Then I ain't anything either. I was goin' to go straight but what's the use. I need this money worse than you. Goodby. B."

To the astonishment of all present, Trenmore's face suddenly cleared and with a whoop of joy he rushed toward the door.

"Moral tone, is it? Wait till I show this to the old scalawag below there. Now whom will he blame for the moral tone, when he reads this letter? And I never thought of Bertram, the thievin' little crook!"

Waving the missive triumphantly, he thundered down the stairs. Viola burst into almost hysterical laughter and Drayton was forced to laugh with her. "That shot of Scarboro's rankled," he said. "Let's go down and hear them argue it out."

In the dining room, however, yet another surprise awaited them. Terry was there, a picture of chagrin, but no Scarboro.

"The old villain skipped out," he said disgustedly, "while we were tearing about after the other scoundrel! And what's worse, he took the dust with him! Well, I'd not chase after either of them if 'twas to win me a kingdom."

Very thoughtfully the three made their way to the library. Drayton picked up the crystal vial which Trenmore had flung away. One of its silver heads was dented to a yet more savage expression. Otherwise the Cerberus was unharmed. He offered it to Trenmore, but his friend waved the vial aside.

"I don't want it," he said grimly. "Sure, Bobby my lad, I think I'll just give the thing to yourself and Viola for a wedding present—if you fear no ill luck from it."

"A wedding present!" stammered Drayton. "See here, Terry, I—Viola, child, I love you too well to marry you! You don't know of the disgrace into which I have fallen, nor, far worse, of the infamy of which I discovered myself capable. On the edge of death and in those strange surroundings, it didn't seem to matter so much; but we are back in a real world again and—and by heaven! I think for me the other was the better place!"

Viola went to him and with her two hands on his arm looked up into his face. "Bobby," she said, "I know what you mean. My brother told me of your sorrows and griefs, while we stood waiting for the examinations to begin, in the Green Room of the temple. He told me everything. Do you think I love you the less that you have suffered?"

"You don't understand" he said hoarsely. Somehow he held himself from taking her in his arms. He looked to Trenmore, but that large, discreet gentleman had wandered over to the window and was staring out into the night. Drayton choked. "You might as well marry that thief Bertram!" he forced out.

"Marry Bertram!" She laughed softly and hid the flush of her cheek against his coat. "Why, but so I would marry Bertram did I love him as I love you, Bobby, darling!"

No attempt to persuade him of his own moral innocence could have had the least effect. That last naive assertion, however, was too much for Drayton. His arms swept about her.

Trenmore, looking over his shoulder, grinned and hastily resumed his scrutiny of the empty pavement outside.

"And so," he murmured, "we'll just take our worlds as we find them, Bobby, my lad! And we'll see what can be done out there in Cincinnati. The scoundrels that downed him have gold. But I've gold myself. We'll give them a chance to down a fighting Irishman. And maybe—who knows?—there's a Red Bell hung for them, too, in the Dome of Justice. Aye, we'll go spy out the land and think well and then strike hard! The way they'll be wishing they'd crept in their holes and stayed there."

And with a smile of pleased anticipation for that Olympian battle he sniffed afar, Trenmore turned to the immediate and more difficult task of exerting his Celtic wit and eloquence to persuade Robert Drayton to let him undertake it.

THE END

1919

THE CURIOUS EXPERIENCE OF THOMAS DUNBAR (1904)

I came back into conscious existence with a sighing in my ears like the deep breathing of a great monster; it was everywhere, pervading space, filling my mind to the exclusion of thought.

Just a sound—regular, even soothing in its nature—but it seemed to bear some weird significance to my clouded brain. That was thought trying to force its way in.

Then waves and waves of whispering that washed all thought away—till I grasped again at some confused and wandering idea.

It was the definite sensation of a cool, firm hand laid on my brow that lifted me up at last through that surging ocean of sighs. As a diver from the depths I came up—up—and emerged suddenly, it seemed, into the world.

I opened my eyes wide and looked straight up into the face of a man. A man—but everything was swimming before my eyes, and at first his face seemed no more than part of a lingering dream.

And fantastic visions of the Orient! What a face! It was wrinkled as finely as the palm of a woman's hand, and in as many directions.

It was yellow in hue, and round like a baby's. And the eyes were narrow, and black, and they slanted, shining like a squirrel's.

I thought that of them at first; but sometimes when you just happened to look at him, they seemed to have widened and to be possessed of strange depths and hues.

In height he was not more than four feet five, and, of all contrasts, this little, weazened curiosity with the coun-tenance of a Chinese god was clad in the very careful and appropriate afternoon attire of a very careful and appropriate American gentleman!

The long sighing was still in my ears, but no longer at war with thought. I lay in a neat white bedstead in a plainly furnished room. I lifted my hand (it took an astonishing effort to do it), rubbed my eyes, and stared at the man who sat beside me.

His expression was kind, and in spite of its ugliness there was something in the strange face which encouraged me to friendliness.

"What—what's the matter with me?" I asked, and I was surprised to note the question was a mere whisper.

"Nothing now, except that you are very weak."

His voice was full, strong, and of a peculiar resonant quality. He spoke perfect English, with a kind of clear-cut clip to the words.

"You had an accident—an automobile went over you—but you're all right now, and don't need to think about it."

"What is it—that whispering noise? Are we near the sea?"

He smiled and shook his head. His smile merely accentuated the wrinkles—it could not multiply them.

"You are very near my laboratory—that is all. Here, drink this, and then you must rest."

I obeyed him meekly, like a child, weak of mind and body.

I wondered a little why I was with him instead of at a hospital or with friends, but I soon dropped off. I was really quite weak just then.

Yet before I slept I did ask one more question.

"Would you tell me—if you don't mind—your name?"

"Lawrence."

"Lawrence what?" I whispered. "Just——?"

"Yes," he smiled (and his face ran into a very tempest of wrinkles), "just Lawrence. No more."

Then I slept.

And I did little but sleep, and wake, and eat, and sleep again, for some five days. And during this time I learned marvelously little of my host and his manner of life.

Most questions he evaded cleverly, but he told me that it was his auto which had nearly ruined my earthly tenement; Lawrence had himself taken me from the scene of the accident without waiting for an ambulance, telling the police and bystanders that I was an acquaintance. He had carried me to his own house, because, he said, he felt somewhat responsible for my injuries and wanted to give me a better chance for my life than the doctors would allow me.

He seemed to be possessed of a great scorn for all doctors. I knew long after that he had studied the profession very thoroughly, and in many countries, and truly held the right to the title he contemptuously denied himself.

At the time I considered only that he had cured me up in wonderfully short order, considering the extent of the injuries I had received, and that I had suffered not at all. Therefore I was grateful.

Also he told me, on I forget what occasion, that his mother was a Japanese woman of very ancient descent, his father a scholarly and rather wealthy American. And for some eccentric reason of his own, his dwarfed son had chosen to eschew his family patronym and use merely his Christian name.

During the time I lay in bed I saw no servants; Lawrence did all things necessary. And never, day or night, did the humming and sighing of the machines cease.

Lawrence spoke vaguely of great dynamos, but on this subject, as on most others, he was very reticent. Frequently I saw him in the dress of a mechanic, for he would come in to see me at all hours of the day, and I imagine must have inconvenienced himself considerably for my welfare.

I had no particular friends to worry about my whereabouts, and so I lay quiet and at peace with the world for those five days in inert contentment.

Then an hour came—it was in the morning, and Lawrence had left me to go to his laboratory—when I became suddenly savagely impatient of the dull round. Weak though I was, I determined to dress and get out into the open air—out into the world.

Mind you, during those five days I had seen no face save that of my dwarfed host, heard no voice but his. And so my impatience overcame my good judgment and his counsels, and I declared to myself that I was well enough to join once more in the rush of life.

Slowly, and with trembling limbs that belied that assertion, I got into my clothes. Very slowly—though in foolish terror lest Lawrence should catch me putting aside his mandates—I hurried my toilet as best I could. At last I stood, clothed and in my right mind, as I told myself, though I had already begun to regret my sudden resolve.

I opened the door and looked into the bare, narrow ball. No one in sight, up or down.

I made my way, supporting myself, truth to tell, by the wall, toward a door at the far end, which stood slightly ajar.

I had almost reached it when I heard a terrible screaming. It was harsh, rough, tense with some awful agony, and to my startled senses preëminently human.

I stopped, shaking from head to foot with the shock. Then I flung myself on the door, from behind which the noise seemed to issue. It was not locked, and I plunged almost headlong into a great room, shadowy with whirring machinery under great arc lights.

Before a long table, loaded with retorts and the paraphernalia of the laboratory, stood Lawrence. His back was toward me, but he had turned his head angrily at my sudden entrance, and his queer, narrow eyes were blazing with annoyance.

In the room were two or three other men, evidently common mechanics, and none save Lawrence had more than glanced round. The screaming had ceased.

"Well?" his voice was little better than a snarl.

"That—that noise!" I gasped, already wondering if I had not made a fool of myself. "What was it?"

"Eh? Oh, that was nothing—the machinery—why are you——"

He was interrupted by a crash and splash from the far end of the place, followed by an exclamation of terror and horror, and a nice collection of French and English oaths from the men.

Lawrence had been holding in his hand while he spoke to me what looked like a peculiar piece of metal. It was cylindrical in shape, and little shades of color played over its surface continually.

Now he thrust this into my hands with a muttered injunction to be careful of it, and rushed off to the scene of the catastrophe. I followed him, at my best pace, with the thing in my hand.

At the end of the room were two immense vats of enameled iron, their edges flush with the floor, half filled with some livid, seething acid mixture, through which little currents writhed and wriggled.

The farther side of the largest vat sloped up at an angle of about thirty degrees, a smooth, slimy slide of zinc about ten feet from top to bottom and extending the full length of the vat.

The surface of this slide was covered to about half an inch in thickness with some kind of yellowish paste, whose ultimate destination was the mixture in the vat.

Above towered an engine of many wheels and pistons, and this operated two great pestles or stamps, slant-faced to fit the slide; these, running from one end of the zinc to the other, worked the paste with a grinding motion, as an artist mixes his paints with a palette knife.

The grinding motion was quite swift, but the lateral movement was comparatively slow. I should say that it must have taken about four minutes for the two stamps to pass from one end of the fifteen-foot vat to the other.

In the vat floated a plank. On the surface of the slide, almost in the middle, sprawled a man, his arms spread out on either side, not daring to move an inch on the slippery paste, for the slightest motion meant a slip downward into the hissing acid.

Worst of all, there seemed to be no means of getting across to him. The great engine occupied one side entirely to the wall—on the other the second vat barred passage.

Beyond the vats the room extended some little distance, and there was a door there, open, through which one could see a fenced yard piled high with ashes and cinders.

And the great stamps, twenty cubic feet of solid metal in each, were making their inevitable way toward the man. When they reached him—well, their smooth surface would afford him no finger hold, even if their rapid movement allowed him to clutch them. They must push him down—they might stun him first, but most certainly they would push him down.

I need hardly say that I did not take in the full significance of all this at the time—it was only afterward that I fully understood the details.

Even as Lawrence ran he shouted:

"Stop that engine! Quick, men!"

I saw two stalwart workmen spring at the levers of the stamp machine—saw them twisting at a wheel—heard another crash, and a deep groan from all! The guiding mechanism had slipped a cog, or broken a rod, or something.

In my excitement, shaking so from weakness that I could hardly stand, I had half fallen against a piece of machinery that seemed to be at a standstill. Unconsciously my fingers grasped at a sort of handle.

I heard a whirring noise, felt something like a tremendous shock, and a burning pain. I let go the handle in a hurry, just as Lawrence wheeled on me with the cry, "For God's sake, you fool——"

But I could give no heed either to what I had done or to him. My eyes were still fixed on the unfortunate man on the slide.

The stamps were not more than five feet from his body now, and their low rattle and swish sounded in my ears loud as the tread of an army.

"A rope!" cried Lawrence in despair.

And then, in my horror, and in the sheer impossibility of standing by quiescent and seeing a fellow-being done to death in this manner, I did a mad thing.

Wild with resentment, as if it were a living thing I could have fought, I flung myself on the great, swiftly revolving fly-wheel of the engine, seized its rim in my fingers, and braced back with all the force in my arms and shoulders.

By all precedent and reason my hands should have been crushed to a jelly in the maze of machinery, but to my intense astonishment the wheel stopped under my grasp with no very great effort on my part.

For a moment I held it so (it seemed to me to pull with no more force than is in the arms of a child), and then there was a loud report somewhere within the intestines of the monster, I saw a guiding rod as thick as my wrist double up and twist like a wire cable, things generally went to smash inside the engine, and the stamps stopped—not three inches from the man's head!

And even as they ceased to grind, men came running in at the door on the farther side of the vats—they had had to go clean round the work-shop to reach it—and were at the top of the slide with a rope which they let down.

In a moment the fellow was drawn to safety out of the reach of as horrible a death as a man can die—death in a bath consisting largely of sulphuric acid!

I stood as one in a stupor, still grasping the eccentric, dazed by the suddenness of it all—hardly able to believe that the danger was over.

A touch on my shoulder roused me, and I turned to look down into the narrow eyes of Lawrence. He was gazing at me with something very like awe in his expression.

"Well," I said, smiling shakily, "I'm afraid I've spoiled your engine."

"Spoiled the engine!" he said slowly, but emphatically. "What kind of a man are you, Mr. Dunbar? Do you know that that is a three hundred horse-power Danbury stamp? That the force required to stop that wheel in the way you did would run a locomotive—pick up the whole mass of that engine itself as easily as I would a pound weight?"

"It stopped very easily," I muttered.

For some ridiculous reason I felt a little ashamed—as if such an exhibition of strength were really a trifle indecent. And I couldn't understand.

Of course, I thought, he exaggerated the power used, but though I am naturally quite strong, still I could, before my accident, boast of nothing abnormal—and was I not just up from a sick bed, only a moment ago barely able to stand or walk without support?

I found that I was nervously clenching and unclenching my hands, and became suddenly conscious that they felt as if they had been burned—the minute I began to think about it the pain became really excruciating.

I glanced at them. They were in a terrible condition—especially my right. They looked as if they had been clasped about a piece of red-hot iron.

"What is it?" asked Lawrence quickly. He bent over my hands, peering at them with his little black eyes.

Then he looked up quickly, and I saw the dawning of a curious expression in his wrinkled face—a strange excitement, a pale flash of triumph, I could have sworn.

Then, "Where is it?" he cried imperatively, his voice sharp and strenuous. "What have you done with it?"

He dropped my hands and fell quickly to his knees on the floor, his head bent, and began searching—feeling about in the shadows of the engines.

"Here—you there!" he cried to one of the men. "A light here! God! If it should be lost now—after all these years—all these years!"

"What?" said I stupidly.

"The new element," he cried impatiently. "Stellarite, I call it. Oh"—glancing up quickly—"of course you don't know. That little piece of metal I gave you to hold—the iridescent cylinder—don't you remember?"

He spoke irritably, as if it was almost impossible for him to restrain himself to civil language.

"Oh, yes—that." I looked around vaguely. "Why, yes, I had it in my hand—of course. I must have dropped it when I grabbed the fly-wheel. It's on the floor somewhere probably; but, if you don't mind, could I have something for my hands? They hurt pretty badly."

Indeed, the air was full of black, swimming dots before my eyes, and iridescent cylinders had very little interest for me just then.

He almost snapped at me.

"Wait! If it's lost—but it couldn't be. Ah, the light at last. Now we can see something."

Still he was hunting, and now the men were helping him. I looked on dully.

Then an unreasonable anger seized me at their neglect —their indifference to my very real agony. I leaned forward, and, in spite of the added pain the raw flesh of my hand gave me, I took hold of Lawrence's collar and started to shake him.

He felt curiously light—rather like a piece of cork, in fact. I picked him up from the ground as you would a kitten and held him at arm's length.

Then suddenly I realized that what I was doing was somewhat unusual, and let go of his collar. He lit on his feet like a cat.

I expected anger, but he only said impatiently, "Don't do that—help me hunt, can't you?" quite as if it were an ordinary incident.

The queerness of it all came over me in full force; I felt as if I were in a dream.

I stooped down and helped him search. But it was no use. The little cylinder of stellarite seemed to have disappeared.

Suddenly Lawrence rose to his feet, his face, whose multitudinous wrinkles had a moment before been twitching with mingled triumph and despair, wiped clean of emotion, like a blank slate from which all significance has been erased.

"Come, Mr. Dunbar," he said quietly, "it is quite time those hands of yours were seen to. You, Johnson, Duquirke, go on hunting. But I'm afraid it's no use, boys. That vat of acid is too near."

"You think——"

"I'm afraid it rolled in," he said.

I was silent, dimly conscious that I stood, as it were, just inside the ring of some great catastrophe whose influence, barely reaching me, had this little wrinkled man in the grip of its vortex.

I followed him to a small office, opening off the laboratory; fitted up much like a doctor's, it was, with its cabinet of shining instruments. He explained its convenience while he bound up my hands with all the skilled gentleness of an experienced surgeon.

"Accidents are always on view in such a place as mine out there," he observed, with a nod of his head toward the laboratory.

"I wish you'd tell me what I've done," I said at last when the thing was over.

I felt no weakness, nor any desire for rest, which was odd, seeing the excitement I had been through and my recent illness.

"Two things, then, to be brief," he replied, smiling rather sadly, I thought. "You've accidentally stumbled on a magnificent fact, and you've at the same time destroyed, I fear, all results that might have flowed from that fact."

I stared at him, puzzled.

"You lifted me just now like a feather," he said abruptly. "You think, possibly, that I don't weigh much—I'm not a giant. Duquirke," he called, "come here a minute, will you, please?"

Duquirke appeared, a very mountain of man, all muscle, too. I am up to the six-foot mark myself, and fairly broad in the shoulders, but this fellow could better me by three good inches in any direction.

"You can't use your hands, of course," said Lawrence to me; "but just stoop down and stretch out your arm, will you? Now, Duquirke, just seat yourself on his arm. That's it. Oh, don't be afraid—he can hold you all right. Ah, I thought so!"

We had both obeyed him, I in some doubt, the Canadian with stolid indifference. But what was my amazement to find that this great big man weighed really comparatively nothing.

I rose, still with my arm outstretched, with perfect ease, and there the fellow sat, perched precariously, his mouth open, his eyes fixed on his master in almost a dog-like appeal.

"What are you all made of?" I gasped. "Cork?"

I let my arm drop, really expecting to see the man fall light as a feather—instead of which he tumbled with a crash that shook the house, and lay for a minute, swearing violently.

Then he got to his feet in a hurry and backed out of the door, his eyes on me to the last, his tongue, really unconsciously I believe, letting go a string of such language as would have done credit to a canal-boat driver.

"What is the matter with you all," I cried, "or"—my voice sank with the thought—"with me?"

"Sit down," said Lawrence. "Don't lose your head."

His eyes had widened, and the strange colors I had sometimes caught a glimpse of were blazing in their depths. His wrinkled face was almost beautiful in its animation—lighted as by a fire from within.

"There's nothing at all astonishing or miraculous about any of it—it's the simple working of a law. Now listen. When we heard La Due fall (the fool had tried to walk across a plank laid over that death trap to save going round the shop—he was well repaid by the fright), I handed you the cylinder of stellarite. I did not lay it on my work-table, because that is made of aluminum, and this cylinder must not come into contact with any other metal, for the simple reason that stellarite has such an affiliation for all other metals that for it to touch one of them means absorption into it. All its separate molecules interpenetrate, or assimilate, molecules, and—stellarite ceases to have its 'individual being.' So I gave it to you, because I wanted my hands free, and ran down to the vats with you at my heels. I confess I would never have been so careless if I had not allowed myself to become unduly excited by a mere matter of life and death."

He paused regretfully.

"However, to continue, you for some reason seized hold of the lever of a dynamo of very great voltage and started the armatage revolving, at the same time stepping on to the plate of its base. Now, in the ordinary course of things you would probably be at this moment lying on that couch over there—dead!"

I looked at the couch with sudden interest.

"But you are not."

I murmured that such was indeed the case.

"No—instead of that thunderbolt burning the life out of you, like that"—he snapped his fingers melodramatically—"it passed directly through your body into the cylinder of stellarite, which, completing the circuit, sent the current back through your chest, but possessed of a new quality."

"And that quality?"

"Ah, there you have me! What that quality was I fear it is now too late for the world ever to know. Well, you dropped the lever, and, I think, the cylinder, too, when I shouted. A moment after you seized the flywheel of the stamp machine, stopped it as if it had been the balance of a watch—and, well incidentally you saved La Due's life."

He ceased, the light faded out of his wrinkled face, his eyes darkened and narrowed. His head sank forward onto his chest.

"But to think of it—years—years of effort thrown away just at the moment of conquest!"

"I don't understand," I said, seeming to catch little glimpses of his full meaning, as through a torn veil. "Do you intend to say—"

"I intend to say," he snapped, with a sudden return of irritability, "that in that minute when you held the stellarite and the lever of the dynamo you absorbed enough of the life principle to vivify a herd of elephants. Why, what is strength, man? Is a muscle strong in itself? Can a mere muscle lift so much as a pin? It's the life principle, I tell you—and I had it under my hand!"

"But this stellarite," I protested. "You can make more, surely?"

"Make!" he scoffed. "It's an element, I say! And it was, so far as I know, all there was in all the world!"

"Maybe it will be found yet," I argued. "Or—if it went into the acid vat, would it have been absorbed by the metal—or what?"

"No—at the touch of that bath it would evaporate into thin air—an odorless, colorless gas. I have but one hope—that it rolled against some of the iron machinery and was absorbed. In that case I may be able to place it by the increased bulk of the assimilating metal. Well, I can but go to work again, test every particle of machinery in the vicinity of the vats—and work—and work. If I had but known before that it was electricity and animal magnetism that were needed to complete the combination—but now, it means years of patience at best."

He shook his head dismally.

"And I?" I mused, rather to myself than to him.

"Oh—you!" he smiled, and his face ran into that tempest of wrinkles. "You can pose as Samson, if you like! Your strength is really almost limitless!"

1904

FRIEND ISLAND
(1918)

It was upon the waterfront that I first met her, in one of the shabby little tea shops frequented by able sailoresses of the poorer type. The uptown, glittering resorts of the Lady Aviators' Union were not for such as she.

Stern of feature, bronzed by wind and sun, her age could only be guessed, but I surmised at once that in her I beheld a survivor of the age of turbines and oil engines—a true sea-woman of that elder time when woman's superiority to man had not been so long recognized. When, to emphasize their victory, women in all ranks were sterner than today's need demands.

The spruce, smiling young maidens—engine-women and stokers of the great aluminum rollers, but despite their profession, very neat in gold-braided blue knickers and boleros—these looked askance at the hard-faced relic of a harsher day, as they passed in and out of the shop.

I, however, brazenly ignoring similar glances at myself, a mere male intruding on the haunts of the world's ruling sex, drew a chair up beside the veteran. I ordered a full pot of tea, two cups and a plate of macaroons, and put on my most ingratiating air. Possibly my unconcealed admiration and interest were wiles not exercised in vain. Or the macaroons and tea, both excellent, may have loosened the old sea-woman's tongue. At any rate, under cautious questioning, she had soon launched upon a series of reminiscences well beyond my hopes for color and variety.

"When I was a lass," quoth the sea-woman, after a time, "there was none of this high-flying, gilt-edged, leatherstocking luxury about the sea. We sailed by the power of our oil and gasoline. If they failed on us, like as not 'twas the rubber ring and the rolling wave for ours."

She referred to the archaic practice of placing a pneumatic affair called a life-preserver beneath the arms, in case of that dreaded disaster, now so unheard of, shipwreck.

"In them days there was still many a man bold enough to join our crews. And I've knowed cases," she added condescendingly, "where just by the muscle and brawn of such men some poor sailor lass has reached shore alive that would have fed the sharks without 'em. Oh, I ain't so down on men as you might think. It's the spoiling of them that I don't hold with. There's too much preached nowadays that man is fit for nothing but to fetch and carry and do nurse-work in big child-homes. To my mind, a man who hasn't the nerve of a woman ain't fitted to father children, let alone raise 'em. But that's not here nor there. My time's past, and I know it, or I wouldn't be setting here gossipin' to you, my lad, over an empty teapot."

I took the hint, and with our cups replenished, she bit thoughtfully into her fourteenth macaroon and continued.

"There's one voyage I'm not likely to forget, though I live to be as old as Cap'n Mary Barnacle, of the *Shouter*. 'Twas aboard the old *Shouter* that this here voyage occurred, and it was her last and likewise Cap'n Mary's. Cap'n Mary, she was then that decrepit, it seemed a mercy that she should go to her rest, and in good salt water at that.

"I remember the voyage for Cap'n Mary's sake, but most I remember it because 'twas then that I come the nighest in my life to committin' matrimony. For a man, the man had nerve; he was nearer bein' companionable than any other man I ever seed; and if it hadn't been for just one little event that showed up the—the mannishness of him, in a way I couldn't abide, I reckon he'd be keepin' house for me this minute.

"We cleared from Frisco with a cargo of silkateen petticoats for Brisbane. Cap'n Mary was always strong on petticoats. Leather breeches or even half-skirts would ha' paid far better, they being more in demand like, but Cap'n Mary was three-quarters owner, and says she, land women should buy petticoats, and if they didn't it wouldn't be the Lord's fault nor hers for not providing 'em.

"We cleared on a fine day, which is an all sign—or was, then when the weather and the seas o' God still counted in the trafficking of the humankind. Not two days out we met a whirling, mucking bouncer of a gale that well nigh threw the old *Shouter* a full point off her course in the first wallop. She was a stout craft, though. None of your featherweight, gas-lightened, paper-thin alloy shells, but toughened aluminum from stern to stern. Her turbine drove her through the combers at a forty-five knot clip, which named her a speedy craft for a freighter in them days.

"But this night, as we tore along through the creaming green billows, something unknown went 'way wrong down below.

"I was forward under the shelter of her long over-sloop, looking for a hairpin I'd dropped somewheres about that afternoon. It was a gold hairpin, and gold still being mighty scarce when I was a girl, a course I valued it. But suddenly I felt the old *Shouter* give a jump under my feet like a plane struck by a shell in full flight. Then she trembled all over for a full second, frightened like. Then, with the crash of doomsday ringing in my ears, I felt myself sailing through the air right into the teeth o' the shrieking gale, as near as I could judge. Down I come in the hollow of a monstrous big wave, and as my ears doused under I thought I heard a splash close by. Coming up, sure enough, there close by me was floating a new, patent, hermetic, thermo-ice-chest. Being as it was empty, and being as it was shut up air-tight, that ice-chest made as sweet a life-preserver as a woman could wish in such an hour. About ten foot by twelve, it floated high in the raging sea. Out on its top I scrambled, and hanging on by a handle I looked expectant for some of my poor fellow-women to come floating by. Which they never did, for the good reason that the *Shouter* had blowed up and went below, petticoats, Cap'n Mary and all."

"What caused the explosion?" I inquired.

"The Lord and Cap'n Mary Barnacle can explain," she answered piously. "Besides the oil for her turbines, she carried a power of gasoline for her alternative engines, and likely 'twas the cause of her ending so sudden like. Anyways, all I ever seen of her again was the empty ice-chest that Providence had well-nigh hove upon my head. On that I sat and floated, and floated and sat some more, till by-and-by the storm sort of blowed itself out, the sun come shining—this was next morning—and I could dry my hair and look about me. I was a young lass, then, and not bad to look upon. I didn't want to die, any more than you that's sitting there this minute. So I up and prays for land. Sure enough toward evening a speck heaves up low down on the horizon. At first I took it for a gas liner, but later found it was just a little island, all alone by itself in the great Pacific Ocean.

"Come, now, here's luck, thinks I, and with that I deserts the ice-chest, which being empty, and me having no ice to put in it, not likely to have in them latitudes, is of no further use to me. Striking out I swum a mile or so and set foot on dry land for the first time in nigh three days.

"Pretty land it were, too, though bare of human life as an iceberg in the Arctic.

"I had landed on a shining white beach that run up to a grove of lovely, waving palm trees. Above them I could see the slopes of a hill so high and green it reminded me of my own old home, up near Couquomgomoc Lake in Maine. The whole place just seemed to smile and smile at me. The palms waved and bowed in the sweet breeze, like they wanted to say, 'Just set right down and make yourself to home. We've been waiting a long time for you to come.' I cried, I was that happy to be made welcome. I was a young lass then, and sensitive-like to how folks treated me. You're laughing now, but wait and see if or not there was sense to the way I felt.

"So I up and dries my clothes and my long, soft hair again, which was well worth drying, for I had far more of it than now. After that I walked along a piece, until there was a sweet little path meandering away into the wild woods.

"Here, thinks I, this looks like inhabitants. Be they civil or wild, I wonder? But after traveling the path a piece, lo and behold it ended sudden like in a wide circle of green grass, with a little spring of clear water. And the first thing I noticed was a slab of white board nailed to a palm tree close to the spring. Right off I took a long drink, for you better believe I was thirsty, and then I went to look at this board. It had evidently been tore off the side of a wooden packing box, and the letters was roughly printed in lead pencil.

"'Heaven help whoever you be,' I read. 'This island ain't just right. I'm going to swim for it. You better too. Good-by. Nelson Smith.' That's what it said, but the spellin' was simply awful. It all looked quite new and recent, as if Nelson Smith hadn't more than a few hours before he wrote and nailed it there.

"Well, after reading that queer warning I begun to shake all over like in a chill. Yes, I shook like I had the ague, though the hot tropic sun was burning down right on me and that alarming board. What had scared Nelson Smith so much that he had swum to get away? I looked all around real cautious and careful, but not a single frightening thing could I behold. And the palms and the green grass and the flowers still smiled that peaceful and friendly like. 'Just make yourself to home,' was wrote all over the place in plainer letters than those sprawly lead pencil ones on the board.

"Pretty soon, what with the quiet and all, the chill left me. Then I thought, 'Well, to be sure, this Smith person was just an ordinary man, I reckon, and likely he got nervous of being so alone. Likely he just fancied things which was really not. It's a pity he drowned himself before I come, though likely I'd have found him poor company. By his record I judge him a man of but common education.

"So I decided to make the most of my welcome, and that I did for weeks to come. Right near the spring was a cave, dry as a biscuit box, with a nice floor of white sand. Nelson had lived there too, for there was a litter of stuff—tin cans—empty—scraps of newspapers and the like. I got to calling him Nelson in my mind, and then Nelly, and wondering if he was dark or fair, and how he come to be cast away there all alone, and what was the strange events that drove him to his end. I cleaned out the cave, though. He had devoured all his tin-canned provisions, however he come by them, but this I didn't mind. That there island was a generous body. Green milk-coconuts, sweet berries, turtle eggs and the like was my daily fare.

"For about three weeks the sun shone every day, the birds sang and the monkeys chattered. We was all one big, happy family, and the more I explored that island the better I liked the company I was keeping. The land was about ten miles from beach to beach, and never a foot of it that wasn't sweet and clean as a private park.

"From the top of the hill I could see the ocean, miles and miles of blue water, with never a sign of a gas liner, or even a little government running-boat. Them running-boats used to go most everywhere to keep the seaways clean of derelicts and the like. But I knowed that if this island was no more than a hundred miles off the regular courses of navigation, it might be many a long day before

I'd be rescued. The top of the hill, as I found when first I climbed up there, was a wore-out crater. So I knowed that the island was one of them volcanic ones you run across so many of in the seas between Capricorn and Cancer.

"Here and there on the slopes and down through the jungly tree-growth, I would come on great lumps of rock, and these must have came up out of that crater long ago. If there was lava it was so old it had been covered up entire with green growing stuff. You couldn't have found it without a spade, which I didn't have nor want.

"Well, at first I was happy as the hours was long. I wandered and clambered and waded and swum, and combed my long hair on the beach, having fortunately not lost my side-combs nor the rest of my gold hairpins. But by-and-by it begun to get just a bit lonesome. Funny thing, that's a feeling that, once it starts, it gets worse and worser so quick it's perfectly surprising. And right then was when the days begun to get gloomy. We had a long, sickly hot spell, like I never seen before on an ocean island. There was dull clouds across the sun from morn to night. Even the little monkeys and parakeets, that had seemed so gay, moped and drowsed like they was sick. All one day I cried, and let the rain soak me through and through—that was the first rain we had—and I didn't get thorough dried even during the night, though I slept in my cave. Next morning I got up mad as thunder at myself and all the world.

"When I looked out the black clouds was billowing across the sky. I could hear nothing but great breakers roaring in on the beaches, and the wild wind raving through the lashing palms.

"As I stood there a nasty little wet monkey dropped from a branch almost on my head. I grabbed a pebble and slung it at him real vicious. 'Get away, you dirty little brute!' I shrieks, and with that there come a awful blinding flare of light. There was a long, crackling noise like a bunch of Chinese fireworks, and then a sound as if a whole fleet of Shouters had all went up together.

"When I come to, I found myself 'way in the back of my cave, trying to dig further into the rock with my finger nails. Upon taking thought, it come to me that what had occurred was just a lightning-clap, and going to look, sure enough there lay a big palm tree right across the glade. It was all busted and split open by the lightning, and the little monkey was under it, for I could see his tail and his hind legs sticking out.

"Now, when I set eyes on that poor, crushed little beast I'd been so mean to, I was terrible ashamed. I sat down on the smashed tree and considered and considered. How thankful I had ought to have been. Here I had a lovely, plenteous island, with food and water to my taste, when it might have been a barren, starvation rock that was my lot. And so, thinking, a sort of gradual peaceful feeling stole over me. I got cheerfuller and cheerfuller, till I could have sang and danced for joy.

"Pretty soon I realized that the sun was shining bright for the first time that week. The wind had stopped hollering, and the waves had died to just a singing murmur on the beach. It seemed kind o' strange, this sudden peace, like the cheer in my own heart after its rage and storm. I rose up, feeling sort of queer, and went to look if the little monkey had came alive again, though that was a fool thing, seeing he was laying all crushed up and very dead. I buried him under a tree root, and as I did it a conviction come to me.

"I didn't hardly question that conviction at all. Somehow, living there alone so long, perhaps my natural womanly intuition was stronger than ever before or since, and so I knowed. Then I went and pulled poor Nelson Smith's board off from the tree and tossed it away for the tide to carry off. That there board was an insult to my island!"

The sea-woman paused, and her eyes had a far-away look. It seemed as if I and perhaps even the macaroons and tea were quite forgotten.

"Why did you think that?" I asked, to bring her back. "How could an island be insulted?"

She started, passed her hand across her eyes, and hastily poured another cup of tea.

"Because," she said at last, poising a macaroon in midair, "because that island—that particular island that I had landed on—had a heart!

"When I was gay, it was bright and cheerful. It was glad when I come, and it treated me right until I got that grouchy it had to mope from sympathy. It loved me like a friend. When I flung a rock at that poor little drenched monkey critter, it backed up my act with an anger like the wrath o' God, and killed its own child to please me! But it got right cheery the minute I seen the wrongness of my ways. Nelson Smith had no business to say, 'This island ain't just right,' for it was a righter place than ever I seen elsewhere. When I cast away that lying board, all the birds begun to sing like mad. The green milk-coconuts fell right and left. Only the monkeys seemed kind o' sad like still, and no wonder. You see, their own mother, the island, had rounded on one o' them for my sake!

"After that I was right careful and considerate. I named the island Anita, not knowing her right name, or if she had any. Anita was a pretty name, and it sounded kind of South Sea like. Anita and me got along real well together from that day on. It was some strain to be always gay and singing around like a dear duck of a canary bird, but I done my best. Still, for all the love and gratitude I bore Anita, the company of an island, however sympathetic, ain't quite enough for a human being. I still got lonesome, and there was even days when I couldn't keep the clouds clear out of the sky, though I will say we had no more tornadoes.

"I think the island understood and tried to help me with all the bounty and good cheer the poor thing possessed. None the less my heart give a wonderful big leap when one day I seen a blot on the horizon. It drawed nearer and nearer, until at last I could make out its nature."

"A ship, of course," said I, "and were you rescued?"

"'Tweren't a ship, neither," denied the sea-woman somewhat impatiently. "Can't you let me spin this yarn without no more remarks and fool questions? This thing what was bearing down so fast with the incoming tide was neither more nor less than another island!

"You may well look startled. I was startled myself. Much more so than you, likely. I didn't know then what you, with your book-learning, very likely know now—that islands sometimes float. Their underparts being a tangled-up mess of roots and old vines that new stuff's growed over, they sometimes break away from the mainland in a brisk gale and go off for a voyage, calm as a old-fashioned, eight-funnel steamer. This one was uncommon large, being as much as two miles, maybe, from shore to shore. It had its palm trees and its live things, just like my own Anita, and I've sometimes wondered if this drifting piece hadn't really been a part of my island once—just its daughter like, as you might say.

"Be that, however, as it might be, no sooner did the floating piece get within hailing distance than I hears a human holler and there was a man dancing up and down on the shore like he was plumb crazy. Next minute he had plunged into the narrow strip of water between us and in a few minutes had swum to where I stood.

"Yes, of course it was none other than Nelson Smith!

"I knowed that the minute I set eyes on him. He had the very look of not having no better sense than the man what wrote that board and then nearly committed suicide trying to get away from the best island in all the oceans. Glad enough he was to get back, though, for the coconuts was running very short on the floater what had rescued him, and the turtle eggs wasn't worth mentioning. Being short of grub is the surest way I know to cure a man's fear of the unknown.

"Well, to make a long story short, Nelson Smith told me he was a aeronauter. In them days to be an aeronauter was not the same as to be an aviatress is now. There was dangers in the air, and dangers in the sea, and he had met

Friend Island (1918)

with both. His gas tank had leaked and he had dropped into the water close by Anita. A case or two of provisions was all he could save from the total wreck.

"Now, as you might guess, I was crazy enough to find out what had scared this Nelson Smith into trying to swim the Pacific. He told me a story that seemed to fit pretty well with mine, only when it come to the scary part he shut up like a clam, that aggravating way some men have. I give it up at last for just man-foolishness, and we begun to scheme to get away.

"Anita moped some while we talked it over. I realized how she must be feeling, so I explained to her that it was right needful for us to get with our kind again. If we stayed with her we should probably quarrel like cats, and maybe even kill each other out of pure human cussedness. She cheered up considerable after that, and even, I thought, got a little anxious to have us leave. At any rate, when we begun to provision up the little floater, which we had anchored to the big island by a cable of twisted bark, the green nuts fell all over the ground, and Nelson found more turtle nests in a day than I had in weeks.

"During them days I really got fond of Nelson Smith. He was a companionable body, and brave, or he wouldn't have been a professional aeronauter, a job that was rightly thought tough enough for a woman, let alone a man. Though he was not so well educated as me, at least he was quiet and modest about what he did know, not like some men, boasting most where there is least to brag of.

"Indeed, I misdoubt if Nelson and me would not have quit the sea and the air together and set up housekeeping in some quiet little town up in New England, maybe, after we had got away, if it had not been for what happened when we went. I never, let me say, was so deceived in any man before nor since. The thing taught me a lesson and I never was fooled again.

"We was all ready to go, and then one morning, like a parting gift from Anita, come a soft and favoring wind. Nelson and I run down the beach together, for we didn't want our floater to blow off and leave us. As we was running, our arms full of coconuts, Nelson Smith stubbed his bare toe on a sharp rock, and down he went. I hadn't noticed, and was going on.

"But sudden the ground begun to shake under my feet, and the air was full of a queer, grinding, groaning sound, like the very earth was in pain.

"I turned around sharp. There sat Nelson, holding his bleeding toe in both fists and giving vent to such awful words as no decent sea-going lady would ever speak nor hear to!

"'Stop it, stop it!' I shrieked at him, but 'twas too late.

"Island or no island, Anita was a lady, too! She had a gentle heart, but she knowed how to behave when she was insulted.

"With one terrible, great roar a spout of smoke and flame belched up out o' the heart of Anita's crater hill a full mile into the air!

"I guess Nelson stopped swearing. He couldn't have heard himself, anyways. Anita was talking now with tongues of flame and such roars as would have bespoke the raging protest of a continent.

"I grabbed that fool man by the hand and run him down to the water. We had to swim good and hard to catch up with our only hope, the floater. No bark rope could hold her against the stiff breeze that was now blowing, and she had broke her cable. By the time we scrambled aboard great rocks was falling right and left. We couldn't see each other for a while for the clouds of fine gray ash.

"It seemed like Anita was that mad she was flinging stones after us, and truly I believe that such was her intention. I didn't blame her, neither!

"Lucky for us the wind was strong and we was soon out of range.

"'So!' says I to Nelson, after I'd got most of the ashes out of my mouth, and shook my hair clear of cinders. 'So, that was the reason you up and left sudden when you was there before! You aggravated that island till the poor thing druv you out!'

"'Well,' says he, and not so meek as I'd have admired to see him, 'how could I know the darn island was a lady?'

"'Actions speak louder than words,' says I. 'You should have knowed it by her ladylike behavior!'

"'Is volcanoes and slingin' hot rocks ladylike?' he says. 'Is snakes ladylike? T'other time I cut my thumb on a tin can, I cussed a little bit. Say—just a li'l' bit! An' what comes at me out o' all the caves, and out o' every crack in the rocks, and out o' the very spring o' water where I'd been drinkin'? Why snakes! Snakes, if you please, big, little, green, red and sky-blue-scarlet! What'd I do? Jumped in the water, of course. Why wouldn't I? I'd ruther swim and drown than be stung or swallowed to death. But how was I t' know the snakes come outta the rocks because I cussed?'

"'You, couldn't,' I agrees, sarcastic. 'Some folks never knows a lady till she up and whangs 'em over the head with a brick. A real, gentle, kind-like warning, them snakes were, which you would not heed! Take shame to yourself, Nelly,' says I, right stern, 'that a decent little island like Anita can't associate with you peaceable, but you must hurt her sacredest feelings with language no lady would stand by to hear!'

"I never did see Anita again. She may have blew herself right out of the ocean in her just wrath at the vulgar, dis-gustin' language of Nelson Smith. I don't know. We was took off the floater at last, and I lost track of Nelson just as quick as I could when we was landed at Frisco.

"He had taught me a lesson. A man is just full of man-nishness, and the best of 'em ain't good enough for a lady to sacrifice her sensibilities to put up with.

"Nelson Smith, he seemed to feel real bad when he learned I was not for him, and then he apologized. But apologies weren't no use to me. I could never abide him, after the way he went and talked right in the presence of me and my poor, sweet lady friend, Anita!"

Now I am well versed in the lore of the sea in all ages. Through mists of time I have enviously eyed wild voyag-ings of sea rovers who roved and spun their yarns before the stronger sex came into its own, and ousted man from his heroic pedestal. I have followed—across the printed page—the wanderings of Odysseus. Before Gulliver I have burned the incense of tranced attention; and with reverent awe considered the history of one Munchausen, a baron. But alas, these were only men!

In what field is not woman our subtle superior?

Meekly I bowed my head, and when my eyes dared lift again, the ancient mariness had departed, leaving me to sorrow for my surpassed and outdone idols. Also with a bill for macaroons and tea of such incredible proportions that in comparison therewith I found it easy to believe her story!

1918

BEHIND THE CURTAIN (1918)

It was after nine o'clock when the bell rang, and descending to the dimly lighted hall I opened the front door, at first on the chain to be sure of my visitor. Seeing, as I had hoped, the face of our friend, Ralph Quentin, I took off the chain and he entered with a blast of sharp November air for company. I had to throw my weight upon the door to close it against the wind.

As he removed his hat and cloak he laughed good-humoredly.

"You're very cautious, Santallos. I thought you were about to demand a password before admitting me."

"It is well to be cautious," I retorted. "This house stands somewhat alone, and thieves are everywhere."

"It would require a thief of considerable muscle to make off with some of your treasures. That stone tomb-thing, for instance; what do you call it?"

"The Beni Hassan sarcophagus. Yes. But what of the gilded inner case, and what of the woman it contains? A thief of judgment and intelligence might covet that treasure and strive to deprive me of it. Don't you agree?"

He only laughed again, and counterfeited a shudder.

"The woman! Don't remind me that such a brown, shriveled, mummy-horror was ever a woman!"

"But she was. Doubtless in her day my poor Princess of Naarn was soft, appealing; a creature of red, moist lips and eyes like stars in the black Egyptian sky. 'The Song-stress of the House' she was called, ere she became Ta-Nezem the Osirian. But I keep you standing here in the cold hall. Come upstairs with me. Did I tell you that Beatrice is not here tonight?"

"No?" His intonation expressed surprise and frank disappointment. "Then I can't say good-by to her? Didn't you receive my note? I'm to take Sanderson's place as manager of the sales department in Chicago, and I'm off tomorrow morning."

"Congratulations. Yes, we had your note, but Beatrice was given an opportunity to join some friends on a Southern trip. The notice was short, but of late she has not been so well and I urged her to go. This November air is cruelly damp and bitter."

"What was it—a yachting cruise?"

"A long cruise. She left this afternoon. I have been sitting in her boudoir, Quentin, thinking of her, and I'll tell you about it there—if you don't mind?"

"Wherever you like," he conceded, though in a tone of some surprise. I suppose he had not credited me with so much sentiment, or thought it odd that I should wish to share it with another, even so good a friend as he. "You must find it fearfully lonesome here without Bee," he continued.

"A trifle." We were ascending the dark stairs now. "After tonight, however, things will be quite different. Do you know that I have sold the house?"

"No! Why, you are full of astonishments, old chap. Found a better place with more space for your tear-jars and tombstones?"

He meant, I assumed, a witty reference to my collection of Coptic and Egyptian treasures, well and dearly bought, but so much trash to a man of Quentin's youth and temperament.

I opened the door of my wife's boudoir, and it was pleasant to pass into such rosy light and warmth out of the stern, dark cold of the hall. Yet it was an old house, full of unexpected drafts. Even here there was a draft so strong that a heavy velour curtain at the far side of the room continually rippled and billowed out, like a loose rose-colored sail. Never far enough, though, to show what was behind it.

My friend settled himself on the frail little chair that stood before my wife's dressing-table. It was the kind of chair that women love and most men loathe, but Quentin, for all his weight and stature, had a touch of the feminine about him, or perhaps of the feline. Like a cat, he moved delicately. He was blond and tall, with fine, regular features, a ready laugh, and the clean charm of youth about him—also its occasional blundering candor.

As I looked at him sitting there, graceful, at ease, I wished that his mind might have shared the litheness of his body. He could have understood me so much better.

"I have indeed found a place for my collections," I observed, seating myself near by. "In fact, with a single exception—the Ta-Nezem sarcophagus—the entire lot is going to the dealers." Seeing his expression of astonished disbelief I continued: "The truth is, my dear Quentin, that I have been guilty of gross injustice to our Beatrice. I have been too good a collector and too neglectful a husband. My 'tear-jars and tombstones,' in fact, have enjoyed an attention that might better have been elsewhere bestowed. Yes, Beatrice has left me alone, but the instant that some few last affairs are settled I intend rejoining her.

And you yourself are leaving. At least, none of us three will be left to miss the others' friendship."

"You are quite surprising tonight, Santallos. But, by Jove, I'm not sorry to hear any of it! It's not my place to criticize, and Bee's not the sort to complain. But living here in this lonely old barn of a house, doing all her own work, practically deserted by her friends, must have been—"

"Hard, very hard," I interrupted him softly, "for one so young and lovely as our Beatrice. But if I have been blind at least the awakening has come. You should have seen her face when she heard the news. It was wonderful. We were standing, just she and I, in the midst of my tear-jars and tombstones—my 'chamber of horrors' she named it. You are so apt at amusing phrases, both of you. We stood beside the great stone sarcophagus from the Necropolis of Beni Hassan. Across the trestles beneath it lay the gilded inner case wherein Ta-Nezem the Osirian had slept out so many centuries. You know its appearance. A thing of beautiful, gleaming lines, like the quaint, smiling image of a golden woman.

"Then I lifted the lid and showed Beatrice that the one-time songstress, the handmaiden of Amen, slept there no more, and the case was empty. You know, too, that Beatrice never liked my princess. For a jest she used to declare that she was jealous. Jealous of a woman dead and ugly so many thousand years! Or—but that was only in anger—that I had bought Ta-Nezem with what would have given her, Beatrice, all the pleasure she lacked in life. Oh, she was not too patient to reproach me, Quentin, but only in anger and hot blood.

"So I showed her the empty case, and I said, 'Beloved wife, never again need you be jealous of Ta-Nezem. All that is in this room save her and her belongings I have sold, but her I could not bear to sell. That which I love, no man else shall share or own. So I have destroyed her. I have rent her body to brown, aromatic shreds. I have burned her; it is as if she had never been. And now, dearest of the dear, you shall take for your own all the care, all the keeping that heretofore I have lavished upon the Princess of Naam.'

"Beatrice turned from the empty case as if she could scarcely believe her hearing, but when she saw by the look in my eyes that I meant exactly what I said, neither more nor less, you should have seen her face, my dear Quentin—you should have seen her face!"

"I can imagine." He laughed, rather shortly. For some reason my guest seemed increasingly ill at ease, and glanced continually about the little rose-and-white room that was the one luxurious, thoroughly feminine corner—that and the cold, dark room behind the curtain—in what he had justly called my "barn of a house."

"Santallos," he continued abruptly, and I thought rather rudely, "you should have a portrait done as you look tonight. You might have posed for one of those stern old hidalgos of—which painter was it who did so many Spanish dons and donesses?"

"You perhaps mean Velasquez," I answered with mild courtesy, though secretly and as always his crude personalities displeased me. "My father, you may recall, was of Cordova in southern Spain. But—must you go so soon?

First drink one glass with me to our missing Beatrice. See how I was warming my blood against the wind that blows in, even here. The wine is Amontillado, some that was sent me by a friend of my father's from the very vineyards where the grapes were grown and pressed. And for many years it has ripened since it came here. Before she went, Beatrice drank of it from one of these same glasses. True wine of Montilla! See how it lives—like fire in amber, with a glimmer of blood behind it."

I held high the decanter and the light gleamed through it upon his face.

"Amontillado! Isn't that a kind of sherry? I'm no connoisseur of wines, as you know. But—Amontillado."

For a moment he studied the wine I had given him, liquid flame in the crystal glass. Then his face cleared.

"I remember the association now. 'The Cask of Amontillado.' Ever read the story?"

"I seem to recall it dimly."

"Horrible, fascinating sort of a yarn. A fellow takes his trustful friend down into the cellars to sample some wine, traps him and walls him up in a niche. Buries him alive, you understand. Read it when I was a youngster, and it made a deep impression, partly, I think, because I couldn't for the life of me comprehend a nature—even an Italian nature—desiring so horrible a form of vengeance. You're half Latin yourself, Santallos. Can you elucidate?"

"I doubt if you would ever understand," I responded slowly, wondering how even Quentin could be so crude, so tactless. "Such a revenge might have its merits, since the offender would be a long time dying. But merely to kill seems to me so pitifully inadequate. Now I, if I were driven to revenge, should never be contented by killing. I should wish to follow."

"What—beyond the grave?"

I laughed. "Why not? Wouldn't that be the very apotheosis of hatred? I'm trying to interpret the Latin nature, as you asked me to do."

"Confound you, for an instant I thought you were serious. The way you said it made me actually shiver!"

"Yes," I observed, "or perhaps it was the draft. See, Quentin, how that curtain billows out."

His eyes followed my glance. Continually the heavy, rose-colored curtain that wag hung before the door of my wife's bedroom bulged outward, shook and quivered like a bellying sail, as draperies will with a wind behind them.

His eyes strayed from the curtain, met mine and fell again to the wine in his glass. Suddenly he drained it, not as would a man who was a judge of wines, but hastily, indifferently, without thought for its flavor or bouquet. I raised my glass in the toast he had forgotten.

"To our Beatrice," I said, and drained mine also, though with more appreciation.

"To Beatrice—of course." He looked at the bottom of his empty glass, then before I could offer to refill it, rose from his chair.

"I must go, old man. When you write to Bee, tell her I'm sorry to have missed her."

"Before she could receive a letter from me I shall be with her—I hope. How cold the house is tonight, and the wind breathes everywhere. See how the curtain blows, Quentin."

"So it does." He set his glass on the tray beside the decanter. Upon first entering the room he had been smiling, but now his straight, fine brows were drawn in a perpetual, troubled frown, his eyes looked here and there, and would never meet mine—which were steady. "There's a wind," he added, "that blows along this wall—curious. One can't notice any draft there, either. But it must blow there, and of course the curtain billows out."

"Yes," I said. "Of course it billows out."

"Or is there another door behind that curtain?"

His careful ignorance of what any fool might infer from mere appearance brought an involuntary smile to my lips. Nevertheless, I answered him.

"Yes, of course there is a door. An open door."

His frown deepened. My true and simple replies appeared to cause him a certain irritation.

"As I feel now," I added, "even to cross the room would be an effort. I am tired and weak tonight. As Beatrice once said, my strength beside yours is as a child's to that of a grown man. Won't you close that door for me, dear friend?"

"Why—yes, I will. I didn't know you were ill. If that's the case, you shouldn't be alone in this empty house. Shall I stay with you for a while?"

As he spoke he walked across the room. His hand was on the curtain, but before it could be drawn aside my voice checked him.

"Quentin," I said, "are even you quite strong enough to close that door?"

Looking back at me, chin on shoulder, his face appeared scarcely familiar, so drawn was it in lines of bewilderment and half-suspicion.

"What do you mean? You are very odd tonight. Is the door so heavy then? What door is it?"

I made no reply.

As if against their owner's will his eyes fled from mine, he turned and hastily pushed aside the heavy drapery.

Behind it my wife's bedroom lay dark and cold, with windows open to the invading winds.

And erect in the doorway, uncovered, stood an ancient gilded coffin-case. It was the golden casket of Ta-Nezem, but its occupant was more beautiful than the poor, shriveled Songstress of Naam.

Bound across her bosom were the strange, quaint jewels which had been found in the sarcophagus. Ta-Nezem's amulets—heads of Hathor and Horus the sacred eye, the uraeus, even the heavy dull-green scarab, the amulet for purity of heart—there they rested upon the bosom of her who had been mistress of my house, now Beatrice the Osirian. Beneath them her white, stiff body was enwrapped in the same crackling dry, brown linen bands, impregnated with the gums and resins of embalmers dead these many thousand years, which had been about the body of Ta-Nezem.

Above the white translucence of her brow appeared the winged disk, emblem of Ra. The twining golden bodies of its supporting uraeii, its cobras of Egypt, were lost in the dusk of her hair, whose soft fineness yet lived and would live so much longer than the flesh of any of us three.

Yes, I had kept my word and given to Beatrice all that had been Ta-Nezem's, even to the sarcophagus itself, for in my will it was written that she be placed in it for final burial.

Like the fool he was, Quentin stood there, staring at the unclosed, frozen eyes of my Beatrice—and his. Stood till that which had been in the wine began to make itself felt. He faced me then, but with so absurd and childish a look of surprise that, despite the courtesy due a guest, I laughed and laughed.

I, too, felt warning throes, but to me the pain was no more than a gage—a measure of his sufferings stimulus to point the phrases in which I told him all I knew and had guessed of him and Beatrice, and thus drive home the jest.

But I had never thought that a man of Quentin's youth and strength could die so easily. Beatrice, frail though she was, had taken longer to die.

He could not even cross the room to stop my laughter, but at the first step stumbled, fell, and in a very little while lay at the foot of the gilded case.

After all, he was not so strong as I. Beatrice had seen. Her still, cold eyes saw all. How he lay there, his fine, lithe body contorted, worthless for any use till its substance should have been cast again in the melting-pot of dissolution, while I who had drunk of the same draft, suffered the same pangs, yet stood and found breath for mockery.

So I poured myself another glass of that good Cordovan wine, and I raised it to both of them and drained it, laughing.

"Quentin," I cried, "you asked what door, though your thought was that you had passed that way before, and feared that I guessed your knowledge. But there are doors and doors, dear, charming friend, and one that is heavier than any other. Close it if you can. Close it now in my face, who otherwise will follow even whither you have gone— the heavy, heavy door of the Osiris, Keeper of the House of Death!"

Thus I dreamed of doing and speaking. It was so vivid, the dream, that awakening in the darkness of my room I could scarcely believe that it had been other than reality. True, I lived, while in my dream I had shared the avenging poison. Yet my veins were still hot with the keen passion of triumph, and my eyes filled with the vision of Beatrice, dead—dead in Ta-Nezem's casket.

Unreasonably frightened, I sprang from bed, flung on a dressing-gown, and hurried out. Down the hallway I sped, swiftly and silently, at the end of it unlocked heavy doors with a tremulous hand, switched on lights, lights and more lights, till the great room of my collection was ablaze with them, and as my treasures sprang into view I sighed, like a man reaching home from a perilous journey.

The dream was a lie.

There, fronting me, stood the heavy empty sarcophagus; there on the trestles before it lay the gilded case, a thing of beautiful, gleaming lines, like the smiling image of a golden woman.

I stole across the room and softly, very softly, lifted the upper half of the beautiful lid, peering within. The dream indeed was a lie.

Happy as a comforted child I went to my room again. Across the hall the door of my wife's boudoir stood partly open.

In the room beyond a faint light was burning, and I could see the rose-colored curtain sway slightly to a draft from some open window.

Yesterday she had come to me and asked for her freedom. I had refused, knowing to whom she would turn, and hating him for his youth, and his crudeness and his secret scorn of me.

But had I done well? They were children, those two, and despite my dream I was certain that their foolish, youthful ideals had kept them from actual sin against my honor. But what if, time passing, they might change? Or, Quentin gone, my lovely Beatrice might favor another, young as he and not so scrupulous?

Every one, they say, has a streak of incipient madness. I recalled the frenzied act to which my dream jealousy had driven me. Perhaps it was a warning, the dream. What if my father's jealous blood should some day betray me, drive me to the insane destruction of her I held most dear and sacred.

I shuddered, then smiled at the swaying curtain. Beatrice was too beautiful for safety. She should have her freedom.

Let her mate with Ralph Quentin or whom she would, Ta-Nezem must rest secure in her gilded house of death. My brown, perfect, shriveled Princess of the Nile! Destroyed—rent to brown, aromatic shreds—burned—destroyed—and her beautiful coffin-case desecrated as I had seen it in my vision.

Again I shuddered, smiled and shook my head sadly at the swaying, rosy curtain.

"You are too lovely, Beatrice," I said, "and my father was a Spaniard. You shall have your freedom!"

I entered my room and lay down to sleep again, at peace and content.

The dream, thank God, was a lie.

1918

UNSEEN—
UNFEARED (1919)

I

I had been dining with my ever-interesting friend, Mark Jenkins, at a little Italian restaurant near South Street. It was a chance meeting. Jenkins is too busy, usually, to make dinner engagements. Over our highly seasoned food and sour, thin, red wine, he spoke of little odd incidents and adventures of his profession. Nothing very vital or important, of course. Jenkins is not the sort of detective who first detects and then pours the egotistical and revealing details of achievement in the ears of every acquaintance, however appreciative.

But when I spoke of something I had seen in the morning papers, he laughed. "Poor old 'Doc' Holt! Fascinating old codger, to any one who really knows him. I've had his friendship for years—since I was first on the city force and saved a young assistant of his from jail on a false charge. And they had to drag him into the poisoning of this young sport, Ralph Peeler!"

"Why are you so sure he couldn't have been implicated?" I asked.

But Jenkins only shook his head, with a quiet smile. "I have reasons for believing otherwise," was all I could get out of him on that score. "But," he added, "the only reason he was suspected at all is the superstitious dread of these ignorant people around him. Can't see why he lives in such a place. I know for a fact he doesn't have to. Doc's got money of his own. He's an amateur chemist and dabbler in different sorts of research work, and I suspect he's been guilty of 'showing off.' Result, they all swear he has the evil eye and holds forbidden communion with invisible powers. Smoke?"

Jenkins offered me one of his invariably good cigars, which I accepted, saying thoughtfully: "A man has no right to trifle with the superstitions of ignorant people. Sooner or later, it spells trouble."

"Did in his case. They swore up and down that he sold love charms openly and poisons secretly, and that, together with his living so near to—somebody else—got him temporarily suspected. But my tongue's running away with me, as usual!"

"As usual," I retorted impatiently, "you open up with all the frankness of a Chinese diplomat."

He beamed upon me engagingly and rose from the table, with a glance at his watch. "Sorry to leave you, Blais-dell, but I have to meet Jimmy Brennan in ten minutes."

He so clearly did not invite my further company that I remained seated for a little while after his departure; then took my own way homeward. Those streets always held for me a certain fascination, particularly at night. They are so unlike the rest of the city, so foreign in appearance, with their little shabby stores, always open until late evening, their unbelievably cheap goods, displayed as much outside the shops as in them, hung on the fronts and laid out on tables by the curb and in the street itself. To-night, how-ever, neither people nor stores in any sense appealed to me. The mixture of Italians, Jews and a few negroes, mostly bareheaded, unkempt and generally unhygienic in appear-ance, struck me as merely revolting. They were all humans, and I, too, was human. Some way I did not like the idea.

Puzzled a trifle, for I am more inclined to sympathize with poverty than accuse it, I watched the faces that I passed. Never before had I observed how stupid, how bestial, how brutal were the countenances of the dwellers in this region. I actually shuddered when an old-clothes man, a gray-bearded Hebrew, brushed me as he toiled past with his barrow.

There was a sense of evil in the air, a warning of things which it is wise for a clean man to shun and keep clear of. The impression became so strong that before I had walked two squares I began to feel physically ill. Then it occurred to me that the one glass of cheap Chianti I had drunk might have something to do with the feeling. Who knew how that stuff had been manufactured, or whether the juice of the grape entered at all into its ill-flavored composition? Yet I doubted if that were the real cause of my discomfort.

By nature I am rather a sensitive, impressionable sort of chap. In some way to-night this neighborhood, with its sordid sights and smells, had struck me wrong.

My sense of impending evil was merging into actual fear. This would never do. There is only one way to deal with an imaginative temperament like mine—conquer its vagaries. If I left South Street with this nameless dread upon me, I could never pass down it again without a recurrence of the feeling. I should simply have to stay here until I got the better of it—that was all.

I paused on a corner before a shabby but brightly lighted little drug store. Its gleaming windows and the luminous green of its conventional glass show jars made the brightest spot on the block. I realized that I was tired, but hardly wanted to go in there and rest. I knew what the company would be like at its shabby, sticky soda fountain. As I stood there, my eyes fell on a long white canvas sign across from me, and its black-and-red lettering caught my attention.

SEE THE GREAT UNSEEN!

Come in! This Means You!

Free to All!

A museum of fakes, I thought, but also reflected that if it were a show of some kind I could sit down for a while, rest, and fight off this increasing obsession of nonexistent evil. That side of the street was almost deserted, and the place itself might well be nearly empty.

II

I walked over, but with every step my sense of dread increased. Dread of I knew not what. Bodiless, inexplicable horror had me as in a net, whose strands, being intangible, without reason for existence, I could by no means throw off. It was not the people now. None of them were about me. There, in the open, lighted street, with no sight nor sound of terror to assail me, I was the shivering victim of such fear as I had never known was possible. Yet still I would not yield.

Setting my teeth, and fighting with myself as with some pet animal gone mad, I forced my steps to slowness and walked along the sidewalk, seeking entrance. Just here there were no shops, but several doors reached in each case by means of a few iron-railed stone steps. I chose the one in the middle beneath the sign. In that neighborhood there are museums, shops and other commercial enterprises conducted in many shabby old residences, such as were these. Behind the glazing of the door I had chosen I could see a dim, pinkish light, but on either side the windows were quite dark.

Trying the door, I found it unlocked. As I opened it a party of Italians passed on the pavement below and I looked back at them over my shoulder. They were gayly dressed, men, women and children, laughing and chattering to one another; probably on their way to some wedding or other festivity.

In passing, one of the men glanced up at me and involuntarily I shuddered back against the door. He was a young man, handsome after the swarthy manner of his race, but never in my life had I seen a face so expressive of pure, malicious cruelty, naked and unashamed. Our eyes met and his seemed to light up with a vile gleaming, as if all the wickedness of his nature had come to a focus in the look of concentrated hate he gave me.

They went by, but for some distance I could see him watching me, chin on shoulder, till he and his party were swallowed up in the crowd of marketers farther down the street.

Sick and trembling from that encounter, merely of eyes though it had been, I threw aside my partly smoked cigar and entered. Within there was a small vestibule, whose ancient tesselated floor was grimy with the passing of many feet. I could feel the grit of dirt under my shoes, and it rasped on my rawly quivering nerves. The inner door stood partly open, and going on I found myself in a bare, dirty hallway, and was greeted by the sour, musty, poverty-stricken smell common to dwellings of the very ill-to-do. Beyond there was a stairway, carpeted with ragged grass matting. A gas jet, turned low inside a very dusty pink globe, was the light I had seen from without.

Listening, the house seemed entirely silent. Surely, this was no place of public amusement of any kind whatever. More likely it was a rooming house, and I had, after all, mistaken the entrance.

To my intense relief, since coming inside, the worst agony of my unreasonable terror had passed away. If I could only get in some place where I could sit down and be quiet, probably I should be rid of it for good. Determining to try another entrance, I was about to leave the bare hallway when one of several doors along the side of it suddenly opened and a man stepped out into the hall.

"Well?" he said, looking at me keenly, but with not the least show of surprise at my presence.

"I beg your pardon," I replied. "The door was unlocked and I came in here, thinking it was the entrance to the exhibit—what do they call it?—the 'Great Unseen.' The one that is mentioned on that long white sign. Can you tell me which door is the right one?"

"I can."

With that brief answer he stopped and stared at me again. He was a tall, lean man, somewhat stooped, but possessing considerable dignity of bearing. For that neighborhood, he appeared uncommonly well dressed, and his long, smooth-shaven face was noticeable because, while his complexion was dark and his eyes coal-black, above them the heavy brows and his hair were almost silvery-white. His age might have been anything over the threescore mark.

I grew tired of being stared at. "If you can and—won't, then never mind," I observed a trifle irritably, and turned to go. But his sharp exclamation halted me.

"No!" he said. "No—no! Forgive me for pausing—it was not hesitation, I assure you. To think that one—one, even, has come! All day they pass my sign up there—pass and fear to enter. But you are different. *You* are not of these timorous, ignorant foreign peasants. You ask me to tell you the right door? Here it is! Here!"

And he struck the panel of the door, which he had closed behind him, so that the sharp yet hollow sound of it echoed up through the silent house.

Now it may be thought that after all my senseless terror in the open street, so strange a welcome from so odd a showman would have brought the feeling back, full force. But there is an emotion stronger, to a certain point, than fear. This queer old fellow aroused my curiosity. What kind of museum could it be that he accused the passing public of fearing to enter? Nothing really terrible, surely, or it would have been closed by the police. And normally I am not an unduly timorous person. "So, it's in there, is it?" I asked, coming toward him. "And I'm to be sole audience? Come, that will be an interesting experience." I was half laughing now.

"The most interesting in the world," said the old man, with a solemnity which rebuked my lightness.

With that he opened the door, passed inward and closed it again—in my very face. I stood staring at it blankly. The panels, I remember, had been originally painted white, but now the paint was flaked and blistered, gray with dirt and dirty finger marks. Suddenly it occurred to me that I had no wish to enter there. Whatever was behind it could be scarcely worth seeing, or he would not choose such a place for its exhibition. With the old man's vanishing my curiosity had cooled, but just as I again turned to leave, the door opened and this singular showman stuck his white-eyebrowed face through the aperture. He was frowning impatiently. "Come in—come in!" he snapped, and promptly withdrawing his head, once more closed the door.

"He has something in there he doesn't want should get out," was the very natural conclusion which I drew. "Well, since it can hardly be anything dangerous, and he's so anxious I should see it—here goes!"

With that I turned the soiled white porcelain handle, and entered.

The room I came into was neither very large nor very brightly lighted. In no way did it resemble a museum or lecture room. On the contrary, it seemed to have been fitted up as a quite well-appointed laboratory. The floor was linoleum-covered, there were glass cases along the walls whose shelves were filled with bottles, specimen jars, graduates, and the like. A large table in one corner bore what looked like some odd sort of camera, and a larger one in the middle of the room was fitted with a long rack filled with bottles and test tubes, and was besides littered with papers, glass slides, and various paraphernalia which my ignorance failed to identify. There were several cases of books, a few plain wooden chairs, and in the corner a large iron sink with running water.

My host of the white hair and black eyes was awaiting me, standing near the larger table. He indicated one of the wooden chairs with a thin forefinger that shook a little, either from age or eagerness. "Sit down—sit down! Have no fear but that you will be interested, my friend. Have no fear at all—of anything!"

As he said it he fixed his dark eyes upon me and stared harder than ever. But the effect of his words was the opposite of their meaning. I did sit down, because my knees gave under me, but if in the outer hall I had lost my terror, it now returned twofold upon me. Out there the light had been faint, dingily roseate, indefinite. By it I had not perceived how this old man's face was a mask of living malice—of cruelty, hate and a certain masterful contempt. Now I knew the meaning of my fear, whose warning I would not heed. Now I knew that I had walked into the very trap from which my abnormal sensitiveness had striven in vain to save me.

III

Again I struggled within me, bit at my lip till I tasted blood, and presently the blind paroxysm passed. It must have been longer in going than I thought, and the old man must have all that time been speaking, for when I could once more control my attention, hear and see him, he had taken up a position near the sink, about ten feet away, and was addressing me with a sort of "platform" manner, as if I had been the large audience whose absence he had deplored.

"And so," he was saying, "I was forced to make these plates very carefully, to truly represent the characteristic hues of each separate organism. Now, in color work of every kind the film is necessarily extremely sensitive. Doubtless you are familiar in a general way with the exquisite transparencies produced by color photography of the single-plate type."

He paused, and, trying to act like a normal human being, I observed: "I saw some nice landscapes done in that way—last week at an illustrated lecture in Franklin Hall."

He scowled, and made an impatient gesture at me with his hand. "I can proceed better without interruptions," he said. "My pause was purely oratorical."

I meekly subsided, and he went on in his original loud, clear voice. He would have made an excellent lecturer before a much larger audience—if only his voice could have lost that eerie, ringing note. Thinking of that I must have missed some more, and when I caught it again he was saying:

"As I have indicated, the original plate is the final picture. Now, many of these organisms are extremely hard to photograph, and microphotography in color is particularly difficult. In consequence, to spoil a plate tries the patience of the photographer. They are so sensitive that the ordinary darkroom ruby lamp would instantly ruin them, and they must therefore be developed either in darkness or by a special light produced by interposing thin sheets of tissue of a particular shade of green and of yellow between lamp and plate, and even that will often cause ruinous fog. Now I, finding it hard to handle them so, made numerous experiments with a view to discovering some glass or fabric of a color which should add to the safety of the green, without robbing it of all efficiency. All proved equally useless, but intermittently I persevered—until last week."

His voice dropped to an almost confidential tone, and he leaned slightly toward me. I was cold from my neck to my feet, though my head was burning, but I tried to force an appreciative smile.

"Last week," he continued impressively, "I had a prescription filled at the corner drug store. The bottle was sent home to me wrapped in a piece of what I at first took to be whitish, slightly opalescent paper. Later I decided that it was some kind of membrane. When I questioned the druggist, seeking its source, he said it was a sheet of 'paper' that was around a bundle of herbs from South America. That he had no more, and doubted if I could trace it. He had wrapped my bottle so, because he was in haste and the sheet was handy.

"I can hardly tell you what first inspired me to try that membrane in my photographic work. It was merely dull white with a faint hint of opalescence, except when held against the light. Then it became quite translucent and quite brightly prismatic. For some reason it occurred to me that this refractive effect might help in breaking up the actinic rays—the rays which affect the sensitive emulsion. So that night I inserted it behind the sheets of green and yellow tissue, next the lamp, prepared my trays and chemicals, laid my plate holders to hand, turned off the white light and—turned on the green!"

There was nothing in his words to inspire fear. It was a wearisomely detailed account of his struggles with photography. Yet, as he again paused impressively, I wished that he might never speak again. I was desperately, contemptibly in dread of the thing he might say next.

Suddenly he drew himself erect, the stoop went out of his shoulders, he threw back his head and laughed. It was a hollow sound, as if he laughed into a trumpet. "I won't tell you what I saw! Why should I? Your own eyes shall bear witness. But this much I'll say, so that you may better understand—later. When our poor, faultily sensitive vision can perceive a thing, we say that it is visible. When the nerves of touch can feel it, we say that it is tangible. Yet I tell you there are beings intangible to our physical sense, yet whose presence is felt by the spirit, and invisible to our eyes merely because those organs are not attuned to the light as reflected from their bodies. But light passed through the screen which we are about to use has a wave length novel to the scientific world, and by it you shall see with the eyes of the flesh that which has been invisible since life began. Have no fear!"

He stopped to laugh again, and his mirth was yellow-toothed—menacing.

"Have no fear!" he reiterated, and with that stretched his hand toward the wall, there came a click and we were in

black, impenetrable darkness. I wanted to spring up, to seek the door by which I had entered and rush out of it, but the paralysis of unreasoning terror held me fast.

I could hear him moving about in the darkness, and a moment later a faint green glimmer sprang up in the room. Its source was over the large sink, where I suppose he developed his precious "color plates."

Every instant, as my eyes became accustomed to the dimness, I could see more clearly. Green light is peculiar. It may be far fainter than red, and at the same time far more illuminating. The old man was standing beneath it, and his face by that ghastly radiance had the exact look of a dead man's. Beside this, however, I could observe nothing appalling.

"That," continued the man, "is the simple developing light of which I have spoken—now watch, for what you are about to behold no mortal man but myself has ever seen before."

For a moment he fussed with the green lamp over the sink. It was so constructed that all the direct rays struck downward. He opened a flap at the side, for a moment there was a streak of comforting white luminance from within, then he inserted something, slid it slowly in—and closed the flap.

The thing he put in—that South American "membrane" it must have been—instead of decreasing the light increased it—amazingly. The hue was changed from green to greenish-gray, and the whole room sprang into view, a livid, ghastly chamber, filled with—overcrawled by—what?

My eyes fixed themselves, fascinated, on something that moved by the old man's feet. It writhed there on the floor like a huge, repulsive starfish, an immense, armed, legged thing, that twisted convulsively. It was smooth, as if made of rubber, was whitish-green in color; and presently raised its great round blob of a body on tottering tentacles, crept toward my host and writhed upward—yes, climbed up his legs, his body. And he stood there, erect, arms folded, and stared sternly down at the thing which climbed.

But the room—the whole room was alive with other creatures than that. Everywhere I looked they were—centipedish things, with yard-long bodies, detestable, furry spiders that lurked in shadows, and sausage-shaped translucent horrors that moved—and floated through the air. They dived here and there between me and the light, and I could see its brighter greenness through their greenish bodies.

Worse, though, far worse than these were the *things with human faces*. Mask-like, monstrous, huge gaping mouths and slitlike eyes—I find I cannot write of them. There was that about them which makes their memory even now intolerable.

The old man was speaking again, and every word echoed in my brain like the ringing of a gong. "Fear nothing! Among such as these do you move every hour of the day and the night. Only you and I have seen, for God is merciful and has spared our race from sight. But I am not merciful! I loathe the race which gave these creatures birth—the race which might be so surrounded by invisible, unguessed but blessed beings—and chooses these for its companions! All the world shall see and know. One by one shall they come here, learn the truth, and perish. For who can survive the ultimate of terror? Then I, too, shall find peace, and leave the earth to its heritage of man-created horrors. Do you know what these are—whence they come?"

His voice boomed now like a cathedral bell. I could not answer him, but he waited for no reply. "Out of the ether—out of the omnipresent ether from whose intangible substance the mind of God made the planets, all living things, and man—man has made these! By his evil thoughts, by his selfish panics, by his lusts and his interminable, never-ending hate he has made them, and they are everywhere! Fear nothing—they cannot harm your body—but let your spirit beware! Fear nothing—but see where there comes to you, its creator, the shape and the body of your FEAR!"

And as he said it I perceived a great Thing coming toward me—a Thing—but consciousness could endure no more. The ringing, threatening voice merged in a roar within my ears, there came a merciful dimming of the terrible, lurid vision, and blank nothingness succeeded upon horror too great for bearing.

IV

There was a dull, heavy pain above my eyes. I knew that they were closed, that I was dreaming, and that the rack full of colored bottles which I seemed to see so clearly was no more than a part of the dream. There was some vague but imperative reason why I should rouse myself. I wanted to awaken, and thought that by staring very hard indeed I could dissolve this foolish vision of blue and yellow-brown bottles. But instead of dissolving they grew clearer, more solid and substantial of appearance, until suddenly the rest of my senses rushed to the support of sight, and I became aware that my eyes were open, the bottles were quite real, and that I was sitting in a chair, fallen sideways so that my cheek rested most uncomfortably on the table which held the rack.

I straightened up slowly and with difficulty, groping in my dulled brain for some clew to my presence in this unfamiliar place, this laboratory that was lighted only by the rays of an arc light in the street outside its three large windows. Here I sat, alone, and if the aching of cramped limbs meant anything, here I had sat for more than a little time.

Then, with the painful shock which accompanies awakening to the knowledge of some great catastrophe, came memory. It was this very room, shown by the street lamp's rays to be empty of life, which I had seen thronged with creatures too loathsome for description. I staggered to my feet, staring fearfully about. There were the glass-doored cases, the bookshelves, the two tables with their burdens, and the long iron sink above which, now only a dark blotch of shadow, hung the lamp from which had emanated that livid, terrifically revealing illumination. Then the experience had been no dream, but a frightful reality. I was alone here now. With callous indifference my strange host had allowed me to remain for hours unconscious, with not the least effort to aid or revive me. Perhaps, hating me so, he had hoped that I would die there.

At first I made no effort to leave the place. Its appearance filled me with reminiscent loathing. I longed to go, but as yet felt too weak and ill for the effort. Both mentally and physically my condition was deplorable, and for the first time I realized that a shock to the mind may react upon the body as vilely as any debauch of self-indulgence.

Quivering in every nerve and muscle, dizzy with headache and nausea, I dropped back into the chair, hoping that before the old man returned I might recover sufficient self-control to escape him. I knew that he hated me, and why. As I waited, sick, miserable, I understood the man. Shuddering, I recalled the loathsome horrors he had shown me. If the mere desires and emotions of mankind were daily carnified in such forms as those, no wonder that he viewed his fellow beings with detestation and longed only to destroy them.

I thought, too, of the cruel, sensuous faces I had seen in the streets outside—seen for the first time, as if a veil had been withdrawn from eyes hitherto blinded by self-delusion. Fatuously trustful as a month-old puppy, I had lived in a grim, evil world, where goodness is a word and crude selfishness the only actuality. Drearily my thoughts drifted back through my own life, its futile purposes, mistakes and activities. All of evil that I knew returned to overwhelm me. Our gropings toward divinity were a sham, a writhing sunward of slime-covered beasts who claimed sunlight as their heritage, but in their hearts preferred the foul and easy depths.

Even now, though I could neither see nor feel them, this room, the entire world, was acrawl with the beings created by our real natures. I recalled the cringing, contemptible fear to which my spirit had so readily yielded, and the faceless Thing to which the emotion had given birth.

Then abruptly, shockingly, I remembered that every moment I was adding to the horde. Since my mind could conceive only repulsive incubi, and since while I lived I must think, feel, and so continue to shape them, was there no way to check so abominable a succession? My eyes fell on the long shelves with their many-colored bottles. In the chemistry of photography there are deadly poisons—I knew that. Now was the time to end it—now! Let him return and find his desire accomplished. One good thing I could do, if one only. I could abolish my monster-creating self.

V

My friend Mark Jenkins is an intelligent and usually a very careful man. When he took from "Smiler" Callahan a cigar which had every appearance of being excellent, innocent Havana, the act denoted both intelligence and caution. By very clever work he had traced the poisoning of young Ralph Peeler to Mr. Callahan's door, and he believed this particular cigar to be the mate of one smoked by Peeler just previous to his demise. And if, upon arresting Callahan, he had not confiscated this bit of evidence, it would have doubtless been destroyed by its regrettably unconscientious owner.

But when Jenkins shortly afterward gave me that cigar, as one of his own, he committed one of those almost inconceivable blunders which, I think, are occasionally forced upon clever men to keep them from overweening vanity. Discovering his slight mistake, my detective friend spent the night searching for his unintended victim, myself, and that his search was successful was due to Pietro Marini, a young Italian of Jenkins' acquaintance, whom he met about the hour of two a.m. returning from a dance.

Now, Marini had seen me standing on the steps of the house where Doctor Frederick Holt had his laboratory and living rooms, and he had stared at me, not with any ill intent, because he thought I was the sickest-looking, most ghastly specimen of humanity that he had ever beheld. And, sharing the superstition of his South Street neighbors, he wondered if the worthy doctor had poisoned me as well as Peeler. This suspicion he imparted to Jenkins, who, however, had the best of reasons for believing otherwise. Moreover, as he informed Marini, Holt was dead, having drowned himself late the previous afternoon. An hour or so after our talk in the restaurant news of his suicide reached Jenkins.

It seemed wise to search any place where a very sick-looking young man had been seen to enter, so Jenkins came straight to the laboratory. Across the fronts of those houses was the long sign with its mysterious inscription, "See the Great Unseen," not at all mysterious to the detective. He knew that next door to Doctor Holt's the second floor had been thrown together into a lecture room, where at certain hours a young man employed by settle-ment workers displayed upon a screen stereopticon views of various deadly bacilli, the germs of diseases appropri-ate to dirt and indifference. He knew, too, that Doctor Holt himself had helped the educational effort along by providing some really wonderful lantern slides, done by micro-color photography.

On the pavement outside, Jenkins found the two-thirds remnant of a cigar, which he gathered in and came up the steps, a very miserable and self-reproachful detec-tive. Neither outer nor inner door was locked, and in the laboratory he found me, alive, but on the verge of death by another means than he had feared.

In the extreme physical depression following my awakening from drugged sleep, and knowing nothing of its cause, I believed my adventure fact in its entirety. My mentality was at too low an ebb to resist its dreadful suggestion. I was searching among Holt's various bottles when Jenkins burst in. At first I was merely annoyed at the interruption of my purpose, but before the anticlimax of his explanation the mists of obsession drifted away and left me still sick in body, but in spirit happy as any man may well be who has suffered a delusion that the world is wholly bad—and learned that its badness springs from his own poisoned brain.

The malice which I had observed in every face, includ-ing young Marini's, existed only in my drug-affected vision. Last week's "popular-science" lecture had been recalled to my subconscious mind—the mind that rules dreams and delirium—by the photographic apparatus in Holt's workroom. "See the Great Unseen" assisted materially, and even the corner drug store before which I had paused, with its green-lit show vases, had doubtless played a part. But presently, following something Jenkins told me, I was driven to one protest. "If Holt was not here," I demanded, "if Holt is dead, as you say, how do you account for the fact that I, who have never seen the man, was able to give you an accurate description which you admit to be that of Doctor Frederick Holt?"

He pointed across the room. "See that?" It was a life-size bust portrait, in crayons, the picture of a white-haired man with bushy eyebrows and the most piercing black eyes I had ever seen—until the previous evening. It hung facing the door and near the windows, and the features stood out with a strangely lifelike appearance in the white rays of the arc lamp just outside. "Upon entering," continued Jenkins, "the first thing you saw was that portrait, and from it your delirium built a living, speaking man. So, there are your white-haired showman, your unnatural fear, your color photography and your pretty green golliwogs all nicely explained for you, Blaisdell, and thank God you're alive to hear the explanation. If you had smoked the whole of that cigar—well, never mind. You didn't. And now, my very dear friend, I think it's high time that you interviewed a real, flesh-and-blood doctor. I'll phone for a taxi."

"Don't," I said. "A walk in the fresh air will do me more good than fifty doctors."

"Fresh air! There's no fresh air on South Street in July," complained Jenkins, but reluctantly yielded.

I had a reason for my preference. I wished to see people, to meet face to face even such stray prowlers as might be about at this hour, nearer sunrise than midnight, and rejoice in the goodness and kindliness of the human countenance—particularly as found in the lower classes.

But even as we were leaving there occurred to me a curious inconsistency.

"Jenkins," I said, "you claim that the reason Holt, when I first met him in the hall, appeared to twice close the door in my face, was because the door never opened until I myself unlatched it."

"Yes," confirmed Jenkins, but he frowned, foreseeing my next question.

"Then why, if it was from that picture that I built so solid, so convincing a vision of the man, did I see Holt in the hall before the door was open?"

"You confuse your memories," retorted Jenkins rather shortly.

"Do I? Holt was dead at that hour, but—*I tell you I saw Holt outside the door!* And what was his reason for committing suicide?" Before my friend could reply I was across the room, fumbling in the dusk there at the electric lamp above the sink. I got the tin flap open and pulled out the sliding screen, which consisted of two sheets of glass with fabric between, dark on one side, yellow on the other. With it came the very thing I dreaded—a sheet of whitish, parchmentlike, slightly opalescent stuff.

Jenkins was beside me as I held it at arm's length toward the windows. Through it the light of the arc lamp fell—divided into the most astonishingly brilliant rainbow hues. And instead of diminishing the light, it was perceptibly increased in the oddest way. Almost one thought that the sheet itself was luminous, and yet when held in shadow it gave off no light at all.

"Shall we—put it in the lamp again—and try it?" asked Jenkins slowly, and in his voice there was no hint of mockery.

I looked him straight in the eyes. "No," I said, "we won't. I was drugged. Perhaps in that condition I received a merciless revelation of the discovery that caused Holt's suicide, but I don't believe it. Ghost or no ghost, I refuse to ever again believe in the depravity of the human race. If the air and the earth are teeming with invisible horrors, they are not of our making, and—the study of demonology is better let alone. Shall we burn this thing, or tear it up?"

"We have no right to do either," returned Jenkins thoughtfully, "but you know, Blaisdell, there's a little too darn much realism about some parts of your 'dream.' I haven't been smoking any doped cigars, but when you held that up to the light, I'll swear I saw—well, never mind. Burn it—send it back to the place it came from."

"South America?" said I. "A hotter place than that. Burn it."

So he struck a match and we did. It was gone in one great white flash.

A large place was given by morning papers to the suicide of Doctor Frederick Holt, caused, it was surmised, by mental derangement brought about by his unjust implication in the Peeler murder. It seemed an inadequate reason, since he had never been arrested, but no other was ever discovered.

Of course, our action in destroying that "membrane" was illegal and rather precipitate, but, though he won't talk about it, I know that Jenkins agrees with me—doubt is sometimes better than certainty, and there are marvels better left unproved. Those, for instance, which concern the Powers of Evil.

1919

THE ELF-TRAP
(1919)

In this our well-advertised, modern world, crammed with engines, death-dealing shells, life-dealing serums, and science, he who listens to "old wives' tales" is counted idle. He who believes them, a superstitious fool. Yet there are some legends which have a strange, deathless habit of recrudescence in many languages and lands.

Of one such I have a story to tell. It was related to me by a well-known specialist in nervous diseases, not as an instance of the possible truth behind fable, but as a curious case in which—I quote his words—"the delusions of a diseased brain were reflected by a second and otherwise sound mentality."

No doubt his view was the right one. And yet, at the finish, I had the strangest flash of feeling. As if, somewhere, some time, I, like young Wharton, had stood and seen against blue sky—Elva, of the sky-hued scarf and the yellow honeysuckles.

But my part is neither to feel nor surmise. I will tell the story as I heard it, save for substitution of fictitious names for the real ones. My quotations from the red notebook are verbatim.

Theron Tademus, A.A.S., F.E.S., D.S., et cetera, occupied the chair of biology in a not-unfamed university. He was the author of a treatise on cytology, since widely used as a textbook, and of several important brochures on the more obscure infusoria. As a boy he had been—in appearance—a romantically charming person. The age of thirty-seven found him still handsome in a cold, fine-drawn manner, but almost inhumanly detached from any save scientific interests.

Then, at the height of his career, he died. Having entered his class-room with intent to deliver the first lecture of the fall term, he walked to his desk, laid down a small, red note-book, turned, opened his mouth, went ghastly white and subsided. His assistant, young Wharton, was first to reach him and first to discover the shocking truth.

Tademus was unmarried, and his will bequeathed all he possessed to the university.

The little red book was not at first regarded as important. Supposed to contain notes for his lecture, it was laid aside. On being at last read, however, by his assistant in course of arranging his papers, the book was found to contain not notes, but a diary covering the summer just passed.

Barring the circumstances of one peculiar incident, Wharton already knew the main facts of that summer.

Tademus, at the insistence of his physician—the specialist aforesaid—had spent July and August in the Carolina Mountains not far north from the famous resort, Asheville. Dr. Locke was friend as well as medical adviser, and he lent his patient the use of a bungalow he owned there.

It was situated in a beautiful, but lonely spot, to which the nearest settlement was Carcassonne. In the valley below stood a tiny railroad station, but Carcassonne was not built up around this, nor was it a town at all in the ordinary sense.

A certain landscape painter had once raised him a house on that mountainside, at a place chosen for its magnificent view. Later, he was wont to invite thither, for summer sketching, one or two of his more favored pupils. Later still, he increased this number. For their accommodation other structures were raised near his mountain studio, and the Blue Ridge summer class became an established fact, with a name of its own and a rather large membership.

Two roads led thither from the valley. One, that most in use by the artist colonists, was as good and broad as any Carolina mountain road could hope to be. The other, a winding, narrow, yellow track, passed the lonely bungalow of Dr. Locke, and at last split into two paths, one of which led on to further heights, the second to Carcassonne.

The distance between colony and bungalow was considerable, and neither was visible to the other. Tademus was not interested in art, and, as disclosed by the red book, he was not even aware of Carcassonne's existence until some days after his arrival at the bungalow.

Solitude, long walks, deep breathing, and abstinence from work or sustained thought had been Dr. Locke's prescription, accepted with seeming meekness by Tademus.

Nevertheless, but a short time passed till Wharton received a telegram from the professor ordering him to pack and send by express certain apparatus, including a microscope and dissecting stand. The assistant obeyed.

Another fortnight and Dr. Locke in turn received an urgent wire. It was from Jake Higgins, the Negro caretaker whom he had "lent" to Tademus along with the bungalow.

Leaving his practice to another man's care, Dr. Locke fled for the Carolina Blue Ridge.

He found his caretaker and his bungalow, but no Tademus.

By Jake's story, the professor had gone to walk one afternoon and had not returned. Having wired Locke, the caretaker had otherwise done his best. He notified the county sheriff, and search parties scoured the mountains. At his appeal, too, the entire Carcassonnian colony, male and female, turned out with enthusiasm to hunt for Tademus. Many of them carried easel and sketch-box along, and for such it is to be feared that their humane search ended with the discovery of any tempting "tit" in the scenic line.

However, the colony's efforts were at least as successful as the sheriff's or indeed those of anyone else.

Shortly before Tademus' vanishment, a band of gypsies had settled themselves in a group of old, empty, half-ruined shacks, about a mile from Locke's bungalow.

Suspicion fell upon them. A posse visited the encampment, searched it and questioned every member of the migrant band. They were a peculiarly ill-favored set, dirty and villainous of feature. Nothing, however, could be found of either the missing professor or anything belonging to him.

The posse left, after a quarrel that came near to actual fighting. A dog—a wretched, starved yellow cur—had attacked one of the deputies and set its teeth in his boot. He promptly shot it. In their resentment, the dog's owners drew knives.

The posse were more efficiently armed, and under threat of the latter's rifles and shotguns, the gypsies reconsidered. They were warned to pack up and leave, and following a few days' delay, they obeyed the mandate.

On the very morning of their departure, which was also the eighth day after Tademus' disappearance, Dr. Locke sat down gloomily to breakfast. The search, he thought, must be further extended. Let it cover the whole Blue Ridge, if need be. Somewhere in those mountains was a friend and patient whom he did not propose to lose.

At one side of the breakfast room was a door. It led into the cleared-out bedroom which Locke had, with indignation, discovered to have been converted into a laboratory by the patient he had sent here to "rest."

Suddenly this door opened. Out walked Theron Tademus.

He seemed greatly amazed to find Locke there, and said that he had come in shortly after midnight and been in his laboratory ever since.

Questioned as to his whereabouts before that, he replied surprisingly that throughout the week he had been visiting with friends in Carcassonne.

Dr. Locke doubted his statement. And reasonably.

Artists are not necessarily liars, and every artist and near-artist in the Carcassonne colony had not only denied knowledge of the professor, but spent a good part of the week helping hunt for him.

Later, after insisting that Locke accompany him to Carcassonne and meet his friends there, Tademus suddenly admitted that he had not previously been near the place. He declined, however, either to explain his untruthful first statement, or give any other account of his mysterious absence.

One week ago Tademus had left the bungalow, carrying nothing but a light cane, and wearing a white flannel suit, canvas shoes, and a Panama. That was his idea of a tramping costume. He had returned, dressed in the same suit, hat and shoes. Moreover, though white, they looked neat as when he started, save for a few grass stains and the road's inevitable yellow clay about his shoe-soles.

If he had spent the week vagrant-wise, he had been remarkably successful in keeping his clothes clean.

"Asheville," thought the doctor. "He went by train, stopped at a hotel, and has returned without the faintest memory of his real doings. Lame, overtaxed nerves can play that sort of trick with a man's brain."

But he kept the opinion to himself. Like a good doctor, he soon dropped the whole subject, particularly because he saw that Tademus was deeply distressed and trying to conceal the fact.

On plea of taking a long-delayed vacation of his own, Locke remained some time at the bungalow, guarded his friend from the curiosity of those who had combed the hills for him, and did all in his power to restore him to health and a clear brain.

He was so far successful that Tademus returned to his classes in the fall, with Locke's consent.

To his classes—and death.

Wharton had known all this. He knew that Tademus' whereabouts during that mysterious week had never been learned. But the diary in the red book purported to cover the summer, including that week.

To Wharton, the record seemed so supremely curious that he took a liberty with what was now the university's property. He carried the book to Dr. Locke.

It was evening, and the latter was about to retire after a day's work that began before dawn.

"Personal, you say?" Locke handled the book, frowning slightly.

"Personal. But I feel—when you've finished reading that. I have a rather queer thing to tell you in addition. You can't understand till you've read it. I am almost sure that what is described here has a secret bearing on Professor Tademus' death."

"His heart failed. Overwork. There was no mystery in that."

"Maybe not, doctor. And yet—won't you please read?"

"Run through it aloud for me," said the doctor. "I couldn't read one of my own prescriptions tonight, and you are more familiar with that microscopic writing of his."

Wharton complied.

Monday, July 3.

Arrived yesterday. Not worse than expected, but bad enough. If Locke were here, he should be satisfied. I have absolutely no occupation. Walked and climbed for two hours, as prescribed. Spent the rest of day pacing up and down indoors. Enough walking, at least. I can't sit idle. I can't stop thinking. Locke is a fool!

Thursday, July 6.

Telegraphed Wharton today. He will express me the Swift binocular, some slides, cover-glasses, and a very little other apparatus. Locke is a fool! I shall follow his advice, but within reason. There is a room here lighted by five windows. Old Jake has cleared the bedroom furniture out. It has qualities as a laboratory. Not, of course, that I intend doing any real work. An hour or so a day of micrological observation will only make "resting" tolerable.

Tuesday, July 11.

Jake hitched up his "ol' gray mule" and has brought my three cases from the station. I unpacked the old Stephenson-Swift and set it up. The mere touch of it brought tears to my eyes. Locke's "rest-cure" has done that to my nerves!

After unpacking, though, I resolutely let the microscope and other things be. Walked ten miles up-hill and down. Tried to admire the landscape, as Locke advised, but can't see much in it. Rocks, trees, lumpy hills, yellow roads, sky, clouds, buzzards. Beauty! What beauty is there in this vast, clumsy world that is the outer husk for nature's real and delicate triumphs?

I saw a man painting today. He was swabbing at a canvas with huge, clumsy brushes. He had his easel set up by the road, and I stopped to see what any human being could find hereabout worth picturing.

And what had this painter, this artist, this lover of beauty chosen for a subject? Why, about a mile from here there is a clump of ugly, dark trees. A stream runs between them and the road. It is yellow with clay, and too swift. The more interesting microorganisms could not exist in it. A ram-shackle, plank bridge crosses it, leading to the grove, and there, between the trees, stand and lean some dreary, half-ruined huts.

That scene was the one which my "artist" had chosen for his subject.

For sheer curiosity I got into conversation with the fellow.

Unusual gibberish of chiaroscuro, flat tones, masses, et cetera. Not a definite thought in his head as to why he wished to paint those shacks. I learned one thing, though. He wasn't the isolated specimen of his kind I had thought him. Locke failed to tell me about Carcassonne. Think of it! Nearly a hundred of these insane pursuers of "beauty" are spending the summer within walking distance of the house I have promised to live in!

And the one who was painting the grove actually invited me to call on him! I smiled noncommittally, and came home. On the way I passed the branch road that leads to the place. I had always avoided that road, but I didn't know why until today. Imagine it! Nearly a hundred. Some of them women, I suppose. No, I shall keep discreetly away from Carcassonne.

Saturday, July 15.

Jake informs me that a band of gypsies have settled themselves in the grove which my Carcassonnian acquaintance chose to paint. They are living in the ruined huts. Now I shall avoid that road, too. Talk of solitude! Why, the hills are fairly swarming with artists, gypsies, and Lord knows who else. One might as well try to rest in a beehive!

Found some interesting variations of the ciliara living in a near-by pond. Wonderful! Have recorded over a dozen specimens in which the macronucleus is unquestionably double. Not lobed, not pulverate, as in Oxytricha, but double! My summer has not, after all, been wasted.

Felt singularly slack and tired this morning, and realized that I have hardly been out of the house in three days. Shall certainly take a long tramp tomorrow.

Monday, July 17.

Absent-mindedness betrayed me today. I had a very unpleasant experience. Resolutely keeping my promise to Locke, I sallied forth this afternoon and walked briskly for some distance. I had, however, forgotten the gypsies and took my old route.

Soon I met a woman, or rather a girl. She was arrayed in the tattered, brilliantly colored garments which women of these wandering tribes affect. There was a scarf about her head. I noticed because its blue was exactly the same brilliant hue of the sky over the mountains behind her. There was a stripe of yellow in it, too, and thrust in her sash she carried a great bunch of yellow flowers—wild honeysuckle, I think.

Her face was not dark, like the swart faces of most gypsies. On the contrary, the skin of it had a smooth, firm whiteness. Her features were fine and delicate.

Passing, we looked at one another, and I saw her eyes brighten in the strangest, most beautiful manner. I am sure that there was nothing bold or immodest in her glance. It was rather like the look of a person who recognizes an old acquaintance, and is glad of it. Yet we never met before. Had we met, I could not have forgotten her.

We passed without speaking, of course, and I walked on.

Meeting the girl, I had hardly thought of her as a gypsy, or indeed tried to classify her in any way. The impression she left was new in my experience. It was only on reaching the grove that I came to myself, as it were, and remembered Jake's story of the gypsies who are camping there.

Then I very quickly emerged from the vague, absurd happiness which sight of the girl had brought.

While talking with my Carcassonnian, I had observed that grove rather carefully. I had thought it perfect—that nothing added could increase the somber ugliness of its trees, nor the desolation of its gray, ruined, tumbledown old huts.

Today I learned better. To be perfect, ugliness must include sordid humanity.

The shacks, dreary in themselves, were hideous now. In their doorways lounged fat, unclean women nursing their filthy offspring. Older children, clothed in rags, caked with dirt, sprawled and fought among themselves. Their voices were the snarls of animals.

I realized that the girl with the sky-like scarf had come from here—out of this filth unspeakable!

A yellow cur, the mere, starved skeleton of a dog, came tearing down to the bridge. A rusty, jangling bell was tied about its neck with a string. The beast stopped on the far side and crouched there, yapping. Its anger seemed to surpass mere canine savagery. The lean jaws fairly writhed in maniacal but loathsomely feeble ferocity.

A few men, whiskered, dirty-faced, were gathered about a sort of forge erected in the grove. They were making something, beating it with hammers in the midst of showers of sparks. As the dog yapped, one of the men turned and saw me. He spoke to his mates, and to my dismay they stopped work and transferred their attention to me.

I was afraid that they would cross the bridge, and the idea of having to talk to them was for some reason inexpressibly revolting.

They stayed where they were, but one of them suddenly laughed out loudly, and held up to my view the thing upon which they had been hammering.

It was a great, clumsy, rough, iron trap. Even at that distance I could see the huge, jagged teeth, fit to maim a bear—or a man. It was the ugliest instrument I have ever seen.

I turned away and began walking toward home, and when I looked back they were at work again.

The sun shone brightly, but about the grove there seemed to be a queer darkness. It was like a place alone and aloof from the world. The trees, even, were different from the other mountain trees. Their heavy branches did not stir at all in the wind. They had a strange, dark, flat look against the sky, as though they had been cut from dark paper, or rather like the flat trees woven in a tapestry. That was it. The whole scene was like a flat, dark, unreal picture in tapestry.

I came straight home. My nerves are undoubtedly in bad shape, and I think I shall write Locke and ask him to prescribe medicine that will straighten me up. So far, his "rest-cure" has not been notably successful.

Wednesday, July 19.

I have met her again.

Last night I could not sleep at all. Round midnight I ceased trying, rose, dressed, and spent the rest of the night with the good old Stephenson-Swift. My light for night-work—a common oil lamp—is not very brilliant. This morning I suffered considerable pain behind the eyes, and determined to give Locke's "walking and open air" treatment another trial, though discouraged by previous results.

This time I remembered to turn my back on the road which leads to that hideous grove. The sunlight seemed to increase the pain I was already suffering. The air was hot, full of dust, and I had to walk slowly. At the slightest increase of pace my heart would set up a kind of fluttering, very unpleasant and giving me a sense of suffocation.

Then I came to the girl.

She was seated on a rock, her lap heaped with wild honeysuckle, and she was weaving the flower stems together.

Seeing me, she smiled.

"I have your garland finished," she said, "and mine soon will be."

One would have thought the rock a trysting place at which we had for a long time been accustomed to meet!

In her hand she was extending to me a wreath, made of the honeysuckle flowers.

I can't imagine what made me act as I did. Weariness and the pain behind my eyes may have robbed me of my usual good sense.

Anyway, rather to my own surprise, I took her absurd wreath and sat down where she made room for me on the boulder.

After that we talked.

At this moment, only a few hours later, I couldn't say whether or not the girl's English was correct, nor exactly what she said. But I can remember the very sound of her voice.

I recall, too, that she told me her name Elva, and that when I asked for the rest of it, she informed me that one good name was enough for one good person.

That struck me as a charmingly humorous sally. I laughed like a boy—or a fool, God knows which!

Soon she had finished her second garland, and laughingly insisted that we each crown the other with flowers.

Imagine it. Had one of my students come by then, I am sure he would have been greatly startled. Professor Theron Tademus, seated on a rock with a gypsy girl, crowned with wild honeysuckle and adjusting a similar wreath to the girl's blue-scarfed head!

Luckily, neither the student nor anyone else passed, and in a few minutes she said something that brought me to my senses. Due to that inexplicable dimness of memory, I quote the sense, not her words.

"My father is a ruler among our people. You must visit us. For my sake, the people and my father will make you welcome."

She spoke with the gracious air of a princess, but I rose hastily from beside her. A vision of the grove had returned—dark, oppressive—like an old, dark tapestry, woven with the ugly forms and foliage. I remembered the horrible, filthy tribe from which this girl had sprung.

Without a word of farewell, I left her there on the rock. I did not look back, nor did she call after me. Not until reaching home, when I met old Jake at the door and saw him stare, did I remember the honeysuckle wreath. I was still wearing it, and carrying my hat.

Snatching at the flowers, I flung them in the ditch and retreated with what dignity I might into the bungalow's seclusion.

It is night now, and, a little while since, I went out again. The wreath is here in the room with me. The flowers were unsoiled by the ditch, and seem fresh as when she gave them to me. They are more fragrant than I had thought even wild honeysuckle could be.

Elva. Elva of the sky-blue scarf and the yellow honeysuckle.

My eyes are heavy, but the pain behind them is gone. I think I shall sleep tonight.

Friday, July 21.

Is there any man so gullible as he who prides himself on his accuracy of observation?

I ask this in humility, for I am that man.

Yesterday I rose, feeling fresher than for weeks past. After all, Locke's treatment seemed worthy of respect. With that in mind, I put in only a few hours staining some of my binucleate cilia and finishing the slides.

All the last part of the afternoon I faithfully tramped the roads. There is undoubtedly a sort of broad, coarse charm in mere landscape, with its reaches of green, its distant purples, and the sky like a blue scarf flung over it all. Had the pain of my eyes not returned, I could almost have enjoyed those vistas.

Having walked farther than usual, it was deep dusk when I reached home. As if from ambush, a little figure dashed out from behind some rhododendrons. It seemed to be a child, a boy, though I couldn't see him clearly, nor how he was dressed.

He thrust something into my hand. To my astonishment, the thing was a spray of wild honeysuckle.

"Elva—Elva—Elva!"

The strange youngster was fairly dancing up and down before me, repeating the girl's name and nothing else.

Recovering myself, I surmised that Elva must have sent this boy, and sure enough, at my insistence he managed to stop prancing long enough to deliver her message.

Elva's grandmother, he said, was very ill. She had been ailing for days, but tonight the sickness was worse—much worse. Elva feared that her grandmother would die, and, "of course," the boy said, "no doctor will come for our sending!" She had remembered me, as the only friend she knew among the "outside people." Wouldn't I come and look at her poor, sick grandmother? And if I had any of the outside people's medicine in my house, would I please bring that with me?

Well, yes, I did hesitate. Aside from practical and obvious suspicions, I was possessed with a senseless horror for not only the gypsy tribe, but the grove itself.

But there was the spray of honeysuckle. In her need, she had sent that for a token—and sent it to me! Elva, of the sky-like scarf and laughing mouth.

"Wait here," I said to the boy, rather brusquely, and entered the house. I had remembered a pocket-case of simple remedies, none of which I had ever used, but there was a direction pamphlet with them. If I must play amateur physician, that might help. I looked for Jake, meaning to inform him of my proposed expedition. Though he had left a chicken broiling on the kitchen range, he was not about. He might have gone to the spring for water.

Passing out again, I called the boy, but received no answer. It was very dark. Toward sunset, the sky had clouded over, so that now I had not even the benefit of starlight.

I was angry with the boy for not waiting, but the road was familiar enough, even in the dark. At least, I thought it was, till, colliding with a clump of holly. I realized that I must have strayed off and across a bare stretch of yellow clay which defaces the Mountainside above Locke's bungalow.

I looked back for the guiding lights of its windows, but the trees hid them. However, the road couldn't be far off. After some stumbling about, I was sure that my feet were in the right track again. Somewhat later I perceived a faint, ruddy point of light, to the left and ahead of me.

As I walked toward it, the rapid rush and gurgle of water soon apprized me that I had reached the stream with the plank bridge across it.

There I stood for several minutes, staring toward the ruddy light. That was all I could see. It seemed, somehow, to cast no illumination about it.

There came a scamper of paws, the tinkle of a bell, and then a wild yapping broke out on the stream's far side. That vile, yellow cur, I thought. Elva, having imposed on my kindness to the extent of sending for me, might at least have arranged a better welcome than this.

When I pictured her, crouched in her bright, summer-colored garments, tending the dreadful old hag that her grandmother must be. The rest of the tribe were probably indifferent. She could not desert her sick—and there stood I, hesitant as any other coward!

For the dog's sake I took a firm grip on my cane. Feeling about with it, I found the bridge and crossed over.

Instantly something flung itself against my legs and was gone before I could hit out. I heard the dog leaping and barking all around me. It suddenly struck me that the beast's voice was not like that of the yellow cur. There was nothing savage in it. This was the cheerful, excited bark of a well-bred dog that welcomes its master, or its master's friend. And the bell that tinkled to every leap had a sweet, silvery note, different from the cracked jangle of the cur's bell.

I had hated and loathed that yellow brute, and to think that I need not combat the creature was a relief. The huts, as I recalled them, weren't fifty yards beyond the stream. There was no sign of a campfire. Just that one ruddy point of light.

I advanced—

Wharton paused suddenly in his reading. "Here," he interpolated, "begins that part of the diary which passed from commonplace to amazing. And the queer part is that in writing it, Professor Tademus seems to have been unaware that he was describing anything but an unusually pleasant experience."

Dr. Locke's heavy brows knit in a frown. "Pleasant!" he snapped. "The date of that entry?"

"July twenty-one."

"The day he disappeared. I see. Pleasant! And that gypsy girl—faugh! What an adventure for such a man! No wonder he tried to lie out of it. I don't think I care to hear the rest, Wharton. Whatever it is, my friend is dead. Let him rest."

"Oh, but wait," cried the young man, with startled earnestness. "Good Lord, doctor, do you believe I would bring this book even to you if it contained that kind of story—about Professor Tademus? No. Its amazing quality is along different lines than you can possibly suspect."

"Get on, then," grumbled Locke, and Wharton continued.

Suddenly, as though at a signal, not one, but a myriad of lights blazed into existence.

It was like walking out of a dark closet into broad day. The first dazzlement passing, I perceived that instead of the somber grove and ruined huts, I was facing a group of very beautiful houses.

It is curious how a previous and false assumption will rule a man. Having believed myself at the gypsy encampment, several minutes passed before I could overcome my bewilderment and realize that after losing my road I had not actually regained it.

That I had somehow wandered into the other branch road, and reached, not the grove, but Carcassonne!

I had no idea, either, that this artists' colony could be such a really beautiful place. It is cut by no streets. The houses are set here and there over the surface of such green lawns as I have never seen in these mountains of rock and yellow clay.

(Dr. Locke started slightly in his chair. Carcassonne, as he had himself seen it, flashed before his memory. He did not interrupt, but from that moment his attention was alertly set, like a man who listens for the key word of a riddle.)

Everywhere were lights, hung in the flowering branches of trees, glowing upward from the grass, blazing from every door and window. Why they should have been turned on so abruptly, after that first darkness, I do not yet know.

Out of the nearest house a girl came walking. She was dressed charmingly, in thin, bright-colored silks. A bunch of wild honeysuckle was thrust in the girdle, and over her hair was flung a scarf of sky-like blue. I knew her instantly, and began to see a glimmering of the joke that had been played on me.

The dog bounded toward the girl. He was a magnificent collie. A tiny silver bell was attached to his neck by a broad ribbon.

I take credit for considerable aplomb in my immediate behavior. The girl had stopped a little way off. She was laughing, but I had certainly allowed myself to be victimized.

On my accusation, she at once admitted to having deceived me. She explained that, perceiving me to be misled by her appearance into thinking her one of the gypsies, she could not resist carrying out the joke. She had sent her small brother with the token and message.

I replied that the boy deserted me, and that I had nearly invaded the camp of real gypsies while looking for her and the fictitious dying grandmother.

At this she appeared even more greatly amused. Elva's mirth has a peculiarly contagious quality. Instead of being angry, I found myself laughing with her.

By this time quite a throng of people had emerged on the lawns, and leading me to a dignified, fine-looking old man who she said was her father, she presented me. In the moment, I hardly noticed that she used my first name only, Theron, which I had told her when we sat on the roadside boulder. I have observed since that all these people use the single name only, in presentation and intercourse. Though lacking personal experience with artists, I have heard that they are inclined to peculiar "fads" of unconventionality. I had never, however, imagined that they could be attractive to a man like myself, or pleasant to know.

I am enlightened. These Carcassonnian "colonists" are the only charming, altogether delightful people whom I have ever met.

One and all, they seemed acquainted with Elva's amusing jest at my expense. They laughed with us, but in recompense have made me one of themselves in the pleasantest manner.

I dined in the house of Elva's father. The dining-room, or rather hall, is a wonderful place. Due to much microscopic work, I am inclined to see only clumsiness—largeness—in what other people characterize as beauty. Carcassonne is different. There is a minute perfection about the architecture of these artists' houses, the texture of their clothes, and even the delicate contour of their faces, which I find amazingly agreeable.

There is no conventionality of costume among them. Both men and women dress as they please. Their individual taste is exquisite, and the result is an array of soft fabrics, and bright colors, flowerlike, rather than garish.

Till last night I never learned the charm of what is called "fancy dress," nor the genial effect it may exert on even a rather somber nature, such as I admit mine to be.

Elva, full of good-natured mischief, insisted that I must "dress for dinner." Her demand was instantly backed by the whole laughing throng. Carried off my feet in a way to which I am not at all used, I let them drape me in white robes, laced with silver embroideries like the delicate crystallization of hoar-frost. Dragged hilariously before a mirror, I was amazed at the change in my appearance.

Unlike the black, scarlet-hooded gown of my university, these glittering robes lent me not dignity, but a kind of—I can only call it a noble youthfulness. I looked younger, and at the same time keener—more alive. And either the contagious spirit of my companions, or some resurgence of boyishness filled me with a sudden desire to please; to be merry with the merry-makers, and—I must be frank—particularly to keep Elva's attention where it seemed temporarily fixed—on myself.

My success was unexpectedly brilliant. There is something in the very atmosphere of Carcassonne which, once yielded to, exhilarates like wine. I have never danced, nor desired to learn. Last night, after a banquet so perfect that I hardly recall its details, I danced. I danced with Elva—and with Elva—and always with Elva. She laughed aside all other partners. We danced on no polished floors, but out on the green lawns, under white, laughing stars. Our music was not orchestral. Wherever the light-footed couples chose to circle, there followed a young flutist, piping on his flute of white ivory.

Fluttering wings, driving clouds, wind tossed leaves—all the light, swift things of the air were in that music. It lifted and carried one with it. One did not need to learn. One danced! It seems, as I write, that the flute's piping is still in my ears, and that its echoes will never cease. Elva's voice is like the ivory flute's. Last night I was mad with the music and her voice. We danced—I know not how long, nor when we ceased.

This morning I awakened in a gold-and-ivory room, with round windows that were full of blue sky and crossed by blossoming branches. Dimly I recalled that Elva's father had urged me to accept his hospitality for the night.

Too much of such new happiness may have gone to my head, I'm afraid. At least, it was nothing stronger. At dinner I drank only one glass of wine—sparkling, golden stuff, but mild and with a taste like the fragrance of Elva's wild honeysuckle blooms.

It is midmorning now, and I am writing this seated on a marble bench beside a pool in the central court of my host's house. I am waiting for Elva, who excused herself to attend to some duty or other. I found this book in my pocket, and thought best to make an immediate record of not only a good joke on myself, but the only really pleasant social experience I have ever enjoyed.

I must lay aside these fanciful white robes, bid Elva good-by, and return to my lonely bungalow and Jake. The poor old man is probably tearing his hair over my unexplained absence. But I hope for another invitation to Carcassonne!

Saturday, July 22.

I seem to be "staying on" indefinitely. This won't do. I spoke to Elva of my extended visit, and she laughingly informed me that people who have drunk the wine and worn the woven robes of Carcassonne seldom wish to leave. She suggested that I give up trying to "escape" and spend my life here. Jest, of course; but I half wished her words were earnest. She and her people are spoiling me for the common, workaday world.

Not that they are idle, but their occupations as well as pleasures are of a delicate, fascinating beauty.

Whole families are stopping here, including the children. I don't care for children, as a rule, but these are harmless as butterflies. I met Elva's messenger, her brother. He is a funny, dear little elf. How even in the dark I fancied him one of those gypsy brats is hard to conceive. But then I took Elva herself for a gypsy!

My new friends engage in many pursuits besides painting. "Crafts," I believe they are called. This morning Elva took me around the shops—shops like architectural blossoms, carved out of the finest marble.

They make jewelry, weave fabrics, tool leather, and follow many other interesting occupations. Set in the midst of the lawns is a forge. Every part of it, even to the iron anvil, is embellished with a fernlike inlay of other metals. Several amateur silversmiths were at work there, but Elva hurried me away before I could see what they were about.

I have inquired for the young painter who first told me of Carcassonne and invited me to visit him there. I can't recall his name, but on describing him to Elva she replied vaguely that not every "outsider" was permanently welcome among her people.

I didn't press the question. Remembering the ugliness which that same painter had been committing to canvas,

I could understand that his welcome among these exquisite workers might be short-lived. He was probably banished, or banished himself, soon after our interview on the road.

I must be careful, lest I wear out my own welcome. Yet the very thought of that old, rough, husk of a world that I must return to, brings back the sickness, and the pain behind my eyes that I had almost forgotten.

Sunday, July 23.

Elva! Her presence alone is delight. The sky is not bluer than her scarf and eyes. Sunlight is a duller gold than the wild honeysuckle she weaves in garlands for our heads.

Today, like child sweethearts, we carved our names on the smooth trunk of a tree. "Elva—Theron." And a wreath to shut them in. I am happy. Why—why, indeed should I leave Carcassonne?

Monday, July 24.

Still here, but this is the last night that I shall impose upon these regally hospitable people. An incident occurred today, pathetic from one viewpoint, outrageous from another. I was asleep when it happened, and only woke up at the sound of the gunshot.

Some rough young mountaineers rode into Carcassonne and wantonly killed Elva's collie dog. They claimed, I believe, that the unlucky animal attacked one of their number. A lie! The dog was gentle as a kitten. He probably leaped and barked around their horses and annoyed the young brutes. They had ridden off before I reached the scene.

Elva was crying, and no wonder. They had blown her pet's head clean off with a shotgun. Don't know what will be done about it. I wanted to go straight to the county sheriff, but Elva wouldn't have that. I pretended to give in but if her father doesn't see to the punishment of those men, I will. Murderous devils! Elva is too forgiving.

Wednesday, July 26.

I watched the silversmiths today. Elva was not with me. I had no idea that silver was worked like iron. They must use some peculiar amalgam, or it would melt in the furnace, instead of emerging white-hot, to be beaten with tiny, delicate hammers.

They were making a strange looking contraption. It was all silver, beaten into floral patterns, but the general shape was a riddle to me. Finally I asked one of the smiths what they were about. He is a tall fellow, with a merry, dark face.

"Guess!" he demanded.

"Can't. To my ignorance, it resembles a Chinese puzzle."

"Something more curious than that."

"What?"

"An—*elf-trap*!" He laughed mischievously.

"Please!"

"Well, it's a trap anyway. See this?" The others had stepped back good-naturedly. With his hammer he pressed on a lever. Instantly two slender, jaw-like parts of the queer machine opened wide. They were set with needlelike points, or teeth. It was all red-hot, and when he removed his hammer the jaws clashed in a shower of sparks.

"It's a trap, of course." I was still puzzled.

"Yes, and a very remarkable one. This trap will not only catch, but it will recatch."

"I don't understand."

"If any creature, man, say—" he was laughing again— "walks into this trap, he may escape it. But sooner or later—soon, I should think—it will catch him again. That is why we call it an elf-trap!"

I perceived suddenly that he was making pure game of me. His mates were all laughing at the nonsense. I moved off, not offended, but perturbed in another way.

He and his absurd silver trap-toy had reminded me of the gypsies. What a horrible, rough iron thing that was which they had held up to me from their forge. Men capable of creating such an uncouthly cruel instrument as that jag toothed trap would be terrible to meet in the night. And I had come near blundering in among them—at night!

This won't do. I have been happy. Don't let me drop back into the morbidly nervous condition which invested those gypsies with more than human horror. Elva is calling me. I have been too long alone.

Friday, July 28.

Home again. I am writing this in my bungalow-laboratory. Gray dawn is breaking, and I have been at work here since midnight. Feel strangely depressed. Need breakfast, probably.

Last night Elva and I were together in the court of her father's house. The pool in the center of it is lighted from below to a golden glow. We were watching the goldfish, with their wide, filmy tails of living lace.

Suddenly I gave a sharp cry. I had seen a thing in the water more important than goldfish. Snatching out the small collecting bottle, without which I never go abroad, I made a quick pass at the pool's glowing surface.

Elva had started back, rather frightened.

"What is it?"

I held the bottle up and peered closely. There was no mistake.

"Dysteria," I said triumphantly. "Dysteria ciliata. Dysterlus giganticus, to give a unique specimen the separate name he deserves. Why, Elva, this enormous creature will give me a new insight on his entire species!"

"What enormous creature?"

For the first time I saw Elva nearly petulant. But I was filled with enthusiasm. I let her look in the bottle.

"There!" I ejaculated. "See him?"

"Where? I can't see anything but water—and a tiny speck in it."

"That," I explained proudly, "is dysterius giganticus. Large enough to be seen by the naked eye. Why, child, he's a monster of his kind. A fresh-water variety, too!"

I thrust the bottle in my pocket.

"Where are you going?"

"Home, of course. I can't get this fellow under the microscope any too quickly."

I had forgotten how wide apart are the scientific and artistic temperaments. No explanation I could make would persuade Elva that my remarkable capture was worth walking a mile to examine properly.

"You are all alike!" she cried. "All! You talk of love, but your love is for gold, or freedom, or some pitiful foolish nothingness like that speck of life you call by a long name—and leave me for!"

"But," I protested, "only for a little while. I shall come back."

She shook her head. This was Elva in a new mood, dark brows drawn, laughing mouth drooped to a sullen curve. I felt sorry to leave her angry, but my visit had already been preposterously long. Besides, a rush of desire had swept me to get back to my natural surroundings. I wanted the feel of the micrometer adjuster in my fingers, and to see the round, speckled white field under the lens pass from blurred chaos to perfect definition.

She let me go at last. I promised solemnly to come to her whenever she should send or call. Foolish child! Why, I can walk over to Carcassonne every day, if she likes.

I hear Jake rattling about in the breakfast-room. Conscience informs me that I have treated him rather badly. Wonder where he thought I was? Couldn't have been much worried, or he would have hunted me up in Carcassonne.

August 30.

I shall not make any further entries in this book. My day for the making of records is over, I think. Any sort of records. I go back to my classes next month. God knows what I shall say to them! Elva.

I may as well finish the story here.

Every day I find it harder to recall the details. If I hadn't this book, with what I wrote in it when I was—when I was there, I should believe that my brain had failed in earnest.

Locke said I couldn't have been in Carcassonne. He stood in the breakfast-room, with the sunlight striking across him. I saw him clearly. I saw the huge, coarse, ugly creature that he was. And in that minute, I knew.

But I wouldn't admit it, even to myself. I made him go with me to Carcassonne. There was no stream. There was no bridge.

The houses were wretched bungalows, set about on the bare, flat, yellow clay of the Mountainside. The people— artists, save the mark!—were a common, carelessly dressed, painting-aproned crowd who fulfilled my original idea of an artists' colony.

Their coarse features and thick skins sickened me. Locke walked home beside me, very silent. I could hardly bear his company.

He was gross—coarse—human!

Toward evening, managing to escape his company, I stole up the road to the gypsy's grove. The huts were empty. That queer look, as of a flat, dark tapestry, was gone from the grove.

I crossed the plank bridge. Among the trees I found ashes, and a depression where the forge had stood. Something else, too. A dog, or rather its unburied remains. The yellow cur. Its head had been blown off by a shotgun. An ugly little bell lay in the mess, tied to a piece of string.

One of the trees—it had a smooth trunk—and carved in the bark—I can't write it. I went away and left those two names carved there.

The wild honeysuckle has almost ceased to bloom. I can leave now. Locke says I am well, and that I can return to my classes.

I have not entered my laboratory since that morning. Locke admires my "willpower" for dropping all that till physical health should have returned. Will-power! I shall never, as long as I live, look into a microscope again.

Perhaps she will know that somehow, and send or call for me quickly.

I have drunk the wine and worn the woven robes of her people. They made me one of them. Is it right that they should cast me out, because I did not understand what I have since guessed the meaning of so well?

I can't bear the human folk about me. They are clumsy, revolting. And I can't work.

God only knows what I shall say to my classes.

Here is the end of my last record—till she calls!

There was silence in Locke's private study. At last the doctor expelled his breath in a long sigh. He might have been holding it all the time.

"Great-Heavens!" he ejaculated. "Poor old Tademus! And I thought his trouble in the summer there was a temporary lapse. But he talked like a sane man. Acted like one, too, by Jove! With his mind in that condition! And in spite of the posse, he must have been with the gypsies all that week. You can see it. Even through his delusions, you catch occasional notes of reality.

"I heard of that dog-shooting, and he speaks of being asleep when it happened. Where was he concealed that the posse didn't find him? Drugged and hidden under some filthy heap of rags in one of the huts, do you think? And why hide him at all, and then let him go? He returned the very day they left."

At the volley of questions, Wharton shook his head.

"I can't even guess about that. He was certainly among the gypsies. But as for his delusions, to call them so, there is a kind of beauty and coherence about them which I—well, which I don't like!"

The doctor eyed him sharply.

"You can't mean that you—"

"Doctor," said Wharton softly, "do you recall what he wrote of the silversmiths and their work? They were making an elf-trap. Well, I think the elf-trap—caught him!"

"What?"

Locke's tired eyes opened wide. A look of alarm flashed into them. The alarm was for Wharton, not himself.

"Wait!" said the latter. "I haven't finished. You know that I was in the classroom at the moment when Professor Tademus died?"

"Yes?"

"Yes! I was the first to reach him. But before that, I stood near the desk. There are three windows at the foot of that room. Every other man there faced the desk. I faced the windows. The professor entered, laid down his book and turned to the class. As he did so, a head appeared in one of those windows. They are close to the ground, and a person standing outside could easily look in.

"The head was a woman's. No, I am not inventing this. I saw her head, draped in a blue scarf. I noticed, because the scarf's blueness gave me the strangest thrill of delight. It was the exact blue of the sky behind it. Then she had raised her hand. I saw it. In her fingers was a spray of yellow flowers—yellow as sunshine. She waved them in a beckoning motion. Like this.

"Then Tademus dropped.

"And there are legends, you know, of strange people, either more or less than human, who appear as gypsies, but are not the real gypsies, that possess queer powers. Their outer appearance is rough and vile, but behind that, as a veil, they live a wonderful hidden life of their own.

"And a man who has been with them once is caught—caught in the real elf-trap, which the smiths' work only symbolized. He may escape, but he can't forget nor be joined again with his own race, while to return among them, he must walk the dark road that Tademus had taken when she called.

"Oh. I've scoffed at 'old wives' tales' with the rest of our overeducated, modern kind. I can't ever scoff again, you see, because—

"What's that? A prescription? For me? Why, doctor, you don't yet understand. I saw her, I tell you. Elva! Elva! Elva, of the wild honeysuckle and the sky-like scarf!"

1919

Gertrude Barrows Bennett (1884–1948) was the first American woman to publish widely in fantasy and science fiction. Her stories, which would influence later writers from H. P. Lovecraft to C. L. Moore, appeared in popular pulp magazines including *Argosy*, *All-Story Weekly*, and *Weird Tales*. Other than "The Curious Experience of Thomas Dunbar," published (as by "G. M. Barrows") when she was seventeen, virtually all of Bennett's work—written under the pen name Francis Stevens—dates from 1917 to 1920. Her best-known novels are *The Citadel of Fear* (1918) and *Claimed!* (1920).

Lisa Yaszek is Regents' Professor of Science Fiction Studies in the School of Literature, Media, and Communication at Georgia Tech. Her books include *Sisters of Tomorrow: The First Women of Science Fiction* (2016) and *The Future is Female!* series (2018–present). A past president of the Science Fiction Research Association, Yaszek serves as an editor for the Library of America.